ASPEN F, SAPPHIRE

HAVOC

The Calamity Series Book Two

WADDOOCESS
PUBLISHING

For my three beautiful daughters, life isn't easy.
There will be times that you feel like you just can't go on.
Times where grief and depression might become consuming.
Times where anxiety and life itself becomes overwhelming.
Times where you might think you can't keep going.
Times where you just don't want to go on.
It's okay to feel that way sometimes.
Let yourself feel those big feelings.
And then pick yourself up,
Dust yourself off,
And remember
I love you.
-Mom

"For the havoc reigning upon the realm was naught compared to the havoc manipulating her mind."

Contents

Trigger Warnings

This book, as well as the rest of books of this series, may contain many different things that could be triggering to some.

This includes but is not limited to: adult language, sex, violence, death, abuse in varying forms, monsters, magic, kidnapping, talk of rape/attempted rape, anxiety, depression, and assault.

Intended for audiences of 18+ years of age. LGBTQ+ relationships and aspects will be part of this series. I believe that everyone deserves love and happiness regardless of their sexual orientation, gender, culture, and race.

If you disagree then my books are not for you.

Please always know that no matter what, you are loved and wanted. Your life matters. Call, Text, or Chat 988 or dial 1-800-273-8255 for the National Suicide Prevention Lifeline. This lifeline is available 24/7 for free. They provide confidential support for anyone in distress.

HAVOC

;

Definition

Havoc

n *oun*

1. great destruction or devastation.
2. great confusion or disorder.

Chapter One

***

Zeke

She's gone. I couldn't feel her anymore.

Empty. I... I'm... empty.

I could feel the panic bubbling up inside me again. Vilulf and I rode our horses as fast as we could. The wind whistled as it whipped past us, and the pounding of the horse's hooves jarred my bones. My hair kept whipping me in my face as I encouraged my horse to go faster. Pushing his limitations but I didn't care. I had to get to her. I had to save her. This was this unexplainable urge to get to her coming from deep inside of me.

The twins were just behind us, struggling to keep pace with me. The rest of our men were following, but we were still hours away from her.

She was hurt and in pain. I wasn't there to protect her. I should have been there for her. The panic started up inside me again, but I couldn't lose my shit. It would be catastrophic, and I couldn't let that happen. Not yet at least. I had to make it to her.

The last thing I felt from her was pain and then she was gone. It felt as if she had been ripped straight out of my chest. She couldn't be gone though. She was too strong to be gone. Whatever had happened to her, she would come back from it. She had to come back.

I choked down the sob that almost broke free from my throat. I would not lose my shit. I wouldn't let that happen.

Where the fuck had Helvig been and why couldn't I connect with him? He really couldn't be gone too. No. There was no fucking way. Helvig was... well he was the best of the best. He had to be the most powerful being in this realm. It's the only reason why I left her with him. I knew that whatever the fuck the mad king had done to take away all magic also made it to where Helvig couldn't fully transform, but he still had more power than anyone in this realm. There's no way anyone would have been able to overpower him, and I knew he wouldn't have betrayed me.

Fuck. What if he did betray me? What if he took her out of this realm? Shit. No. At the very least he wouldn't have betrayed her. I saw how close they had become and if I had been anyone other than a fucking king, I might have been insecure about it. I also knew that Helvig wouldn't actually want her because he would be leaving as soon as he fucking could. However, I still saw it. I saw the way he looked at her like she was his god's damn world. She had that effect on everyone around her though. She pulled me in the same exact way, just by being herself. She was intoxicating. Everything about her was from the way that she spoke to her smell. If I could bottle her smell up I would. She didn't see it, but I did. I saw how all her guards eyed her. How that fucking fuck boy, Lance, looked at her. Helvig would have given his life for her. I know he would have. He was fiercely loyal in general but there was something about their friendship that told me he would burn down this realm for her.

Fuck. Fuck. Fuck. FUCK!

What the fuck happened! My thoughts were all over the place. I had to find them. I had to find her. I tried searching for the bond with him and found nothing. There should have been a connection. There should have been something there but there wasn't even a flicker. Was he dead? Fuck. He couldn't be dead. Him being dead was the only explanation though. How else could something have happened to her.

I couldn't fathom someone overpowering Helvig. It would take 100 men or even more before they posed a real challenge. I tried searching him out again and again. I just couldn't believe that he was gone yet I still couldn't find my connection to Helvig. Fuck. I felt like I was unraveling from my very existence.

I wouldn't have left her if I didn't think she was safe. He would have at the very least partially transformed the moment anything went wrong. It would have freaked Cordelia out and possibly blinded her but... but she would have been safe. He should have brought her directly to me and he didn't. Someone had to have taken him out first in order to get to her. It was the only thing that made sense. Helvig would have defended her to his last breath. My thoughts kept replaying on a loop. I couldn't focus on anything. Every time I started to think about her the emptiness in my chest seemed to expand. Everything felt wrong. Everything was wrong. The way the wind blew was wrong. The way the air smelt, empty of her, was wrong. So completely wrong.

Something inside me told me that she was still alive. It was like a faint flicker of light somewhere inside me. Maybe in my soul. Sure, I had to be my soulmate. I was sure of that. That little flicker worried me. One soft breath and it could go out, but it was there. It was still there, and it was hope. It was that small hope that she was okay that kept me from losing my mind.

The longer it was taking to get to the castle the more I was vibrating from my fury that someone did something to her. That she was hurt and probably scared. I had felt her fear and I felt the tremendous loss that went through her. That only reaffirmed my suspension that Helvig was killed.

Fuck. If I could only fucking shift. I could already be with her. I would have been there so much faster, and I would have fucking electrocuted everyone around her. It would have been exhilarating.

My fury was building at my tumultuous thoughts. Storm clouds started rolling in and lightning struck off in the distance. A storm was brewing, and my emotions were fueling it.

Blood trickled down my chest from a wound I didn't even feel. Light rain started and washed the blood across my torso and around my sides. Quickly, it was turning into a downpour.

"TAKE A BREATH BROTHER! WE WILL GET TO HER!" Vilulf shouted over the thunder and the sound of our horses.

"SHE WILL BE GONE BY THE TIME WE GET THERE! EVERYONE THAT IS ABLE TO SHIFT NEEDS TO IMME-DIATELY AND GO AHEAD OF US," I commanded. With a nod of his head, I felt him through our bond. He sent the command out and within moments the sky had turned to night. The sun was completely blocked off and the sky full of dragons, phoenix's, griffins, sphinx, and ravens. They shot through the sky and headed towards Dorchia. Urmahlullu, half man half lion, and Centaurs ran past us. Rovini's castle would be surrounded in minutes. No one in and no one out.

Vilulf stayed next to me as we pushed our horses as fast as they could go. Every time my thoughts started to get away from me he would reel me back in.

Unfortunately, my emotions were all over the place. I was barely keeping myself together. Thunder boomed and then lightning cracked in the distance. It started to rain harder and the rain only made my mood worse.

After hours of riding through the rain, we crested a hill, and I finally glimpsed the mad king's castle. The spires were covered in dragons and ravens. Griffins made their perch on the wall surrounding the castle grounds while the air was filled with patrolling phoenix's. Sphinx, Centars, and the Urmahlullu prowled the forest and castle grounds.

We made our way to the front gate and a large dragon dropped down behind us. My breath fogged in the cool air, but I didn't feel it even though I was only wearing my sleeping pants. I hadn't even taken a moment to put on my boots. I jumped off my horse and turned to Lykke. He handed me my double blades and I turned to run up the front steps. I hadn't felt Cordelia in hours now and part of my soul felt numb. The fury had settled and made a home inside me.

We stormed the castle only to find it filled with warriors waiting for me and it was the welcome I needed. I was blood thirsty after that long ride... after feeling her ripped from me.

I lunged forward and began my assault. I tore through them leaving a path of destruction behind me. "WHERE IS SHE?!" I roared as I sliced through limbs. Blood coated my body and face. It trickled from my blades in a steady stream. No one answered me with any other than screams. I saw Emon standing at the top of the stairs, and I focused on him.

"WHERE IS SHE?!" I roared again rushing the stairs. I mowed through the pathetic excuse for guards in my way like a wolf surrounded by a flock of sheep and came face to face with Emon. I grabbed him by his throat and asked him one last time where Cordelia was. I could hear my men fighting in the background, but Emon held my focus.

He began laughing hysterically, "She's gone, and you'll never find her. We took her from the library and she's on her way to her soon to be husband… KING DAEMONGER," he continued laughing as the shadows began to shift and change form. Hydras and other creatures of the dark were coming from everywhere out of the shadows. Unseelie fae began pouring into the room.

At least that fucker was dead. I had wanted to kill him for a while, but it hadn't sated the rage I was feeling. Instead, it seemed to have only fueled it. Brutus had Cordelia and who knows what that fucker was going to do to her. I didn't know him much. The few interactions I had with him had been very bad. After all Cordelia wasn't the first thing, he had taken from me.

My fury had been building and thinking about all that Brutus had taken from me tipped me over the edge. I couldn't keep it restrained any longer. I needed to shift, and I couldn't because of the fucker that took my fiancé. I screamed and let everyone here feel my wrath. My feet left the floor as my arms rose. Everything went blurry and then bright. Lightning came from within me and struck every repulsive creature within the castle walls. It lasted for what felt like en eternity. Endless electricity poured from me like I was just a conduit with no control. I felt every connection and every life I took. Nothing could sate my rage. It wasn't until the last man crumbled that I felt the power within me ebb. Vilulf grabbed me as my feet hit the ground. He held me up while my legs shook, and my vision slowly returned to normal. Fuck. I was losing it. I needed a moment to pull myself together.

"I have you," he said as I tried to stand and regain my composure. "I already sent the twins to the library. I could smell that Helvig was here within the last few hours. We will find him and then we will know what exactly happened," Vilulf said trying to reassure me. It didn't reassure me at all though. I couldn't even appreciate his attempt.

I pushed away from him and began climbing the stairs to the library with shaking legs. It took all the energy I had left in me. Vilulf was saying something to our men around us, but I couldn't hear him over my pulse in my ears. I glanced behind me and saw the carnage I left in my wake. I heard the sound of the dragons leaving the roof. Vilulf was sending them out to scout and look for her without me asking. I was lucky to have him on a good day. On a day like today, I don't know what I would do without him.

Her faint scent was all I could focus on. It was so faint it made my heart break more.

"Thanks for making the order for them to look for her," I choked out. My voice was cracking and the reality that she wasn't here began to set in. We really were too late.

"She is our Queen, Ezekiel. We will get her back," Vilulf

said firmly clasping my shoulder.

We didn't speak the rest of our way to the library. I felt his worry and anger through our bond. Normally he was able to keep his emotions restrained but we were all barely keeping our shit together.

The library doors were open, and I could see the bodies of creatures everywhere.

"It looks like there was one hell of a fight that took place in here," Trygg said.

"Shit man. Helvig must have gone ballistic, but I don't understand why he didn't shift," Lykke replied. "Didn't you say that the one time you saw him shift he was the most powerful being you had ever seen? I still don't know what you mean by that."

"Where is he?" I asked, looking around the library ignoring my brother's questions. I didn't have an answer for him. I knew he wasn't here, but I had to ask where he was anyway. The shelves were knocked over. Books and bodies were everywhere. A few men that I recognized from around the castle were dead laying up against a gated section. Their eyes had been burned and only black sockets were left. Blood and guts littered the ground. I saw the puddle of blood that I knew was Helvig's. I could smell Cordelia's blood in the air too. She had only been gone from here for a few hours and she was hurt. My stomach clenched with the fear I had been trying to choke down.

"He isn't here. His blood is in the back corner and there's a small trail of it to that desk over there by the gated section," Trygg said solemnly. "The desk is covered with his blood and had large chunks taken out of it. It looks like he was tortured before they took him. If I had to guess they knocked him out

11

somehow, took her, tortured him for information and then took him as well."

Fuck. I rubbed my neck and looked around the room. He was right, it looked like they had tortured him. There were tools used only for torture tossed around and his clothes laid in shreds next to them. My body was shaking, and I didn't think I could take much more. I looked back at my men and said, "Spread out and see what you can find. We leave here in an hour." I needed to get out of here. The smell of the bodies and blood was getting to me. I had seen a lot in my lifetime but knowing that all of this around me was part of Cordelia being hurt and taken made me ready to lose control.

I turned to walk out of the library when Vilulf grabbed my arm. "You need to take a minute. You are on the edge of losing your shit and you aren't even thinking things through. She isn't dead. We would feel it. We will get her back… we just need a plan. Get your fucking shit together soon because your soulmate is depending on it. You can't lose your cool like you just did downstairs. Ever since Brutus left that scar, you haven't been able to control the lightning in this form. You know how dangerous it is. We can't afford to waste time healing you, if you let it consume you like that again."

"I know. I know," I said, scrubbing my hand down my face. Normally, I didn't have to deal with emotions. I was in control, and I never had the urge to use lightning in this form. "I'll meet you in the main hall. Sweep the castle. Capture anyone you come across for further questioning. We are officially at war with the Kingdom of Daemonger and the Kingdom of Rovini."

"Speaking of this Kingdom…" Vilulf motioned around "where do you think the king ran off to?"

"If I were a betting man, I would say he and his slimy sons are wherever Cordelia is," I turned and began walking down the hall. The same halls that I had walked down with Cordelia now felt unrecognizable.

My body had gone into auto pilot, I walked through the halls without even knowing what I was doing or where I was going. My chest ached and I could barely see. I tried to find our bond again and it was empty— it was just gone. I couldn't feel her. I had gotten used to feeling her emotions tickling the back of my mind constantly as they changed. Now I felt like there was a hole inside me. All of the good, the joy, and the warmth inside me was gone. I was a shell of a pathetic man without her. I had never heard of a soulmate bond disappearing when both people were still alive. Did they do something to her that caused our bond to disappear? My gut twisted wondering what she had gone through here.

Eventually, I found myself standing outside of her room. I reached for the handle and let out a long breath. Turning the handle, I didn't know what I would find. I did not expect to find her room empty though. Her room was completely empty of everything except her bed and large furniture. Her clothes were gone. Her brush was gone. Even the books that normally sat on her nightstand were missing. They had been prepared for this. They weren't just kidnapping her. They were moving her, and it was planned. Her father, brothers, and all of their staff were missing. It was at that moment I realized her father never had any intentions of us marrying. He had always planned to have her marry Brutus. The question was what Brutus' intentions were. He couldn't have known she was my soulmate. I had only told a select few people and I knew none of them wouldn't have said anything.

I stood in her room staring at her bed trying to fit all the pieces together in my mind. I had to get her back and I needed a plan. If they were heading straight to Brutus, they would be out of Rovini territory and already in Daemonger territory by now.

I gathered the few items of mine I had left behind and walked out of the room. I was still coated in blood as I pulled on a fresh shirt. I walked down her hallway to the black doors that led to the main castle. It was only then I noticed the ancient writing around the door. I studied it for a long time. It wasn't anything I recognized and that said a lot. Part of my training as a child was to learn lots of languages from the realm. The ones that I couldn't speak, I could at least be able to identify and make some of it out. This language looked old.

I found Vilulf in the main entrance and nodded to him, "Get someone to tell me what the language is around those black doors. I want to know what it says. I don't recognize it, but it looks unseelie. Then we will meet at the Northern border camp. We have a battle to win and war to wage," I said with firm determination. A plan was beginning to form in my head.

"I won't lie. It worries me a bit that you don't know what language it is," Lykke said. "I will find someone who can identify it and translate whatever it says."

"I just want to make sure we are all on the same page with this. We are officially waging war against Brutus and King Rovini as well as anyone that chooses to ally with them?" Vilulf asked.

An image of Cordelia thanking me for coming for her when she was attacked in the training yard popped into my head.

"I will always come for you. It is my duty to protect you. I know you don't fully believe that we are soulmates, but I do. I know we are. Now that I have found you, I can't lose you. I would tear this realm apart to get to you. I would fill it with death and chaos until we were reunited." I had told her in response.

"I once told Cordelia that I would fill this realm with death and chaos if she were ever taken from me. I think it's time I live up to that promise," I said to Vilulf.

Chapter Two

Cordelia

I watched through narrowed eyes as King Daemonger sliced the head of three women down in the valley. Their heads rolled across the ground as two men in front of me laughed.

"Happy Tyche," one man yelled out, way too excited over seeing the women's heads roll.

My stomach twisted and I felt like I was going to puke. They beheaded these women because it was Tyche. That can't be right. Looking at Quinlan I asked, "Is today the start of Tyche?"

"Yeah. I think that they—"

An unseelie creature interrupted him, stating in a low ghostly voice, "Happy Tyche, Queen. It is custom to behead a woman as an offering to the Goddess Tyche in hopes to receive her favor." A chill slowly crept up my spine at his words.They did this every year for Tyche. How many innocent women were sacrificed over the years? Bile filled my throat.

"It looks like King Daemonger is hoping to increase his favor and fortune three times over," another creature squealed in a high-pitched voice that hurt my ears.

My heart ached as the realization hit me. I was supposed to marry Zeke during Tyche. That thought rolled through me leaving no part of my mind untouched. We should have been starting our new lives together. Helvig would have been there with us, celebrating and being the best friend anyone could have asked for. I was so sad that Zeke likely knew what today was and was hurting too. Quickly though, my sadness turned to anger. Red hot anger. Before I could even think about it, I spoke.

"As soon as I am Queen, this will be the first of many traditions I change," I seethed. It didn't matter whether I was to be Queen here or with Zeke. Either way, I would not let traditions like murdering women in hope it would increase luck continue on.

The creatures all started murmuring and protesting what I had said.

"Maybe you should wait until you are safe before starting to upset them," Draug said, smirking and rolling his eyes. His beard was long and overgrown, but I could still see the smirk underneath it.

I watched King Daemonger and his army as we descended the mountain. I didn't know how large Zeke's army was, but I knew how large my fathers was. His and Brutus' combined was scary. How would Zeke ever be able to take down an army this large? There were so many beasts and creatures that I had never seen before. Some with large wings others with serpent like bodies.

Resolve slowly crept in. I knew what I was going to have to do.

If I wanted to get my meadow for my future children and peace in the realm, I would have to take the disease out myself. Starting with the source of the disease. King Daemonger and my father, King Rovini. They thought that bringing me here would be a good thing. Little did they know, I would be an end to them all. A small smile played on my mouth as I thought about how shocked my father would be when his plans all fell through. First, I would have to put King Daemonger and my father against each other. It would not only slow down my father's assault on the realm but distract Brutus from Zeke. Secondly, I would need to figure out what temple my father's magic was in. I needed to take his magic for myself to ensure that he could never reach it.

"What are you thinking about?" Zander whispered in my ear, tickling me. "Your emotions have gone from sad, to angry, to dare I say amused?" Sharing a horse with Zander was surprisingly comfortable.

"You know what they say, there is no fury like a woman scorned, or something like that," I said chuckling.

"Yah women are scary just in general and then when you piss one off...its a bad day for everyone. My dad always said that if mom wasn't happy then no one would be happy," Quinlan chimed in. I could just see a man that looked just like Quinlan making that comment to a little boy.

We laughed and I couldn't help but think about how much I already cared for these three men around me and soon Alba. She was special. I didn't know why but I could feel it in my bones.

Quinlan looked up at me and smiled that pretty boy smile, "I bet if you get pissed off enough, everyone around here will end up cowering in fear. I won't though but Zander will for sure. You already have him wrapped around your fingers," he laughed as Zander reached down and smacked him in the back of his head making his blond hair toss around.

"Yeah. You wouldn't be cowering because you would be too busy shitting yourself. I on the other hand would be kneeling before our Queen. There's a difference," Zander said to him. "I bet Cordelia ends up bringing everyone to their knees."

Quinlan laughed even harder and with that same pretty boy smile that I was learning quickly was a telltale sign of trouble and said, "I remember the last time I knelt before a woman. She was naked and I had the best meal of my life".

At that Draug finally chimed in with a straight face, smoothing his long red beard with one hand, "Might have been the best of your life but it was probably barely mediocre for her." This had us all roaring. The look on Quinlans face had me laughing even harder. It wasn't until I stopped laughing that I realized the caravan had stopped moving and we were at the base of the mountain walking up the path that led to the Castle entrance. Shops and homes lined the path and looked like they had seen better days.

There were unseelie creatures everywhere watching us. The villagers had stopped whatever they were doing and bowed as I rode past them. They looked tired and poor. Most of their clothes were dirty, old and ripped. I reached my hand over to Zander's leg and briefly gave it a squeeze. I could feel my anxiety and worry bubbling up inside me. My stomach started to twist, and my bowels felt loose. This was

19

the beginning of how I would take down King Daemonger. Starting now, everything I did would impact not only these people but the realm around us.

We continued to follow the caravan up the dirty road until I saw what looked to be a tailor store next door to a dress shop. I motioned for Zander to take us towards them.

"Hello!" I said waving to a nearby group of women and young girls outside of the dress shop. "I am Cordelia Rovini."

They all bent at their knees and lowered themselves to the ground bowing to me.

"Please, you don't need to bow. Stand and tell me your names," I said as friendly as I could be. They glanced at each other before they slowly rose. I slid my leg over the saddle and hopped down from the horse. Quinlan and Draug were immediately on each side of me by the time I righted myself.

An old lady stepped forward before them and said, "My name is Esther, your majesty. These are my granddaughters Loren, Valerina, and Sylvia. They work in my shop here," she motioned to the dress shop.

"Nice to meet you all! I am honored to meet the owner of this lovely shop. I will be needing some items for my wardrobe and for my lady in wait's wardrobe as well. It seems many of my items were lost in the travels. How do I book an appointment to come and get my measurements taken?" I asked, trying to be as friendly as possible. I need to get the villagers on my side. I needed them to like me and trust me. Plus, it would be great to get new jumpsuits made. I would no longer wear the dresses that my father saw fit for me. I would from now on wear whatever it is that I want to wear.

"You do not need an appointment, my lady. You can come whenever it pleases you and we will make you our number one priority," she said beaming while her gray curly hair bounced as she spoke.

The caravan had continued forward to the Castle while we stood and talked.

"Oh, I could never do that. I wouldn't ever want to take away from your business and other people's time. Could I schedule an appointment for tomorrow afternoon?" I asked eagerly.

"Of course, my lady. Do you have any preference on materials or styles? I bet a more fitted style looks marvelous on you."

"Actually, have you ever made a woman's jumpsuit? I prefer pants over dresses, but I still want a feminine look to it. I like it thin enough that it isn't heavy and doesn't weigh me down... but it flows enough that I have room to move and run if I want. I don't want to be hindered if I need to jump on a horse or climb something," I said thinking about all the things I would need to be able to do if I ever got the chance to escape here.

Her eyes widened and she was speechless. Ah yes, by the looks of the town here I'm sure most women do not wear pants.

"You are the Queen. Why would you ever need to climb something?" Loren said, rolling her eyes. She looked to be about 10 and clearly hadn't learned manners yet. I was just glad no one was around us. I wouldn't want her getting in trouble for speaking out.

"Loren," Sylvia hissed as she fell to her knees and started begging, "I am so sorry for my sister's insolence. Please forgive her. She will be punished at home accordingly. Please my queen, I am so sorry".

Valerina and Esther were both on their knees. Lorens face was as white as a ghost and her hand was over her mouth. I was horrified at their reaction. Did they think I would have her killed right here for speaking out? What kind of place was this? What kind of abuse were they used to seeing?

"It's okay," I said softly. "She was merely curious. There is nothing to forgive. I would teach her better in regard to other people. Other members of the royal family would not be so understanding. Please get up." It made me uncomfortable to have people on their knees before me. Actually, this whole situation made me incredibly uncomfortable. I just wanted to get some new clothes and make nice with these people.

I looked at Quinlan and he was holding back a laugh at my expression. Draug stepped forward and helped Esther to her feet. "Up you go, my lady," he said.

The women looked confused and I turned to say something to Zander when I saw that a crowd had gathered. Zander was still atop the horse and had his hand resting on his blade as he surveyed the crowd around us. He was always alert and ever the predator ready to attack and protect me at a seconds notice.

The crowd all had mixed expressions of shock and curiosity. I stepped closer to Quinlan out of instinct and said to the women, "I look forward to tomorrow afternoon then."

I smiled brightly trying to hide the inner panic I felt at the situation that just occurred and the surrounding crowd. "I think I would like to walk the rest of the way," I said to no one in particular. I didn't want to get back on the horse and be so high above everyone. Zander smiled and dismounted easily. He walked with the horse behind me while Draug and Quinlan were on each side of me. I smiled and waved to people as we walked. This was okay. I was getting a feel for them, and they were getting a feel for me.

"It would be similar to this, walking through the streets of a village back home," Draug said and I knew he meant the Havaror Kingdom. "Only there wouldn't be any fear. Everyone would be eager and curious to get a glimpse at their Queen. Here they seem to be worried about what kind of Queen you will be." I thought about when Helvig and I had made a bet. If he lost, he would have had to walk around the village introducing me to his people and quacking like a duck. A small smile had started to spread across my lips at the image of Helvig walking like a duck and quacking, but it quickly fell as the void in my chest opened wide. Everything went blurry around me as I felt tears fill my eyes. I missed him more than I had ever thought I was capable of missing someone. I might have even missed him more than Zeke but that wasn't something I was ready to think about.

"Was that reaction to Loren speaking out normal?" I asked him, trying to change the path my thoughts had taken. If I started down the path of thinking about Helvig I would be a blubbering mess within minutes. "Do they all live each day in fear that one simple thing will mean they're killed or brutally punished?"

Quinlan grimaced and said, "The rules and traditions here are far more barbaric than anywhere else in the realm. You have to keep in mind that they called Brutus Daemonger's father Daemonger the Violent."

"People here could die just because King Daemonger says so. He doesn't need an explanation. Nor would he provide them with one." Draug said with sadness in his eyes.

"Have any of you ever been here before or have any of you

ever met King Daemonger?"

"No." Zander said softly from behind us.

I shared the empathy they had for the people here. No one should live their lives in that kind of fear. That wouldn't even be really living their life. I decided at that moment that I already hated Brutus Daemonger.

We walked slowly and stopped to speak with small shop owners and Draug even handed out some coins that he had in his pockets. I would have to get a good look at the treasury here. Then I could have an endless supply of coins to hand out. As I watched Draug hand a very dirty little boy a coin, I heard hooves on the bricks. Looking up I saw Voronion and Elbereth, along with two dozen soldiers heading straight towards us. For the god's sake, what the hell were they doing now?

"YOU SHOULD HAVE ALREADY BEEN TO THE CAS-TLE TO MEET YOUR KING!" Elbereth shouted. Ugh she just rubbed me the wrong way. Who the hell did this bitch think she was?

Voronion narrowed his eyes and gave her a sideways glance before speaking, "King Daemonger is waiting for you to make your appearance. He does not like to be kept waiting."

"Of course, he doesn't. I don't know one person that actually enjoys waiting for something. I don't think anyone has ever said 'Oh gee I am looking forward to waiting,'" I scoffed and rolled my eyes. Yes, I was purposefully being petulant. I felt Zander's presence behind me before I saw him. He was stiff and in a defensive mode before I could even register why.

Quinlan did exactly what I expected him to though. He laughed loudly at my words causing Draug to stiffen his spine making his powerful essence seem almost overwhelming. The tension in the air was almost palpable.

"How dare you speak to him that way. I might not be allowed to hurt you specifically, but no one said anything about your companions," Elbereth scoffed with a cruel smirk spreading across her face. Suddenly, Quinlan was on his knees gasping for air. His eyes were wide and momentary fear flashed through them.

"Elbereth, that is enough," Voronion said, rolling his eyes as if all of this was beneath him.

Elbereth didn't stop though. Instead, she stared me straight in my eyes and smiled wider. She looked crazed. Panic began to seize me. Oh no, I couldn't lose Quinlan. "LET HIM GO," I screamed at her. My voice cracked, betraying my emotions I was trying to hide.

She lifted her hand in the air palm open wide. I felt a weird pulse in the back of my mind and then I could hear Quinlan in my mind, "It will all be okay, my queen." At that moment she closed her hand in a fist and yanked it downward. Quinlan quit moving and fell flat on his face, his blond hair spread out in a mess. It all happened so fast. Within seconds he was on his face in the dirt.

A gasp went through the crowd.

"Quinlan!" I shouted falling to my knees and rolling him over. He wasn't breathing. Suddenly I was transported to the night I was taken. All I could hear was that sound from the library. The sound of flesh splattering. The sound of Helvig being murdered by these people. Helvig was gone. Quinlan is gone now too. My heart tore open and I couldn't breathe. My chest felt like it was seizing up and my breaths came in short spurts. No. No. No. No. A sob broke through me and I felt all the breath leave my lungs. Not from something Elbereth was doing but from the overwhelming emotions rolling through me. She had killed him. Quinlan was my guard. MINE. Just as Helvig was my guard that day. My friend that day. Another one of my men had been hurt and there was nothing I could do about it. I was weak and couldn't save him.

Zander was at my side attempting to help me up, but my sadness had already started to turn to anger. All I saw was red. Draug had knelt down on Quinlans other side and was trying to take his pulse. I didn't need to wait for him to tell me Quinlan was dead. I felt him disappear from me only a few moments after he appeared. I knew in my soul that he was dead. I let Zander pull me to my feet but before he could say anything to me, I turned and threw my dagger. In one swift motion, I grabbed his blade and moved faster than I had ever moved before. My dagger stabbed her in her chest in the exact spot the arrow had pierced me. I had thrown it so hard that it knocked her back. Screaming, she flew off her horse backwards and landed hard on the ground.

"STAND UP AND FIGHT ME LIKE A REAL WOMAN. HOW DARE YOU USE YOUR MAGIC ON SOMEONE WHO COULD NOT DEFEND THEMSELF AGAINST IT. STAND UP AND FIGHT ME!" I screamed at her, my voice was shrill and filled with fury. The roaring in my ears wouldn't stop. It couldn't stop. Not with the sound of flesh, Helvig's flesh, splattering in my mind over and over again. Not with the sight of Quinlan falling to the ground replaying over and over. My mind that once held Quinlan's final words was now empty of him.

The crowd had gone silent and backed up. The soldiers had started to surround us.

"Cordelia, my Queen. Do you really think this is necessary over his death? It's not like—" Voronion had started but I didn't care what he had to say.

"I SAID STAND UP AND FIGHT ME. DO NOT MAKE ME TELL YOU AGAIN," I screamed even louder. My throat ached from just how loudly I had yelled at her.

Elbereth smiled as she stood up. The breath began leaving my lungs and my eyes widened for a moment. She took the bait and did exactly what I expected her to do. She would want to make this slow and painful for me… I was counting on that. I kept thinking about the air around me moving into my lungs. I was slow moving but it was working. She was trying to take all the air out and I kept refilling it. My lungs burned and my chest felt like it could explode from all the pressure changes. A malicious smile crept onto my lips.

"STOP IT NOW ELBERETH AND I WON'T SENTENCE YOU TO DEATH FOR HARMING THE QUEEN. STOP IT NOW," Voronion scolded. His voice sounded shocked and almost panicked. If she killed me, I wonder what would happen to him. He had turned in his saddle and was facing her. He didn't even see my approach.

I slowly walked closer to her grinning from ear to ear. A look of shock flashed across her beautifully cruel face making me smile wider almost wildly.

"You… you should be dead…" she mumbled. "How… How are you doing that? You don't have magic. Your father said you don't, and I haven't felt any," She gasped. The realization that she was not a threat to me anymore was setting in. I thoroughly enjoyed watching her scramble. Maybe there was something dark inside me but after she killed Quinlan, I wanted her to feel afraid.

I was close enough now that I could smell the metallic scent of her blood in the air. I lifted Zander's blade and swung. Meeting little resistance, I cut straight through her neck and spine. Wet warm blood splattered my face as her head fell off her body. Suddenly my lungs filled with air. I choked for a moment on all the air and then bent down and removed my dagger from her chest. It made a wet suctioning sound as I pulled it from her chest. Carefully, I wiped it across her dress making sure to remove as much blood as possible. I guess that made a fourth woman beheaded on Tyche.

I turned my head and saw the silent shocked faces of the crowd around us. I stood slowly and walked back towards my men. My chest ached from her magic and from the loss of another one of my men. No one spoke as I handed Zander back his blade. He took it, eyeing me curiously.

The crowd started cheering and Voronion looked horrified at what just took place. His mouth was open like he wanted to say something, but nothing came out. He just sat there staring at me. I walked to the horse and mounted it.

Zander walked up beside me and put one hand on his hip. The smirk on his face said it all. "You do remember that Quinlan is a Phoenix, right? He will be fine in less than 20 minutes now. That was pretty cool though because she was really annoying. I'm glad we won't have to deal with that anymore," he chuckled and shrugged his shoulders in such a casual way. As if he was used to seeing something like this and it was all normal, but shock registered through me. I had forgotten that Quinlan was a Phoenix. I was so caught up in my emotions that she was hurting him. He tried to tell me but feeling him die just moments later... It rocked me.

He would be fine though. He was a fucking phoenix.

I hadn't lost him like I lost Helvig. The pain from Helvigs loss was still so volatile, and I wasn't even sure why. I had considered Helvig a friend, but his loyalty lay with Zeke. He was Zeke's man and not mine. He was Zeke's friend first. Yet the pain from losing him felt bottomless. I kept my face from betraying my rollercoaster of emotions.

I looked from Zander to Draug to Quinlan who was starting to breathe again. These were MY men. They weren't Zeke's men… I mean they were, but they were also MINE. They would remain my guards as long as they wanted to. No one else would ever replace them.

I made eye contact with Voronion and said, "No one touches my men or those I care for and gets to live. No one torments these villagers and most of all no one uses magic on an innocent person that can't defend themselves."

Chapter Three

Voronion just sat there, blinking at me. The crowd around us was cheering for me and I didn't know why exactly. Had Elbereth tortured people here? Did they know what kind of person she was, and they were happy she was gone? Did they just like violence? I mean they just watched me attack and slaughter her and no one seemed afraid now.

I directed my horse over to Quinlan. He was still laying on the ground with his eyes closed barely breathing. My heart ached and I felt tears pricking my eyes. I couldn't imagine what it must feel like to die and the process that it took Quinlan to wake back up. I could only imagine how painful it must have been for him.

"Voronion, stop gaping at me like a fish out of water and do something useful. Go get a cart or something for us to put Quinlan in," I said, rolling my eyes. He was absolutely useless, and I didn't understand why someone like Brutus would bother keeping him around.

"Uhh. Yes, my queen," he said, still shocked. I wasn't sure if it was from what he witnessed or from how I was talking to him. Either way, I didn't really care.

I hopped down from my horse and knelt next to Quinlan. I slid my fingers through his blond hair moving it away from his neck. My hands shook as I checked for a pulse, something deep inside me needed reassurance that he would be okay. Electricity buzzed through my fingers at our skin touching. The only other time I had felt it was when I touched Zeke. I had never felt a jolt like that with anyone else until now.

Quinlan's eyes opened, and he gasped. Suddenly, he was jolted up into the air. Within the blink of an eye, he became a large Phoenix. His beak was bright yellow, his eyes burned with the fire of 1000 suns, and his tail stretched like ribbons. His feathers were varying shades of red, orange, and yellow and depending on how the sun was hitting his feathers, the colors changed from one shade to another. He was beautiful and I had never seen anything like him before.

He let out a terrifying shriek pulling me from my thoughts. The crowd around us screamed and scattered. I wasn't afraid though. I knew Quinlan was there and he wouldn't hurt me. Zander launched himself on top of me knocking us over and wrapping me in his arms. His shoulder took the brunt of the impact, but it still made my teeth clatter. My whole body buzzed with electricity where Zander was touching me. The Phoenix version of Quinlan shrieked again, and I could just see him over Zander's shoulder.

Before I could ask Zander what the fuck, fire engulfed Quinlan and then burst from him like an explosion from the inside out.

"Tuck your head under me. Your eyes will burn from the

ash and smoke," Zander yelled into my ear. His words and his voice sent shivers up my spine. I took one last look at Quinlan's phoenix form and buried my face into Zander's chest.

I could feel the heat from Quinlan's phoenix flames around us and it was almost suffocating. The air smelt like burnt flesh and my lungs burned worse than before.

The shrieking had started out very faint and then grew louder and louder. I heard what sounded like a body hitting the ground. Quinlan must have shifted back into his human form and fell to the ground.

I shoved Zander off and rushed towards where Quinlan had been.

"Cordelia, don't he'll burn you still!" Zander shouted as he scrambled to his feet trying to chase after me.

My eyes burned from the smoke and my lungs felt too full like they couldn't expand anymore.

"He's in pain. I can't stand to hear his screaming. We have to help him," I said to him.

There wasn't any more fire in the sky. Instead, just smoke and ash falling like snow in the middle of a storm.

"You can't help him. Not from this. He will still burn you! You have to wait until his body cools down," Zander tried reasoning with me, but I wouldn't hear him.

I started crawling on my hands and knees when I saw Draug heading towards me. "My Queen, you have to stop. He will never forgive himself for burning you."

"How can you just stand there and listen to him scream like that? He's in so much pain and agony," tears rolled down my cheeks.

Draug looked in disbelief and just shook his head. "What

screams? What screams, Cordelia?"

I ignored Draug and started feeling out with my hands searching for Quinlan in all the ash. I knew deep down inside me that he was somewhere close to me. Crawling on what felt like hot coals, my knees began to hurt. Each time I moved, I felt the hot prick of ash and cinders kissing my skin. Tears flooded my eyes that burned like they had been touched by the flames and streamed down my face.

Quinlans screams were so loud I thought my ear drums were going to burst. He had to be so close to me. I scooted once more and dug into the ashes causing it to puff in the air clouding my visibility even more. My hands burned as I dug through the hot snow-like ash. Finally, I felt Quinlan and grabbed onto what I thought was his arm. I pulled as my hand sizzled from the intensity of his heat. The air began smelling like fresh meat over an open fire and it took me a moment to realize that smell was coming from me. It was my flesh burning from where our skin touched.

"Quin. Quinlan! I am here. It's okay. I am here." I pulled his head and body into my lap. His eyes and mouth were closed but I could hear his screams. I stared at his closed mouth for a moment as I realized I could hear him inside my head. I followed his voice in my head and tried talking to him. *I am here. I have you. I am here.* I kept trying to communicate with him over and over again.

The fabric of my clothes burnt away in the spots it touched him. My skin felt hot but somehow, I wasn't burning any deeper than a mere flesh wound. I wished I could take his pain from him. I would rather feel his pain than him go through this. It was because of me that he had been killed in the first place. I made him laugh and Elbereth took her anger

33

out of him.

My tears splattered on his forehead as I sat there holding him. I felt Zanders gentle hands on me. I had been so focused on Quinlans pain that I hadn't felt Zanders worry for me. I could feel it now though. I didn't know if he was pushing it through this bond of ours or if he was just worried about me that much that it overflowed my mind.

Zander sat behind me and wrapped his body around me, careful to not pull me away from Quinlan. Draug was on the other side of Quinlan and slowly reached to place his hand on top of mine.

"He will be okay. He knows we are here. He will be okay in time. Just give him time," Draug said, trying to ease my fear and panic.

I felt Zander growl behind me and then wings flew up and spread out behind us. The movement cleared some of the smoke from around us and I saw that we had been surrounded by horrendous unseelie creatures. I wasn't afraid though. It only made me feel more protective over Quinlan in this vulnerable state. If they tried anything right now, I would murder them all and I wasn't sure if their deaths would even haunt me.

Zander let out a guttural roar as his wings wrapped around the four of us; creating a barrier and some privacy from the large crowd that surrounded us.

Quinlan's breathing seemed fuller now and I felt his muscles twitch. I held on tight to him and leaned forward placing my head on his chest. I listened to his heartbeat grow steady and strong. We sat like this for what felt like hours but must have only been minutes. Zander kept making soothing circles on my thigh with his fingers and there was a purring sound that

I thought came from Draug. It was rhythmic and sad as it reached out to touch my soul and calmed me.

It wasn't until I felt two hands touch my head and cheeks that I opened my eyes. Quinlan cleared his throat and said, "Cordelia, my beautiful queen, I tried to tell you I would be okay. I'm so sorry I scared you."

Tears fell freely from my eyes and each one stung more than the last. I turned my head and looked up into his eyes.

"You were in so much pain and it was because of me," I barely choked out. "It felt like you were dying over and over again. I'm so sorry. I'm so, so sorry."

I sobbed as all of my emotions came to a boiling point. My anger at everything that had happened to me. All of the unspeakable things that I had yet to process from my childhood. The loneliness I had felt my whole life until I met Zeke and Helvig. The pain and grief from losing Helvig and not being able to save him… Not being strong enough to save him. The betrayal of my family. The soul deep ache I felt for Zeke. My worry and panic for Quinlan. Lastly, the love I felt for these three men. Draug sat holding my hand still purring to me while Zander protected us and gave me the privacy I needed in this moment while holding me close. Quinlan's very first thought was to apologize to me as he ran his fingers through my hair. How was I so lucky to have them?

We sat like this for a few moments while I let all of my emotions out and wiped away my tears. I had to pull myself together. "I thought I had lost you too," I said to Quinlan and pulled away from him. He sat up carefully and said, "It's okay, one day I'll get that bitch back for suffocating me."

Zander chuckled and Draug laughed out, "Well actually Cordelia beat you to that."

"Yeah, she kind of lost it when you died. She threw her dragger knocking Elbereth off her horse and stole my blade. Elbereth tried to suffocate her too, but Cordelia just smiled at her, dare I say wickedly, and walked forward. She raised my blade and cut her down with one swipe," Zander recounted with a gleam in his eyes.

"Well, that explains the blood across you," Quinlan said, eyeing me, "I am disappointed that I missed you being a badass."

Draug pulled his hand away from mine and cleared his throat, "I think we have caused quite the scene. We should probably make our way to the castle before King Daemonger decides to kill us all."

I'd like to see him try to kill me or my men. I wouldn't hold back if it came down to me protecting them.

Zander released his hold on me and pulled his wings up. I blinked my eyes at the sunlight that now blinded me. His wings had been blocking out the crowd and now with them gone, everyone was staring at us.

Unseelie creatures, fae, and monsters moved around us as if waiting for an order to pounce. I stood slowly. My whole body ached like I had been the one to die. My joints were stiff, and I felt a little weak. Quinlan stood and shook out his arms and legs, shaking the ash off of his body.

I watched as the soot fell from his body exposing that he was completely naked now. I felt heat rush into my cheeks. Let's just say whoever ended up with him would be one lucky woman or man.

Zander was at my side with one hand holding my elbow. "Are you feeling, okay?" he asked. Concern was oozing through the bond.

36

"I'm fine," I lied to him.

Coooooorrrrdelia.... we need to have a little chat. Quinlan said to me in a sing-song voice.

I turned to him and said, "What?"

He grinned like he couldn't have been happier by my clipped response.

"What?" I said again a little harsher than I meant to be. He was obviously fine since he was back to his annoying self. Why was I feeling so poorly when he was the one that just died and came back? I knew he had been in serious pain. So why is he acting like he's totally fine?

Quinlan winked at me. Without moving his lips, he said, *"I didn't say that out loud. Just like you kept telling me that you were here. I know I didn't hear you with my ears."*

Surprise flickered through me as Quinlan's voice filled my mind.

"What's happening right now?!" Zander commanded. "I don't like the way your emotions are all over the place."

"We will talk about it later. When there's less people around," I said to them both as I stared at Quinlan.

Oh, and I like hearing you call me Quin. Only my mom has ever called me that. I like the way you say it though. It definitely provokes different feelings than my mom. This was going to get real old real fast.

How was this happening?

We have a connection, possibly even a bond. That's how. He was choosing to speak into my head rather than out loud like a normal person.

OH GODS. COULD HE HEAR ALL MY THOUGHTS?

Nope. Not all of your thoughts. Just the ones you're projecting towards me like a crazy woman. You are literally shouting inside my head. So, if you would like to take it down a notch or two that would be great. I did just die after all. My head is throbbing, and I could use some sleep. He put a hand on his hip and my eyes couldn't help but take all of him in.

Zander cleared his throat, "So, I don't want to interrupt whatever is happening, but Draug is coming over with your horse, we are literally surrounded by the villagers and unseelie fae, and you are just staring at Quinlan with your mouth hanging open and he is naked. So that's probably not a good look." At that moment I felt the sour taste of jealousy through our shared bond. Zander was jealous that there was something going on between Quinlan and me. I couldn't help but laugh a little at that thought.

Then I felt the light fruity taste of amusement through Quinlans bond with me. It was interesting that not only did I feel their emotions, but I processed the emotions as if I was tasting it. Each emotion had its own flavor.

WHAT THE ACTUAL FUCK WAS HAPPENING.

I stood frozen for a moment. It wasn't until Draug brought the horse to me and smiled brightly that I was able to pull myself together. I felt nothing from him, and I couldn't hear his thoughts.

"Your horse, my lady," he said.

"Thanks," I said sheepishly, taking the leather reins. I didn't know how to feel about any of this. I felt like a child who was clueless about the world around her. None of this seemed possible. Growing up so sheltered from magic and now being thrust into things that I was clueless about made me unsure how to proceed. I hadn't even heard about being able to mind-speak with someone until I met Zeke and yet here, I was just having a conversation with Quinlan.

My poor sweet horse was covered in soot now and definitely deserved all the best treats when she got to her stall. Apparently, when a Phoenix dies it is really dramatic, who would have known that. Although it fits perfectly with Quinlans personality. Maybe that was something they could have mentioned when I first found out he was a Phoenix. Just so I would be prepared in case it happened. The road was covered in ash and soot. Two buildings nearby had scorch marks in the front of their doors and all the windows that had been open were now closed. I would guess that ash had still managed to get in. This section of the village was utterly destroyed. I would have to remember to pay them for the damages.

Yah, you should definitely use King Daemongers funds to pay for the damages. I mean, after all, it was his consort who caused my death. Not my fault it's messy. Quinlan smiled at me.

Dude if you don't get out of my head, I swear all I will think about is Zeke's dick.

Quinlan laughed out loud and Draug and Zander turned to look at him.

"Okay. I know something is going on. I just can't figure out what it is," Draug said to us.

Zander looked at both Quinlan and I assessingly. He studied us both for a moment and then paused. "Wait. You can't," he said. Of course, Zander would be the one to figure it out. He was smart like that.

"We can't what?" I asked.

"For the god's sake. I have been trying to figure out how to do that with you and Quinlan just dies and boom you two can do that," Zander said, shaking his head and crossing his arms. "I have never been jealous of him dying until now."

"Do what?" I asked again just to tease him.

Oh, he totally knows, and he is so jealous. Quinlan's chuckle was out loud and inside my head. This was going to take some time to get used to.

"I think I missed something here," Draug said, raising an eyebrow and smoothing out his beard with his hand.

"Let's go," I said, wanting to get out of here and away from all the people staring at us. Turning to get on my horse, I saw Voronion arrive with another man riding a horse pulling a cart.

"Perfect timing. Now you three can ride and I won't have to deal with feeling guilty about you walking," I smiled like the cat that got the cream.

"What the hell happened while I was gone?" Voronion said annoyed.

"What do you mean?" He had been there when Quinlan was dying. He knew what had happened.

"Did you not take cover? You need a full bath before you are presented to the King. you are covered in ashes and soot and… blood. Gods. You make everything so much more difficult than it needs to be. He is already unhappy with you keeping him waiting. Now this," Voronion complained, gesturing at my body. Oh, so it wasn't the village or the people here that he was concerned about. Of course not, why would he be. He was just concerned about how I would be presented to King Daemonger.

"No. I'm good," I said flatly. Zanders' amusement trickled through our bond just as Quinlans laughter sounded in my head. I needed to find a way to get them out of my head. I already had enough thoughts and feelings, so I did not need theirs either.

This should be good.

"I'm sorry what? That doesn't even make sense. What do you mean 'No you're good'?" Voronion asked.

"I mean I don't need a full bath before I meet King Daemonger. He doesn't like to be kept waiting so we won't keep him waiting," I stated as the horses started to move forward towards the castle. The crowd moved just enough to let the horses through. The villagers were assessing us. They had been cheering one moment and then running in fear. I felt bad for them that their lives were so bad and chaotic here. I would have to do more for them.

"You can't be serious," Voronion said. "If you could see yourself, you would be embarrassed by how you look."

I felt complete outrage from Zander and then I heard Quinlan.

You are a vision right now. Don't let him tell you otherwise.

I didn't have to look at him to know he was speaking in my head only to me.

"I am very serious. You clearly do not know me so do not make assumptions about what I would and would not be embarrassed about. You're lucky that I don't make it worse than it is now. Come on. Let's not keep him waiting any longer," I said with a smile playing on my lips. I wished Zeke was here to see me. To see this and all that had transpired. He would probably love to see me all bloody and covered in ash.

I noticed Quinlan lean over to Draug and whisper something. Draug looked over at me and then winked. His eyes started to change and showed the silver-blue flecks in them. Draug's mouth moved as he looked at me. He smiled widely and leaned over to Quinlan.

Zeke wishes he could have been here to see you kill Elbereth. He also wishes he was here to help you navigate the new bonds you are creating. Oh, and to help you clean up.

Quinlan's eyes held a heated look to them.

I started to choke on my own spit at the last part. I cannot believe that Zeke said that to Draug who said that to Quinlan who then told me.

"Are you okay?" Voronion asked skeptically. He raised one eyebrow curiously.

Coughing a couple more times, I choked out, "Yes, I'm perfectly fine."

We rode in silence the rest of the way up to the castle. I watched the villagers staring at us as we passed them by. Some looked in awe and others seemed angry. The roads were filthy, filled with trash, abandoned houses, and garbage. Plants were dead and the closer we got to the castle the worse everything around us seemed to be. My lungs were finally starting to feel normal again. Breathing in all that smoke and ash was really rough. I hadn't thought any of that through. I just needed to get to Quinlan. That's all my brain could process. Deep down inside me there was this part that knew I would be fine no matter what happened. So, the rest of me just threw caution to the wind and went for whatever my emotions were pushing me towards. Time and time again Ragnor tried to beat that instinct out of me. Yet, time and time again my emotions fueled me. I wished I had been able to get to Helvig. I would have done anything to save him that day. Maybe that's why I was so desperate to get to Quinlan.

The closer we got the more breathtaking the castle became. It was huge with spires that were magnificent in a dark and ominous kind of way. They looked like they touched the sky. The vines growing on the castle must have taken years to grow and take over such a large area. I didn't see any flowers. Just some bushes and trees that looked half dead. Unseelie fae and shadow creatures were everywhere around the castle grounds. They seemed to be lurking in every shadow watching us. The air smelled slightly like mold and decay which made my nose itch.

As we passed through the gated archway, I straightened my spine. I could do this. I could face King daemonger, find his weakness, kill him, kill off my father, and bring peace to the realm. No big deal. I had this in the bag.

Excuse me. you plan to do what? Does King Havaror know about this? I think you need to talk this over with us. Our job is to keep you safe until extraction. Whenever that may be. You plan to kill King Daemonger and your father? Who will rule their kingdoms? Are you wanting to take over like your father has? What's your angle here? Quinlan was back to shouting in my mind. I could feel the start of a headache already.

Get out of my thoughts. No. I don't want to take over the realm like my father. I want to bring peace to the realm. I want this war to end. I want to rid this realm of the disease that is evil like my father and the violent Daemonger line. I don't need Zeke's permission to do that or anyones permission for that matter. I don't have to discuss this with anyone if I choose not to. If I put myself in danger, then that is my problem. NOT yours, Zanders, or Draugs. I have been surviving by myself for years now. Also, if you are going to butt into my head you could at least do it quieter.

I was furious with him. I didn't need anyone's permission before I acted. He needed to butt out of the conversations I had with myself, and I needed to figure out how to keep him out.

We will be talking about this later. Along with Zeke. I think there's so much more at play here than we know. Like the fact that you and I can do this. It isn't normal. I'm not complaining. It just isn't normal.

Quinlan gave me a pointed look for emphasis.

GET OUT OF MY HEAD!

We approached the stone steps of the castle just as elderly man stepped forward. He held his hand out to me.

"My lady," he said, starting to bow but stopped when he took in my appearance. His eyebrows were raised in surprise. Quickly he bowed like he just remembered that he was supposed to do so. He was probably expecting something very different from how I looked currently.

I hopped down from my horse without giving him a second look.

"Please find my companion here, some pants and take this sweet horse to the stables. She deserves the best treats available."

He looked over my shoulder and his eyes widened. "Yes, of course," he practically ran away.

This was it. I would be walking in to meet Brutus face to face. I decided I would not call him King Daemonger to his face. I would only refer to him as Brutus and Brutus only. He might hate it and want to kill me for it, but I didn't care. He was no king of mine.

Zander was at my side giving me a tight smile. "Are you ready for this?"

Draug approached slowly and nodded.

"As ready as I'll ever be," I said to them. How prepared can one be when going to meet someone with a reputation as bad as his.

The old man that was finding Quinlan some pants appeared

with clothes in his hands.

Quinlan dressed quickly and came to us.

"Going forward," I said. "It's us four and Alba, okay? We stick together. We have to watch each other's backs, and most importantly we leave no one behind."

"My queen," Draug said, taking in a sharp breath. "Our job is to ensure your safety. No matter the cost."

"No. Not anymore. I can't lose any of you," I said, biting down the flood of emotions that came with the thought of losing one of my men… the thought of losing Helvig.

Voronion approached and sighed loudly, "If you are done with this chatter, I believe King Daemonger is anxiously awaiting to meet his betrothed queen."

"Let's go then," I said with a smile. "Quit holding us up, Onion." I decided at some point on the ride up here that would be Voronions new nickname, Onion. Mostly because I hated onions and for some reason, I just hated him.

Voronions eyes grew wide "Excuse me, my lady, I don't like being—"

"Come on Onion, you're holding us up again. Let's go," I barked out. Quinlan let out a laugh that he tried to cover up with a coughing sound. He ended up sounding like he was choking.

"Yes of course, my lady," he said. If I was going to be quote his queen quote, then it looks like it was time for me to start acting my part. The new bitch queen it would have to be.

We approached the doors and I saw my reflection in the polished marble. My hair was wild, my clothes were burnt and falling apart, I had ashes and soot all over me, blood splatter was across my face and chest and matted in my hair, I still had that bandage on me from when I was shot with an arrow, so ya… I looked fucking great. Hopefully, I looked ridiculous enough that he didn't want to spend much time with me.

Chapter Four

I walked next to Voronion with my men behind us. The double doors opened slowly as we approached.

"King Daemonger will be waiting for us in the throne room," he said.

"Oh good. I'm excited to see what my throne will look like," I said sarcastically as we crossed the threshold. A chill went up my spine and I felt cold pressure pushing on my head. Something told me to turn and run but I ignored it. There was dark magic here. I could feel the evil pulse of it. The ceilings were high as if this place had been made for a giant race of evil men.

All the doorways were arched and tall... just as tall as the ceilings actually. There were exposed bricks everywhere. Like someone had fought hard in this hall and the walls took the damage.

We walked silently to the end of the hall where two guards were standing along with two shadow creatures. I didn't have a way to describe them. They were all black with the head of a wolf, body and legs of a centipede, and tail of a monkey. They were huge. At Least 8 feet tall if not taller. I didn't think they were unseelie. They seemed to be something that I had never encountered before. Something… other.

I narrowed my eyes on them. I recognized the men as my father's personal guard and of course fucking Ragnor. My bad feeling only got worse as we approached them.

"Is he in here as well?" I said to no one in particular.

"Who?" Voronion asked.

"Yes, Princess Cordelia," one of the guards replied. They knew I meant my father.

"Perfect," I said coldly. He was going to hate how I looked right now. The only thing I wish I could have changed was my ripped dress. I would have loved to be in pants. That would have really added the final touch considering my father hated when I wore pants. He always wanted me in dresses posed as the perfect little princess.

"Alright then, Let's have it. I hope you're ready for a show boys," I said to them, winking over my shoulder.

They opened the doors and I held my head high, narrowing my eyes slightly, and holding my mouth firm. I was strong. I was brave. I am Queen Cordelia Havaror and nothing would change that. Okay so Zeke and I weren't technically married yet and it might never happen but we were soulmates, right? I felt like I should be able to just take his name whenever I felt like it. Although, the thought didn't bring me the courage I thought it would.

My father was standing on the dais while talking to a few men. One of which took my breath away and not in the love at first sight kind of take your breath away. More of a holy shit is this real-life kind of take your breath away.

He was larger than all the other men. He almost seemed too large to be real. Half of his head was shaved and tattooed with swirling markings that went down his neck and under his shirt. The other half of his head had long black hair with white tips. He had strong, sharp features, and his eyes were solid black. There was no white in his eyes at all. It made it hard to tell exactly where he was looking. He was made of full, thick muscles. Zeke was nowhere near as jacked as this guy. Gods he was like... well a god. I almost couldn't believe Zeke and him were related but I saw the similarities in the subtle parts of him. Their jaw lines were similar, their eye shapes and noses were the same. Aside from the similarities he shared with Zeke there was something familiar about him. As I approached, I realized that the white tips of his hair were actually a pale purple. It was so pale that from a distance it just appeared white.

My father turned and dropped the glass that was in his hand. It shattered as it hit the pristine marble floor. "MY GODS. Cordelia, what has happened to you!" he said. As if he really cared if something had happened to me. He only cared about appearance.

"I don't know what you mean," I said innocently tossing my hair over my shoulder exposing my bandaged shoulder even more.

"You are.. You are horrendous," he stated, blinking like if he just blinked enough times maybe It would change how I looked. It only made me grit my teeth.

"Oh," I said softly, looking down at myself. "Some stuff happened on the way here like being attacked, murder, death... you know, the usual kind of welcoming to a new Kingdom." I glared at them.

49

King Daemonger, um Brutus, narrowed his eyes and stepped forward.

"Is that Elbereths blood I smell on you?" Brutus questioned with his black eyes boring into me. It was a little creepy to say the least. How he knew the smell of Elbereths blood was beyond me.

"It is," I said flatly, shrugging one shoulder. I reached into the saddle bag I had brought in with me and pulled out her head. I had used my magic to move her head into the bag while everyone was distracted. I tossed it at my father's feet. I could have tossed it to Brutus, but I didn't think he would care as much as my father would. He seemed like this sort of thing would only amuse him and I didn't want to be anyone's entertainment.

"Why... Why is her blood all over you?" he said calmly, cocking his head to one side. I couldn't tell if he was just curious or if this was the calm before the storm. It wasn't like he hadn't just watched me toss her head onto the floor. His black eyes continued to study me.

My father gasped as her head hit the floor by his feet with a thud, "Cordelia! How dare you disrespect me and King Daemonger with this nonsense!"

I ignored my father and looked around the room taking in every detail when my eyes caught Lance's. He truly was beautiful and part of me missed our friendship. He had been my only companion for years. Then it hit me. He shouldn't have been here. I dismissed him. You have to be fucking kidding me? After I dismissed him, he probably ran straight to my father. I shouldn't have been surprised but I was. Maybe he had never been loyal to me. Maybe it was truly all for my father. After all, he did nothing to stop them hurting me and killing Helvig.

"I cut her head off and it got a little messy," I deadpanned. "Consider it a thank you for bringing me here." My father and brothers, along with the men standing by my father, gasped at my continued disrespect. They were worse than a room full of girls. All this gasping was pathetic.

Brutus laughed, "You cut down Elbereth before she was able to take the breath from your lungs?"

"I believe that is exactly what I just said," I stated, turning towards Brutus and narrowing my eyes slightly in annoyance.

Brutus laughed again. He looked towards Voronion. "Is this true?" he asked with amusement dancing in his eyes.

"Well, your majesty, Elbereth attacked Cordelia's Phoenix guard and then yes, Cordelia did indeed behead her," Voronion said hesitantly.

I moved slightly and placed my hands on my hips. I noticed there was only one throne beside the men. I smiled brightly as an idea came to me and slowly moved towards it stepping in between them without excusing myself. Sitting down I crossed my legs as my skirts separated and slid all the way up my thigh. The room fell completely silent, and everyone stared at me sitting on Brutus' throne. It was large and cold. Made of all black metal except for the cushion on the bottom and back. Those were blood red and honestly not as comfortable as they looked at all.

I felt Zander's anxiety rise but I also felt a sense of pride coming from him.

Gods. You are such a little devil. I had no idea you had this side to you. You aren't just poking the bear. You're straight up kicking him in his nuts.

Quinlan's laughter glided through my head along with his

words.

Stop distracting me. I'm trying to be a badass.

"She was a really terrible person. I think the realm will be much better off without her," I said casually, relaxing into the seat. I had a kind of bored lounging position. Brutus laughed even louder.

Brawntly looked horrified by my actions. "Cordelia, don't you think you should go get cleaned up before we have discussions?" he said softly. Ah yes, my darling brother "always looking out for me," but really his intentions were to please my father.

"Not particularly. Brutus," I said his name with a bite. "Do you have an issue with the blood or ash on me?"

"Not at all," he said with a twinkle in his eye. Okay I think I was having the wrong effect on him because he looked proud.

"Perfect. Let's discuss the next steps here," I said "Brutus, do you believe in soulmates?"

The air in the room seemed to turn to ice and everyone stopped moving again. I didn't realize that talking about soulmates would be taboo. I guess after everything with his parents and Zeke's parents it would make sense.

"Yes. I do. Why?" His tone was menacing but yet I felt no fear.

"I was just curious. Considering, I know I'm not your soul mate, yet here I am being brought here forcefully, attacked multiple times, and now I'm supposed to just wed you and live happily ever after," I said yawning. I didn't bother covering my mouth. "When do you plan on us marrying?"

"I think you two should wed as quickly as possible," my father chimed in. "Cordelia, you should really get out of King Daemongers throne. Especially sitting like that."

"Oh, this is your throne? I assumed it was here for me," Sitting up straight I motioned for a servant to come forward and he did just as I wanted. "I need you to commission someone to build me a throne the exact same size as this one. I would like it to be made of Onyx with Diamonds and blue sapphires in it. I want the cushions to be a black. I don't care much for this red color. Also, I would like it a bit more comfortable than this one," the servant's eyes widened, and he glanced over towards Brutus.

"You don't need his permission to do as I say," I snapped.

Brutus had nodded his approval anyway and the servant scampered off.

"A throne? You can't be serious. You are a princess. You aren't even married to King Daemonger and you think you can just order a throne to be made for you," Brawntly practically shouted. He was trying really hard to keep himself composed but I could see it in the thick of his jaw just how angry he was or was it jealousy?

My father looked at me like I had three heads and the men around them shook their heads.

Standing, I rolled my neck slightly, "Actually, dear brother, I am the Queen." I mean I actually wasn't a queen but that didn't matter. Fake it till you make it right.

"Now the last name you would like to call me by may differ because you don't want to recognize my betrothal to King Ezekiel Havaror but it does not change the fact that I am a Queen. So you may call me Queen Cordelia Havaror now or you may call me Queen Cordelia Daemonger after mine and Brutus' wedding. Either way. I am still a queen. It matters not which title you grant me." I walked past him to where the servants stood by what looked like wine.

Did you and King Havaror have a union before the gods? Quinlan's voice sounded surprised but his face betrayed none of our internal conversations.

No but they don't need to know that. I'm just trying to stir the pot so to speak. Zeke believes that he and I are soulmates so that's all that matters.

"This betrothal to King Havaror that you speak of," Brutus said, "Is this why he has taken down five of my outposts bordering our Kingdoms?"

I turned looking at him like he was a complete idiot. I cocked one hip against the table and raised my glass to my mouth before pausing. "I would assume so. After all, he was gone preparing our castle for my homecoming when I was attacked and brutally taken. Which brings me to another point, I think if you are going to steal another man's bride, you should at least have big enough balls to do it with him present. I mean what kind of man sends 50 or more fucking creatures to attack a woman. It's kind of pathetic if you ask me. Are you afraid of him? Is that why you didn't want to face him? It's the only explanation I can come up with. I don't think he will ever stop coming for me. Even if you were to kill him, his Kingdom will recognize me as their queen because not only did he choose me, but we are soulmates, and they will continue to come for me," I took a long sip of my wine. The room was so silent you could hear the sound of the village outside the open windows.

"Please give my men some," I said, nodding to the servant and raising my glass up. "Quinlan could use some after Elbereth attacked us."

"YOU CANNOT JUST WALTZ IN HERE COVERED IN BLOOD AND SOOT LOOKING LIKE A HOMELESS

WHORE. SIT IN THE KING'S THRONE. CALL HIM BY HIS GIVEN NAME, MAKE DEMANDS AND HALF ASSED THREATS, AND THEN HAVE THE SERVANTS POUR YOUR GUARDS WINE. THIS IS RIDICULOUS. FATHER, DO SOMETHING ABOUT HER!!!!" Brawntly was throwing a prince sized tantrum and it was hysterical. It made me wonder how mad he was that I would actually outrank him now.

"Oh, my dearest brother. It's cute that you are so outraged," I smiled at him. "Brutus, I do hope I haven't offended you. I figured we would be on a first name basis since you went to such trouble to get me here." My voice was so sickeningly sweet that you could make a dessert from it.

"I actually find this completely refreshing and quite hilarious. Unfortunately, I don't know anything about the trouble you encountered getting here. I had only been informed that you were on your way here two days ago," he said laughing. "However, what was that bit about Elbereth attacking you? Voronion, you didn't inform me of this. I would like to know the details of this situation. I thought I had made it quite clear no harm was to come to my betrothed."

Voronion looked at me like he was half afraid of this conversation. "Well, my King, Cordelia here had made a comment regarding keeping you waiting, and it set Elbereth off. Cordelia's guard Quinlan had laughed and Elbereth used her suffocating power to kill him in front of Cordelia," Voronion trailed off at that last part.

"Well actually if we are giving him the full details of this situation and not a shortened version, " I said a little snarkily. "Elbereth had previously attacked me with that same suffocating power when I first awoke in camp. This time I said something that made a guard of mine laugh. She suffocated him in front of me. Then I stabbed her with a dagger for killing Quinlan and she used that power of hers against me again. This time though, I just walked straight up to her while she was using it and cut her down. You're welcome for my gift. Consider it a betrothal gift and sign for what's to come." I crossed the room again and handed my glass to Brawntly. "You are too uptight. Try removing the stick from your ass and relaxing a bit. You would think by how you are acting that you were the one attacked, taken forcefully, attacked again, and then again." I patted Brawntly on his shoulder and continued on.

"So, tell me how you were able to walk while she was suffocating you," Brutus said, crossing his arms and eyeing me skeptically.

"Well, that is the question now isn't it. However, I don't ever reveal my secrets especially when it is something that saved my life," I answered with a wink. Maybe Brutus wasn't quite as terrible as I thought he was going to be.

"GODS DAMMIT CORDELIA," my father shouted. "Enough with this game you are playing at, child," His anger was palpable. He probably figured out that I had used my magic that he forbade me to ever use.

"I'm sorry but you're joking right. You think I am playing a game? You all have been playing a game for months. I have been open and honest from the moment I walked in here," I spat. "It was less than a pleasure meeting you Brutus." Malice dripped from my voice as I spoke to Brutus. Our eyes met for a moment, and I held his stare. One of his servants came up next to him and he broke eye contact. I felt shivers run down my spine as they spoke in a quiet language I didn't understand.

I turned and walked out of the room with my guards falling in line behind me. "Voronion, I would like for someone to show me my rooms and bring food for myself and my men. Seeing as how late it is, we will just take the food in my chambers. I would like Alba placed in a room next to ours," I didn't bother looking back at him. I knew he would do as I say.

Within a few moments, two servants came up next to us and said in unison "Your rooms are this way, Queen Cordelia. Your guards' rooms as well as the lady in wait's are down this hall." They pointed in the opposite direction of my rooms.

I stopped walking. "Yeah, that's not going to happen. Either their rooms are next to mine down this hall, or my room can be next to theirs down that hall."

The servants looked at me and began speaking in unison, "My Queen, your rooms connect to King Daemongers. They are the only rooms down that hallway. The guards' rooms are in the guest section." It was very creepy how they talked at the same time saying the exact same thing. I paused taking in their appearance. My father had pretty much removed anything that wasn't human or fae from our kingdom, so I wasn't used to seeing such a variety of beings. The servants here were bald with a bulging brow bone and had scales for skin. They moved with a serpent-like grace as if they were always poised and ready to strike.

"That's fine. I'll take a room in the guest section then," I turned on my heels and started down the hallway. "Do any of these rooms connect with one another?"

"This set here connects. It's only three rooms that connect together though. The fourth one directly across the hall does not connect to anything." They looked at me with concern. I felt a fleeting guilt thinking that they might get in trouble if I didn't take the room joining Brutus.

"Perfect, thanks. We will take these three. We will sort out who has which room between ourselves. Lady Alba can have the private one. Please find her and help her to her room when she is ready. You are dismissed," I said, stopping just out front of the first connecting room.

"Yes, our queen," they said and quickly bowed. They hesitated before walking away. My men stood staring and waiting for them to leave before they said anything.

"That was hot as fuck. All of it. Totally hot. When you sat in his throne," Quinlan said and then started biting his knuckles. "Ooof. I thought I was going to cum right there." I just stared at him as I processed what exactly he had just said.

"Who the fuck just says shit like that!" Zander turned, jokingly shoving Quinlan.

Draugs booming laughter got my mind working again, "Yeah that was definitely something else. You just took control of that room and all the men. Like a true Queen of this realm." He placed his fingers to his lips briefly.

Zander stood there looking angry, but I couldn't feel his anger. I realized I couldn't feel him at all.

Quin. I said inwardly trying to find my bond with him. Silence. I stared at Quinlan while I tried searching for him mentally.

Quinlan, can you hear my thoughts again? I asked through what I thought was our bond. It was silent. It felt like I was hitting a brick wall before I even left my mind and tried to enter his.

"Who wants what room? We need to get this sorted,"

58

Zander finally spoke.

"What if Cordelia gets the main room in the middle and we just rotate between the other rooms. That way she's never alone while sleeping and one of us is on each side of her rooms," Quinlan said.

"Yah. I like that idea. I don't want to be left vulnerable in the middle of the night. Ragnor has woken me up way too many times in the middle of the night for punishments," I said with a shiver running down my spine. "It's settled then". The men froze at my words but nodded their agreement.

Chapter Five

꩜

I opened the wide brown door to my new rooms. I knew they were only temporary, but I didn't know how long I would end up being here before Zeke arrived. Temporary felt like eternity. Walking in, it smelled like musty flower water. That smell when you have flowers in a vase for too long and finally dump the old water out. I walked in and looked around at these so-called guest rooms. The first section was a greeting area that had a small table and two chairs, the next room had an office desk, bookshelves, a fireplace, and a couch. There was a large doorway with double doors on the back wall. Through those doors was the bedroom. It was large and spacious. A four-post-canopy bed that was twice the size of my bed in Drochia stood in the middle of the room. Large windows lined one wall, a fireplace with two oversized chairs in front of it lined another wall, and a couch sat near the third wall. There were three more sets of doors in this room. The first one on the right side led to a smaller bedroom, another set of doors on the left side of my room also led to another bedroom, and then on the back wall was the bathroom and walk-in closet.

Before I could even really get a full grasp on the room and all the doors, Quinlan plopped down on the bed and said, "I have dibs on this bed tonight."

"It's my bed but I will be happy to share it with you tonight," I said laughing at him. The room fell silent at my words, and it hit me just how that could be taken. Looking over my shoulder at my guys, I said, "ONLY the bed. So, find your own blankets."

I briefly thought about Zeke and how he would feel about me sharing my bed with his men. Sharing a bed with Helvig had been one thing. It had seemed different than sharing a bed with these men. Helvig was safe. Not saying that my men weren't safe. It was just different. Ultimately, he would just have to trust me and his men. He knows we are soulmates so if anything, he would maybe be jealous but that would be all. I walked straight to the bathroom and stripped out of my nasty dress.

I needed a hot bath and to scrub my skin. I wanted every last bit of Elbereth off of me. The bathroom was not what I had expected though. The whole back wall was one giant window. You could see the whole valley and village from here. There wasn't a bath but just a faucet that hung from the ceiling. I turned the lever on the wall under it and water fell from it like a rain shower. Forgetting that I was completely naked, I yelled "YOU GUYS HAVE TO SEE THIS!"

Zander, Draug, and Quinlan came bursting into the bathroom ready for a fight.

"There's no bath in here! The water just falls from that faucet up there like a giant rain shower. I have never seen anything like it," I said, staring up at the water coming out of the metal pipe.

Zander cleared his throat and started to say something but stopped before he had even formed one word. Quinlan let out a low whistle and Draug said, "If that is all, we shall take our leave now, my lady."

Still in complete shock at the water just pouring from this pipe I turned looking at them confused by their reaction. "Look, there's just this hole over here that all the water runs into. Have you ever seen anything like this before? We didn't have this in Drochia! Is this common in other kingdoms?"

Looking from the water falling from the ceiling to them to see if they were as shocked and amazed as I was. Draug had his head tilted up looking straight up at the ceiling with his hands on his hips. Zander had one hand on the back of his neck and sucked in a deep breath completely motionless. Quinlan let out another whistle and said, "The gods have truly blessed me today."

"What's wrong?" I asked, perplexed by all of their behavior. I moved to put a hand on my hip when my fingers touched bare skin. I could feel the jagged scar from the night Helvig had stitched me up.

"OH, MY GODS," I shrieked. I turned back around so they only had a view of my ass. I wasn't ashamed of my body, but I just didn't walk around naked in front of strange men. Okay, so I did do that before, but Zeke ended up being my soulmate.

"We shall take our leave now," Draug said again.

"Please do," I said to them. I felt the heat from my embarrassment crawling up my body and heating my cheeks. I called them in here while I was completely naked to look at this bathroom that they had probably before. Gods. What kind of Queen was I going to be? I had shocked them completely and still I just stood here naked not realizing what I had just done. I felt the warm heat from my embarrassment flush my skin. Zander's emotions were tugging on the back of my mind. He was shocked... amused... and OH MY GODS. He was so freaking horny. I bet Draug and Quinlan felt similarly. Of course, I literally just gave them a full show of the goods. I shook my head trying to get over the embarrassment.

I stepped under the hot rain shower in the bathroom and let out a long sigh. The water pelted my skin making me relax. It felt so fucking good. I mean I loved slipping into a warm bath, but this felt amazing too. I didn't see any soaps around, so I thought about my bathroom back in Drochia and the soaps I had there. Just like that, they appeared in my bathroom on the shelf. I had decided at some point that it would be best for me to start using my magic more now. I grabbed my soaps and scrubbed my body and my hair. I ended up washing my hair three times to get all of the blood and gunk out of it. Once all of the blood and dirt was off of me, I just stood there letting the water fall over me. I could really get used to this. Maybe I could convince Zeke to recreate this bathroom but add in a large tub to soak in.

As I stood there, I let myself feel my emotions. I missed Zeke. It felt like my soul ached after everything that had happened. I wondered what he was doing right now, and I wished I could be with him. It was Tyche which meant that we should have been starting our new married lives together. It should have been our wedding night tonight. I closed my eyes and leaned my back up against the wall. I wondered what he would have thought about seeing this rain shower bath thing. Gods. I knew what his reaction would have been if I had called him in here to see it. He wouldn't have paid any attention to the water. He would have been on me immediately. With that thought, memories came flooding back of us together with water splashing all around us.

I pictured his hands roaming over my body as we stood under the hot water. I trailed my fingers along where I imagined he would touch me. I missed being touched so much. I would give anything to feel his fingertips sliding over my body again. I slid my hand down from my breast to myself. He always gave me so much pleasure. Gods. I swear I could smell him. His scent of dark spice and cedar wrapped around me. It took me a moment, but I realized I could also smell fire and smoke and blood.

Opening my eyes, I froze. I was standing in a tent facing the back of Zeke. He was shirtless and wearing his night pants. He was speaking to someone in front of him that I couldn't see. I was afraid to move.

"I swear I can smell her," Zeke said. His voice was shaking "We have to get to her soon. I don't know how much longer I can keep my shit together."

My heart broke for him. He was hurting and I wanted to comfort him. Out of instinct, I reached my hand up and placed it on his bare back. "I miss you so much too," I said, tears falling from my eyes.

Zeke moved so fast that I hadn't even registered what was happening before it had happened. He turned and grabbed me, lifting me up into his arms. His hands were on the backs of my thighs which were spread around him exposing myself to him fully.

His eyes searched my face, and I froze. All the times I had dreamt of him, he had never been able to touch me. I reached my hand up and touched his face running my fingertips along his scar.

"Tell me you see her. Tell me this is real," Zeke said to whoever was standing in the tent. His eyes never left mine though like he was afraid to look away. If he did, I might just go poof and disappear.

"Are you really here?" I barely managed to croak out.

"What... the... fuck," Vilulf said in complete disbelief.

"I am here. Are you really here? How? How are you here?" Zeke said tears rolling down his cheeks like a dam had broken. I had never seen this emotional side to him before. He leaned forward and sucked in deeply. "I've missed your smell more than anyone could imagine."

Slowly I lifted his head and kissed him repeatedly. I couldn't help myself, but I kissed his lips over and over again. I kissed his nose and his cheeks. I kissed each tear that escaped from his eyes. He was real.

"I can't believe you can touch me this time," I said, pulling back from him. "I have been dreaming about you and every time you can't touch me or see me. You are really touching me this time."

Zeke sucked in a sharp breath and said, "You have been with me, haven't you? I thought I was going crazy. I could smell you sometimes. Other times, I swore I heard you." He leaned forward and placed his forehead on mine.

"I missed you so much. I need you to know that I am coming for you. I am doing everything I can. Daemonger has been preparing to wage a war against me for a long time and I was unaware of that until recently. His army is much larger than I had initially anticipated so it is taking us longer than I thought. I'm sorry. I'm so sorry I wasn't there for you. Helvig and I had a plan and if anything were to happen—" I cut him off.

"Please… tell me what happened to Helvig," I said, closing my eyes and bracing myself for the worst. My emotions were all over the place. I started to picture Helvig and that night. I felt the panic and grief of losing him fill me. Even being here with Zeke did nothing to calm my emotions. In just a few brief moments my heart had gone from the joy of being with Zeke to swelling with the overwhelming loss of not being with Helvig.

"Delia, I," Zeke's words were fuzzy. I whipped open my eyes and he was blurry. I was losing him again. Suddenly, I was in my bathroom standing under the rain shower again. A sob tore through me, and I wasn't sure if it was due to being back here away from Zeke or from the fact that I knew Zeke hadn't found Helvig alive.

I turned the shower off and used my magic to get my robe. I wrapped it around myself and tried really hard to keep my shit together. I walked over to the corner near the window and stood looking out over the village at night.

Something was happening to me. That was real. It had to have been real. I wasn't asleep in the shower. I managed to go to him, and I didn't know how I did it. My heart squeezed at the thought that I had the power to be with him right now and I didn't know how to use it. I could have used that same magic to get Helvig out of the library. I could have saved him. My heart felt like I had just broken it into a thousand pieces. Tears fell from my eyes, and I didn't bother trying to stop them.

Zander came bursting into the bathroom, eyes searching frantically until he found me. He stormed over to me and picked me up. Holding me like I was precious to him, he carried me out into my bedroom.

"Whoa. What the fuck are you doing Zander," Quinlan said jumping up off the bed and rushing towards us.

Draug came bursting through the right-side door. "Is everything okay? I felt…" his eyes widened for a moment and looked around the room. "Old magic. VERY old magic."

I was shaking and for a moment, I thought I was really losing my mind. All the stress and pressure I had felt over the years had finally broken me. This was it. I was going crazy. Zander sat on the bed and kept me in his lap. He started making a low comforting sound that was a cross between a purr and a bird chirping in his chest and I snuggled in. He felt like the only reality that I could hold onto for the moment.

Within a few moments I was already feeling better. I looked up and saw Quinlan had perched himself on the edge of the nightstand directly beside me and Draug had knelt on the floor. All three of these men were comforting me and they didn't even know why.

"I have some questions that I need you guys to answer honestly and to the best of your knowledge," I said, wiping the tears from my eyes. I didn't move from Zander's lap. Instead, I snuggled in more which probably wasn't very queenly of me, but I didn't care. I was on the verge of a complete breakdown and there was something about being this close to him that comforted me.

"First, I think we need to tell them our secret," Zander said to me, nudging the top of my head with his chin.

"There better not be anything going on between you two. I def. call dibs if things don't work out with her and King Ezekiel," Quinlan said, completely serious.

An almost hysterical laugh bubbled out of me as Draug punched him i n his leg, "Obviously, there isn't anything romantic going on between them, you idiot. She is the soulmate of our King."

"No, there isn't something going on between Zander and I like that. Also, you can't call dibs. Who said I would even want to be with you if it didn't work out between Zeke and me. Maybe I would prefer Draug?" I said, raising my eyebrows and then glaring at Draug.

Zander cleared his throat and said, "Actually, Cordelia and I have developed a bond. I can feel her presence and all of her many many many emotions. I believe she can also feel mine as well?" Zander questioned.

"Uh, yah that pretty much sums that bond up. I also have some type of bond with Quinlan. Sometimes, I can hear his thoughts and he can hear mine. We have also talked to each other through our minds as well," I said.

"I knew it," Zander breathed. "I thought I noticed something going on between the two of you."

"Yah, our bond is way cooler than yours dude," Quinlan joked.

"When did you guys notice these bonds clicking into place?" Draug asked us all.

"For me, it was after I spoke with Zantos and saw Zander as a dragon. Then with Quinlan it was right before Elbereth killed him. I heard him telling me everything would be alright but honestly, I didn't even register that until everything was done," I said thinking back. "Did you guys notice the bonds at the same time or was it different for you?"

Zander shifted slightly and said "I had felt your presence the moment you were in the camp. I didn't start feeling your emotions until after you touched my wing. It was like the moment you touched them; I could feel how in awe of them you were. I think that is what got Zanto's attention. Feeling your emotions, that is," Zander rubbed small circles on my leg. I shifted slightly and laid my head on Quinlans knee. He began running his fingers through my hair. There was something about my men that made me feel safe. It wasn't like the feelings I had around Lance, or Helvig, or even Zeke. No, these men made me feel like I could drop all my walls and expose my soul to them, and they would guard it with their lives.

"Give me just a moment," Draug said.

He got up and went to the receiving area in my rooms. He came back with a tray of food and set it down on the bed next to me. He went back and got wine glasses and a bottle of wine. I was so glad dinner had arrived while I was in the shower. I was starving all of a sudden.

"And for you Quinlan?" Draug said as he poured everyone a glass of wine.

"I heard Coredlia screaming at Elbereth and something inside of me needed her to know that I would be okay. I felt her pain of losing someone. It was sharp and so agonizing. I needed her to know that she wasn't losing me, and I wasn't leaving her anytime soon. So, I just told her it would be okay. Those were my final thoughts before I felt death take me," Quinlan said, running his fingers through my hair again. I nuzzled my head a little more into his leg. I did think I had lost him, and that thought had been unbearable. Losing Helvig left an unhealing wound in my chest that was ripped open more when I thought I was losing Quin.

"Hmm. I see," Draug said, taking a long drink from his wine

glass. "Then after she saw you both in both of your forms, the bonds developed more than what they had started out as." Draug cleared his throat uncomfortably and poured himself another glass.

"Draug?" I said, picking up on the tension radiating from him. "Are you okay? I'm sorry that we don't have a bond yet. I'm sure one will come eventually."

Draug looked at me and smiled slightly, "I think you and I already have some type of bond started. I know every time you need to eat. That sounds a little weird and kind of lame compared to those two, but I think it's your pain I'm feeling. Whether it be hunger pain or the emotional pain you felt just a few moments ago, or the physical pain you felt when the arrows shot through you. I have felt it all. The weight you are carrying has to be very heavy, my dearest queen." For a moment Draugs words scared me. If he could feel my emotional pain, he would know the grief I felt for Helvig and everything else that came with that. I wasn't comfortable sharing that with anyone and I was grateful he hadn't asked more questions.

"Oh," I said rather speechless. "I hadn't realized. I haven't felt anything from you though."

"I haven't been in any pain. I have also felt very old magic a handful of times since you arrived at the camp." Draug said, waiting for me to respond with an explanation like he knew I wasn't telling them the full story. Except I didn't know what to say to him. I felt a little guilty that I hadn't told anyone about my magic or what I could do. However, my magic wasn't very old. So, it wouldn't have been me he was feeling.

"What do you mean by very old magic?" Quinlan asked.

"I have been in this realm for a very long time. The last time

I felt this magic was when the gods were still…" Draug sighed as if he was trying to watch his words. "When they were still awake and that my friend was a very long time ago. Unless there is a god wandering around these halls then something isn't quite adding up."

Zander had stopped making circles on my leg. "Do you think a god is," he paused briefly. "Awake and doing something here? Doing something to her?" The way Zander and Draug were staring at each other made me think they were having a whole conversation with just their eyes.

Draug sighed and pinched the bridge of his nose. "I honestly don't know. I'm not saying it is a god's magic. It's just whatever it is has very old magic. My biggest concern is why is it here now and what does it want with Cordelia. Every time I have felt it has been near or around you," he said, looking at me skeptically.

Guilt flooded through me at Draugs words. They were concerned about the magic they had felt around me and here I was keeping this secret about my own magic. There was a small possibility that my magic was what Draug was feeling. He could simply be wrong about it being old.

Zander stiffened slightly as the guilt started eating at me. "Cordelia, what is it that you aren't telling us?"

Awe fuck. These damned bonds sucked.

"What? What do you mean?" I gawked at him. He was just going to throw me out there like this.

"You are feeling guilty about something. It gets worse every time someone has mentioned the magic around you or it being a possible god. What do you feel guilty about?" Zander asked in an encouraging tone. Oh, so he thought being nice after exposing my emotions was going to work. Fucking prick. I took a moment and sighed really dramatically. This whole bond thing was feeling really annoying at the moment.

I pulled away from them and got off the bed. I walked near the fireplace and stared at it for a moment. I hadn't ever told anyone about my ability. Not even Zeke and now I needed to tell them. Yet part of me felt like I was betraying Zeke because I hadn't told him about this. I hadn't even told Helvig and he knew everything else about me. My heart clenched at the fact that I would never have a chance to tell Helvig about this.

I turned to my men and saw the three of them had moved to the end of my oversized bed. They sat in a row watching me attentively. I checked on my bond with Zander and all I felt from him was curiosity, encouragement, and love. He cared for me deeply and would accept me no matter what and I had to focus on that. I looked at Draug and then Quinlan. They both just nodded their heads giving me time and the spacc I needed to speak.

"Alright. I guess I'm really going to tell you guys this. You have to promise me something before I do though," I said with apprehension running through me.

"Anything," Zander responded immediately, and I knew he was serious. Somehow, I knew that Zander really would promise me anything I needed.

"Whatever you need, my queen" Draug stated.

Quinlan's voice popped into my head, "If it's too hard for you to say out loud, you can say it to me first. I can try to explain whatever it is to them. They won't be upset with you. I promise you that. I know that's what you're worried about, but we won't be upset with you. We all have secrets, and we have them for reasons we can't always explain and that's okay."

I sucked in a breath at his kind words. Closing my eyes, I decided he was right. I felt like I didn't need to hear their promises, I knew in my heart that they wouldn't betray me, and they would accept me.

"I'm going to tell you something that I haven't even told Zeke yet. I just hadn't found the right moment and then all of this happened," I gestured to the room around us.

I started to think about my father's reaction and the pain that left me, and I felt anxious...like I was going to vomit up all of my stomach contents. Love poured through the bond from Zander a moment later. I could hear Draug purring lightly. I looked at Quinlan and said through our bond just a moment before I spoke it out loud "I have my own magic and I have been using it on and off ever since I arrived at camp."

Chapter Six

I had just told them that I had magic and they just sat there waiting like that news in itself wasn't mind-blowing. Leave it to my men to make this so anticlimactic.

"Okay," Draug said tentatively. "What kind of magic can you do?"

I figured it would just be easier to show them than try to explain it. I opened my hand and thought about the cup that Quinlan was holding, Zander's shirt, and Draug's plate. Suddenly, they were sitting in my open hand. Their eyes widened and then I moved the items to the bed with one thought. In my next thought, I place each item on the wooden floor in front of the men.

"You can move things with your mind?" Zander asked, not surprised at all. Pure amusement filtered to me from him causing me to narrow my eyes at him.

"Yes. I just have to think about what I want to do and then it happens. I also have to see the items originally before I can move them. I can't just steal King Daemonger's treasures. I haven't seen them, so I don't know where they are or what they look like."

"How long have you been able to do this? Just since you bonded with King Ezekiel?" Draug asked hesitantly. He reached down and touched each item. Assessing that they were real.

"I for one think that's really fucking cool and super handy," Quinlan said. "I mean you guys have to be thinking about how awesome this is and the kind of stuff she can do."

I smiled at their reactions. "No, I have been able to do this since I was a small child. Also, Zeke and I haven't actually bonded yet," I admitted quietly, looking away from them and into the fire that popped and cracked. I didn't know which truth was worse. I tried to keep my emotions even when I thought about the first time I had ever used my magic.

Zander was too keen or maybe he was just searching my emotions for any little blip. "Why does talking about your magic make you so anxious?" he asked me. "Are you not proud of what you can do?"

I hated thinking about the reasons why I didn't use my magic. The emotions it brought up felt unbearable, but I knew they needed to know. How could I expect them to help me and risk their lives, if I can't be open and honest with them? It was hard because of how I grew up compared to them. They were used to seeing magical beings... shit they are fucking were magical beings. So, the fact that I could do magic wasn't a big deal to them but under my father's thumb it was a huge deal.

"The first time I had used my magic I was a little girl. Around the age of 5, I think. I was at the dinner table and wanted the dessert I had seen in the kitchen and then poof it was on my plate. My father reacted very poorly to this to say the least. I was punished. My father's right-hand guard, Ragnor, took me and punished me. He sought a soothsayer that told him my magic came from my hair. So, he cut all my hair off, including my body hair. He told me if I ever used it again very bad things would happen. So, I didn't use my magic again for years. Then it was only every once in a while. It wasn't always easy for me to use it. Sometimes it wouldn't work at all. Other times it came to me without me meaning to use it," I explained, a shiver running down my spine even though I was skipping the worst of the details.

"Why did your father have such a terrible reaction to magic?" Quinlan asked. I searched his face waiting to see the disappointing or similar reaction to everyone else's when I was child. However, I never saw it. All three of my men weren't angry or upset that I hadn't told them. They mostly seemed confused by all of this.

"I don't know exactly but I have a few speculations. I can still remember the look on his face. He hated me that day and for a while afterwards. I was scared for my life for days. A few weeks ago, I overheard a private conversation my father was having. Apparently, his father stole his magic from him and hid it somewhere in this realm," I could only assume that was why he was angry.

Draug sucked in a deep breath and slowly released it. He kept running his hand through his beard. He gingerly stood stretching and started pacing back and forth. As I watched his graceful movements, I realized it wasn't really a pace but more like a prowl. "It's no secret your father hates anything to do with magic. Maybe he felt threatened by it because he doesn't have his own?"

Quinlan sat perched on the edge of the bed messing with his hair as he watched Draug prowl.

My eyes slid to Zander and met his eyes with an intensity I felt in the depth of my soul. Zander stood gracefully and narrowed his eyes at me. I crossed my arms over my chest holding myself. Zander narrowed his eyes even more and I felt the scrutiny in his gaze.

"Cordelia," Zander said but I couldn't look at him. "Cordelia. Look at us." I turned towards the fire again and closed my eyes tightly. I was waiting for the other shoe to drop... for one of them to hate me or be angry with me. If they hated me... gods if Zander hated me... I wouldn't be able to handle it. Not right now at least I was still dealing with so many emotions regarding the kidnapping, losing Helvig, and being separated from

Draug spoke up then, "My Queen, I have questions. Questions I only intend to ask to better understand."

I sighed knowing this was inevitable, "Okay. What are your questions?"

"What happened while you were in the shower that caused you to use your magic? I felt a huge pulse of magic before I came bursting in here. I'm assuming you had used your magic just then. What did you do exactly? How often have you used your magic? Who all knows about what you can do?" His body language showed that he was indeed just curious and not angry with me.

"Uhm I was in the shower. I thought about Zeke and how much I missed him. I opened my eyes and I was standing in a tent facing Zeke's back. He turned around and saw me. He picked me up and it was real. Well at least it felt so incredibly real. He was confused and asked me how I was there. Vilulf was there too, and he looked shocked that I was there. Before we could really even talk, I was back in the shower. I swear I hadn't fallen asleep. I was naked and dripping with water in his tent. I've had similar things happen only just recently, but Zeke could never hear me or see me until just now."

"Oh. Well, that makes sense" Draug said "I think there's a pretty easy—"

"What the fuck. Why don't I have cool powers that can move things and move people through time and space? No, instead I get to live a bazillion painful deaths. Yay fucking me!" Quinlan crossed his arms and was actually pouting. His actions made all of us burst out laughing. This only made Quinlan pout even more which in return made us laugh harder.

"Anyways..," Draug stated as he tried to regain his composure "I think this directly relates to your powers. You were thinking about moving stuff from one place to another. More specifically, you were thinking about being with King Havaror, I would assume? You moved yourself to be with him. Now I know you say you have to see things but maybe because of your bond, you don't need to know where he is exactly. I know you said you don't have a bond but I'm willing to bet that you have at least a bond that is similar to one of our bonds. You might not have the mating bond yet, but I bet there is something there." Draug sighed and looked at Quinlan who was still pouting.

"You said it started recently? The whole going to King Havaror?" Zander asked.

"Uh yeah, I don't have any control of that. It just happens but it started the day of the pyre," I shrugged. Draugs eyes narrowed like he was trying to put puzzle pieces together.

"Quit pouting and listen up," Zander said to Quinlan. "I have an idea. It might not work but I think it's something we should at least try."

I perked up at the thought that there could be something we could do.

"I think Cordelia should go into the bathroom with one of us and try to move herself to this room with us waiting."

Draug walked towards the bathroom and then stopped, "I think because you two have a stronger bond with her, you should stay in here. maybe she can use your bonds to bring her to this room." I got up and smiled widely at Zander. He was brilliant and I was excited to be trying something new. Actually, I was elated that my men were so accepting over my magic. I guess I had been so sheltered by my father that I forgot about other parts of the realm still utilizing magic.

I tied the knot of my robe a little tighter and walked into the bathroom. Draug was leaning up against the wall with a thoughtful expression on his face, "I guess just do whatever you were doing when you went to Zeke. I mean you don't need to be showering but think the same thoughts."

I inwardly cringed and felt my face heat because I was thinking very inappropriate thoughts about Zeke when I found myself in his tent.

"Uhm Okay. Sure." I said, closing my eyes and picturing Quinlan and Zander in the next room. I couldn't think any appropriate things about them so maybe just picturing them waiting for me would be enough. I thought about how much I wanted this to work and opened my eyes. I was still facing Draug. He raised one eyebrow and said, "So I'm gonna guess that it didn't work?"

"Let me try again," I sighed and closed my eyes again. I

thought about the comfort I felt when I snuggled up in Zander's lap and Quinlan played with my hair. I hadn't ever been taken care of until I met Zeke and now, I seemed to be surrounded by men who wanted to take care of me.

I opened my eyes and still saw Draug. "Shit. I don't know how I did it before," I was really starting to feel frustrated. This could solve all my problems. If I could literally just poof and disappear from here and be with Zeke without poofing back here, that would be fucking fantastic. Well, it wouldn't solve all of them, but it would solve most of them.

Zander popped his head into the bathroom. "I have a thought. When you were in here before I felt your emotions all over the place. However, they were all intense feelings. You felt intense sadness and intense longing. What if it is the intensity of your emotions that opens a connection to King Havaror?"

"Okay... I can believe that," I said, trying to remain hopeful. I closed my eyes and tried to feel intense emotion for Quinlan. I thought about how funny he could be and how grateful I was for him. I thought about how scared I was when I thought he had died. When I thought I lost him just like I lost Helvig. I could feel that ache in my chest for Helvig opened wide and for just a few moments, I allowed myself to feel it. To feel how much I missed him and how much I wished he was here to help me through this. I opened my eyes and stared into Zander's gaze. I sighed deeply. How can I not know how to use my own magic? It's my freaking magic and yet I'm unable to replicate what I did— what I've been doing by accident.

"Maybe it's time we all head to bed tonight. It's getting late and I think we are all exhausted. Who knows, maybe moving yourself takes up a lot of your energy. Maybe you can't just do it over and over. You might need to recharge some before you can do it again," Draug said with a shrug of his shoulder.

"I agree with Draug. I think we should all get some rest. Who knows what tomorrow will bring us and we should all be on top of our game," Zander said, looking directly at me. It made me squirm. It was like he was trying to read into my innermost thoughts. Thank the gods his connection with me was emotional. If he had the ability Quinlan did... I didn't know if I would have been able to ever get him out of my head. I checked mine and Quinlans bond because it had been a while since he yelled at me for projecting my thoughts into his head. It felt like a small tether connecting us. Almost like I could pull on it and it would vibrate.

Quinlan? I thought of his name but attempted to keep that thought to myself. It was tricky feeling his mind brushing up against mine and keeping what I wanted in my own head. I imagined a glass window between us keeping our minds separated.

We exited the bathroom and I found Quinlan asleep on my bed. The sight shouldn't have been unexpected but yet it caught me by surprise, "How can he just be asleep like that?"

"Well.. he did die today. I'm sure he's exhausted," at Draugs words I smiled slightly thinking about how lucky I was that he was still here with me. That was today that I had almost lost Quinlan. He would have been another person I would have mourned for the rest of my life. Today felt like it took years to end. I was so thankful to finally be going to bed.

I climbed into bed behind Quinlan while Draug and Zander walked in opposite directions to the conjoining rooms. "Just shout if you need anything," Draug said. Zander just nodded as he walked through the doorway. I didn't need to shout when it came to Zander. He would feel my heightened emotions before I could open my mouth if anything bad did happen.

I pulled the blanket a little but it didn't budge. Quinlan was asleep on top of the blanket and I didn't think I would be able to wake him. I sighed and slipped under the covers. I scooted as close to him as I could get and snuggled into his strong back. He was warm and it felt nice against my cold cheek.

I couldn't help but feel disappointed. I was a complete and utter failure. If I could figure out how to move myself or other people then my men could be safe. We wouldn't be here and they wouldn't have to be ready to defend me from all the potential dangers around us. I could be with Zeke and help him formulate plans and help end the war my father has started. Sometimes it felt like all the things Emon and Ragnor had said to me over the years were right. I really was a failure and would amount to nothing. I couldn't even do the one thing that my men and Zeke were depending on me to do. I could get us all out of here. We could escape so easily if I just figured out how to use my own damn magic.

I closed my eyes and felt the hopelessness seep in. I was truly pathetic. I had the ability to save Helvig and yet I didn't know about it. I hadn't used my magic enough because I was afraid of the repercussions. If I hadn't been so weak and pathetic, Helvig would still be alive. The guilt of his death felt suffocating. I was a coward and because of that Helvig was dead.

I closed my eyes and thought about Helvig and wished he was here so I could talk to him about what was happening. I wanted to tell him about my magic and the secret I had been keeping from him. I wanted his thoughts on how I could move from one place to another at my will and how to do it without being poofed back to wherever I was.

Mostly though, I wanted the comfort I felt being with him.

Tinkling bells filled the air just before her beautiful voice began. My darling girl.

Your sadness is causing you to miss what is right in front of you. You're letting your mind run rampant with these thoughts and they are dangerous. Why is it that people see physical pain and know how to heal it, yet the mental pain is always overlooked until ruinous damage has been done?

Be true to yourself and you will find that everything isn't as terrible as it seems.

I awoke with a sheen of cold sweat across my skin. I've always been true to myself. How much more true to myself could I be? I walked into that throne room today and was a total badass. I snuggled into Quinlans back again as I attempted to fall back asleep. My last thought before everything faded away was, "Fuck these cryptic messages."

Chapter Seven

I awake on and off all night. At one point I laid there without sleep coming to me for what felt like hours. The bed was soft and the sheets were silky. Quinlan was naturally warm and I didn't feel too terrible about him sleeping without a blanket. I mostly felt terrible that I had the capability to get us all out of here but I didn't know how to use it exactly. I kept racking my brain trying to figure out how to make my magic work. I tried over and over to go to Zeke again. No matter what I did, I couldn't trigger it again.

Quinlan rolled over and wrapped an arm around me pulling me to his chest. If someone would have told me 6 months ago that this is how my life would be, I wouldn't have believed them. Mostly for the fact that I thought I had been a strong woman and didn't need anyone ever. Now I was coming to realize that I was not strong. I depended on my men more than I ever thought possible. The comfort and hope they gave me was unparalleled.

"Go to sleep, my Queen." he yawned. "You cannot solve

all of our problems in one night. You are not worthless. You are quite the opposite to many people. We will figure this out together. Calm your mind and think happy thoughts. Tomorrow you will get your new dresses and we can explore the village some. Eventually we will try to figure out how your magic works but for now just enjoy being yourself openly. You don't have to hide yourself any longer, especially from us. You are our Queen." He nuzzled his chin and neck up against my head and pulled me tight.

Tears pricked my eyes at his sweet words. I was thankful to have these genuine men around me but there was part of me that still wanted to run from it. The two men that had come to mean the most to me were not here. One was probably dead and it was my fault. The other, well I had thought he would have been here with me. I never would have thought he would have allowed me to be held captive for so long. It had been weeks and yet he still wasn't here. If you would have asked me months ago how long it would take him to get to me, I would have told you that he wouldn't hesitate. He would have been here immediately. I didn't know if it was disappointment or anger that I felt and I wasn't sure if it was with him or with myself. I snuggled further into Quinlan and closed my eyes. Briefly, I wondered what Zeke was doing now and what he thought about earlier. I pictured myself snuggled up in his arms and slowly I drifted off to sleep.

The smell of cedar and dark spices surrounded me. I went to move the sheet only to discover it wasn't on me any more. I opened my eyes to reach down and grab it when I realized I wasn't in my room anymore. It was pitch black and I could hardly see. I groaned, breathing in a deep breath when Zeke's scent registered in my mind. I looked beside me and he was asleep on his back with his head turned away from me. I must have used my magic in my sleep to be with him. Somehow I triggered it again and I still didn't know how.

I stared at him for a few moments before I reached out and touched his cheek. I traced his scar from his temple down past his ear and down his neck to where the blanket touched his skin. He barely stirred. I slid closer to him and leaned down to kiss him. I stopped just a few inches above his face. He was so beautiful even in his sleep. He looked exhausted. His normally shaved face was pebbled with scruff from not shaving. His brow was dirty and I imagined he hadn't been taking care of himself. I hoped he wasn't out on the front lines fighting every battle but I knew deep down that he was. He was a good man but a part of me felt like he wasn't my man or maybe that I wasn't his. After all we had been a part for so long now. A pang of guilt hit me and I pushed it away.

I kissed the top of his scar and worked my way down to his neck trailing kissing the whole way. I moved slightly to adjust how I was laying next to him when something caught my attention. On the table behind Zeke's bed lay a sickle like sword. I stared at it for a moment. My heart hammering in my chest trying to break free of the constricting cage it was in. The night I had been attacked in the courtyard came flooding back to me. Helvig and Zeke had come to my rescue. Zeke with his double blades and Helvig with that one sickle sword. I choked on a sob as I stared at it.

Zeke's hands slid to my hips and he pulled me on top of him. I glanced down at him and stared straight into his blue-silver wide eyes.

"Please tell me this is real. I think I'm going crazy. I keep smelling you and hearing you. Earlier today I swore you were in my arms one moment and then gone the next. If you aren't real, I don't know how much more of this I can handle. It's torturing me." His voice was groggy and raw as he stared into my eyes searching for an answer.

My throat felt like it had closed and I choked back another sob that had bubbled up from deep within me. "Zeke, it's me and it's been me each and every time," I whispered. "I don't know how long I have here and for that I am so sorry." Tears began to fall from my eyes and land on his cheeks. I didn't know what exactly I was crying for at this point. I felt overwhelmed by everything my brain was trying to process.

"How? How are you doing this?" He asked, wiping my tears from my face with his thumbs. "Please don't cry. I'm sorry, I didn't mean to upset you."

Sitting up with me in his lap, I buried my head into the crook of his neck and kissed him. "There's so much I have to tell you. I was keeping a rather large secret from you. I just... I just hadn't figured out exactly how to tell you. I was afraid your reaction would be like how my father had reacted and I wouldn't have been able to handle that. He had been so angry with me the first time it happened and I was punished for it. I was told to never use magic again. For years I didn't but recently I have been using it a lot more and now I can somehow come to you. I don't know exactly how but I'm trying to figure that out." I was stumbling over my words hoping he would make sense of it all.

"You have magic?" he questioned. At least he was able to figure that out from my rambling.

"I do. I can move things from one place to another just by thinking about it. I hadn't ever moved myself or a person until the other day. I had just missed you so much and wanted to be with you so badly. Next thing I knew I was watching you but it was all hazy and blurry. Like I was in a dream state or something. The first few times I thought I had just been dreaming. Then it happened while I was in the shower. I wasn't doing it on purpose and I don't know how exactly it works. I was sleeping in bed next to Quinlan one moment and the next I was waking up here."

"You were in bed with Quinlan?" I felt Zeke's whole body stiffen beneath me.

"We were just sleeping. Don't be jealous. It's for my safety, one of the guys will sleep next to me every night. They're going to rotate so I won't ever be left vulnerable," I said pushing on his shoulder.

"I can't help but feel jealous that they get to sleep next to you when I have been dreaming about being with you every single night." He nuzzled the top of my head and then kissed my hair gently. "So you have magic. Well that's really cool."

"Yah.. any ideas on how I can learn to do this on command?"

"Hmm," he mumbled as he ran his hands up my legs to where the robe had slipped open. Slowly, he kissed down the side of my cheek to my neck.

"I have missed you so much. I can't even think straight right now. I have an almost uncontrollable urge to lay you down right here and show you just how much I have missed you. I just want to worship you. The smell of you makes every part of my body very aware of your presence on my lap," his breathing was ragged and his words hoarse.

I let the robe slip from my shoulders and expose my breasts. "I've missed you too," I admitted, all thoughts about my magic disappearing. I just wanted to feel him. In moments like this, he made me feel cherished and I needed that more than anything else right now.

I ran my hands down his chest and pushed him down. "I want to show you just how much I missed you." An overwhelming desire to ride him bloomed inside of me. Maybe it was finally our bond encouraging us to come together. Maybe our soulmate bond would finally slip into place and I could stop questioning it. Although for some reason the idea of our bond slipping into place didn't bring the happiness it once did.

"My little mouse," he breathed just as I freed him from his pants.

"Yes, my King?" I said as I rolled my hips and slowly let him slide into me.

He sucked in a sharp breath as he stared at where our bodies met. He watched me as I slowly rode him, pulling up until he was almost completely out of me. Just before he could slip free, I would glide back down his length and rock my hips. I felt the ecstasy building inside of me. I began riding him harder until I couldn't take it anymore. I slid my hand to my clit and started rubbing myself.

Zeke let out a growl and I felt his hand replace mine. Opening my eyes, I stared into his eyes as the pleasure built. "Zeke, I…" I moaned out.

He reached with his other hand and played with my breasts, squeezing and rolling my nipple between his fingers. He rolled us over and instinctively, I wrapped my legs around him and grabbed his shoulders bracing myself. I was so close and I needed him to take me over that glorious edge into euphoria.

He was touching all over me, kissing my neck as he pounded and ground into me. Each time he pushed into me brought me closer and closer to that edge. "I love you, Cordelia, Queen of the Havaror Kingdom. I love you so much." He said his voice was husky and full of lust.

I broke and felt myself plummeting off the edge. I called out his name and felt his pulsing orgasm inside me. We were both breathing heavily but he was still kissing all over me. He laid himself on top of me bracing his weight on his forearms. "I have missed the way you smell so much. Sometimes it's all I can think about. I can't believe you're here. Maybe if we stay connected just like this, you will stay, " he said, kissing my jawline and then sucking on one ear lobe before burying his nose into my hair. I turned my head so he could have better access to my hair and caught a glimpse of that sickle sword. Guilt flooded through me but before I could focus on it, Zeke was starting to gently roll his hips.

"I think it's worth a try," he said, whispering in my ear. I grinned back at him trying to let go of the guilt I had felt.

This time together was much different than the first time. Zeke was slower and more tender. Each thrust was deliberately used. He held me in his arms as he made love to me and I kissed him like he was the only source of oxygen and I was suffocating. I met him thrust for thrust. Sweat was glistening off of him and we were no longer being quiet. The whole camp probably heard the moans coming out of his tent but I didn't care.

"Gods. Your smell is like an aphrodisiac," he said, placing his head into the crook of my neck and inhaling. After kissing up and down my neck he began to suck eliciting a moan from my lips. Gently he began using one hand to rub my core. He knew my body so well. My orgasm shattered me but he didn't stop.

"Cordelia," Zeke breathed "You are the most beautiful woman in the world. I am the luckiest man alive." He kissed my throat down to my breasts. Looking me in my eyes, he said, "I have no doubt you will figure out how to use your magic and then we can do this every day."

He slowly sucked one nipple into his mouth as his thrusts became harder. He moved to my other breast and just before he took it into his mouth, he said "I will never give up on you. I will worship you always."

Something about his words sent warning bells ringing in my mind. I didn't know why but before I could reply, he sucked my breast into his mouth and began thrusting into me desperately, almost frantically. I lost all thoughts as my brain turned into mush from the intensity of the moment. I held his head to my breast and attempted to meet his thrusts but he was becoming wild. He drove me to the edge once again.

Without warning, he moved us so I was on top of him. He keep thrusting and fucking me from below. My mind was in complete bliss and I could barely sit up. He slid his hands into mine to help me brace myself. I started meeting his thrusts and then I took control as he backed off. He watched me on top of him riding him with wild abandon. I was on the edge and I wanted to take him with me. I tightened around him with every stroke. Once I began grinding on him, I felt his cock pulse with his orgasm. Feeling his pulsing cock filling me again sent me over the edge.

I was mid orgasm when I began falling forward, my hands smacking his chest.

Quinlan choked out, "DEAR GODS".

My eyes snapped open and stared straight into Quinlan's gaze. His look of shock quickly changed to one of lust as he looked down my body and back up to my face. I was stunned speechless. Shocked. I was completely frozen in place naked and on top of Quinlan. "This is the best way I have ever woken up in my entire life." he said, attempting to make a joke.

His words snapped me out of it and I flew off of him. I grabbed the pillow off the bed just as Draug and Zander came running into the room. I used it to cover the important parts seeing as I had lost my robe in Zeke's tent.

"I was with Zeke I swear," I said, stammering before anyone could speak. Gods. This looked really bad. Oh my gods. I was having one of the best orgasms of my life on top of Quinlan. I felt my cheeks and ears get hot. This was so fucking embarrassing. First I gave them a good look at my goods in the bathroom and then this.

"I can smell his scent on you," Draug said, looking shocked. "You really were with him. Not that I hadn't believed you before… but that is definitely proof he said pointing at my legs." I didn't have to look down to know that Zeke's cum was currently oozing down my legs. Considering it wasn't from just one of his orgasms and he had rather large loads, it was no surprise. Still I felt horrified at the notion that I was standing here naked with cum dripping down my legs in front of my men.

Zander looked from me to Quinlan and then back to me. I felt the light tickle of his amusement in my mind. Before I could stop myself, I threw my pillow at him and shouted, "It isn't funny you fucker."

Turning I stormed into the bathroom to clean up. I took my time and the longer I stayed in the bathroom the more I didn't want to go out and face Quinlan. I was beyond embarrassed and didn't know how to move past what had happened.

I stood letting the water run over me thinking about everything that had happened in the last few weeks. The one constant was how much I wished I could go back in time and save Helvig. I thought about his sword and briefly felt ashamed that I hadn't asked Zeke if he found Helvig. I just wanted him to distract me from everything else we had to worry about which only made me feel more guilty. Instead of working out the details of a plan, I was too busy getting dicked down. Was the sex with Zeke great? Yes. Should it have been my priority when seeing him? No. Not even close.

By the time I left the bathroom, Quinlan wasn't in the bedroom. I didn't know if he would be coming back but a large part of me didn't want him to. I felt guilty for spending all that time with Zeke and doing everything except talking. Helvig's sickle sword had been right there and yet I hadn't even asked about him. Tears filled my eyes and I let a sob out into my pillow. I wasn't sure why I was even crying but I couldn't stop. Eventually sleep took me.

The room was dark and smelled so musty that I had a hard time breathing. Like an old cellar that hadn't been opened in years. It was so cold bumps immediately covered my skin and I could see my breath in the dim torch light. I didn't know where I was or how I had gotten here. I heard what sounded like someone wheezing and if I squinted my eyes, I could barely make out a body on the other side of the room.

My instincts set in as I slid into the shadows and out of the dim light. All those nights sneaking out of the castle came in handy as I crept through the darkness towards the person. The closer I got the larger they became. I heard them wheeze and then a coughing fit followed. The cough was wet and sounded like they wouldn't last very long. I slid past another torch without them noticing. They were situated in a dark spot that made it hard for me to make out any details. I was pretty sure it was a man and it looked as though he was chained to the wall. His arms were spread wide at an awkward angle behind him and he was leaning forward with his head hanging down. That had to hurt his arms and shoulders to be putting so much pressure on them. Something was pulling me to this man. If only I could step closer, I might be able to help him. Did I want to help him? I didn't know who he was or what he had done to be chained like this. He could be a dangerous criminal.

Before I could make a decision, I saw his head start to lift. I pressed myself up against the wall hoping to blend into the dark. He sucked in a wheezing breath and then let out a rough moan. He was in pain. Lots of pain. I couldn't stand here any longer. Even if he had done terrible things, I didn't think he deserved this. No one deserved this. He might deserve death but I couldn't stand around any longer. Just when I went to take a step everything began fading away.

Chapter Eight

The sun was starting to rise on the horizon as I dressed. One of the servants had come by and dropped off my trunks. Lucky for me, Rosemary had left me a letter and a large vial of contraception with instructions. Apparently, my father was sending her to his winter estate to begin preparing it for his eventual arrival. I missed her too. In all the craziness that was my life, Rosemary had been there for me. I asked the servant to retrieve Alba for me this morning. I knew her rooms were literally just across the hall but she had seemed wary around me. I didn't want her to wake up to me and start her day off on the wrong foot. I needed today to be a good day. From what little sleep I did get last night, I felt on edge. The figure chained in that dungeon seemed to haunt me and I didn't have any idea why I would dream up something like that.

The men were all getting ready and I had a good feeling about today as long as I didn't think about the dream that plagued me last night. Maybe it's because I was with Zeke last night or maybe it was just going to be a good day. Either way, I knew today would be promising. I needed it to be promising.

Zander was the first one ready and came into my rooms to find me. I was sitting at a desk eating breakfast when he walked in. "I didn't feel like meeting everyone for breakfast. I thought we could eat it here and then head into the village. I know I told them I would meet them in the afternoon at the dress shop but I was kind of hoping I could be the first one there. Just get it done and out of the way, ya know?" I said to Zander between bites of my blueberry muffin.

He picked up a sausage link and popped it into his mouth. "That sounds like a good plan. I would also like to avoid all those fuckers too," he said as he picked up another sausage link and popped it into his mouth. Sun light shone in through a window catching the hint of blue in Zander's hair.

Quinlan came walking in while still pulling on his shirt. I found it hard to look at him after last night. After I cleaned up, I went straight to bed facing away from his side. I mean he woke up to me straddling him completely naked mid-orgasm. How do you just continue on like it never happened because that's what I was planning on doing. I checked our bond and instead of imagining a piece of glass, I imagined a brick wall. Nothing in and nothing out today.

Draug came walking in right behind him. "You have to tell them." The amusement on Draug's face made me curious while the look on Quinlan's face was that of pure embarrassment.

"I swear it's never happened before. Never in my life. I normally go for hours even with my own hand." The sharp lines of his face and strong jaw that normally made him look like a typical pretty boy only seemed to enhance his embarrassment now.

Zander set down his drink, turning to look at them and honestly, my interest was peaked now too. Looking at Quinlan, I took a sip of my orange juice and tried to hear his thoughts. I removed some bricks from the wall and tried peeking through our bond into his mind.

Oh gods. How am I supposed to fucking explain this. She was a freaking goddess on top of me. Her head was thrown back in pure ecstasy and she jerked her hips once. I freaking exploded. I have never cum that hard in my entire life. I wasn't touching myself and she wasn't even touching me. My clothes were still on. Thank fuck considering I would have been really embarassed for the premature ejaculation. How the hell do I explain that to Zander and my fucking Queen that was the one to make me the explode in the first place.

I choked and spit my orange juice out spraying it all over the side of Zanders face who had just been leaning over to get a plate right as Alba came walking in to witness it all.

I burst out laughing and Zander said, "please tell me what you find so fucking amusing about spitting orange juice across me?" His normally stoic expression had changed to one of annoyance. Apparently he was not in the mood today.

Alba sucked in a shocked gasp probably at Zanders harsh tone with me but I couldn't stop laughing.

"Oh gods…. It burns. It burns so badly… It's coming out of my nose," I was crying from laughing so hard with orange juice leaking out of my nostrils. I was almost in hysterics. "I made Quinlan orgasm the best orgasm he's ever had in his whole life without even touching him," I said with a burst of laughter so hard I was practically screaming. I don't know why I was still laughing. I wasn't meaning to laugh at Quinlan but I couldn't stop it. I really did think the hysteria was finally setting in. I was definitely going crazy from all of this.

Poor Alba gasped again and put her hand over her mouth. We all ignored her. She was the definition of a princess in most moments and now was one of those.

Zander stood and turned towards Quinlan while wiping the orange juice from his face. "How is that possible? She's definitely not your mate. I mean you haven't found your mate but she is King Havaror's mate."

Quinlans mouth was still open from my shocking revelation and finally said "It is not very nice to be eavesdropping on private conversations, Cordelia!!! "

"Maybe because she is our Queen?" Draug said skeptically. "Maybe that doesn't apply because she is our Queen...I think we should try to look into this or something. Maybe the curse is finally broken? Maybe it doesn't apply to her because of her magic? I love a good riddle and I haven't ever heard of anything like this happening."

"MAGIC," Alba practically shouted. "I knew that there was a curse on the people from the Havaror Kingdom but I never believed it to be true! You mean that you all really can't ejaculate with someone other than your mate?"

Part of me was completely horrified by this conversation... another fucked up part of me was a little amused.

Draugs cheeks were bright red and Quinlan's mouth just opened and closed again. For once, he was speechless.

"Unfortunately for the Havaror people, it is very true," Zander was just casually wiping away the orange juice from his face and neck. My amusement quickly faded as I realized what Zander wasn't saying. His mate was gone. He would never be with her again.

"Before anyone starts researching queens and orgasms, let's go into the town. I really hate these dresses and I need to get my pants and jumpsuits as soon as possible. I need to clothe Alba in the fabrics she deserves. She is a Queen as well. Wysteria may be currently occupied by my father but it is still her birth right to rule it one day. I intend for her to do that when all of this is said and done," I declared standing from the table and turning towards Alba. "Yes. I have magic. I can move things like this—" I raised my hand and held Albas slippers. Then I moved them to the floor in front of her. She let out another gasp flipping her blond hair over her shoulder and I really hoped this wasn't going to be her reaction to everything. "I also managed to move myself to King Havaror last night. Him and I were preoccupied when I moved back to my bed by accident and when I opened my eyes, I was straddling Quinlan. Apparently, he orgasmed in the 5 seconds I was above him. Questions?" I smiled at her waiting for her response.

Alba looked at Quinlan who looked completely mortified. Then a bellowing laugh came from her. It was rather surprising to hear such a hearty laugh come from this petite woman. "Yes. I have many. So if you have magic and can move yourself to King Havaror, why are you here? Why wouldn't you want to just go to him and stop the war and save lives?"

"Good question…" I crossed my arms and leaned against the table. My dress billowed out around me and I inwardly groaned at it. "I have been able to move objects for a long time. I'm rather good at it and can control it well. Up until a few days ago, I was never able to move myself. Each time it has happened has been completely by accident and I don't know what is triggering it to happen. I also don't control how long I am gone for or when I come back. I would love to be able to save lives and if I had the ability to, I would." I gave her a small smile.

You could almost see the wheels turning in Albas head. Then her smile fell and she looked angry. "So you were fucking King Havaror and then come back here and fuck him," she gestured to Quinlan. "He has an orgasm and then you make fun of him for it! What a queen you are! I didn't take you for a cheater or one to take advantage of her position over others!" She was shouting at me by this point and I think she misunderstood what had happened.

Quilan had visibly shrunk in on himself. Draug was frozen in shock and Zander started to move forward towards her. His anger was pouring off of him in heavy waves. I reached up and grabbed his arm. He was ever my protector.

I pulled Zander behind me slightly and angled myself to Alba. Suddenly her face turned pink and she fell to her knees, "I am so sorry my queen. You have been more than kind to me and I should have never spoken to you like this. I should have never questioned you or judged you. Please I beg for your forgiveness." She was beginning to cry now and my respect for her had grown and then shrunk within moments.

I bent down and touched her shoulder. "Please get up," I kept my voice soft. "I am not angry with you. You will not be punished and you do not need to apologize to me."

"That's bullshit. She owes you a plethora of apologies," Zander said clearly fuming.

"Shut up," I said over my shoulder to him. Alba started to stand and she looked absolutely petrified. Much like a wounded animal waiting for more abuse.

"Here, in front of my men and myself, I want the real Alba. Always. Your real emotions and words. I want your friendship. I don't want a fake friendship with you. I'm sure there's plenty of people in this court here that I can find fake friendships in. However, I was to be friends with Alba Wyster, rightful queen of Wysteria. Here, I am just Cordelia. A woman trying her best to end this war and heal this realm. Please never fall to your knees or beg for forgiveness like that again. I did not cheat on King Havaror. I was with him one moment and then I was straddling Quinlan, who was fully clothed might I add. I was shocked for a couple seconds and then flew off of him as fast as I could. I also would never want to use my position over someone for sex or sexual favors. I want someone that wants me for me." I brushed a tear from her cheek and then stepped forward embracing her. Her sobs left her shaking and I just held on tighter. She might be just as broken as I am or possibly even more so.

Just as I pulled away from Alba, Quinlan finally managed enough courage to speak. "I want everyone to forget this conversation even happened. We can look into it but we are all going to pretend that we are just researching for like the fun of it or some shit. Not because of me or my situation. Got it?" Quinlan said to everyone still pouting but breaking the mood that had fallen over us.

"Not a chance," Zander said, chuckling, "We will all remember this for the rest of our lives."

Draug clapped Quinlan on the back. "Listen, it's never happened to me but I did hear once about teenage boys who…"

Quinlan shoved Draug and stormed out of the room and into the hall.

"Cut it out. He's embarrassed enough about it. Plus I bet if either of you were in the same situation something similar would have happened." I said, shrugging my shoulders and walking towards the hall. "Although, I can't wait to tell Zeke about this new development." I winked as I turned stepping into the hallway.

"GOOD GODS! You can't seriously want to tell King Havaror about that. I don't want to die." Quinlan threw his hands into the air as Zander stepped into the hall.

"Maybe he will take pity on you for your lack of stamina," Zander said, clasping Quinlan on the back.

Draug chuckled and shut the door behind us.

Walking past the dining hall, I heard my father talking with King Daemonger. I felt a cold chill run up my spine and couldn't help but feel like they were up to no good. I picked up the pace heading straight for the front door.

"I think I want to practice using my magic today. So if random things just start appearing in random places, no one needs to freak out."

We stepped out into the sun and it instantly felt like it was warming me from the inside out. Sometimes when I was a little girl, I would climb out onto the roof and hide from my brothers. I would lay in the sun and just soak it in. My brothers weren't always very kind to me. They used to tease me and tell me I was adopted because of my hair color. Not that there's anything wrong with people being adopted, but as a child it hurt. They would purposefully trip me and play pranks on me. As we grew older and started training with each other, they would be encouraged to try and hurt me. Brawntly was always the most kind to me. Maybe because he is the oldest and couldn't be bothered with childish things.

Maybe it was because he is a decent person. I would like to think that an actual decent person would have stopped the torment though.

Draug made an almost purring sound as he soaked in the sun. I was still incredibly curious about what he was exactly but I was waiting for him to reveal himself to me. However, I would still watch him and try to figure it out.

Our party walked down the old stone path to the village below. I noticed that not all of the village was in despair like what I had previously thought. There were a few buildings that looked halfway decent. A few thorny plants grew and most of the bushes were bare. It was a sign that the cold season was fast approaching. While some buildings looked decent, others were very rough. Some had broken windows and roofs falling apart. Others looked as though they had been lit on fire. The people matched the buildings. Some people looked to be pretty decent. They were clean and in nice clothes. Others were in rags and very dirty. I took a mental note at the locations the poor seemed to hang out. We would need to do something for them before the winter sets in.

We stopped at a few shops on our way to the dress boutique. One shop sold desserts and pastries. Of course, I had to stop there and get some chocolates. Another shop was full of crystals, stones, rocks, and small orbs. One of them looked similar to the divination orb that Zeke had given my father. It was much smaller though. About the size of a marble. Honestly, It might have been a marble but I bought it anyway because it made me think of that day. I slid it into my pocket and we continued on

I noticed trash here and there, so I used my magic to move

it into the bin I saw just outside of the castle. It wasn't a big deal but I was using my magic every few minutes which was the most I had used it ever. Maybe by the time we made it to the dress boutique, I would have this road cleaned up. The closer we got to the boutique and the further away from the castle, the worse off the buildings looked. It confused me because I would have sworn it was the opposite when we came through previously. My heart still ached for the people here that were struggling to survive.

Zander leaned down and whispered into my ear "We can figure out a plan to help them too."

I stopped walking as realization set in. "My goal is to leave. I'll be leaving all these people at King Daemongers mercy and he isn't very merciful. What kind of Queen am I to just leave them and let them suffer?"

Quinlan looked around us and then said, "You aren't leaving them. You are trying to survive and then you want to save them from this hell they are currently living. War is a terrible thing, I would bet they have lost many family members to your fathers cause. King Daemonger has been helping to supply troops. I'm sure that's why there's so many abandoned buildings."

Alba's sad expression didn't help my guilty conscience.

Maybe Quinlan had a point though. I continued walking when another thought crossed my mind. "Why don't one of you just fly me out of here? I mean, you're a fucking dragon and you're a phoenix. Surely, one of you could fly me out of here." Surprisingly enough, this did not evoke another gasp from Alba. Really though, they could have flown me out of camp days ago. As soon as they found out I was there, boom they could have gotten me to Zeke.

"My Queen," Draug started. I couldn't help but roll my eyes. Usually when he started things off like that, I was going to hear something I didn't really care to hear. "We are outnumbered. The second one of us changes and takes off into the sky, they will be on us. King Daemonger has unseelie fae, beings from other realms, and well creatures that I don't even know what they are everywhere watching the skies. This is NOT like your home in Drochia. Shifters of all kinds live in the Daemonger Kingdom just like the Havaror Kingdom. Not to mention the dragons he has in his army. I'm not sure exactly how many but I know it's at least five. Five full grown dragons against us, with you and Alba riding on someone's back? It isn't worth the risk of you falling, being burnt, or being hurt."

"Oh. I guess that makes sense," I said letting everything he said sink in. Disappointment quickly washed away the hope that had begun to bloom.

"Believe me, if we could have safely gotten you out of camp or away from here we would have. None of us want to see you be a prisoner here," Quinlan said with a pitiful smile on his face. His eyes were saddened and he looked tired. After yesterday's events and last night, he didn't get much sleep. He really needed to rest up after dying. A flash of my dream from last night at his use of prisoner. I wasn't really a prisoner, well I was but I wasn't treated like one and for that I was lucky.

"Maybe there's a reason the fates have brought you here," Alba said with a shrug. The fates. What a fucking joke they were.

Just as we approached the dress boutique, we saw a hag walk in. My skin felt tingly and I was instantly on edge. I glanced at my men but they seemed completely unbothered.

We walked up the few wooden steps and opened the door.

"Ahh Nimae, I have your dress ready this morn— Your Majesty," the old shop owner, Esther, said startled.

"Thank you, Esther. I am here for the Queen too though," the old hag said, doing a hand motion when she said Queen. While she was turning towards me, my men instantly stepped in front of me.

Draug's harsh tone cut through the air, "What business do you have with the Queen?"

"Ahh I see you do have yourself quite the bandit of misfits don't you." She said completely ignoring him. A smirk splayed across her face exposing her rotting teeth.

She was shorter than me by a good 8 inches so compared to where her height reached my men she looked almost miniature. Her hair was gray and long. It had sticks and twigs sticking out from it in random places, but she had it in a loose braid. She had large moles on her chin and nose. Her nose was long and crooked and her eyes looked like they saw everything and nothing at the same time. They were completely white with no pupils or color to them at all.

"How can I be of service to you?" I asked her as I stepped between Draug and Zander. Alba stepped up beside me. Whether it was out of protectiveness or nervousness, I didn't know.

"Oh, I have been looking forward to meeting you since the first day I saw you. I was a young woman then. Those were the days when my suitors looked like the men you surround yourself with. All of them wanted a piece of me and when they broke my heart, I turned them into cats," She said, cackling and reminiscing.

"You turned them into cats?" I asked, my eye brows pinched

together.

"Well of course, serve them right too. You know you're not the only one with magic around here," she said, placing her curved wooden cane on the ground and stepping closer. I saw Esther's eyes widen as she glanced from the hag to me.

"You have magic?" I asked curiously. I probably should have asked how she knew I had magic but I figured rumors had spread the night I first used my magic in front of my father and the staff.

"Yes, my dearie. Listen up because I only have a few moments. The only way to ever improve and to be able to do what you seek is to use it and practice. You have to hone your skills. Otherwise, you'll never escape him. He's going to hurt you. That we cannot change." She said looking me directly in the eyes. Her eyes showed sorrow. Like two pools filled to the brim ready to flow over. She didn't allow them to flow over though. She straightened her back… well as straight as she could manage and said, "I have seen it go two ways. He will break you and continue to hurt you until you are a shell of the woman you are now. Or he will hurt you and you will shatter completely. This realm will fall." She waved her hands at that last part dismissively like she hadn't just dropped a huge fucking shockwave on us.

I started to ask her what she meant because honestly both options sounded the same and equally terrible. She shook her head and continued. "You seek answers to questions that are not important at the moment. I saw you in a conservatory. There are things in there you will need and answers to questions you have yet to ask. Oh and when a goddess speaks to you in your dreams you should heed her words. Let him go. He will find his true mate soon and if you hold on it will only cause you pain." She picked up her bag and smiled at Esther. "I won't be needing to come back seeing as she finally showed up."

"Wait, what do you mean he will hurt me? Who?" I was shocked and a little confused. A conservatory? What could I need from there? It was taking a moment for my brain to catch up to everything she was saying.

Draug , Zander and Quinlan looked confused, concerned, and skeptical.

"The counterfeit king of course," she said, placing her hand on my cheek before stepping around me to open the door, "Oh I almost forgot! You should look into King Rovini's beloved Queen's death. The story that's been told isn't true. Seek the truth about her and that will lead you to the truth about your father and your mother. Maybe try asking King Daemonger's alchemist. He was there after all. When King Daemonger wants to see you, don't hesitate. Do not put it off. You have much to discuss and he isn't the enemy you think he is."

She stepped out of the boutique and the door closed behind her.

"Wait!" I shouted rushing to the door. I had LOTS of questions. She couldn't just say these things and leave. I mean who does that. Just says a bunch of rather vague shit and goes about their day.

I opened the door and she was gone. I froze and looked around. How could she just be gone. She was only a few steps in front of me. She wasn't anywhere on the road either. She was just gone. Poof. Just like that. My mouth was wide open and my eyes had to have been the size of dinner plates. What the fuck was all of that. My brain was reeling trying to piece together what she said and where she just went.

Chapter Eight

I turned around to find my men also peering out of the doorway looking for the old hag.

"She was a very, very old witch," Draug said, shrugging his shoulders slightly. "It has been a few centuries since I have seen a witch like her."

Chapter Nine

I was a little shocked that Draug seemed so casual about what just happened. I mean she just said some crazy shit and disappeared and he just shrugged. Literally lifted one shoulder and dropped it. How could he be so calm and casual about all of that? About everything that had happened recently?

Placing my hands on my hips I gave him my full attention. "You do know she said someone was going to hurt me and possibly do it more than once," I said to him. I watched as his eyes widened slightly.

"I know," he whispered, "We won't allow that to happen."

"I will give my life 1000 times over before that happens," Quinlan said firmly, "That is a promise."

"What? No! I do not want you ever giving your life even once for mine," I said. I started to lay into him about how ridiculous it was for any of them to sacrifice their lives for me when I caught myself. That wasn't what was important at the moment. Me ranting about it isn't going to change it right now and we have other more important things to handle.

"It truly is never a dull moment with you," Alba barely whispered. She didn't even know that half of it but she wasn't wrong.

Esther cleared her throat, "Well I have to say I am a little saddened that she won't be back. She has been coming here every morning for a very long time. Sometimes she just stands in the spot you found her in not moving. Eventually she would say 'Nope, must not be today' and then just walk out. I kind of thought she was crazy. Now I know for sure that she is."

Esther's words caused me to burst out in a fit of laughter. The sound of my loud laughter almost echoed through the otherwise silent room. Esther's eyes crinkled as she grinned, "Now, I figured you would come early. You seemed anxious to get measured. Come. We will get you all straightened out. I already have some items that could be of interest to you."

I went to take a step forward when I realized that Zander hadn't said anything. I searched for his emotions as I turned towards him. White hot pain and hurt was pulsing through him. There was anger and lots of regret.

"Zander," I said softly, reaching for his hand and squeezing it. "Zander. Come back to me". I knew where his mind had gone. King Daemonger was responsible for his soulmate's death. After what the hold hag had said, it probably left Zander a mess. It was his job to protect me and he took that very seriously. To hear that I needed to meet with King Daemonger and someone was going to hurt me at least once and there wasn't anything we could do about it had to pain him. Well it frightened me to say the least. Any smart person would be frightened.

What worried me the most was what kind of hurt would be inflicted on me? Would it be a physical pain? Emotional? Maybe even psychological? How bad would it be? I knew one thing though, I needed to learn how to move myself at my own will. So if whoever were to ever do something, I could escape. I bet that's how it only happens once. I get hurt and then remove myself from whatever the situation is. Fear slid its icy fingers through me as I thought about how I can't move myself yet and I don't know when this person is going to hurt me. If I don't figure this out, he would hurt me repeatedly and all would be lost.

Zander, well it had taken him to a dark place. I knew dark places like that. Sometimes Ragnor's words would trigger a dark place inside me. He made me believe the things he said about me. It felt like I was drowning in the emotions and I always had to figure out how to pull myself out of it. I was alone for most of my life and I had figured it out. Zander though, he had me. He wasn't alone and didn't have to figure his way out of that. I squeezed his hand again, "Zander, please come back to me, your Queen, Cordelia. I am here and I am safe. I need you to come back to me."

Slowly his eyes met mine and I saw the pain he was trying to hide. My heart squeezed for him. I stepped forward and wrapped my arms around his waist. I buried my head into his chest and stood there holding him. Ever so slowly, he moved his arms and placed them around me. I felt his muscles loosen and then I felt him suck in a breath of air. I stepped back from him, and nodded my head. Zander was becoming more than a guard to me. He was quickly becoming a dear friend. Although no one could ever replace Helvig, maybe my friendship with Zander would help heal the wound Helvig left. He didn't need me to dwell on what had happened. I turned to Esther who eyed me carefully, "I am so excited to see what you have for me." I knew that this whole encounter was strange and probably looked inappropriate for me, the future queen here, to be hugging a guard.

Her eyebrows lifted and she motioned towards the back. Okay. "You guys stay right here. I will be back." I winked at my men. All three of them started to protest but I held up my hand. I didn't want them coming in the back while I was measured and tried things on. If I needed them, I could scream. Plus they had already see way more of me than anyone needed to. "Come on Alba. You're getting fitted too."

After being measured, measured again, and then one more time I was ready to get out of the dress shop. Alba was currently going through everything they had just done to me. I could hear my men in the front room talking about the old hag and what they could do to keep me safe. It's why I hadn't gone out to join them. If we were to believe her words, I was going to get hurt no matter what. The only way that I could ensure it would just be one time was to train. I would need to train physically and with my magic.

I stared at Alba wondering why that strange feeling of seeing her before had come back. Well it wasn't so much as a feeling like I had seen her but more of a deja vu feeling while looking at her. There wouldn't have been any way that I had seen her before the camp. I had never left our kingdom and my father didn't allow other royalty to visit us. He claimed that if he did then that would mean he recognized their claim to a throne when the only throne that was legitimate was his. So why did I get this feeling when I watched her.

I sighed and started thinking about all the things the old hag had said. There was one thing we were all ignoring. It was the part about me listening to the goddess from my dreams and that he was going to meet his true mate soon enough. No one had asked or spoken about it. Unfortunately I already knew what she meant. It had been obvious this whole time but I had wanted to ignore all the signs. Zeke and I weren't soulmates. I wasn't his true mate. It's why I wasn't able to ever catch him in that dream I had. I had chased him and chased him, yet he was always just out of reach. It's why she kept telling me to let him go. I had wanted to be selfish for once in my life and hold on to him as long as possible. I really did care for him and I tried convincing myself that even if he found his soulmate he would still choose me. I knew it was impossible. The bond they would have would outshine anything he and I had. It wouldn't be fair of me to expect him to choose me. The next time I went to him, I would have to tell him. I would explain to him that I really care about him but a goddess told me we weren't mates and I had to let him go. I would then tell him that the old hag said he would be meeting his mate soon and that I wanted him to be happy and choose her without feeling any guilt about me.

Surprisingly the hole in my chest didn't increase at these thoughts. Maybe it was because I knew deep down that this day was inevitable. I had come to terms with it the day Helvig had openly talked about it. He said it wouldn't be fair and part of me thinks he knew that Zeke and I weren't soulmates somehow. Yet, he didn't want to push me about it and was trying to protect me. That thought did make the hole in my chest swell and ache. I miss him more than I ever thought possible. Gods. I had been such a fool. Tears pricked my eyes and I did my best to hold them back.

At that moment Zander came charging in the back, almost frantic. "Is everything alright?"

Would they continue to guard me once I told them? I would no longer be their queen. Well not that I was truly their Queen now. I would no longer be betrothed to their king. I could only hope their loyalty wouldn't change but yet I could understand if everything changed and between us. I felt a panic start to set in. I would be alone again. I would have no one again. I would be left with Brutus and who knows what I would have to endure then. What if he was the counterfeit king? What if he was the one that was going to hurt me?

"Yeah… Yes," I choked out. "After we leave here, I would like to go back to the castle. I have some things I need to speak privately with Alba and you three about."

Zanders' eyes held mine for a moment. I felt the worry and concern come through our bond. He didn't say anything. He just nodded and said, "I'll let the guys know."

I smiled weakly at him. It was forced and I knew he could tell. Zander always knew and I wasn't sure if I liked that or not. "Are you alright, my Queen?" Albas voice caught me by surprise.

"Honestly?" I said ignoring the women working around us in the room.

"Of course," Alba said with an eyebrow raised.

"No. I don't think I'll ever be alright again but that is for another day to worry about. Can you please stop calling me your queen? I want to be your friend rather than your queen." I dropped her gaze and turned to stare out of the window. The village was bustling now. No matter what happened to me, I wouldn't fail these people. I wouldn't fail the people of this realm.

Quinlan? Can you listen to what I'm about to tell you but keep a straight face?

Of course I can! The fact that you would even question that, ugh, woman. I am the master of all things serious. Quin's laughter filtered through my mind and it was hard to keep the smile from my face.

I want to tell you this first. Kind of like a practice round. But I need you to keep it a secret until I tell the others. Can you promise me you won't speak of this conversation or of what I'm about to tell you? Watching as Alba was being fitted, I held my breath as I waited for his response.

I promise. Always. Anything you need. I am here. His voice sounded soft like he was trying to soothe my worry.

I have had these dreams for most of my life. A goddess visits me. I cannot see her but I can hear her. Usually she tells me something of importance but it's vague and oddly worded and she never just comes right out with whatever it is she wants me to know. It's always like putting together a puzzle. It's cryptic and annoying as hell. However, once I figure it out it or whatever she tells me comes to fruition, it's all painfully obvious what she was trying to tell me. Well she's been visiting me for weeks. Always the same or similar message. Telling me to let him go. At one point in time I was chasing Zeke, his brothers Lykke and Trygg, Vilulf, and Helvig. No matter how fast I ran, I could never catch up to Zeke. I've had a feeling now for a while that Zeke and I were not soul mates. I addressed this with him before I was kidnapped and he assured me that he thought we were meant to be together and even if we weren't soulmates he would still choose me. He would always choose me. At the time I felt relief and happiness. I felt loved by him and I didn't want to give that up. Maybe that was selfish of me. I just haven't ever had someone care for me like he has and the thought of losing that killed me. However, the old hag's words keep repeating over and over in my head. Those words combined with the goddess... It's time I face the truth. Zeke and I are not soulmates. We are not true mates. I have to let him go and I have to do that before he finds his true mate. Which according to the old hag, will be soon. So the next time I somehow manage to go to him. I have to explain all this to him. I have to end things. I care about him so much but he deserves to be able to choose his true mate without feeling guilty. So whenever I am able to have this conversation with him, I will no longer be betrothed to him. I will no longer be your queen. You will not have to guard me and risk your lives for me. You will no longer be duty bound to your queen or future queen that is. However, I hope that you will still be my friend.

My heart felt raw. Like I was standing there holding my bleeding heart out in the open. Zander stepped back into the room and narrowed his eyes at me. I knew he could feel the emotions tormenting me. I sighed real deep and gave him a half smile and shook my head. His mouth formed a tight line and he took slow steps towards me.

In front of everyone, Zander wrapped his arms around me this time and pulled me into his chest. I fought as hard as I could to not cry. There was something so comforting about Zander that made me know deep down I was safe with him. He had no idea what was going on with me but he was here and that's what mattered most. He started speaking to the women and Alba. Asking if they were almost done and telling them we would be leaving in 5 minutes. He leaned close to my ear and whispered, "It's okay. You've been through a lot lately but just know that I'm here for you."

117

Quinlan's voice filtered through the fog that my brain had been in.

You're wrong you know. You might not be Queen Havaror of the Havaror Kingdom. That much is true, but you will always be Queen Cordelia of the Realm. There is something special about you. You have to see that. No one can just form bonds with people like you have. No one is like you. A goddess visits you frequently and an old hag has been waiting for you to come into this dress shop for years. You have to see there is so much more to you that you just don't know yet. I will forever be duty bound to protect you, whether or not you marry King Ezekiel does not change that. You are my Queen and my friend. Nothing will ever change that.

At Quinlans words a choked sob broke from me. Zander pulled me in tighter to him as Draug burst into the room. "We are leaving now. Finish up. Let's go." What was wrong with me? Why was everything making me so emotional? I used to be able to keep my emotions in check. Having emotions and showing them made you weak according to Ragnor. Every time I would cry, he would punish me if he saw it. I couldn't afford to be weak. Not right now. I might be surrounded by my men but that doesn't mean that I'm safe. If anything, I was far from safe after hearing the words from the hag earlier.

After putting myself back together, I pulled away from Zander and straightened my shoulders. Esther's voice was carefully measured, "We will have your new clothes by the end of the week. We can deliver them straight to the castle for you."

"That sounds lovely, thanks," Alba replied for me.

We exited the shop and headed straight towards the castle. The heaviness in my chest grew the closer we got. I kept my head straight forward and tried not to let my emotions show physically and mentally. I knew Zander had been checking my emotions and I didn't want to freak him out anymore than I already had. I could feel the villagers' eyes on us as we passed. It was odd seeing so many unseelie fae in one place. Some were so close to human looking I had to look twice. Others had obvious unseelie characteristics like horns and antlers. Others though… Others were like beasts I had never seen before. They were so far removed from humans and fae; made up of animal like bodies. Some had multiple heads and others seemed to be as black as shadows at night. I didn't think the unseelie welcomed me very much. My father had always hated them even going as far as holding tournaments in the past that involved killing as many as you could. I knew I had won over a good portion of the fae and humans when I killed Elbereth but the unseelie, they would be tough to win over.

How do you want to go about telling everyone? You know I will help you out and back you up with anything you need. You just let me know and I will do whatever. If you want me to explain it I will.

Quinlans words were the reassurance that I didn't know I needed. He had my back. Even if the others didn't, he would still be here when all the rest of the world fell around me.

I think when we get back, we should go straight to our rooms. I'll start explaining everything and if things start to head for the worse or if I get choked up or something, then you can just step in. Don't worry about asking. You can just explain to them I told you already. If someone gets upset by that then too bad for them. After that, I will have to meet with King Daemonger and see what exactly his expectations are for me. I am also going to see what it would take for him to stop the war with Zeke. Maybe if we can get

Zeke and Brutus on the same side, we can take down my fathers army. If I have to marry him, then that is a sacrifice I am willing to make.

Quinlan glanced at me as I said those final words to him. I tried not to look at him but his sigh made me glance over. I wished I wouldn't have. The look on his face showed me all the pity he was feeling and it made my insides twist up. This would be my new goal to get Brutus and Zeke on the same side. Originally, I wanted to find the temple my father had been searching for. Now, I didn't think that was as important as combining the two armies to try and face off against him. Quinlan's pity as he looked at me made my stomach roll.

I didn't want anyone to feel pity in this situation. It was fine. If I wasn't Zeke's soulmate then there would be someone else out there waiting to find me. I held my head high as we climbed the stairs. Before we reached the top, the guards opened the doors and Voronion stepped out.

"Ahh Cordelia," he said bowing. "King Daemonger is requesting your presence in his receiving room. Just you, your guards can remain in the hall." He glanced at my men and then back to me.

"Actually, there is something I must do before I meet with him. I will see him when I am done and yes, sure, my guards can remain in the hall." I smiled as we continued walking. I didn't know what Brutus wanted with me but I had to talk to my men.

"I must insist that you come at once. He requested your presence now. Not whenever it is convenient for you," Voronion turned towards the guards at the door of the castle. I could see he wasn't going to give up on this one. If I was going to be here long term now, I would have to learn when to fight my battles and this was not one of those situations.

"Of course," I said coolly. "Draug, Zander, and Alba please go with Quinlan to my room. I will meet you there once I am done with Brutus."

Zander started to protest but I quickly gave him a look that said do not push.

Then I nodded at Quinlan.

Go and tell them what I told you. Explain to them about the goddess and my dreams. Then about the words the old hag said and what Zeke had said previously. Let them know the next time I go to Zeke I am telling him and ending things. Explain to them that I understand if this changes things for them and I do not fault them for that. If they or yourself have questions obviously reach out to me but give me a moment to respond. I do not want Brutus to know that I can communicate with you this way... at least not yet.

Quinlan nodded back and motioned for the rest to follow him. Alba looked nervously at me and I gave her a reassuring smile.

"I have to admit, I assumed your men would have thrown more of a fit to stay with you," Voronion said in a tone that made my neck hairs rise.

"Yeah well I am their Queen and they do trust me. They aren't going to go against me. Now shall we meet with Brutus?" I walked past Voronion and into the grand entryway.

"Yes, his rooms are right this way. So tell me what do you think of the village here? Isn't it rather lovely. I know it isn't as glamorous as other villages but King Daemonger has made it his personal mission to spruce the place up. I think it's a waste of time and resources but he insists on moving displaced commoners from Kingdoms your father has conquered to this village." Voronion almost sounded annoyed that Brutus was attempting to help these people which was incredibly surprising and a good tidbit to keep in mind.

"I think it needs a lot more work. I already told my men that I was planning on helping the people there, so I guess it's a good thing that Brutus is already attempting that. One less thing that I will have to fight with him about," I rolled my neck and stretched my arms. It was mostly out of habit but I realized I looked like I was gearing up for a fight when Voronion raised an eyebrow at me.

"Do you work out, Onion?" I chuckled as I said my new nickname for him. "You don't look like you work out very often. Do you at least train to be able to defend your King?" I was shameless in my prying for information and he knew it.

"I don't need to train to defend my King. There isn't any amount of training that someone can do that would out mancuver me," His grin was wide and almost malicious.

"A little full of yourself?" I laughed trying to calm my nerves but something inside of me was screaming to be careful around him.

"Oh no. I think you just underestimate what someone with magic is truly capable of," His tone was menacing now and I felt a chill go up my spine. I felt my magic falter and instantly a sharp spike of pain sliced through my head.

At that moment, the double doors at the end of the hallway opened and Brutus came charging forward but before I could take another step everything went black.

I found myself in the dark and musty room again. Bumps immediately covered my skin and I prepared myself for the cold I knew would seep into my bones. I still didn't know where I was but I knew that someone else was still here. My head throbbed and I wobbled on my feet for a moment. I heard the wheezing and thought it sounded even worse than the last time I was here.

I slid into the shadows once again. I watched them carefully as I made my way closer. I knew I had to move quicker than I did before. I didn't know how long I would stay dreaming and I had a feeling the Goddess was responsible for this dream. What she was showing me, I still didn't know.

His arms were still spread wide but this time I noticed the painful angle of his arms. His right shoulder looked like it was dislocated and blood was dripping in a steady rhythm from his wrist. He grunted and sucked in a deep breath. Suddenly, he jerked his body and let out a scream. I watched in shock and horror as he repeated this over and over again. Blood began pouring from his wrist but I saw the crack spreading in the wall behind him. He was attempting to break free even though he was tearing his arm apart.

I stole all my courage and stepped forward silently. He stopped yanking his arm and began vomiting all down the front of himself. The pain must be unbearable.

"Hello?" I whispered not wanting to startle him.

I watched as he slowly lifted his head, moaning in pain. All the breath left my lungs when I met his emerald eyes. His head dropped back down but I knew. I knew who he was.

"Helvig?!" Panic flooded my veins. "Gods. Helvig!" I rushed to him and lifted his head with my hands. "I'm here. I'm here. Oh Gods. How long have you been here? What happened? What hurts?" I was rambling and I couldn't stop myself. My hands were searching his body for wounds. My mind was racing and I couldn't focus as tears flooded my eyes. My heart tore wide open and I felt like I was dying seeing him like this.

"My zon" he let out a hard cough. "My zonlicht, you must leave this place."

Chapter Ten

I awoke on a soft velvet couch facing an unfamiliar fireplace. My head was throbbing and I could hear shouting in the distance. I felt like I was coming out of a fog. I tried to sit up but my head spun and I fell gently back to the couch. I closed my eyes and tried to focus on the conversation I could hear rather than the too realistic dream I just had.

"I HAVE REPEATEDLY TOLD YOU THAT YOU WILL NOT USE YOUR POWERS ON HER! I FORBID YOU TO SEARCH HER MIND AND YET THE FIRST MOMENT YOU HAD ALONE WITH HER YOU DIRECTLY DISOBEYED AN ORDER FROM ME. DO YOU THINK THAT JUST BECAUSE YOU ARE MY FUCKING BROTHER THAT I WILL ALLOW THIS?" Brutus was yelling.

"I think you are a fool. There is much more to her than they have told us. I sensed her magic and she willingly let her guards leave her side to come here. If you trust her then you are a fool. Punish me however you wish but I do not regret trying. At least now we know her mind is impenetrable. That just leaves the question of why?" Voronion angrily said back.

"Leave. Assure her guards that she is fine and that she passed out on her way here. Once she is awake I will see what she remembers and what she can tell me," Brutus sounded exhausted. "Don't come back until I summon you."

I heard the door close and Brutus let out a long sigh. When I heard his footsteps approach, I closed my eyes.

"What the hell did you get us into dad?" Brutus said on a sigh.

I opened my eyes to find him standing in front of me and facing the fireplace. He was staring up at the portrait of a tall man with the crown that Brutus now wore and a beautiful woman. They must have been Brutus's parents. King Daemonger the violent and Queen Xola. She looked so happy in this portrait. Actually, a genuine happiness radiated from both of them. I was surprised to see that the similarities between Brutus and Zeke came from their mother. It made sense but still surprising nonetheless. Aside from the few similarities, Brutus looked so much like his father. I did not fear him. I would not be afraid of whatever he had in store for me.

"You wanted to see me," I said, pushing past my throbbing head and trying to mask my voice with a half-bored half annoyed tone.

"I did."

"Would you like to tell me what the hell happened and why Voronion has the power to delve into someone's mind?"

The light outlined his body and I realized just how large he was. He was a beast of a man. I understood now why all the doorways were twice as high as normal doorways. "No.

I needed to see you. I'm afraid that we haven't spent much time together since you've been here and I would like to get to know you," Brutus turned and looked at me assessingly. He sighed and rubbed his neck once before sitting down at the end of the couch by my feet.

Gods, he could crush me with just his hands. I tried not to let the fear of being completely alone with him overwhelm me. I will not fear him. I will not fear him. I repeated that over and over until I started to believe it. I stared at a wingback chair trying to avoid looking at him. I didn't need my men who were already unhappy and on edge feeling anything from me right now. I didn't know how much they felt when Voronion was a dick and decided to try to get in my head. Awkward and silent minutes passed.

I started to try to sit up when he finally spoke again, "Don't try to sit up just yet. You'll get dizzy and feel worse." The sigh he released was somewhere between annoyed and exhausted. "I am going to assume that your betrothed didn't tell you about his or his brothers powers since you are asking about Voronion?" He looked at me questioningly.

"Well considering we didn't get to spend much time together before I was kidnapped, no. He didn't tell me," I couldn't help the bite in my bitter words. "So both Zeke and Voronion have powers? What about their other siblings?" I knew I had no right to feel angry because I didn't tell Zeke about my powers. Yet the taste of bitterness crept up my throat anyways. First I didn't even know about Voronion or Brutus. Now they all have fucking magic. What else did he never mention? We did have time. We had plenty of time for him to tell me these things just like we had time for me to tell my secrets. I chose not to tell him about my magic which means that he was choosing to keep all these secrets from me.

"As far as I know they all have powers. My father believes it came from their mother," he stated looking up at the portrait once again.

"You mean your mother, that you killed?" Yah. That's right buddy boy. I know what kind of psychopath you are… the kind that kills their own mom. Most people wouldn't want to bring something like that up, yet here I was, provoking him.

"No. According to my father the Zola that he married and had created me with was not the Xola that married King Havaror and had a slew of children with him. I would never kill my own mother," he shrugged his shoulders.

I narrowed my eyes and glared at him. According to the story that Zander told me none of what Brutus said made sense. "You act as though your father and mother created you out of love and then she went off and married King Havaror and had his children. Are you saying that you didn't kill Xola after dining with her?"

"That isn't really relevant right now. What is relevant is that Voronion disobeyed a direct order from me and tried to search your mind. Much to his surprise you had completely blocked him from it. Which caused him to try harder and resulted in your passing out. Did you block him on purpose?" he wouldn't look at me. Instead he just stared into the fire. His elbows rested on his knees and his hands dangled between his legs. He looked tired and vulnerable.

"No. I didn't know what he was doing and I didn't mean to block him. I don't know how I blocked him. He just made some vague statement about his powers and then I felt a sharp pain in my head before passing out." I don't know why I felt like I needed to be honest with him. It was the truth though and maybe if I was honest with him, he would be honest with me.

"I see. What of your magic then? Your father told me that you didn't have any magic, yet clearly you have quite a bit." The annoyance rang clear in his words and made me bristle. How could he be annoyed with me over my magic? Was it because my father lied to him or was it because I actually had magic?

"I don't know why my father would lie to you about it other than he didn't want me to use my magic ever. The day I discovered my magic, I was a little girl and did something in front of my father. Well... putting it mildly, he freaked out. He had me punished and I was never allowed to use my magic again. I did when I was older but I used it very infrequently. After my kidnapping, I decided that I would no longer suppress who I am. I can move things. I just have to think about what it is that I want and where I want it. I have only ever been able to do it with things that I have seen before. If I hadn't seen it, I wouldn't be able to move it." I yawned as if it was no big deal. I hadn't realized just how tired I was until now. I felt exhausted down to my bones. My whole body ached and I wanted nothing more than to crawl into my bed and go to sleep. Today had been a long day.

"You're going to be exhausted. Essentially, Voronion assaulted your mind trying to break in. It will take time for you to recover. I am going to go out on a limb and say that you and some of your guards have bonded?" I watched as he crossed his arms and raised his eyebrows. His question took me by surprise.

"What makes you think that?"

"Within moments of your passing out, your guards were

barreling down the hallway screaming. They killed 7 of my men before I stepped in and ordered my guards to stand down. There would be no other way for them to know that something had happened to you unless you were bonded." Surprisingly, he didn't sound accusatory. Just merely curious.

"Yes. We have. I won't go into details about my bonds, who they are with, or what they do because unlike other people, I will protect my men at all costs. If they came here looking for me earlier, where are they now? What did you do to them?" I asked. Guilt and worry started creeping in. I tried to find my connection to Quinlan but all I felt was a spike of pain in my head that had me on the verge of puking. Oh Gods. What if he put them in a dungeon? What if they had been beaten for their actions? I could feel my chest start to tighten and the fear was running wild through me.

"They have been escorted back to your rooms and I have assured them that you will be fine," he said. "Although, I don't think they truly believed me and they were incredibly hesitant on leaving you but I insisted. I have never met a more unhappy group of men."

The expected relief from his words didn't come. Instead the images of my men fighting to try to get to me flashed through my mind along with images of Helvig from my dream. I took a moment to try and get my shit together. What was happening to me? I didn't panic under pressure, yet here I was ready to crack. Is this what it feels like to actually care about people? If so, I needed to start separating my feelings because I couldn't risk panicking everytime something bad might have happened to one of them.

"Of course they weren't happy about leaving me with you. Why would they trust that you have the best intentions with me? What is it that you want to know and what exactly are your intentions with me? Do you truly intend to marry me because I'm starting to wonder what else you have up your sleeve with your line of questioning?" I asked coldly, glancing over at him and watching as he ran his hand through his hair. It reminded me of the same thing that Zeke did when he was nervous about something.

Brutus was more handsome than I first thought. His features were sharper and more defined than Zeke. He also had a hardness to him that I had never seen on Zeke. Even when Zeke was angry and tough, he never had such coldness in him. My eyes followed Brutus' tattoo that covered the half of his head that was shaved. The swirling pattern looked like vines when I first saw it but after seeing it this close I realized it was actually branches that came together near the middle of his head forming half a tree. I briefly wondered if the tree continued on the other side of his. I followed it down his neck until it tucked into his maroon colored shirt. The tattoo was thicker on his neck and looked like the top part of the tree trunk. Squinting, I could just make out that it wasn't line work making up his tattoo but what looked to be ancient text. His shirt was tight on his body and he seemed to have muscles on top of muscles. He was Godly. I should have feared him but the longer I was around him the more comfortable I became. Something about Brutus made me feel safe. Were we kindred spirits? I looked away from him and stared back into the fire. I was still angry but that didn't change the fact that I knew I was safe with him. I had good instincts and I need to trust them. If my gut was telling me that Brutus was safe, then I needed to believe that.

I could see him staring at me from the corner of my eye

while he twisted the white tips of his hair in his fingers. His hair was long, down to his mid chest. "Look at me, please," he demanded softly. The softness in his voice took me by surprise. I looked at him and stared directly into his pitch black eyes.

"Are you afraid of me?' he asked curiously. I pushed through the ache in my head that was now just a dull pain and leaned forward narrowing my eyes, "I am afraid of nothing."

That wasn't the truth though. I was afraid of a lot of things like my men getting hurt trying to protect me. Losing them. Not being good enough. My father succeeding at taking over the realm. The list of things I was afraid of was long but Brutus wasn't on that list. Was he dangerous? Yes. Very. I wasn't stupid.

Brutus let out a short laugh and his eyes crinkled around the edges.

"I truly believe that."

"Are you going to answer my questions? What do you want to know about me, Brutus?" Maybe, I should have been more careful around him but I wasn't in the mood for games and my patience was already wearing thin.

"Brutus? I hadn't realized we were on a first name basis. Alright, I guess that's good. Cordelia. Cordelia." He said my name like he was tasting the weight it carried in the air. "You know, you have a really beautiful name. I would say it's also a very appropriate name, don't you think?" His sly grin set my teeth on edge.

"I'm not sure what you mean by appropriate," I scrunched my face slightly confused by that… by all of this. What game was he playing at? "Why is my name appropriate to you?"

"Do you not know what your name means?" His eyes

widened with surprise.

"I know what my name means. My name means daughter of the sea."

I still wasn't understanding how that made my name appropriate. I could feel my anxiety rising. He sure did talk a lot for someone who never made any sense.

"Indeed it does. I suppose Queen Rovini was very prognosticate when she named you." Brutus stated casually.

"My mother was never Queen Rovini," I said sharply. Did he not even know that I wasn't Queen Rovini's daughter and that I had a different mother than my brothers.

"Obviously," Brutus said with a chuckle. "I would like to know what you like? What do you spend your time doing? What do you enjoy?" He changed the conversation so quickly I swear it gave me whiplash.

"Why?" His question caught me off guard. Why would he want to know that about me?

"If you are to be my wife, I should probably know how to make you happy."

"My freedom would make me happy," I said glaring into his black soulless eyes.

He frowned and turned staring into the fire. After a few long and excruciating silent moments he began, "I am sorry. I didn't know about King Havarors intentions to marry you. I had heard rumors that he was going to be taking a wife soon but those rumors have been going around for a few years now. If you grew to care for him and now are here… well, I am sorry to have done that to you."

He ran his hand through his hair again. "Let's talk about something else. Is there anything you would like to know about me?" His voice almost sounded hopeful and my heart sank a bit. I wasn't expecting an apology from him but he actually seemed remorseful.

"Why would you kill your mo— err Xola Havaror?" This was the question that had been burning my mind ever since Zander told me the story about them.

Chapter Eleven

ⴻⵯⵑⵯ

I t was the question I had been dying to know the answer
to and couldn't stop myself from asking. I needed to
know why he killed her. The reason might not matter
to most people but it mattered to me. One day I might have
to make a hard decision about my father and I would like to
hope that it wouldn't make me a bad person. Well I would
like to hope that people wouldn't think of me as terribly as
they think of Brutus.

"Wow. You just go for the throat don't you," he said,
scrubbing a hand down his face again. "That is a long story.
Are you sure there isn't anything else you would like to talk
about? Like my favorite color? My favorite book? My
hobbies?"

"I have plenty of time," I said flatly. I wasn't letting him
wiggle his way out of this. I scooted back on the couch, tucked
my legs under me relaxing into the plush fabric and raised
my eyebrows at him. "I'm waiting for you to tell me how
exactly you could be so cold and kill your own mother after

she welcomed you into her home?"

Brutus stood and folded his arms over his chest. He walked up next to the fire and stared into it for a moment. He moved his hand above the fire, and I watched in awe as the flames danced, forming a scene right in front of my eyes.

"I'm not sure what you think you know about that day, or what you know about me or my parents for that matter, but this story is long, and it started way before my time." He let out a long sigh as the scene in the fire formed. I watched in astonishment as the flames turned into the shape of people. As he spoke, a village formed, and the people danced throughout it.

"My father wasn't always King Daemonger the Violent. He wasn't as brutal and horrible as he ended up being portrayed. He started his rule hoping to change the ways here. He wanted a fresh start for his kingdom and his people. My father helped build the road that connects all the villages in our Kingdom. He helped build this very castle. He wanted something large enough that if our people needed to seek shelter, they could find shelter and safety here."

The flames danced as a man made of fire walked through a village. A woman approached him and they embraced. The village around them faded away and the scene continued to change as Brutus narrated his story. "My father met a young go—woman named Xola in a nearby village. He was immediately smitten with her. They started courting and eventually he proposed to her. She was his soulmate. He said that they knew immediately that they were soulmates. There was no hesitation on either of their parts. He had lived 200 years before he found her. My father would have done anything for her. She accepted his proposal on one condition.

She would be free to do as she pleased and would never be forced to stay with him because of the duty she felt she had to the realm. My father accepted her condition because he would never want to cage her or make her feel as though her purpose wasn't important. He recognized her need to be independent from him and he respected that. He hoped that she would know that she was always safe with him and he gave her everything she asked for. She didn't want a large ceremony so they married in private. She didn't want a public coronation, so he gave her a small intimate one. She told him she didn't want to have children for a long time. She wanted to spend time with just the two of them for a while. He was saddened by this because he always wanted a large family and children. He imagined these halls filled with their children and because he loved her he told her that they could wait as long as she needed before they started having children. They spent the next fifty or so years together building their kingdom. It was beautiful and prosperous. Eventually, Xola needed to leave. Umm… for the duty that she had to the realm. I'll go into detail about that later but it isn't important right now. She told him she was leaving and didn't know when she would be back. My father was confused, hurt, and didn't understand how she could just want to walk away so easily. He understood her importance to the realm and didn't put up a fight about her leaving. She told him it wasn't for forever. So my father stood back and watched her leave. He waited two years before he went out in search of her. He had tried to respect her wishes but the soulmate bond was urging him everyday to go find her. He fought the bond for as long as he could until one day he couldn't fight it anymore. He gathered a small group of his men and set out to find her. He found her in the nearby Kingdom of Tershia."

"I've never heard of Tershia." I was confused by all of his story. Her duty? Her importance? What were the secrets that he was keeping?

"It was one of the first Kingdoms your father took. It was very small. I'm not surprised you don't recognize the name."

"What happened when your father found Xola?"

"She was happy but also thought it was funny that it took him two years to come find her. She told him she grew bored waiting for him and was disappointed that he took so long to come find her. He brought Xola back to our Kingdom where they lived happily for about another hundred years. Then she did it again. She told him she was leaving and this time she told him he better not wait two years to find her. My father was furious that she was leaving again. He waited a few months and set out to find her again. He took a small army with him and followed her throughout the kingdom. He might have murdered anyone he thought was keeping her from him. He grew frantic the longer it took to find her. He moved through the realm in search of her. Eventually he found her again and brought her back. She seemed to enjoy this game that she was playing with him. Most of that I learned from the servants that were here during this time. My father never spoke any ill of her. He swore that she wasn't playing a game and that she was truly performing her duties when I asked him about it. I think she was playing some game but I never met her so I guess I shouldn't make assumptions. They lived here together but things were different. My father had started to grow bitter. The realm was changing and your father was beginning his reign of terror. Magic was growing weaker and chaos was spreading. My father had wanted a family and he had given that up for her wants and needs. I think that he felt like he wasn't enough for her but before she left they decided on trying to create a child. It was the happiest he had ever been. She swore to him that she loved him more than anything and hoped that their child would be everything to him that she couldn't be. The third time she left, he swore he wouldn't go and search her out. He sat and watched the realm change over the years. He was bitter and cold to everyone. Every time someone found their soulmate, he was envious or so the servants said. He started searching for ways to break the soulmate bond because he felt that she was constantly trapped with him. He felt that she needed their bond to be broken so that she could fulfill her destiny without feeling guilty for leaving us behind. With their bond stretched so thin, he became violent towards everyone and took prisoners that he thought might be able to help him break the bond. He wanted to break the bond for her. Most of all though, I think he didn't want to hurt anymore."

Brutus looked at me for a long moment and then sighed. At that moment I felt a connection that I had never felt before. It wasn't physical or sexual in any way but it was this connection like my soul recognized him and loved him for who he was even though I didn't actually know him all that well. He looked at the portrait of his parents and then continued, "My father received a portrait in a letter one day. It was of King Havaror and his soulmate, Xola. She was going to become his wife and Queen. My father lost it. He didn't know how King Havaror could claim that Xola was his soulmate when my father knew for a fact that she was his soulmate. He gathered his army and attacked. He took Xola and brought her back home. He demanded that Xola stay. She needed to correct this and he wanted the realm to know that she was indeed his true soulmate. She refused to acknowledge that they were soulmates. She told him repeatedly she didn't know who he was. She begged for him to release her. My father broke and they found a compromise. My father refused to speak of what happened after I was born. The only thing he said was that he protected me the best he could and that he thought she would stay. It was my Elgra, my nanny, who told me about what happened once I was born. Elgra said that after Xola gave him her blood to finish the creation magic they had used all those years ago, she looked to Elgra and told her to take care of me and to do whatever she wished with the babe because it was not her babe. Elgra tried to get her to feed me and Xola refused. She said her part of the deal was to give my father a few drops of her blood to finish the creation magic and that she never agreed to raise or care for a child that is not hers. After that Elgra couldn't convince Xola to even be in the same room with me. My father sent for a wet nurse to come to the castle immediately. The day my mother left, she looked at my father and said to him "only come find me, once your son is dead and you figured out why my blood worked". Then she laughed and left with King Havaror. So after King Havaror and Xola had a litter of children, my father grew angry. Not for himself but for me. That my mother hadn't wanted me but yet was raising other children. So he found a way to curse the Havaror bloodline and accidentally cursing their whole kingdom. They can only reproduce with their soulmate since he believed that she was his soulmate and not King Havarors. Of course they have found a way around it but I can't blame my father for cursing them. It wasn't their fault but really Xola's fault for the pain and heartache she caused all those years."

That was a lot to take in but he still hadn't answered my question as to why he killed her. I didn't understand a lot of what he was talking about because my father had outlawed magic. I didn't even know that creation magic was something that could be done. I thought babies were only made by having sex. "So now after that lovely back story, answer my question. Why did you kill her?"

"I didn't," he said flatly.

"What? What do you mean you didn't? Who would have killed her if it wasn't you?" I asked, annoyed that he still wasn't answering me.

Brutus moved his hands again and the flames flickered into a new scene.

"It was Xola, Voronion and myself at dinner that night. I asked her about what my father had told me about their soulmate bond and about what Elgra had said. She admitted to most of it so casually. Voronion was outraged. She thought his reaction to how she treated me was hysterical. Really, she was so flippant and careless the whole dinner. She made snide remarks about my father and even insinuated some pretty horrible things about me. They began arguing and things got very heated quickly. In Voronions anger he shoved Xola. She fell backwards and landed on an iron from the fireplace. The metal went straight through her skull killing her instantly. The servants went wild screaming and yelling. King Havaror came running in and drew his sword. He attacked Voronion but Voronion was overwhelmed with grief that he had just killed his own mother. He didn't even try to protect himself. I stepped in and fought with King Havaror. Unfortunately, he wouldn't listen to me about the situation being an accident.

140

It ended with his death as well."

A ripple of shock rolled through my body. Somehow, I knew deep down that what Brutus just told me was true. I could feel it in my bones that he was being honest with me and that scared me. Why should I believe anything he was saying? Yet, I did. I didn't just believe him. I KNEW it was the truth or at least it was his truth. "I don't know what to say," I whispered under my breath. Xola sounded like a terrible person. Voronion had accidentally killed his mother, his father then tried to kill him, and then his father was killed. He lost so much more than just his parents that day though. He lost everything including Zeke.

"You don't need to say anything. It is all history... it's all in the past." He snapped his fingers and a small table with two drinks appeared. I reached forward and grabbed a drink. Bringing it to my mouth, the scent of strong whiskey filled my nostrils right before I threw it back in one swallow.

"Don't worry it's not Aphrodites drink... not that you were worried," he chuckled. Aphrodites drink was a legend. Supposedly, there was a drink that you could give to someone that would make them feel for you the same way they would if you were true mates.

"You know I'm not your soulmate right?" I had to make that clear. I knew Zeke wasn't my soulmate but that didn't mean Brutus had a chance with me.

"Oh believe me, I know." He laughed like he knew something that I didn't and then threw his shot back and grimaced slightly. With a snap of his fingers, the glasses were filled again. We raised them towards each other and downed them once more. Maybe I could get use to the idea of being cordial with Brutus.

"So what do you want from me?" Thinking about spending the rest of my life with him wasn't terrible if he could remain pleasant but this game of avoiding questions was already growing old. He seemed to skirt around topics and only revealed what he wanted me to know. I was the type of person who wanted to know the whole truth immediately. If I ask something, I want to know now, not when you think I'm ready to know.

"That is the million dollar question now isn't it. My intentions are not to marry you and they have never been to marry you. I know that to your father and the outside world, we are betrothed and I have started a war with King Havaror over you. I would only like to marry my soulmate and that I do know is not you. However, I had to get you here to protect you and for now that is my only goal." He stood quickly and began pacing in front of the fire. The flames danced again like they were trying to reach out and touch him.

Chapter Twelve

H e wanted to protect me. WHAT THE FUCK KIND OF ANSWER WAS THAT!

"Protect me? Are you being serious? I was kidnapped and hurt! Helvig, my…my Helvig was killed trying to protect me. They said they tortured him. What he went through was because of you because you want to protect me? Protect me?! WHAT ARE YOU PROTECTING ME FROM? WHY ME?" I was yelling and once I had started I couldn't stop it. It was his fault that Helvig was taken from me. That he was tortured, hurt, and killed. It was his fault that Helvig would forever haunt my dreams. Helvig had been the one trying to protect me. Not Brutus.

"I am sorry to hear about your friend. I wasn't aware that someone was with you while you were taken. That whole thing was left up to your father and I see now that he managed it poorly. He was instructed to deliver you to me unharmed. Believe me, when I heard that you had been hurt I was furious. I should have come to you myself but I can't risk leaving my

Kingdom right now."

"WHAT THE FUCK DO YOU WANT TO PROTECT ME FROM?!" I seethed. I wasn't even hearing the words he was telling me at this point. My emotions had become volatile after his mentioning protecting me and I hadn't been able to ring them in quite yet.

"A goddess came to my father one night. She told him he needed to find and protect the princess with copper eyes and lilac hair. She said that only she would be the key to returning what was stolen and ridding this realm of the evil that plagues it."

I couldn't help the laugh that burst from me. "Are you being serious? A goddess visited King Daemonger, the fucking violent, and instructed him to protect me. That I somehow can rid this realm of the evil that plagues it. Your fucking father was the evil that was plaguing this realm. He tortured and fucking tormented people for fun. Now my father is doing the same fucking thing. What am I supposed to do? Kill my father? What the fuck was stolen and why the fuck am I the one that needs to return it?"

"I would appreciate it if you didn't laugh at this. First of all, that reputation of my fathers isn't true. Those who knew him would tell you that. He saved many lives when he came to this godforsaken realm. Secondly, if a goddess was going to visit anyone and charge them with the duty to protect the princess that will save this realm, then Hypnos-Samnus Daemonger— God and Spirit Demon of Sleep, the one who could walk both the realms of Gods and Demons, rose from the land of eternal darkness for the love of his life, would be the perfect one to do this. Not to mention that he set everything else aside to try and find you and it ended up costing him his life in this realm.

It cost him being here with me. It. Cost. Him. Everything. So again, I would appreciate it if you didn't laugh at my father," Brutus' words were stern and so full of passion that stunned and shocked me into silence.

His father was Hypnos-Samus Daemonger. He was a fucking God? That would make him a child of a God. A fucking Demi-God at the very least.

A. FUCKING. DEMI. GOD. I couldn't handle this. I was in precense of a fucking offspring of a god.

We sat in silence for a long time. I couldn't form any words and my brain felt like it couldn't function properly. Maybe I needed sleep or maybe I needed water. Water was always the answer. Headache? Drink water. Dry skin? Drink water.

I sipped my drink and wondered how someone could have been as cruel as Xola. How could she have done that to her soul mate? How could she have been so cruel to her son? He was only a little babe. How the fuck her soul mate had been a God and that hadn't been good enough for her? He could have forced her to stay. He could have used whatever God magic he had to make her stay here. He probably could have wiped out King Havaror with just a single thought, yet he didn't do that to her. My stomach rolled at the thought of his power. Power that Brutus probably wielded. It would explain his shadows and his ability to manipulate fire. Who knows what other power he could wield.

"I didn't mean to laugh at you or take any of this lightly. It's just a lot and it's all overwhelming." My voice trailed off as I tried to come up with something to distract from this conversation. There were too many emotions attached and we needed something lighter. "What room is this?" I needed to change subjects before my mind exploded. I was struggling to process everything at once and choke down my emotions about Helvig. He had felt so real in that dream and Brutus mentioning protecting me brought up emotions I had been trying so hard to shove down. No. No! I won't think about that. Not right now. Not while my brain feels like it's over loaded with information.

"It is just a sitting room off of my conservatory."

"The conservatory? Can I see that?" I asked as ice filled my veins. The old had had mentioned a conservatory.

Brutus eyed me skeptically. "It is my PRIVATE conservatory. I will show it to you but you cannot come back to it unless I am with you."

I stood and threw back my last shot of whiskey. Brutus held out his arm for me and I hesitated. I didn't know how to feel about this whole situation after talking with him. Ultimately I decided to just take his arm. I wasn't comfortable touching him but I didn't want to offend him either. At least not when I didn't know the extent of his power and our new found friendship was well... new.

He walked us out of the sitting room and through a door that I hadn't seen. We went further down a hall and a large dark door came into view. I hadn't seen this door from where I had originally entered the hall, if this was even the same hall. "I swear these doors are just appearing out of nowhere." I laughed trying to bring a lightness to our tense energy.

"You would be correct. This hall is ever changing. It provides you with the room that you seek only if you truly seek it with good intentions."

"And you have good intentions?" I questioned.

"Always." His smirk took my breath away for a moment. He was so handsome in such a different way than Zeke. One day he would make a woman very happy that woman just wasn't me though.

"Tell me something Cordelia," Brutus said. "Do you think you could ever love someone like me? Do you think I could ever be loved?"

My heart gave a little pitter patter and I gulped. I wasn't sure the answer to that. Romantically love him? No. I think Zeke had been the only man to ever make me feel those types of feelings. Well I might have loved someone else if we would have had a chance but we didn't. My stomach rolled and I felt a little nauseous. How was I supposed to answer that without hurting his feelings? A platonic love? I guess that depended on the type of person he truly was.

"If you help my father take over the realm then no. I don't think I could. There will be so many innocents killed. It makes me sick to my stomach just thinking about it."

"If I don't help your father, do you think you could love me?" Gods fucking sake dude. I'm trying to let you down gently and not make this awkward but here you are pushing the fucking issue.

"I'm not sure what type of feelings I could have for you. I don't know you. I do know that I have a soulmate somewhere and you aren't him. I also know that the love I have for him isn't something I could replicate for someone else," I sighed. "I'm sorry if that hurts you. It wasn't my intention. I do think that there is someone out there waiting for you and they are perfect in all the ways that you didn't know you needed. They will love you and you will love them so much that you didn't even know it was possible to feel that much for another being." The closer we got to the conservatory the more anxious I felt. There was an energy buzzing through the air that made my hairs stand on end.

"Are you sure about King Havaror being your soulmate?" Brutus asked. Confusion was evident by the way he scrunched his brows. We had reached the conservatory and he opened the door.

"Probably," I breathed as we stepped into the large room. I was purposefully trying to avoid his questioning; I didn't want to lie to him but I wasn't ready to tell him the truth. I knew my answer was no but I didn't want him to know that. At least not yet. The ceiling and three walls were made of glass. The height of the ceiling had to have been three stories tall. The room was huge. Fully grown white oak trees were everywhere and I could hear the faint trinkle of a stream nearby. This felt like a miniature version of my clearing at the river.

"How... How do you have white oaks?"

"They're my favorite. I saw them once when I was a little boy. When I got older, I dug a small one up and planted it in here. I took care of it and helped it grow into the tree it is now. Over the years more have grown with the rest of the foliage." I didn't bother looking at him as he spoke. My mind had wandered back to my clearing in the woods and the best memories I had.

"This is beautiful. No. It's stunning." It truly felt like I wasn't in the Daemonger kingdom any longer. A feeling of safety swept over me. I felt at home and I felt peace. The only other time I had felt that way was with Helvig in my clearing. I hadn't felt that way with Zeke because I had been on edge and a complete lustful mess with him.

We walked forward into the room. "I'll show you the stream and then we will leave. I don't like this place to be disturbed.

It's my sanctuary from the rest of the world." Brutus gave me a small smile that looked more like a grimace.

He placed a hand over mine as we walked to the stream. The water was crystal blue and tiny fish swam in it. Next to the stream was the largest white oak I had ever seen.

"That is the one I originally planted in here," he said, gesturing to the large tree.

I walked towards it and ran my hands along the bark that was starting to peel. I missed my woods and I missed my river. I closed my eyes and thought about the night I showed Helvig my special place.

I turned to look at Brutus when I noticed a feather on the ground. It was the size of my arm and white. I reached down to pick it up. Running my fingers along its length, I felt an electric jolt in my finger tips. It didn't hurt. Honestly, it felt nice and the feather itself was so incredibly soft. I picked it up and walked toward Brutus.

He looked at the feather in my hand and frowned. "I heard that birds can carry diseases. You probably shouldn't touch that."

"Oh well," I shrugged. "I want to keep this. It's really cool.What kind of bird did it come from?" I could hear birds off in the distance but I hadn't ever seen a feather like this before.

"Uhm, it could be from a few different birds that live here. I think it's time that we leave though." He said, reaching for my hand.

"I really like it here. I had a place I would sneak off to that is so similar to this place that it's almost crazy. Could I come back another time? Maybe the next time you want to get to know me, we could meet here." I asked, feeling hopeful for the first time in a long time.

"Once you are my wife, You can come here at any time you would like." he stated flatly. I frowned. He had already said he didn't have any intentions of marrying me, so did that mean I wouldn't be coming back here?

"Are you being serious about making me your wife? I thought that you didn't want that? Even with Zeke advancing? You know that he wants me and he won't stop. You know I am not your soulmate, so why are you fighting for me? You don't even know me. I am not just some possession to have and don't give me that whole protecting me bullshit. Let's be honest about the shit job you've done," I blurted out. "Is it because supposedly some fucking goddess visited your father… YOUR FATHER WHO IS A FUCKING GOD HIMSELF. Like what the fuck Brutus. How do people not know that? What the fuck happened to him? Where is he now?"

We reached the door and Brutus stopped walking. His solid black eyes were on me and then I watched in amazement as they started to shift. Silver spots speckled his eyes in the shape of an iris. The rest of his eyes remained pitch black. I strained my neck looking up directly into his eyes as he towered over me.

"Do you want him? Do you even know who you are enough to choose him? I'll answer that for you. You don't. I'm not stupid. He isn't your soulmate. You and I both know that but it seems I'm the only one willing to admit it." He practically shouted pinning me with his gaze. "Do you even know what you are?"

"Of course, I want him. He," I shuttered from the intensity of the moment. "He is my betrothed. What do you mean 'what I am?' Who are you to question whether or not he is my soulmate? I'll answer that, YOU ARE NO ONE. How about you start answering some of the Gods damned questions I've asked!" Shock rolled through Brutus and then confusion. I felt both his shock and confusion in my own emotions. I didn't understand how I could have felt his feelings when I wasn't bonded or connected to him. I looked down and saw that our hands were still connected. I yanked my hand away from him hoping to sever the connection.

"You don't know then?" he said in disbelief. "Your father never told you…"

Brutus reached out and touched my arm. Everything went pitch black and I felt as if I were falling. Suddenly, I was being yanked up by my sternum. I opened my eyes confused. When did I close my eyes? I was standing in front of my bedroom door and Brutus stood still holding my arm. He reached and knocked on my door twice. Then he let go of my arm and vanished into thin air.

What the fuck.

Just as he vanished, the door whipped open. Zander was picking me up before I could even speak.

"Are you okay? What did he do to you? I swear I will kill him. Tell me now. Just say the words and I will hunt him down and kill him." Zander was vibrating with fury. At his words Quinlan and Draug came rushing into the room. Behind them Alba was carefully stepping in. They all began fussing over me and throwing a million questions at me.

"Set me down. Everyone just stop and sit down. I'll explain everything." Zander ignored the fact that I told him to set me down. Instead he sat down on the couch and placed me between his legs. Quinlan did his usual stance

151

of perching himself on the edge of something that had to be uncomfortable, Draug knelt on the floor beside us, and Alba took the seat on the end of the couch by my feet. "Everyone just calm down. Your combined anxiety is making me sick."

"It's their other forms," Alba said. "It makes them act this way over you. Well it doesn't make them. It is just who they are. Zander being a dragon makes him protective and possessive of you. They really can't help it."

She reached over and patted my leg. Her touch was refreshing and calming. I looked around at them and realized they had become everything to me in such a short amount of time. They were my family. It might not have been a family by blood but we were a family nonetheless. I sucked in a deep breath and then began trying to explain everything to them. It was harder than I thought possible. They all had lots of questions that I didn't have any answers for and I realized that I really hadn't gained much information from Brutus at all. Just the fact that his father was a fucking God.

Chapter Thirteen

The following few weeks were filled with spying on Brutus and Voronion, scouring the castle, and actively avoiding my father and his guards. Lance seemed to have been sent somewhere else because I hadn't seen him since that first day.

I had a lot of questions I needed my father to answer but I had to play my cards just right. Otherwise, he would use his knowledge against me and hold it over me. He was the one with the answers after all and part of me thought he was really just manipulating all of us. The look of pure disbelief on Brutus's face when he said that I didn't even know what I was still haunted me. Of course, only I was avoiding my father. My men on the other hand were doing all of the spying for me when it came to him. We had yet to find a way to get information out of this Kingdom but we would soon enough. I spent my days being the perfect fiance and my nights slinking around the castle eavesdropping.

Weeks filled with dreams of Helvig... well more like nightmares filled with him being chained up and tortured. Each time, I just barely reached him before I was jerked awake. I found myself crying most nights with his scent still filling my nostrils. Each night I fell asleep I dreamt of Helvig chained up. Some nights he was being tortured and other nights he was alone. The nights that he was being tortured, he screamed for me to wake up. The men around him would start looking around wondering who he was talking to but I stayed in the shadows frozen to the spot. A war brewing inside myself on whether or not I should intervene. Eventually his screaming would force me to do as he said. I would startle awake breathing heavy with sweat pouring down my body. Some nights I swear I could smell the musty dungeon on my night clothes. During this time, I had hoped I could just get the information to Zeke and then he would be able to pass it on —but I hadn't seen him once. Draug and Zeke communicated some but their bond wasn't as strong as it used to be and Draug couldn't always reach Zeke when he needed to.

Surprisingly, I had actually started to grow really close with Alba. We were becoming such close friends. I had never had a friend that was a girl before. She was the type of friend that I could just sit with and be comfortable or I could spill my heart out and still be comfortable. She never judged me and always seemed to be a consistent positive supporter of all my decisions. Now she didn't blindly support everything I did. She would ask questions and make suggestions but whatever I ended up deciding she would back me 100%. Like when I agreed to having dinner with Brutus each night without a guard. She had given her opinion on it but when I made my decision she supported me. She helped me bring in some of the local florists to spruce the castle to support the local economy. Anything that we could do to help the local villagers, we did and most of it involved spending Brutus' money.

It turned out that Alba had lived a pretty sheltered life too. I didn't blame her father for that though. He truly was just trying to protect her. My father had already started this whole take over the gods damned realm thing and she would have been vulnerable outside of their castle. Although she was sheltered, she knew all about magic and different species. Her father had allowed their kingdom to become a safe haven for those seeking refuge after my father began slaughtering anyone with magic. She was incredibly smart and funny. So fucking funny. I caught Quinlan giving her a lustful eye a few times but as far as I could tell she didn't reciprocate those feelings. She did most of her resonance in plain sight. Turns out no one thought she was a threat so they paid her no attention when she accidentally wandered in the room. The first time I witnessed her do this, she acted all innocent and bashful. When really she was a viper just waiting to strike. She would quietly wait by the door before claiming to be lost and asking for directions. My father's men here really looked at women like they were stupid and far from equal. So it was easy for them to believe she was just ditzy and forgetful. It was rather hysterical actually. Sometimes they would glance her way and keep talking for another half hour.

Each night that Brutus would come for me, he would escort me to some private room somewhere new in the castle and we would eat together. He wouldn't answer most of my questions and that was incredibly frustrating. He seemed to truly want to get to know me. I felt like he was looking for a slip up on my part. To catch me hiding something but all his questions were easily answered. He questioned me a lot about my mother. He would ask a question and then a moment later ask the same question only worded slightly different. Sometimes I felt like he was trying to hint at something. I just didn't know what though. We spent time looking at portraits of gods and goddess. He talked about them like he knew them personally. His father was a god after all but I didn't think Brutus had ever left this realm.

I had questioned him about what exactly he was supposed to protect me from. I figured he wouldn't answer me just like the rest of my questions. He surprised me though and answered honestly. His words were enough to chill my bones. "I'll be honest with you. I have no idea what I am protecting you from. All I know is that my father made it his mission to protect you. He spent years looking for you and told me that if we didn't find you and protect you and prepare you, not only would this realm fall but all the realms connected to the gods. He also hinted that the city of the gods would no longer be safe for anyone." I didn't know Brutus's father but I would assume he wasn't a worst case scenario kind of person. When I tried to question him further about this, he would just shrug and change the conversation. I didn't know what exactly he was preparing me for or when he would begin preparing me. After my time with Brutus, I would head back to my rooms and then seek out whoever was out spying at that time if they weren't back by the time we had previously designated. I had shared everything about Brutus with my men and Alba. They all were skeptical of him but agreed that there was so much more going on here that we didn't know. Nothing really made any sense to us. Why was my father taking over the realm? Who was going to hurt me? What exactly did I need prepared for? Why were the realms going to fall? Why me? What was I supposed to do about it all?

We had learned that my father was desperate to get to that temple. He truly thought his magic must be there because they were guarding it so well. It was the same temple he was trying to access all those weeks ago when I had ruined his plans by telling his enemies his schemes. His behavior had become more erratic and volatile the more his efforts were crushed. Even Brutus seemed to be growing tired of my father. Zeke was attacking not only Brutus' forces to try and gain access to his kingdom but he had also sent a fleet to block the waters and stop all trade ships of my fathers. My father had never seen a need for warships so he had nothing to combat Zekes. My father then became dependent on Brutus for the goods he had been receiving from the sea. What was most interesting was Brutus's clear neutrality in all of this. He did the bare minimum to help my father. It was as if he was just trying to appease him to keep me here. That if he didn't help my father then I would be taken from here too.

Unfortunately I hadn't been able to go visit Zeke again. It had taken me some time to move on from the fact that we were not destined to be together. I truly hoped whoever he ended up with was an amazing person. He deserved that. I wasn't sure if I hadn't accidentally gone to see him because I had come to terms with the fact that we weren't soulmates or if it was something else. I wasn't desperate to see him anymore and I didn't have these huge spikes of emotions like before. I had been growing numb to everything. It was the only way I was able to process everything. I still tried everyday multiple times a day but nothing seemed to trigger it. Once I even tried thinking about us having one final tryst, but I honestly didn't want that and didn't feel that desire for him anymore. So that was incredibly disappointing when even that didn't cause me to go to him.

It was mid afternoon when Alba and I were sitting on my bed together. I had started taking the time out of everyday to spend with her. Just us and no men. Of course that was something neither of us had before, the guys didn't like the idea of not being allowed in the room with us but it allowed her and I a sense of freedom. We could talk about things that maybe we would have held back on in the presence of others. She had just told me one of the funniest jokes I had ever heard. She made me feel more than the shell of a person that I had become. It was brief and fleeting but it was a nice reprieve from everything else.

Alba chuckled, "Want to hear a dirty joke now?"

I leaned forward and whispered, "Of course!"

Alba's laugh rang through the room and finally when she pulled herself together enough she said, "What is the first thing a husband puts in his bride after they get married?" I paused thinking for a moment, "Uhh the wedding cake?"

She clutched her sides and laughed again. "Gods, no. The wedding ring."

It had taken me a moment to understand how it could be his fingers. Once I got it I couldn't help but laugh hysterically. She made me laugh almost as much as Helvig had. It still hurt whenever I thought about him and how I didn't know what exactly had even happened to him in the end.

Some days, I still cried myself to sleep thinking about the day that I was taken. I could still hear the sound of his flesh and it would take me hours to calm down and eventually fall asleep. I realized he wouldn't want me torturing myself with guilt but I still had my moments. I was using my magic daily now and it was becoming second nature to me, almost instinctual. I wish I would have started using it sooner. I could have protected him. I told myself that I had to try and move forward. Yet, I just couldn't let him go. I needed to move forward with the newest plan Alba and I had come up with for trying to get answers out of Brutus.

I had changed earlier into a rather revealing dress that belonged to Alba because our plan was going to be to try to seduce Brutus into giving me answers without having to touch him. She thought it would be easy. I wasn't so sure about that though. Although Brutus and I had dinner each night, he was always a gentleman. He never tried to make a move or even flirt with me. There was a part of me that was starting to look at Brutus like a brother. He never made any advances and never crossed any lines. We laughed and joked yet we weren't quite friends. It reminded me of how Brawntly had been with me only even better. Brawntly, being my father's eldest son, seemed to just put up with me most of the time. Brutus seemed to actually care about me. I was still laughing so hard at Alba's joke that I was now crying and I had to hold my boobs to keep them from falling out. "Zeke would love this joke too. He has the same sense of humor about this stuff that we do. I bet he would turn it even dirtier somehow though."

Suddenly, I was no longer sitting on my bed with Alba instead I was sitting on an active battlefield. I let out a shriek of terror and surprise as I took in the scene around me. At first glance, I couldn't tell who were the good guys and who were the bad guys. There were so many men everywhere. Not just men, I gasped. Dragons. There were dragons attacking each other. Creatures of all kinds were fighting and the sounds from them were like nothing I had ever heard before. I watched a bright red dragon dig its talons into a light gray one. My eyes tracked the blood that sprayed out of the wounds and fell to the ground like a waterfall of blood. The men below were drenched in it, yet they didn't falter in their fight. Small fires were burning from arrows that had been lit and shot across the field. The sounds of the dragons, men screaming, swords clanging, and just the battle itself was overwhelming. I had never seen anything like this before. What I had imagined a battle to look like was nothing compared to being in the midst of one. Where the hell was Zeke or Vilulf? I stood and turned trying to assess the men around me and figure out how I could find Zeke.

A man charged me and raised his sword. A burst of fear shot through me and then instinct swept in. It had be a long while sense I had fought anyone but my instincts were still sharp. I twirled out of the path of his sword and then moved into a fighting stance. Quickly, I thought about his sword laying on my bed. Poof. It was gone from his hands. The man looked shocked and then stumbled backwards mumbling about a witch or something. I would have laughed if it wasn't for another man who came at us. Swinging his sword, he killed the rambling man. Then he turned towards me, attempting to strike but I did the same to his sword that I did the last man, making it disappear into thin air. I turned on my heel and took off running. There was no way I would be able to do hand to hand combat with these men in full armor. All it would take was one distraction and I would be dead.

"ZEKE! KING HAVAROR! EZEKIEL! ZEKE!" I bellowed as loud as I could. He had to be around here somewhere.

"VILULF! ZEKE! VILULF!" I was screaming for Zeke and Vilulf but no one seemed to care or maybe they were just too busy to care about a crazy woman running through the carnage of a battlefield screaming. My dress was blowing in the wind and part of me wishes I hadn't worn something so sexy. It was an olive green dress that hugged me in all the right places. There was a cut out exposing my stomach and a high slit exposing my left leg. It made me stand out like a sore thumb.

Anytime a man came towards me to attack, I just took his sword from him by sending it to my bed. Bodies littered the ground and men that hadn't died immediately were groaning or screaming in agony. I couldn't stop to help anyone because men were constantly trying to attack me. You would have thought that one of these men would be concerned for a woman dressed like I was running through a battlefield.

My stomach twisted at the sight before me, a man's abdomen had been sliced open leaving his insides partially outside of his body. I watched in horror as he slid a dagger across his own throat. My father had caused so many battles and wars; the things happening here, probably happened in all of them. I couldn't help but think of how many men had died just like the men here and I immediately threw up. Watching a man slight his own throat was enough to send me over the edge. I thought I was tough. I thought I was strong. Gods. I didn't know that this was what a battle was truly like. That this carnage was normal and happening day after day. Kingdom after kingdom my father fought and took. So many innocent men had died so brutally just trying to protect their kingdom and their families. I wiped my hand across my mouth and mentally pulled myself together. I couldn't think about all of this right now. I needed to find my allies. I had to find Zeke.

I moved through the battlefield scanning the warriors. I knew what Zeke's armor looked like and I could only assume that Vilulf's would look similar. Once I focused, I could finally tell apart the Havaror warriors and my father's men. It became really clear when the warriors paid me no attention and lots of my father's men either tried to attack me and grab me while screaming what they were going to do to my body. Clearly Zeke's men had morals and integrity whereas my fathers men were vile.

A warrior ripped their own helmet off in front of me and I gasped. A beautiful woman with braided long blond hair and a tattoo covering her neck and stretching up past her ear and onto her temple was in front of me. "Dear Gods. Does Ezekiel or Villy know you're here?" A man swung his sword towards her and I removed it causing a flash of surprise across her face as the sword just vanished. She slid her sword straight across the man's neck severing his head from his body. If there was one thing I could get behind it was a woman who knew how to use a sword.

"No. I haven't found them." I yelled at her. I must have looked half crazed by the way she looked me up and down. "Come, I'll take you to where they last were." She grabbed my hand and started dragging me through the field and over bodies of the fallen. I could tell she had seen lots of battle by the way she scanned the path infront of us. She was assessing everything and choosing her path based on what she saw before her. She was quick and cunning. More times than I would like to admit she caught a man advancing towards us before I did.

"PROTECT QUEEN CORDELIA!" she screamed as a group of men ran towards us with their blades raised. Although I wasn't their queen, I definitely wasn't going to correct her. Instantly, I was surrounded by warriors in matching armor. I didn't even know where they all came from but here they were. Without even consciously thinking about it, I sent the opposing men's swords to my bed. The men were stunned that their swords had just disappeared. I heard her chuckle in front of me and then she shouted, "That's a great power to have. I just love the look on their faces when they realize their weapon just disappeared. Then when the assess the situation, they practically shit themselves."

We began moving quickly again after two of the men around us sliced through our attackers. We reached the crest of a slight hill where I saw Vilulf and Zeke fighting back to back completely surrounded by men. I took off at full sprint pushing through the surrounding warriors and my female companion towards them and before I knew what I was doing, I had, for lack of a better word, poofed all the men's swords and weapons away from them. I took their armor off their bodies and with one thought, their own blades were protruding from their chests. No one would hurt Vilulf or Zeke as long as I was here. The men slowly fell forward as they succumbed to the brutal wound I inflicted on them.

I heard Vilulf yell my name as Zeke began running to me. I turned to survey the battle that was still raging. There had to be hundred of men fighting and so many of them were innocent. They were just fighting for their kingdom, their families, or for our realm. So many good men would lose their lives if I let this continue. Tears filled my eyes as I thought of all the men we had passed that were laying dead already.

With a single thought, all the men that had been attacking Zeke's warriors were armorless and a moment later their swords sticking out of their chests. The Havaror warriors stopped moving and began looking around. I heard Zeke call my name again and I briefly glanced over at him. I looked back at the battlefield and watched as hundreds of men fell to the ground. For a moment, my heart swelled with the power that thrummed through my veins knowing I had just saved Zeke's army. Then the nausea rolled through me at the realization of what I had just single handedly done. I had just murdered all those men. Hundred of men from my fathers army were dead because of me. They were men from my kingdom, loved ones from my beloved village and many other villages, sons, and brothers that would never return home because I had just murdered all of them. I leaned forward placing my hands on my knees and began puking up the rest of my lunch. I felt Zeke's arms wrap around me moments before my legs gave out.

"I killed them. I killed all those men. I was a murderer. Zeke. I'm a monster. I thought they were going to kill you. They were going to kill you!" I shrieked at him as he held me. " I looked at all the warriors who were fighting for their lives and I couldn't let another one of them die but it wasn't my fathers men fault. Most of them were forced to join my fathers army. What am I? They didn't even have a chance. THEY DIDN'T HAVE A CHANCE AGAINST ME!" Tears fell from my eyes and my whole body began shaking. I was lost in the grief over what I had just done. I couldn't breathe and nothing seemed to comfort me. Zeke held me tightly and I pounded my fist into his chest. It didn't help me. Nothing helped me.

Vilulf was shouting orders as the female warrior approached us. She grabbed my face and forced me to look at her. "Look at all the warriors standing right now. They have loved ones too. They are alive because you saved them." Her words weren't as reassuring as they should have been. Yet her words struck a cord with me. Who am I to decide which man gets to live and which man gets to die? My stomach rolled again and I shoved against Zeke. Turning, I threw up less than two feet away from him. He grabbed me and pulled me up against him. "It's okay. I promise it's okay." His words were hollow in my mind. They didn't reassure me.

Zeke barked an order for his tent to be erected immediately and then took off carrying me towards their camp. It looked like it had been half taken down when they were attacked. I watched through blurry vision from my tears as two warriors ran ahead of Zeke and began putting together his tent. By the time we made it there, other men had come and we're putting together Zeke's belongings on the inside. Zeke told them to stand guard and only let Vilulf in. He set me down on his bed and began checking over me for wounds. The image of all those men falling to the ground kept flashing through my mind. He finally spoke his first words to me after seeing that I was completely unharmed. "When I saw you standing there after those men fell, I was a mess. I was in awe of your power and your control over it. I was shocked to see you standing there in this beautiful dress looking like a fucking Goddess amungst us petty men and then the fear set in. You were on a fucking battlefield, Cordelia. Do you know what that did to me?! I have never been so afraid in my life. We have to figure out a way for you to control your power of moving from one place to another. You could have been killed! I could have lost you forever."

I took a deep breath and attempted to pull my thoughts together. I had to pull myself together. Not just for myself but for Zeke. He was clearly feeling emotional and having him carry me was only a burden to him.

"I'm fine," I lied. I wasn't fine and I hadn't been fine for months now. Between the lack of sleep and nightmares of Helivg, I was slowly losing my mind. "I have been trying to come to you for the last few weeks but nothing has worked. I have so much I have to tell you and it isn't good news. I'm sorry. I'm so sorry for all of this." I wiped the tears from my face and mentally put my big girl panties on.

Vilulf came charging in and froze when he saw us. "You should stay for this," I croaked out, before he could turn and leave. He looked at Zeke for guidance and when Zeke nodded to him, Vilulf sat. The tent was spacious but the weight of what I needed to tell them made me feel claustrophobic.

I started with telling them about the dreams I had when a goddess came to me. I told them that I thought she was telling me I needed to let Zeke go. Zeke immediately began protesting, saying that dreams could mean anything and they are up to interpretation. I didn't argue with him though. I simply kept moving forward with what I needed them to know. I told them about everything the old hag had said.

I could see the disappointment in Zeke's eyes as he looked away from me. I was hurting him and I knew it even though he tried to cover it up. I didn't want to hurt him but I had to do this. Then I poured my heart and soul out to them. I told them about how much I cared for Zeke. How we had talked before and how much his words about the bond not mattering meant to me. I told him how I loved him and I needed him to know that. I told him I didn't know if I could survive something terrible happening to him. I told him that I couldn't be his Queen anymore and that his true mate was going to walk into his life very soon. Zeke broke even more when I told him I wanted him to be happy with her and I didn't want him to have any guilt about being with her. Seeing such a masculine man break down the way he did broke something inside of me. Zeke was a good man and he deserved a woman that was just as good.

The tent was silent and my words hung in the air. Zeke hadn't looked at me since I had told him about the old hags words. I never had any one that had cared enough for me to hurt like this. He had started sobbing and I didn't know what to do. I knew I had to tell him but this was hard. Vilulf stood and put a hand on Zeke's shoulder. "I should go and let you two discuss things."

"Don't go," I said on a sigh. I didn't want to do this but I didn't know how much longer I would be here. "There's more I have to tell you and you will want to hear it all."

It must have been the tone of my voice but Zeke finally turned and looked at him. His eyes were wide and tears had left streaks through the dirt on his face. I moved down to the floor and wrapped my arms around him. I held him for a moment and then kissed his cheek before moving back to the bed. I pulled my legs up to my chest and let out a long sigh. Zeke moved forward and took my hand in his. "I wasn't expecting this but the last week or so, things have felt different for me. It was like part of me knew that we weren't made for each other and I needed to make peace with that. Another part of me wanted to fight those thoughts with everything inside me. I don't know where this leaves us but I will still come for you, I promise. I will always come for you."

I knew that would have to change but I didn't have the heart to tell him. So I told him everything Brutus had told me. Everything from his mother, to King Daemonger the violent being a fucking God, to them having this duty to protect me, and that Brutus was powerful. Very powerful. I told him all the plans I knew that my father had and any other relevant information I could think of. Finally, I finished telling him about my bonds with my men and about my new found friendship with Alba.

Vilulf let out a low whistle. "Damn. You have been busy since we last saw you. I need to go send out messengers. If there is anything else you need or if you think of anything more I need to know, please send someone for me immediately. Thank you for this. What you are doing will save thousands of innocent lives." Vilulf gave me a small smile and left the tent quickly leaving Zeke and I alone.

Chapter Fourteen

"I'm sorry," Zeke's breath was warm against my head. "I'm sorry that you have had to go through so much in your life and that I'm not the one for you. I so badly wanted it to be us. I wanted to spend the rest of my life with you by my side. I would do anything for you. Even now. If you ever need anything, please don't hesitate. I love you. I know over time that will fade but I will never stop caring about you. Even if you find your soulmate, your one true mate that completes you, I will still care for you."

His words touched part of my heart that I hadn't realized was so scared he would hate me. "I needed to hear that," I said to him breathlessly. "You know I will always care about you." I needed to change the subject. I couldn't dwell on this without feeling like it was too much. "I haven't figured out how to move between places at my own will. Do you have any ideas? Originally, I thought it was connected to my emotions but I have tried repeatedly to get to you and it didn't work. Then today I was laughing with Alba and simply thought you would love a joke she told. Poof. Here I was in the middle of a fucking battle." I laughed at how absurd the situation was. Zeke slid his arms around me and pulled me into his lap. "I just want to hold you one last time while we talk. I know that once you leave here, that will be it. The next time I see you, we both will have healed and moved forward so for now, please just let me hold you." I had thought about our final moments together. I had even wondered if we would make love one last time. The thought didn't bring forth the heated desire I once had for him and I had been a little perturbed by that. If Zeke couldn't get my blood boiling then who could? This though, him holding me and us talking, it was perfect.

I smiled up at him and then he said, "What if it isn't about emotions but more so about your intentions? Like before you were trying to get here but today your intentions were pure. You thought I would love a joke and probably wished you could tell me it. It was a pure intention with nothing else impacting your wants."

"Any other time I wanted to see you my intentions were good too. I have never wanted to bring you harm or anything like that–" before I could finish my sentence Zeke interrupted. "I know that. That isn't what I mean though. I guess like previously you were on a mission. You had to get that information to me. It was your duty or whatever. This though, this wasn't because you had to. It was because you wanted to. Does that make sense?"

Huh. I had never thought about it that way.

"Actually that makes perfect sense. Maybe once I get better at using my abilities, I will be able to do it at will and not depend on emotion or intentions to use it at all."

Zeke chuckled. "I'm sure you will figure it out. You're smart like that." A comfortable silence fell between us and we sat there for a few moments just existing together.

"What have you been up to since the last time we talked?" I had been curious about what they were doing since the last time I was here. It had been weeks and they must have been doing something important.

"Oh, a little of this and a little of that." He laughed again. I couldn't tell if he didn't want to tell me and was trying to play it off or if he was actually just teasing me.

"Could you be more specific? I want to work together to bring my father down. I want to convince Brutus to join us and remove his forces from my father. If I can do that, well my father will be fucked." My father would lose a large portion of his army. He would be facing a multi front war between Brutus, Zeke, and the last remaining kingdoms. I knew he wouldn't go down without a fight. Actually, I thought my father wouldn't stop until he either had his magic or every last man of his was dead and he had to give up. Even then I could see my father using everything he had to try and win still. Who knows what kind of tricks he has up his sleeves.

"I have been trying to figure out what happened to Helvig," Zeke said so casually that the chasm inside my chest expanded taking me by surprise and it took every ounce of willpower I had to not fall into the darkness once more. Not now. I couldn't do that now. I would have to wait till later to fall apart from the guilt that was eating away at me. "I thought I felt a flicker of our bond once but then it was gone. I don't know if that gives me hope or not. If he is alive then he has probably been tortured this whole time which is really scary. Helvig is the most powerful being I know. So for someone to have not only subdued him enough to take you and capture him but to hold him, gods, that is just too much to think about. I hope he died. I know that sounds terrible but I would much rather him be dead than be tortured. At least in death, his soul would be set free."

I felt like I was choking on the air in my lungs. Could Helvig still be alive? Could he be held somewhere being tortured right now? Gods. That was... too much. Zeke was right. Images from my dreams about him came flashing through my mind. That was just too much. I don't know how he could survive being tortured all this time.

"What exactly is Helvig?"

"I am oath bond to keep that secret. I physically am unable to tell you. What I can tell you though is if they haven't killed him and they have been torturing him this whole time... they better kill him before he gets free. Once he is free and he has regained his strength and his power back, no one will be safe from his revenge. The amount of devastation and chaos he would cause them," Zeke whistled. "We would no longer be afraid of your father. There would be a new reigning king of this realm and a new age. An age of pure havoc. Hopefully, he would somehow be able to reign in his fury. Otherwise, we would all be doomed.Well, I think he had a soft spot for you. Maybe you would be able to reach him in his fury."

A chill went down my spine. I wasn't sure if I believed what Zeke was saying. The Helvig I knew wouldn't cause mass destruction harming innocent people. He would be able to hone his fury and focus it on the ones that deserved it. Helvig was good through and through. I knew that, somehow I just knew it in my bones. But Zeke knew more about Helvig than I did. They had been friends longer and Zeke knew all the secrets that I didn't. The thought that Helvig could be alive but being tortured made me sick but at the same time my heart swelled with hope. Hope that maybe he was alive somewhere. Maybe he had made it back home. He had wanted to go home and maybe he finally was able to. My heart sank at that thought. If he had gone home, I wouldn't ever see him again. Maybe I was selfish but I wanted to see him one last time. I wanted to tell him I was sorry for not using my magic and that it was my fault he was hurt. I wanted to tell him so much but mostly I wanted to look into his emerald eyes one last time. I wanted to see them crinkle with mirth and glow with peridot one more time.

When I was a little girl I had seen my father crying once. I was startled because I had never seen him show such emotion. I asked him why he was crying and he said his best friend had died in a battle a few months prior. He told me that sometimes the loss of a friend can leave an everlasting hole in your heart. For weeks afterwards, I brought my father little bits and bobbles in the shape of a heart. Finally he asked me why I kept bringing them to him. I told him I wanted to help him fill the hole in his heart. My father might not have been the best father. He might have ruined this whole realm and allowed unspeakable horrors to happen. Sometimes though, there was a sliver of a good man that made his way out of the darkness. Although that sliver never lasted long, it was always enough to carry forward the hope to see that side of my father again.

I think Helvigs loss was the kind of loss that my father had talked about. I think it changed me and left a hole in my heart. Honestly, I didn't think that hole would ever heal. I felt a small drop of fear and then panic at the thought of Helvig being tortured. I let out a small gasp and Zeke tightened his hole. "Don't worry about Helvig. If he came back, I think he would spare you. There were times he volunteered to stay with you instead of letting someone else. I think he genuinely enjoyed your friendship. He hadn't ever shown interest and being friends with someone like he did you. Shit. Him and I weren't even as close as you two were. There were times I worried that he was going to take you away from me." I couldn't tell if that made the ache in my chest better or worse but that wasn't what had caused my reaction. There was that drop of fear again only it wasn't mine and it wasn't a small drop anymore. Suddenly all I could think about was Zander.

"I think I can feel Zander. I can feel his fear and his panic about something. I can almost taste it on my tongue. I haven't been able to feel him any other time I have visited you." Just then it sounded like Quinlan was whispering to me. It was so faint I almost missed it. I jumped from Zeke's lap. "QUINLAN. QUIN. CAN YOU HEAR ME?" I was shouting both inside my head and outside of it. Zeke stood confused and looked around the room.

"Sorry, I meant to try and mindspeak to Quinlan," I said, still way too loud out to Zeke.

Quinlans worried voice came into my mind a little louder now.

"Are you okay? Gods. Please tell me that you are okay?"

"I'm okay. I somehow managed to poof to Zeke, only they were in the middle of a battle. I wasn't even anywhere close to him and men were attacking. It was crazy but it's over now and I am okay. I have been speaking with Vilulf and Zeke about everything that has happened."

There was a brief pause and then like a flood gate had opened I felt Zander's relief sweep through me. Then I felt

his satisfaction and pride. He was so proud of something…
almost giddy with delight.

*"We were worried something happened to you. Do you think
you will be able to come back or are you stuck there?"* He tried to
mask his worry but he failed. I knew he didn't like me being
somewhere he couldn't be.

I sighed. *"Honestly, I'm not sure. I haven't tried to come back
yet. There's been a lot going on here but I will try soon. I'm sorry
I worried you all. I really hadn't meant to."* I looked at Zeke and
smiled.

"I need to try and go back. I have things I need to figure
out there. I'll come back to you with any news as soon as I
can. Tell Vilulf I said bye and uhm… What was her name?" I
asked him, realizing I hadn't gotten the name of the female
warrior that helped me.

"Who? Vilulf's sister? Her name is Celeste."

Zeke seemed so calm with everything now. Like he had
already come to terms with how things were going to be
between us.

"Tell Celeste thank you for everything. I hope you know
just how much I care for you. Think about becoming allies
with Brutus. I know there is history there but I think we
need to put that aside and figure everything else out." I gave
him a small smile and thought about my friends back in the
castle and how worried they must have been. Then I started
thinking of the delight Zander felt and curiosity filled me.
What had he been so happy about?

I felt the world tilt slightly and then Draugs' warm summer
scent filled me.

"My Queen," Draugs voice slid over me. I opened my eyes to
find myself standing in an armory with Alba, Brutus, Draug,

Zander, and Quin. It took me a moment to fully adjust. I had appeared right next to Draug, so close that we were almost touching.

Brutus took a step forward and motioned around the room. "I love what you've done with the place."

I frowned, not sure why he thought I had something to do with this room until my sight caught the bed. It was my bed. Oh gods. I had sent all that armor and those swords here. Woops. "Imagine my surprise when I'm minding my own business and suddenly feel magic that is far too old and strong to be in my castle without me knowing. Then a few moments later, I feel it again and again and again. Of course, I had felt it before but it had always vanished before I could locate it. This time it kept happening. So I followed the pull of it and wouldn't you be shocked to know that it led me to your door." Brutus's voice took on an almost deadly tone. His face was unreadable and his body language screamed uncomfortable.

"Oh stop being so dramatic," Quinlan said walking past Brutus. Quinlan apparently had enough of dealing with Brutus. If Brutus had been here the whole time, he had probably questioned them about me. Brutus turned and took a single step towards Quinlan when I pounced. I moved so fast that Brutus didn't even have time to defend himself. In a blink of an eye, I was in front of Brutus poking his chest with my finger.

"Your problem is with me. Not him. You're keeping secrets and so am I. Get over it." Brutus's eyes widened and then he laughed. He actually laughed at me.

Draug's voice skated over me again. "My Queen, let me get you something to eat and drink. You've been gone for nearly four hours. You've missed dinner and clearly fought in a battle." I looked down at myself and realized I was coated in blood and dirt.

"That would be appreciated. I'm going to get cleaned up. We can all talk about what happened when I am done." I turned to walk to the bathing room when I stopped and spoke directly to Brutus. "Why don't you do something useful with yourself and get this place cleaned up." Zanders' amusement slithered into me as I strode into the bathing room. He had been suspiciously quiet during all of that.

So the cat was out of the bag. Brutus was now fully aware of the extent of my magic. I wasn't going to tell him I didn't have full control over it. He didn't need to know that. I would let him think that I could come and go as I pleased. I washed quickly and dressed in loose pants and a fitted top. I walked out of the bathing room while brushing my hair. "Oh good. I see you were indeed useful." I smiled at Brutus with all my teeth.

Alba was relaxing in one of the oversized chairs when our eyes met. "You know, I was startled at first when you disappeared. I sat waiting around to see if you would come back quickly. Then suddenly it started raining bloody dirty swords. Poof, swords were just showing up all around me. I started screaming, of course, and then the guys came running in here. You would have loved the looks on their faces. I thought Quinlan was going to shit himself—" at that moment Quinlan chucked a piece of bread at her. She laughed and threw a three inch thick book at him. He caught it with an oomph but the impact had been so strong it knocked him sideways off the dresser he had been perched on.

"I have told you time and time again, jackass. If you are

going to be stupid then you need to be tough because the dildo of consequences is rarely ever lubed," Alba said to Quinlan. The laugh that burst out of me was so loud that Zander slid a hand over my mouth. "Damn woman. She is not THAT funny." He slowly removed his hand and I leaned up against his chest. Brutus stood in complete shock looking at everyone. He had been alone for a good portion of his life. He didn't seem to have very many friends and his life goal had been to find me and protect me. Honestly, I felt kind of sorry for him.

Draug strode in the room and took in the scene. "Alba told Quinlan about the dildo of consequences again didn't she?" Just hearing Draug utter the word "dildo" had me rolling with laughter again.

Brutus's black eyes were twinkling with merriment. "Never have I been around a group of people so comfortable with each other and so full of life."

A pang of guilt rolled through me. If what Brutus had told me was true about his father and his mother then he had probably lived a very lonely and sad life. People thought of his father as this terrible ruler when in reality he hadn't been. They now thought that Brutus was just as terrible, killing his own mother, when in reality he hadn't.

"Why did you kill those three women? Was it truly just for tithe?" It was the question that had been haunting me for months now. I needed to know the answer to this before I answered any questions he had. I needed to know exactly what kind of person I was dealing with. If he had truly murdered three innocent women for some bizzare tradition during Tithe then I wouldn't be able to trust him. How could I trust someone that thought something like that would be okay? If he really had killed them essentially just because he could then I would never be able to trust him and I would have to change our plans. Screw trying to get him to side with us. He would just have to be another monster I needed to take down.

"I've been waiting for you to ask me about that. No. Those women were involved in kidnapping and selling children to the highest bidder. They didn't care what would happen to those children once they were sold off. Their actions were disgusting. It just so happens that we caught them just in time for the traditional offering that your father's darker side of his army believes in." He casually sat in a large wingback chair and placed his ankle over his knee. "I want to make it very clear to everyone in this room. The Daemonger family reputation and the true character of each of us is very very different."

I let out a breath I had been holding for way too long. Maybe I could trust Brutus and just maybe he would side with us. I had a feeling taking my father down would be much harder than I expected.

Before anyone could respond to him, my chamber doors flew up and two warriors stood. "My King," one said while bowing his head. "King Rovini and his men have left. They didn't alert anyone to their movements and we only just discovered that their trip into the village was a cover for their plan to leave. They are currently crossing the mountains and will be in their own Kingdom within the hour."

My father had left. Just like that. Without saying goodbye. Without forcing his plans regarding my union to Brutus. He just vanished. That was so incredibly like him but also not. Normally, he would have tied up any loose ends and then vanished. Maybe he didn't want me to marry Brutus after all so he hadn't considered it a loose end to tie up. I had also been avoiding him and all his requests to see me. Maybe he had planned on telling me goodbye but I had avoided him for too long. Still a part of me felt hurt that after everything, my father just left me here with Brutus who had a reputation for being a horrible person. How were we going to continue to keep an eye on him? How would I be able to warn the other kingdoms about his plans? Gods. I wouldn't be able to save anyone anymore. So many people would die. It felt like my lungs were collapsing and I wasn't able to breathe.

"FUCK," Brutus said under his breath. "Did he take all of his men with him? Were Balin and Turq able to go with them? Do we have any eyes in their party at all?" Brutus sounded desperate now. Had he not trusted father then if he had people spying on him.

"No my king. Balin and Turq were sent on a fool's errand. King Rovini did leave his right hand, Lord Ragnor, here. We do not know why," One of the men said, looking ashamed.

I felt my whole body stiffen. Ragnor was still here for some reason. Probably to watch over me. Maybe even to torture me because that was truly what he was good at. Ragnor's words flooded my mind. *You are pathetic. You are a waste of resources and flesh. You will never amount to anything. Your father should have just killed you when you were a babe. You are weak. You are nothing. You are nothing. You. Are. Nothing.*

My breathing had become ragged and short. I was shaking violently. I couldn't focus on the world around me. I felt like the walls were closing in and there was a smothering weight on my chest. I couldn't breathe. I couldn't get any air. I was suffocating. My eyes were wild as I searched the room. For what? I wasn't sure.

Before I knew what was happening, Draug had me in his arms and moved us into another room. Zander and Quinlan were right behind him. They had shut and blocked the door so that no one else could come in.

Draug was talking but I couldn't hear him. My thoughts kept circling. So many people would die. I hadn't done enough. I had failed them. Just like I had failed my Helvig. They would die just as my Helvig had died. I had failed again. I felt like I was suffocating and my chest had tightened to a painful grip. I miss Helvig. I missed him so much and for a moment the grief was so overwhelming. I was utterly alone without him.

Suddenly Quinlans voice filled my mind. It was soft and gentle. *I am here. You are not alone. I am here.* He repeated the words over and over.

Zander's emotions flooded my senses. Love. So much love. My eyes began to focus and I could see Draug. Then I could hear him. "Take a deep breath, my Queen. You are projecting your panic and your worry. One big deep breath and then hold it for me while I count to five. Ready? Deep breath now." I complied, sucking in as deep of a breath as I could. "Very good. One. Two. Three. Four. Five. Now slowly release it as I count to five again. One. Two. Three. Four. Five. Another deep breath. One. Two. Three. Four. Five. and release it slowly again." Draug repeated this over and over until my breathing had calmed and I had stopped shaking. We sat in silence for a long time just taking comfort in being with each other. Zander had pulled me into his arms and held me tight against him.

My mind felt like it had been scrambled and my limbs were numb. I was so exhausted. When was the last time I slept a full night? I couldn't focus on what they were saying. Sleep was coming for me quickly and for once I was going to welcome it with open arms.

"I would like to go to sleep now," I mumbled to my men. I knew they would protect me. I knew I could trust them. If not anyone else, it would always be them.

Before anyone could reply, exhaustion overtook me.

Chapter Fifteen

T he room was dark and smelled musty. I knew this place and I hated it. I hated it for the bone chilling feeling it gave me. As if my life was right here and was on the verge of being taken away. It didn't make sense because I knew this was only a dream and I had been in life threatening situations before but this feeling was what true fear was. Each and every time I saw his state worsening, the fear and the guilt consumed me a little more. The cold began to set into my bones before I even began moving towards him. He wasn't moving this time. Gods. Was he dead? Was I dreaming about his death? Why the fuck was I dreaming about him dead?

The answer was simple. Because I had failed everyone. They would all die just like he had died. Would I dream about them too? Would I dream about their deaths?

I walked closer to him so scared of what exactly I would find. My body was shaking so badly it was hard to walk. The smell down here was of death and made my stomach churn.

I reached out to touch him but hesitated. I didn't hear any

183

wheezing anymore and it didn't look like he was breathing. The sight of him caused the air to seize in my lungs. His head was hanging down with his hair dangling in front of him. His shoulder looked dislocated but the chains attached to the wall looked like they were ready to fall apart. He had been fighting for his freedom. Gods. He had been so close to getting the one side out. My heart ached so much it felt like someone had reached into my chest and squeezed it as hard as they could.

I slid my hand across his good shoulder and over to his exposed skin on his collar bone. He was so cold and frail. His bones were protruding from his body making him look skeletal. Wet tears slid down my cheeks before falling to the floor.

"Helvig?" I choked out trying to sound strong but my voice came out barely a whisper. He made a whimpering sound before attempting to lift his head up.

"Shhh please don't move." Ducking down, I looked up at him. His eyes fluttered open for a moment but I wasn't sure if he even saw me. He looked so weak. He had cuts and bruises all over his body that looked and smelled infected. One of his eyes was swollen almost completely shut and I felt my heart shatter a little bit more. I didn't know what to do for him. "Can you speak?"

"Dddd...n't.... Plllese...gah...."

My heart ached at his attempt at speaking. I didn't know what he was trying to tell me. I tried thinking about the chains laying somewhere else and not attached to him but it didn't work. Every dream I tried it and it never worked. I slid my hand up his neck and cupped his jaw slowly raising his head. He moaned a little and then a shiver wracked his body. I carefully leaned my forehead against his and let the tears fall that I had been doing a terrible job of holding back.

"I'm so sorry. This is my fault. I should have been better. I

should have been stronger. Gods. I wish I would have told you my secrets and used my power to get us out of there. I'm sorry I was so weak."

As I spoke to him, it felt like a weight had lifted from my chest. Admitting to him my guilt had been almost freeing. I wouldn't be weak any longer. Instead I intended to be strong for him. Even if it was just a dream. I would make up for my past mistakes in every dream for the rest of my life if I had to. I wouldn't fail my men or Alba.

Finally, a new idea of how to help him popped into my mind. I was such an idiot. Just because I couldn't remove the chains didn't mean I couldn't bring stuff here. I closed my eyes and thought about my travel water flask, a bowl, soap, healing drafts, a pail of broth from the kitchen and a cup. Once everything was sitting next to me, I tore part of my sleeve to use as a rag to clean him.

I tried to be as careful as possible but the grime was stuck to him. I used the healing draft directly on him. I knew it would sting like a bitch but he barely flenched. Hopefully, that would help take care of the infection and heal him. I thought about the ottoman in my room and placed it between him and the wall. It wasn't quite tall enough for him to sit but I was able to manipulate his legs so he was kneeling on it and the pressure was taken away from his shoulders. I knew I needed to reset his shoulder and it was going to hurt. I really didn't want to hurt him. My heart ached at the thought but it needed done so he could heal properly.

"I'm going to fix your shoulder now."

He gave me a slight nod and I moved over to his arm. The tears broke free again and I didn't bother trying to stop them. I wouldn't apologize for what I was about to do even though I knew it would cause him pain. He and I both knew it was a necessary evil. Gently, I grabbed his arm and with one quick motion, I popped it back into place. Helvig made a gargled scream. It was a good thing I saved the broth and water for last. He probably would have just thrown them up.

I took a small step away from him trying to assess if he had any other injuries that I might have missed. He reached out with the arm I had just relocated and grabbed my hand. I stood there frozen for a moment. He had enough slack in that chain that he could move quite a bit. I slid my fingers through his intertwining them, relishing the feel of our skin touching. His hands were rough and dirty but I felt something when our hands touched.

"I'm not leaving unless I'm forced to. I won't leave you if I have anything to do with it. I know this is just a dream and it kills me that I'm not actually with you. I wish I could truly be with you wherever you are. Even in death, I would have followed you if I could have." Speaking this truth out loud for the first made me realize just how much I had cared for Helvig. I hadn't even admitted it to myself until now, but I would have followed him into the void.

Helvig opened his eyes again the best that he could and I swear he was looking at my soul. I felt raw and broken and his stare made me feel like he was seeing all of it, all of me for who I was. Not like everyone else. They saw me for what I could do for the realm, not for me. He gently pulled me closer to him and attempted to speak but his words came out grumbled and rough. I reached down and grabbed the water flask, gently placing it against his lips helping him drink from him. It was slow and careful at first and then he was guzzling it. I pulled it away and set it down, trading it for the broth.

"Not so fast. You'll make yourself sick and that won't do any good."

I carefully gave him spoonfuls of broth. The whole time his beautiful emerald eyes, well the eye that wasn't swollen almost completely shut, never left mine. I talked to him quietly. Telling him about everything that had happened since I was taken. I even told him about Zeke and how we weren't soulmates. He had attempted to speak a few times but his voice was almost non-existent. He had probably been screaming while he was tortured. After he was halfway through the broth, I set it down and used my cloth to wipe his face.

I hated that my brain tortured me with him like this. These dreams felt so real but every time that I woke up, he was gone and I was back to reality without him. I wasn't sure what was worse. Dreaming of him like this or living in reality without him.

"You were right. The night we talked about soulmates, I don't know if you remember it, but you had talked about it being better to end it if Zeke and I weren't actually soulmates. It was hard to end it but I almost felt relieved that it was over. Honestly, I don't regret the time I spent with him but part of me wishes I would have come to terms that we weren't meant to be sooner. Maybe things would have been different. Maybe you would still be with me." I ran my fingers along his jawline and down his neck. Then over to his good shoulder and grabbed a hold of the chains to try and pull them from the wall for him. Suddenly my vision blurred and I felt sick. It was wrong. So wrong. It felt like all my magic and power had been taken from me. I started to panic but I couldn't let go of them. It wasn't until Helvig touched my cheek with his other hand that I managed to let go.

He let out a hard cough. "My Zonlicht, go."

Two days had gone by before I mustered up enough courage to tell Quinlan through our bond what had happened with Zeke. I told him in detail from the time I realized I was on a battlefield to me appearing before them in what I had

187

mistaken as an armory. He had listened but was far more quiet than usual. His normal banter and mischievousness was gone and it was my fault. I didn't tell him about my dreams about Helvig. I just couldn't bring myself to open that wound any more than the dreams already had. I knew I was spiraling but I couldn't stop myself.

I would fail the people of this realm. I would no longer be able to get information for them. They would suffer because I had been selfish and ignored my father. If I would have faced him, I would have known he was leaving. I could have convinced him to stay or figured something else out. I didn't even know where he was going. I could have at least gotten that much information out of him. We might not have been doing much over the last few weeks aside from gathering intel but at least we were doing something. Now though, I had nothing. All because I was too much of a coward to speak to my father.

I wished Rosemary were here. The last time my thoughts had become so overwhelming that the world seemed to crush me, Rosemary had helped me through it. She had been my rock. Afterwards, she had helped me learn the signs that this was going to happen. She helped me recognize the feelings of hopelessness and the thoughts that seemed to trigger it. If she would have been here the last few weeks, she would have seen me spiraling. She would have been able to catch me before I fell.

Alba had been sitting in the chair next to my bed quietly. She hadn't asked me questions or blamed me for anything. She hadn't even pestered me about what had happened with Zeke. She had just been a quiet presence in my room.

"I'm sorry," I finally croaked out to her. Her brows

narrowed as she looked up from her book. "What the hell are you sorry for?"

"For not being able to keep my shit together. I just—" Alba cut me off as she set her book down. "Cordelia, do you even know what is wrong with you? Not what you have done wrong but what illness you have?" Her words surprised me because I was healthy. I was fit. I ate well. I didn't have any illnesses. I was uncomfortable not only because of the conversation but the bed sheet was too scratchy, the light from the window was too bright, and I swear I could hear someone breathing on the other side of the door.

"That's what I thought. You, my dear friend, have an illness of the mind. My mother had it too. Her mind would go so fast and it would trick her into thinking horrible thoughts that then made her body respond in ways it normally wouldn't. I believe my mother's doctor called it anxiety. She had a few other mental issues as well but I think that one was most prevalent."

Anxiety? There were definitely times that my mind was reeling over things that most people would only flinch at. Rosemary had told me I needed to learn to let things go and that I had to stop letting them pile up and crush me. That was much easier said than done.

"Zander feels guilty. He said over the last few weeks, he had felt your excessive apprehensiveness and panic over things. He feels like he should have recognized the signs and been able to help you more." Alba was staring at me intently. My guilt only seemed to increase at her words.

Silence stretched out between us until I finally sighed and said, "It isn't Zander's fault that something is wrong with me. I'm just wired wrong. I don't know. I don't expect him to be able to fix this or point out the warning signs. It isn't his problem to deal with." A whisper inside my head told me that I had let Zander down. He was feeling guilty for my problem. I should have been able to keep it together. If not for myself but for my men and for Alba. I had failed them yet again. I mentally sighed and packaged my emotions up into boxes to deal with another day.

A small smile tugged at Alba's lips, "I wish I knew how to help you. I am no doctor and I hadn't paid attention to what the doctors did for my mother. Now that she is gone, I wish I would have paid more attention to her for more reasons than just this."

A soft knock on the door came and Alba stood. "I have to do my nightly stuff. I'll come by around 8 tonight so we can catch up more." I knew that meant she was going to spy on someone. She leaned down and hugged me. It caught me slightly off guard because we hadn't really every hugged before. Sure we had become friends, laughing and joking but we hadn't been the touchy feely type of friends. So I gave her a small smile and nodded. She opened the door and Brutus came striding in.

"I think it is time you and I had a talk," he said as he took the chair Alba had just been sitting in.

"Great. I can't wait." I was attempting to tease him and lighten the mood but my attempt seemed to fall flat.

Brutus leaned his head back and closed his eyes. He sighed the most dramatic sigh I think I had ever heard in my life. "My father believed that you were his niece, my cousin, and that you are the child of a god and goddess. He believed that you were stolen and would eventually be used against this realm. That your magic is powerful and unlike anything seen before." I stared at him for a moment before blinking my eyes. Was this real? What the fuck was Brutus going on about now? I didn't think I heard him correctly. No. I knew I must have not heard him correctly. It wasn't that I didn't fully trust him, it was just that well I didn't fully trust him. How was I just supposed to forget everything I had ever been told about him and this kingdom. Then I was just supposed to believe everything he was telling me? How could I even be the child of a god and goddess. My father might have thought he was a god because he descended from one but he most definitely was not godly in any way.

"Why would your father believe something like that?"

"He thought this because he was given a vision of you. I was sitting with him when his eyes turned white and the vision struck. It scared the fucking shit out of me. When my father was released from the vision, he told me that the one we had to find and protect was his brother's child. According to him, you looked exactly like your father but with your mother's lilac hair and copper eyes. I have tried getting information from King Rovini about your biological mother. I have tried to get him to admit that you are not his daughter. However, he always avoided the subject or flat out told me to mind my own business and to stop sticking my nose where it didn't belong. He never once said or claimed to be your father." Brutus opened his and looked at me, frowning as he took in my appearance. "Gods. You look absolutely dreadful. Have you not gotten out of bed since your episode?"

My breath caught in my chest. No. What he was saying couldn't be true. It didn't make any sense. How could I be his cousin? King Rovini was my father and I took after my mother. That's what he told me all the time. My father might be a lot of things but at the end of the day he was my father. He had cared for me and loved me to the best of his abilities. It wasn't perfect but he had been there. He would never talk about my mother but I didn't fault him for that. Whatever happened between them was serious enough that he couldn't face it, but there were times that he stared at me lovingly, and I always imagined he was thinking of my mother. Also, maybe I hadn't gotten out of bed. Every girl needs a few days every once in a while to regroup. "I'm not the daughter of some God and his mistress." My tone was flat and laced with anger. Did he come in here just to rile me up? If so, it was working. I couldn't see the logic in what he was saying. All I knew was that my world had been turned upside in the last few months and now he was attempting to destroy it even more.

"Truemate and Goddess. If what my father thought is true, you would be the daughter of the God of Land and the Goddess of the Sea. Hence why I thought the name that King Rovini's wife picked out was so fitting. Cordelia, daughter of the sea. Your supposed father told everyone that his Queen had told him if she were to ever have a daughter she would have named her Cordelia. So he chose that name for you. I think there is more to it all than what he has told everyone. I think you truly are the long lost daughter of the creators of this realm. If you are feeling up to it, I would like to show you something." His words were gentle but firm. He truly believed what he was saying. My mind was reeling. How could I be the daughter of the god and goddess that created this realm? How did my father—errm King Rovini— take me from them? Did they abandon me? I felt sick but there was this part inside me whispering that what he said was true. A

192

part of me felt like the final puzzle pieces were beginning to click into place and I was trying to fit that so much. I didn't want this to be true. He was my father. All my memories were of him and my brothers and the idea that I had a family out there just tore my heart to pieces.

I thought back to how my father interacted with me compared to my brothers. I had always thought it was because we had different mothers. I thought maybe my father simply didn't know how to raise a daughter and that was why I always seemed on the outside looking in. Like I had always been an afterthought and my heart clenched. Who were my parents and how did I end up with King Rovini?

"Sure. Can you just give me a few moments to get ready?" His words kept whispering through my mind and I couldn't believe what he was saying. Yet there was a part of me that did believe him. A part of me deep down was screaming that he was onto something and I needed to listen to him. If I did, maybe it would fill in so many answers I had been seeking over the years. It would explain why I had magic and my brothers did not.

Brutus waited for me in the hall. I quickly dressed in a long tunic and pants from Alba's closet. I was thankful that I could wear pants whenever I wanted here. The tunic was a little tight and scratchy making me consider changing again. I stared at all the clothes in her closet and I realized that it didn't matter what I wore. I wouldn't be happy with it. There wasn't actually anything wrong with the clothes, I was just being picky and unhappy. Sighing, I let Quinlan know I was going with Brutus for a while. My men had given me some space the last few days and stayed out of the bedroom. I knew they were only trying to help but it had felt like they had given up on me. Almost like they didn't want anything to do with me now that they knew there was something wrong with me. I wasn't their King's soulmate and I wasn't their Queen.

Quinlan just let me know they would be waiting for my return. He didn't say anything else or elaborate on what they would be doing in my absence. He didn't even bother asking what Brutus and I would be doing or where we were going. I didn't like the feeling of loneliness that began to creep in around me. He had told me things wouldn't be different after I talked to Zeke. He had said he would still be here for me. Yet I have never felt more alone than I did now. I probably seemed like a liability to them after my "episode" as Brutus so kindly put it.

I felt lonelier now than I did before I met Zeke. Maybe it was because then I didn't know what I was missing. I knew what it is like to be surrounded by people that cared for you. Maybe they didn't care for me though. Maybe they were just doing the job that Zeke told them to do. Maybe that's all I ever had been to them. A twist of pain shot through my chest and I felt like I couldn't breathe. My breathing became fast and I knew what was happening again. I couldn't think about all the things Rosemary had told me to do. I couldn't focus on anything other than the rising panic. I was going to be alone again. I squeezed my eyes shut and tried to breathe. I didn't want to be alone. I had never doubted Helvig for a moment and I missed him. I wished he was here with me right now to hold my hand and help me through this. I wished he was here to make me laugh and smile. I wished I could see his eyes light up when he looked at me one more time. I stood in my room falling apart on the inside but I only let myself fall apart for a couple short minutes.

After a few moments of focusing on my breathing the crippling tightness began to ebb. I stood up straight and pulled my hair back out of my face. I glazed into the mirror and realized I did look terrible.

I opened my door and found Brutus talking with Draug. "My Queen, are you alright? I felt your pain? I tried to come in but King Daemonger would not grant me access claiming you were just getting ready." Draug's voice held a tone of irritation but was mostly filled with concern. I wondered if Draug would have cared about what was happening to me without our bond. He could feel my pain and I think any decent person would have come to see what was going on. Did he actually care or was it just the link between us? Maybe it wasn't fair of me to question him like this but I was questioning everything at this point.

"I'm okay. I just saw how I looked and felt a bit over-whelmed with everything. Would you like to accompany us?" I asked him, hoping he would say yes and join us. If he did join us that could mean I had just been over thinking things. Before, when everyone thought Zeke and I were soulmates, he would have immediately joined us without hesitation. Actually, I wouldn't have even had to ask. My men would have just been there. Now they were always busy doing something. Of course, it was always an important task like helping those displaced from the war or trying to figure out why my father was moving around his troops so much. Still, I felt like I was losing my friends. I adjusted the sleeve of my tunic that kept scratching my wrist while waiting for a response.

"I actually have something I need to take care of. I will find you later though." He bowed slightly and took off down the hall. I would have to remember to find him after and figure out what was going on. What could Draug have to be so vague about? Maybe it was because Brutus was here. I frowned while watching Draug head down the hallway.

Quin? Brutus motioned for me to begin walking down the hall. Opposite of where Draug had gone.

Yeah? He sounded breathless like he was in the middle of running.

"I want to take you down into our sacred catacombs. There are things hidden that I think you need and would want to see. There's a portrait that I think will help you see why my father believed what he did." The catacombs? Sounded a bit sketchy but I would go with him to see this portrait.

Is everything okay with you? My mind has been awfully quiet without your constant chatter. I tried to tease Quinlan hoping maybe I could fix whatever had been broken between us.

I've just been busy. King Havaror has us searching every inch of the castle creating him a map.

Oh. He doesn't want you guarding me any longer?

He thinks you can take care of yourself. If you end up in trouble, you can just poof yourself to us. Things had changed. I wasn't their priority any longer. It had all been because of Zeke's intentions to marry me. The friendships I thought we had created were built on a false foundation. My battered heart felt like it was breaking even more.

I closed my eyes and took a deep breath. It was okay. I would be fine. I hadn't needed them before Zeke and I wouldn't need them after.

"Cordelia? Are you alright? I've been speaking and you haven't said a word," Brutus eyes were narrowed and a frown marred his tight lips.

"I'm sorry. I was thinking I would very much be interested in the catacombs but first can we see your Alchemist?" I asked as I rubbed my temples, a headache had begun to creep in. "If you are ill, perhaps we should see the healer?" Brutus started to turn. The infirmary was in the opposite direction we were heading.

"No. I would much prefer your Alchemist. I'm hoping they might have an elixir to help me. I have seen the healers and nothing they do helps." It was a small lie and I hoped they wouldn't be punished for failing me. I had seen healers in my father's castle and they hadn't helped. I assumed the healers here would be the same.

"Ah. I see. Sure. We can stop by his laboratory before we head into the catacombs. It's along the way anyways," He said tightly. He couldn't possibly have known that I lied to him. I didn't know what all he could do or what exactly his magic entailed but he definitely didn't know when I was lying… or at least I hoped he didn't.

"I'm sorry if I upset you," I whispered after walking in silence for a while, unsure of how to proceed with spending the day with him. I couldn't handle it if this was how he was going to act the rest of the day. He paused and adjusted the black leather harness he had over his blood red dress shirt.

"You have not upset me. I wasn't speaking because I didn't want to cause you any pain. One of my favorite chefs gets a pain in her head. Even the sound of a whisper can cause it to worsen." He shrugged.

"Oh. It isn't that bad for me. We can still talk." I felt desperate for a distraction from myself. I couldn't be alone with my thoughts. There was too much going through my mind right now and most of it wasn't positive. I had never been a positive person but lately I seemed to be a glass half empty type of person.

"We are already here," Brutus said as he swung open the door behind him. I stepped into the room filled with beakers and strange looking liquids. A man came walking towards me and said "BY THE GODS. Cordelia? My you have grown."

Chapter Sixteen

❧◦❧

The Alchemist's words surprised me. I hadn't met him before yet he knew me.

"I apologize but I don't think we've met before." I glanced at Brutus who looked just as shocked as I felt. I would have remembered a man like. His gray hair stood out straight like he had just been struck by lightning. He had big eyes and a mole on his cheek that was rather distracting.

"Oh. Right. Well we have. I helped Queen Rovini in the castle for a few years when you were just a babe." He said turning and looking over a beaker with a lime green substance.

Wait. What? Again someone was just casually mentioning information that made my whole world tilt. The queen died before I was born. He had to be mistaken. My stomach rolled and I was suddenly grateful that I hadn't eaten.

"You must be mistaking me for one of my brothers. The Queen died before I was born. I never got to meet her. My father met my mother a couple years afterwards and they had me. Unfortunately, I do not know what happened to my mother." I tried explaining as if the words meant nothing even though they felt so heavy on my tongue. Brutus scoffed but I didn't bother looking at him.

The alchemist moved around pouring different colored liquids into each other. "No. I am not mistaken," he spat vehemently. "I was the one that helped the Queen save you. I was the one that helped her give her life in exchange for yours to right the wrong that her husband had committed. King Rovini probably kept you in the dark because he is ashamed and guilty for the choices he made. He probably didn't want you to feel personally responsible for her death. Actually, I take that back. He wouldn't care how you felt. He probably had some other plans for you. You shouldn't feel responsible at all. She freely gave her life to save yours. She was well aware of what she was doing and did it anyway because it was the right thing to do. She would not want you to be saddened by what happened to her."

I felt my world start to shatter even more than it already had. I looked towards Brutus for an explanation but his face was a mask of confusion as well. "I don't understand. Why would she have to give her life to save mine? What did my father do that he would have been ashamed and guilty about?" I looked from Brutus back to the alchemist when he didn't respond immediately. He was extremely focused on whatever it was that he was mixing. Brutus cleared his throat but before he could speak the alchemist said, "He stole you from your parents before you were ready to be of this world. It would have killed you. It should have killed you but the Queen had been frantic. She came to me and begged me to find a way to save you. She said the gods would be angry and we would all feel their wrath if you died. I didn't know who you were or where you came from. She refused to tell me. I still don't know exactly. I told her I would try to find a way. That night I fell asleep while researching a cure. Books had been scattered everywhere. A goddess whose laughter I will never forget visited me. She sounded like the ringing of bells and showed me what to do and how to save you. She told me what the cost would be and said that a life had to be given freely in exchange for yours. I ran to the Queen's rooms to wake her. Only she had also been visited by that same Goddess. She had been standing there holding you when I rushed through her door. She gave me a firm smile and told me what the Goddess had shown her. It was the exact same thing the Goddess revealed to me. She then said that it would be her life she would give to save you. I begged her to find someone else. She refused. She said that it must be her. It was her husband's wrong doings that caused all of this and she would help right the wrongs that she had supported blindly. It took two years before your life had been fully restored and hers had been fully depleted. Her final words to me were to leave and come here– to wait for you here. I don't know how she knew you would be here one day but she did." He gestured to me as if to prove the point that the Queen had indeed known I would come here.

"You never told me about this?" Brutus said whether in shock or awe I couldn't tell. My world was spinning. I was trying to hold it together but none of it made any sense. Why would my father–err I guess he isn't my father if what they are telling me is true– why would he have stolen me? Why did the Queen feel so adamant about saving me? Why was she willing to give her life for mine? I was just a baby and she was a Queen. He stole me from my parents. Parents who probably wanted me. Parents who would have loved me. Parents who would have cherished me and not had me beaten for everything. Parents who wouldn't have left scars on my body.

What's happening? Quinlan sounded so distant. He was shouting but yet so far away in my mind. All my thoughts were pushing his words away from me. My chest was tightening and pure fear filled my veins. If my father had stolen me, he would have done it for a reason. He would have known who my parents were. He would have known about my magic. He had always known. Did he plan on using me for something? Had I always just been a pawn in his game? Whatever game he was playing, he was the only one aware of the rules.

I'm not sure what happened. I was standing there staring at Brutus and then I was in his arms as he was laying me down. The alchemist was having me drink something but I was choking on it. Brutus was screaming at him. The door flew open and my men came rushing in. Zander shifted into a small dragon and then grew bigger and bigger before our eyes. He filled the room knocking tables over and destroying all of the alchemists' hard work. I couldn't breathe. No matter how big of breaths I tried taking, no air would make it way into my lungs. I grabbed at my throat and my eyes widened as the realization that I was going to die from lack of oxygen hit me.

Zanders' dark blue glittering body was shoving between me and the Alchemist and Brutus. I couldn't catch my breath. I couldn't speak. My breathing was erratic and I was shaking. I could hear the blood pounding and pulsating through my head. I felt Zander wrapping around me more than I saw him doing so.

Then I heard Quinlan. His voice was so faint but he was there. *Take a deeper breath. I'm here with you. You are safe. Zander is wrapped around you. No one will touch you. Draug is here too. He's dealing with Brutus. You have to calm down. You have to breathe. Please breathe. Breathe for me. I need you. I can't lose you. Fuck. Cordelia. The whole fucking castle is shaking. What the fuck happened?*

I can't do this. Quin. I. Can't. Do. This. Anymore.

I closed my eyes and reached for Zantos. My hand touched the underside of his throat. Then I felt the change in the air. I opened my eyes and found that we were sitting outside of Zeke's tent. Men were shouting and I heard the sound of swords being pulled. I still couldn't breathe right. I felt like I wasn't getting any air but if I were to breathe any faster my lungs might actually implode. Zantos let out a roar of warning that I felt into my bones. I tried moving from under his protective stance hoping that the men would recognize me and not attack but I stumbled and fell forward onto my knees. My chest was heaving so hard I couldn't get back up to my feet.

Vilulf was at my side pulling me up to him. His eyes were roaming my body looking for wounds.

"You have to tell me what happened. I can't help you unless you tell me what happened." His voice was softer than I had ever heard it before.

"I. Can't. Breathe." I barely choked out as Zantos let out another deafening roar. Tears were streaming down my face. I was scared. I was really truly scared for the first time in my life. I didn't understand why this was happening to me.

Vilulf grabbed my face in his hands and looked me into my

eyes. "I'll make it better. I'm sorry for this though." Then my world went black.

I awoke some time later laying in Zeke's bed with Zander still in dragon form laying on the floor next to me with his head resting on the bed.

Zantos?

How could you tell that it was I and not Zander?

I'm not sure. I just knew.

I have held him back while you slept. He was very distraught over the situation. I assured him that you would be okay but he wasn't listening. So I had to take control.

I'm sorry that I am causing issues between you. I don't know what is happening with me and why it has gotten so bad recently.

Ahh yes, I suppose no one is here to explain any of it to you. I will do my best as I have been around your kind more than anyone else. I believe that your magic has been repressed for a very long time. All magic here has been warded and doesn't operate at full capacity. You know this. However, I believe the necklace you put in the pyre of my brethren was enchanted to suppress your magic further. Since you are now coming into your powers at such a late age, it is all coming to you at once however the wards are still blocking it from functioning properly. All of this is causing havoc and turmoil inside your body. It can cause fluctuations of emotions. I can see by your face that you are not understanding. Imagine a barrel filled with water. You are that barrel and your magic is the water. Your emotions control whether that water stays still or is a whirlpool. Most people that come into their powers under normal circumstances can open and close the tap at will to access their powers when they want and use as much of it as they want. The wards make your tap not work properly. The enchanted necklace made your tap almost completely close up. Between the wards and the influx of emotions, you are unable to control something as simple as breathing because your body is completely overloaded. You have no outlet for your power and tied to your power are your emotions. It is imperative that you bring down the wards blocking your power. The amount of power inside of you that you haven't been able to access is more than I have seen in a very long time. Currently, you have more power inside you than I have seen in this realm in thousands of years. Until then, you need to work on controlling your emotions. When your emotions get out of control, it makes the water in the barrel turn into a whirlpool. You do not have full access to the tap to help control the water. So it is essential you take down the wards soon. This is a matter of life or death. Not your life and death but those around you. If you become too overwhelmed, you could release such immense power that you kill all of those around you.

I don't know what the wards are or how to get them down. I wouldn't even know how to start looking for them. I don't... wait... that was my mother's necklace and–

It was not your mother's necklace.

How do you know?

I knew your mother. She hated jewelry. She would not have worn a necklace.

You knew my mother?! Who is my mother? Why didn't you tell me or Zander?

I know many things. It is not my place to intervene with what the fates have laid out.

Who is my mother?

You have already been told who your mother is, Cordelia, daughter of the sea goddess.

I let out a small gasp. Zantos moved his head towards the door and let out a small huff. Zeke and Vilulf came walking into the tent just then. Zeke looked as handsome as ever but I no longer felt that unwavering attraction to him.

"How are you feeling?" Vilulf spoke first. He glanced at Zeke who just stared at me with a confused look in his eyes. "I'm feeling much better now. I'm sorry for busting in your camp like that. It just kind of happened."

"You smell different," Zeke finally said.

"I... I smell different? How do I smell? Bad?" I laughed out loud. I was expecting a lot of things but I was not expecting him to talk about how I smell.

"No. You smell... amazing. Well part of you does at least. I mean you smell like you but then there's this other smell that I'm just..." Zeke made a show of sniffing the air.

Vilulf eyed Zeke skeptically before turning back to me. "I would like to know what happened to cause you to have that kind of reaction. I had to use the little bit of access to my power that I have to shut your brain down and force you into sleep." Vilulf explained. I hadn't known that he even had powers.

"You have powers? What kind of powers do you have and what exactly did you have to do to me?" I shifted moving closer to Zander– err Zantos.

Do not worry. He will not hurt you. He is of pure heart and comes from a long line of loyal Horai.

Horai?

Yes. They guard the gates to the realm of gods.

Vilulf's next words pulled my attention back to him. "I do. They are limited ever since your father outlawed all use of magic. I don't know what exactly he did but it's like there is a collar around my magic, choking it down. I can access the minds of others. I can put things in your mind and make you think it was your idea. I can erase memories from it, melt it, ruin it, make you live nightmares over and over, project images into it, and make you shut down and fall asleep. If you can think it, I can do it to your mind. Unfortunately whatever your father has done has tampered down what I can do to the bare minimum."

Somehow this new information didn't scare me or cause me to panic. If anyone should be trusted with that type of power, Vilulf would be one of the best people. Out of all the new information my brain was trying to process, this really didn't seem too terrible.

"Have you ever used your powers on me before?"

Vilulf had the decency to look shameful. "I have... a few times. Well every time we met, I dipped into your mind to ensure that what you said was true. I hope you understand that it is my duty to ensure Zeke's safety. I had to make sure that your father wasn't using you to get to him."

I glanced at Zeke and saw he was watching me. He looked like he was trying to put together a puzzle but the pieces weren't fitting. He had begun pacing and was beginning to look like he was in pain.

I didn't know how to feel. Part of me wanted to feel violated that Vilulf had gone into my mind without me knowing. Another part of me understood where he was coming from. Someone protecting Zeke like that was the best case scenario. They could weed out people who wanted to do him harm. I didn't want Zeke to come to harm. I wanted the best for him. I realized I wasn't as upset as I could have been.

"You are not angry with me?" Vilulf shifted on his feet. It was the first time I had seen him look unsure. He was always confident and sure of himself. It made me smile seeing him squirm the way he was.

"No, I am not angry. I apparently am not King Rovini's daughter. Can you just look into my mind and see what happened? Now that I know that you can do that... I think I would rather it than go over everything that happened with Brutus." I shrugged my shoulders and felt Zander through our bond. Zantos must have released his hold on Zander and let him take back over. "Okay, I can do that." Vilulf's eyes took on a slightly glazed appearance. I felt nothing. If he was looking at my mind, I had no idea.

"You're a goddess," Vilulf breathed.

Chapter Seventeen

Vilulf's words rang across the tent. Without hesitation, Zeke let out a small growl and lunged for me. In a flash, Zander shifted from his dragon form to his human form behind me and launched towards Zeke. I let out a small shriek as they clashed together.

"WHAT THE FUCK ARE YOU DOING?" I screamed at them as I moved towards Vilulf.

In one swift movement, Zeke flipped Zander over his shoulder and straight into Vilulf and I. Zander landed on top of us and knocked us down. Vilulf flung his arm out to protect my head from slamming into the ground. The weight of Zander crashing on top of me caused all the air to swoosh out of my lungs. Before anyone could move Zeke was jumping on top of Zander. Vilulf pushed them off of us and ripped them apart. Zeke was still trying to get through Zander to get to me, I realized.

"Get. Away. FROM MY MATE!" Zeke roared. I was momentarily frozen in place from his words. Mate? What the fuck man. We already went over this. I felt all the hairs on my arms raise and the air in the tent seemed charged with electricity. I had a bad feeling about whatever was happening with Zeke.

Vilulf grabbed him by his face and yelled for him to stop. "You'll kill them if you don't control your power. You will kill them both! STOP! FOR THE GODS SAKE JUST STOP DAMN IT!" I wrapped my arms around Zander and thought about going back to Brutus's castle. I felt my magic start to tingle just as Zeke shoved Vilulf causing him to fall into us. The world began to tilt and I knew right then I might not see Zeke for a long time.

In what felt like slow motion, I watched as Zeke was moving towards us but before he could reach us everything went black and then blurred into an array of colors. I moved and pulled Vilulf up to his feet and then held on to both of them. The world around us started to come into focus again at an increasing rate. Suddenly, we were slammed into the marble floor of the Alchemists room.

Vilulf leaned forward and fell down to his hands and knees.

"Are you okay?" I glanced from him to Zander who I just realized was completely naked. Vilulf held up a finger and then emptied the contents of his stomach on the floor. I grimaced at the sight before me.

"I thought you said that Zeke wasn't your mate?" Zander's eyes narrowed as he crossed his arms over his chest.

"He isn't my soulmate. We just talked about all of that. He was fine." I didn't know what had triggered him to be so enraged like that. He had never acted that way before.

Vilulf made another heaving sound and then wiped his face. "I think it was that scent he smelled on you. I think it caused him to act like that. I don't know why. Maybe it made him feel threatened? I won't lie. Whatever it was did not smell very nice to me. Not to mention he really was fine after you talked with him. He said that there was part of him that always knew something was off. It wasn't necessarily wrong but it wasn't completely right either."

While none of that surprised me it still didn't make any sense as to why he attacked Zander and it still didn't explain why he called me his mate when clearly I am not.

"Let's go find Draug and Quinlan. We need to touch base with them and then find Brutus. He said he wanted to show me some stuff but we didn't end up getting that far."

"You need rest. You cannot keep shoving all of your emotions down. You need to deal with everything you are going through so that you don't have another episode like earlier." Zander crossed his arms and stared at me.

It still amazed me how comfortable Zander was just walking around naked. He didn't seem to notice his nudity.

"No," I said, turning to walk from the room.

Vilulf pulled himself together and followed us. "I have to admit that I wasn't expecting to be entering my enemy's castle today."

"Except I don't think Brutus is the enemy any longer. I think that there is a huge misunderstanding and–"

"He will be the enemy for as long as he continues to withhold Zeke's thunderbird!" Vilulf was shaking with anger at my words.

"I'm sorry. What? Zeke's thunderbird?" I had no idea what Vilulf was referring to but I had a feeling whatever it was was going to piss me off.

"King Havaror never told you how he got his scar?" Zander

asked bemused.

"Yes. It happened in a battle after he was told that Brutus killed their mother." Vilulf rested a hand on his hip. It was the most normal gesture I had ever seen him make. He was always the hard warrior. Stiff and alert. Seeing him posture up that way almost made me laugh. It might have been a weird thing to focus on but with all the new information coming at me it was the little things like this that helped me keep it together.

"King Daemonger used his powers to rip Zeke's thunderbird out of him. It tore his soul in half. It almost killed him. Zeke struggles to keep his powers under control without his thunderbird. It was the thunderbird itself that kept Zeke safe when he harnessed electricity and used lightning. Zeke isn't able to shift since his thunderbird is missing from him. It is equivalent to missing your limbs I would assume."

"Wait. What. Zeke could shift into a Thunderbird? Like you shift into a dragon?" I motioned at Zander.

Vilulf sighed, "Yes. He could. The only difference is that Zander and Zantos are two separate beings. Zeke and his thunderbird are one. It tore his soul in half." My eyes had to be the size of dinner plates. I was days away from marrying him at one point in time and I hadn't known any of this. I have been in the castle for weeks and no one thought to mention it. How was I still being left in the dark after all this time? What else was there that I didn't know.

"Brutus will give Zeke back his Thunderbird." I stated, clenching my fists and walking in the opposite direction. "Let's see Brutus first. I will have the others meet us there. Clearly today is a day full of information and surprises."

Quin. We're back and we have Vilulf. I need to speak to Brutus.

There is a lot that we all need to discuss but I need you guys to come meet up with us.

I've been waiting to hear that breathy voice. Tell me. Are you out of breath from doing the dirty with King Havaror or something else?

What the fuck Quin. Just what the fuck.

I did not do the dirty with Zeke. I am breathless because I am exhausted. I am hungry and I am slowly getting more and more annoyed with all the men around me.

Yikes. I was just trying to lighten the mood. You seem stressed.

For fucks sake Quin. I AM STRESSED. Just meet us.

Easy peasy my queen. We are already in King Daemongers war room with him.

You couldn't have led with that?

I figured we would get to it eventually.

So help me. When I see you I'm punching you.

Why punch me? I'm not the one that freaked you out. That would be Brutus. Punch him instead.

You know what. I might punch him too.

"They're in the war room waiting for us." I reached up and started rubbing my temples. I was starting to feel overwhelmed again and my head was pounding now. There was so much happening. Too much. Just too much to keep straight. I needed to make a checklist. Maybe not in any important ranking but atleast just a list would help.

Number one would have to be stopping my father from fully conquering the realm. Then figure out how he is blocking everyone's magic and stop it. Maybe then I would finally start feeling better. After that I would need to find the magic that his father took from him before he does. He definitely doesn't need any more fucking power. Then hide his magic somewhere so that he can't use it for more fucking evil. At some point I definitely need to make Brutus give Zeke back his thunderbird. Speaking of Zeke I need to figure out what the fuck happened to him and why he freaked out like that. Hopefully giving him his thunderbird back will fix that. He knows we aren't meant to be together so him going psycho like that wasn't okay. Once my father has been stopped, I need place Alba on the throne that she rightfully deserves. Then I can finally discover the truth to who my parents really are and why my supposed father would have taken me from them and lie about it my whole life. Oh and I definitely want to hunt Ragnor down and kill him for the part he played in Helvigs death, not to mention everything he ever put me through.

With that one brief thought of Helvig, a knife twisted in my chest. Gods. I wished he were here. Why was I responsible for all of these things? Why was I the one that had to figure this out and save everyone from my psycho dad? It felt like this boulder was sitting right on my chest making it hard to breathe again. I took a slow breath in and held it. I counted to ten before I released it. I could do this. I would figure all of this out. I would save the innocent people that needed help. I would do all of this because it is the right thing to do. I just needed to keep my emotions in check.

"You okay?" Zanders' voice was quiet as he reached over and nudged my shoulder.

"I'm fine. We're almost there and we have a lot to discuss." I didn't have time to not be okay.

"How do you think King Daemonger will react to having the general of his enemy's army in his castle?" Vilulf chuckled.

"It will be fine. You are my guest. Under my protection. I

am under Brutus's protection. So I think in math that means you are under his protection as well."

"Math? Really? I didn't realize you were a scholar."

"I'm not," I laughed.

We turned the last corner and saw Alba standing outside the war room's double doors. I couldn't help the smile that filled my face when she saw us and took off running to me.

"My Gods," she breathed as she wrapped her arms around me. "I was so worried about you. Brutus wouldn't tell us what had happened. The guys have been freaking out since you vanished and took Zander with you. Quin couldn't reach you. Draug could feel your emotional pain and was a mess. It was even worse when it suddenly went blank."

I hugged her back for a brief moment and then pulled away, "Come on. I'll explain everything in a moment. I want to say it all once so let's get in there with everyone.

"They're all waiting. Quinlan said you were grumpy and to quote not poke the bear quote." Gods I swear I was going to stab him one day. He's a phoenix so he would be fine but just one of these days I would take pleasure in stabbing him in his arm or something. "Oh. Hi. Who is this?"

"Like I said before, I will explain everything with everyone present so I don't have to go over it all again." I smiled at her. She was like a breath of fresh air. There was just something about her presence that calmed me. She put me at ease and made the pressure of the world feel a little lighter. I glanced at Vilulf and noticed he had scrunched his nose up at Alba. He looked mildly disgusting and confused. I would have to ask him about that later because we have more important things to deal with right now.

We entered the war council room as the men were arguing.

Draug was toe to toe with Brutus and I was shocked to see his display of emotion. He was normally so calm and collected. Just as we entered Draug pulled his arm back and had actual claws sticking out from his knuckles. With one sharp motion he slashed at Brutus's chest and let out a shocking roar. He fell forward onto his hands and knees and in a flash a Sphinx was standing in front of us.

"CAN EVERYONE FUCKING SHIFT?" I shouted and was ignored.

Brutus reared back just as Draug's blow was to strike his chest. It took me a moment to realize that Brutus had morphed himself into the shadows I had seen surrounding him. Draugs claws went straight through the shadows. Brutus let out a laugh that was drowned out by Draugs' roar. Brutus was nothing more than black mist. Draug launched himself towards Brutus but went straight through him. Brutus whipped a black tendril towards Draug but Draug dodged to the left and it missed by mere inches. If I find out one more person can shift into something…

No. I don't think Vilulf nor Alba can shift into anything.

Quinlan's voice rang through my mind making me realize I had projected my thoughts to him.

I didn't know what had caused this fight to break out but I honestly didn't care. I was done. I was so done with everything. I slammed my fists onto the table making not only the table shake but the room as well. "THAT'S ENOUGH!"

In the blink of an eye, both men were back in their human forms and sitting in seats opposite each other at the circular table. Their eyes were wide and shocked.

"DID YOU JUST FUCKING FORCE ME TO FUCKING SHIFT. HOW FUCKING DARE YOU DO THAT!" Brutus was fuming but I didn't care. I had a shit day. I was tired and my head was throbbing. Taking a steadying breath and I closed my eyes tight. I didn't know how I had forced them to shift back into their fae forms but thank fuck I did. My voice was barely audible and shook with anger, "I do not give a fuck what happened to cause this fight. There is too much we need to go over and plan for you two to be at each other's throats. I need you two to set your differences aside and move past this."

"I apologize, my Queen." Draug said to me but continued to glare at Brutus. I don't think he had taken his eyes off of Brutus the whole time I spoke.

"Oh yes, I am terribly sorry Goddess Cordelia." Brutus's voice was dripping with sarcasm.

Chapter Eighteen

I took a few moments for everyone to calm down. I went to take a seat when I realized that Vilulf had frozen in the doorway. He still looked like someone had struck him. "Vilulf, Come and sit down," I said softly.

He glanced at me briefly and then back up as he walked towards the seat I had pulled out for him. I followed his gaze and saw he was staring at Draug who was still staring daggers at Brutus. He sat down and I leaned over to him. "Are you okay? Did something happen to you that I missed?"

Without looking at me, he whispered, "I'm great." A faint smile played on his lips briefly before he turned fully towards me.

Ohhhhkay. What the actual fuck was happening today.

I stared at him for a few moments trying to figure out just what was going on when Quinlans voice broke me from my thoughts.

Sooo I'm not sure what is happening but I am staring at you. You are staring at Vilulf. Vilulf is staring at Draug. Draug is

*staring at King Daemonger. King Daemonger is looking from
Draug to Zander to you. Alba looks like she's ready to piss herself.*

I cleared my throat and began. "Okay I think a lot of us are
all on different pages regarding what has been going on. First
and foremost, for those of you that haven't seen him before.
This is Vilulf err" I realized I didn't know his last name. "He
is Zeke's right hand man, his second, and his general. He is
a guest here and under my protection." I stood and walked
towards Brutus who had now focused his attention on Vilulf.

"You brought a man who has been trying to break through
my defenses straight into my castle." Brutus' words were
edged with frustration.

I punched him straight in his shoulder.

"What the hell did you do that for?" It clearly hadn't hurt
him but it did surprise him.

"You deserve that for taking Zeke's thunderbird from him
and keeping it all these years. You are going to give it back
to him immediately." The room went deadly quiet except for
Alba's gasp.

"You don't know what you are talking about. I did not
purposefully take it from him. It was an accident. I didn't
even know I had that ability. I cannot give it back to him
though. I do not know how. If I release it, he might not ever
get it back."

"That's bullshit and you know it. You killed your mom. You
did something to Voronion to have him follow you and then
you stole Zeke's bird!" Vilulf had stood from the table making
his chair fall.

"Wrong. All of that is wrong." Brutus didn't even try to
explain anything further. I didn't know if it was because he
didn't think anyone would believe him or if he just didn't care

whether or not they knew the truth.

"Whatever actually happened isn't the point. The point is we will be reuniting Zeke with his thunderbird. Where do you keep it?" I continued walking around the table. I was too anxious to sit. I wasn't anxious about Zeke's thunderbird persay. I was mostly anxious about everything altogether.

"In the conservatory." The conservatory. A memory blasted through me. The conservatory where I had found a feather. Not just any feather but a giant feather. It must have been from Zeke's thunderbird. Dear gods. His thunderbird was right here.

"Once my energy is regained enough. I will return Vilulf back to their camp and–" Vilulf interrupted me, "No. I will stay here. It's fine. I can communicate with King Havaror about anything we need. I will be staying here though." I watched as his gaze swung back to Draug who still hadn't looked away from Brutus.

"Alright. Vilulf is staying. Once my energy is regained enough, I will go to Zeke and bring him to the conservatory. We will try to reunite the two halves of his soul. If for some reason we are unable to, his thunderbird will stay in the conservatory until we figure out a way to fix this situation. Is everyone in agreement?" I said this mostly for their benefit. I had reached a point where I didn't give a damn what anyone else thought. I was going to be doing things my way. Slight deviations like Vilulf staying were fine but the overall plan would be what I wanted.

Everyone nodded in agreement. "Perfect. Now Brutus. Please explain to everyone who your father is, the visions he was given, and what he believed." I reached my seat again and sat down.

You look exhausted.

I am exhausted.

You need to take better care of yourself.

I'm trying, Okay? I'm trying but it feels like everything is constantly working against me.

After Brutus finishes, we should have him make someone bring some food up here.

That is the first thing you've said today that hasn't made me want to stab you.

Feeling a little stabby today? Too bad you didn't have a dagger when you punched Brutus. Now that would have been hilarious.

A small smile tugged at my lips.

Brutus fell easily into the story about his parents. I noticed he glossed over some small details but overall it was the same story he had told me all those weeks ago. When he got to the part where Voronion had shoved Xola and she fell on the iron from the fireplace he stared directly at Vilulf. Vilulf looked confused and then his eyes lit up. There must have been some part of Brutus's story that clicked for him. Did Brutus know about Vilulf's powers and was Vilulf using them right now to know that Brutus was telling the truth? Brutus casually talked about killing Zeke's father in order to protect Voronion who was stricken with grief from his mother's death. He moved on to tell everyone about how a Goddess had visited his father and told him he needed to find and protect the princess with copper eyes and lilac hair. That she would be the key to returning what was stolen and ridding this realm of the evil that plagues it.

Alba cut in and asked, "Why would a Goddess task your father with this though. I mean he was King Daemonger the Violent. I know you say that isn't who he was truly but still why him? Also why did he need Xola's blood and what the hell do you mean to finish creating you. I'm not sure if your father gave you the talk about the birds and the bee's but it does not take blood to create a baby. Some other bodily fluids and a few months for a healthy fae baby but definitely not blood."

Brutus' smile was wicked. "Because my father is Hypnos-Samnus Daemonger— God and Spirit Demon of Sleep, the one who could walk both the realms of Gods and demons. My mother, the real Xola, is the Goddess of Life and Death and all creation. She has to give her blessing for a realm to be created. She collects the souls after death. I believe it is something to do with those powers passed down from my mother that made me able to accidentally tear Ezekiel's soul in half and remove his thunderbird."

"You didn't tell me that you thought your mother was a goddess?" I burst. He hadn't once mentioned that. "I don't think it is as you put it. I know she is a goddess but it didn't seem relevant at the time." He shrugged.

"As for the blood thing. In this realm, it isn't possible for a goddess to carry her offspring. It is a long and complicated process. The baby grows in a delicate sac that has to be suspended in a very safe place. Somewhere safe from the elements, animals, diseases, well pretty much anything. Because the baby is in such a fragile state, blood from the goddess has to be dripped onto the sac every so often to keep what little strength it has. It takes years for the baby to develop enough to be viable out of the sac. Although my father had been using his blood to keep the sac containing me strong, it is the goddess's blood that holds the true strength." Brutus gave me a pointed look as he explained this Alba. The words from the Alchemist came rushing back to me. He had said I should have died. That I wasn't ready for this world yet. He said my father stole me from my parents and it would have killed me. Should have killed me but the Queen had saved me. All of his words lined up with how Brutus said Goddesses and Gods had children. The Queen had told him that the gods would be angry and they would all feel their wrath if I died. Well no wonder why. If I was truly the daughter of a Goddess, they would be angry if someone killed me.

Brutus continued talking, this time glancing around the room. Whatever else he had to tell them, he was nervous about it. "My father believed that the princess with copper eyes and lilac hair was his niece, my cousin. He believed that the princess had been stolen and was the child of a god and goddess. More specifically, his brother's daughter. My father was given a vision of the princess he was supposed to find. He said she had looked exactly like his brother only with his wifes lilac hair and copper eyes. I have questioned King Rovini regarding Cordelia's biological mother repeatedly. I have even questioned him on whether or not he is her biological father. He never once claimed to be her father and usually told me to mind my own business."

The room was silent again as we let all of what Brutus had said sink in.

"Brutus, could we get some food sent up here?" I asked. He nodded and lifted his hands. Suddenly he dropped them down to his side and the table shuddered. All of our seats scooted back a few feet as the round table slowly spun and widened. I watched in amazement as the table grew larger and larger. Then food started appearing out of thin air and landing on the beautiful table. He was such a showoff.

Once everyone started filling their plates, I took a deep breath and explained to everyone what the Alchemist had claimed. I then filled Brutus in on the fact that Zeke and I were not soulmates. He had the audacity to laugh at me. "Why are you laughing?" I could feel the anger inside myself rising up again. It's like these men liked to do things that just pissed me off.

"It was rather obvious that you two were not true mates. If you were, you would have been frantic to get to him. Instead you were rather distracted with other things and getting to him wasn't your priority. Don't get me wrong, being concerned with what your father is doing should be your number one priority. Considering I had my suspicions that you are indeed a goddess, it made sense for King Havaror to believe that you two were true mates."

Vilulf crossed his arms over his chest. "Why would it make sense for King Havaror to believe that they were mates if they were not actually mates?"

"All goddesses are alluring to fae, humans, and even lesser gods. If a goddess so chooses, she can release a pheromone that can amplify attraction, lust, and pretty much all emotions regarding desire and love. Obviously, Cordelia here didn't know she had that ability. So when she found herself attracted to King Havaror, she unknowingly released those pheromones. He would have had to be already deeply attracted to her for them to have such a pull on him and continue to work even over great distances." My mouth fell open. Pheromones. Our relationship was because of fucking pheromones. Talk about a slap in the face.

I felt like my brain wasn't working properly anymore. My mind was in a state of great confusion over who could shift into what forms, who my parents were, what my father was planning, how to stop him, all the fucking information Brutus was providing, and now he was adding in that I have pheromones because I'm a goddess that can make men essentially fall in love with me.

You look like you're going to be ill.

I feel like I'm going to be ill. How will I ever know if someone has true feelings for me? What if I am forever forcing someone to be with me when they truly might not choose to if I didn't have these pheromones.

Quinlan spoke up then. "Are the pheromones always at work or is it something she can turn on and off?"

Brutus raised an eyebrow, "I'm not really sure to be completely honest but I think it is something she can learn to turn on and off. She can learn how to use it like her magic."

Relief washed through me. Okay. So maybe I did stand a chance at finding my true mate one day. I wouldn't have to worry about whether or not it was a situation like with Zeke again.

"Enough talk about pheromones please," I said, shaking my head. "We need to figure out a few things. First of all, Brutus, you and King Havaror need to start working together and stop fighting. Secondly, we need to figure out how my father is blocking our powers from fully working. Then we need to figure out why his father took his magic from him and where it is. There must be a damn good reason as to why his father would do that to him. Then we need to decide what to do with his magic."

Draug turned to look towards the desserts appearing on the table now. I watched as he glanced at me and did a small nod. Then he glanced at Vilulf and froze. Vilulf was as still as a statue and for a moment as they both just stared at each other. Then Vilulfs mouth tilted up in a smirk while Draug cleared his throat and began piling food onto his plate. Before I could say anything, Zander spoke up for the first time since entering this room and it was at that moment that I realized he was still naked.

"King Rovini wouldn't be able to use his magic to block everyone else's magic since he doesn't have it. So he would have to rely on collective magic from other people or a spell from witches or maybe even druids could be involved. I'm not really sure of that part. There are a lot of variables. Whatever it is, they would have to renew it though for it to last this long. Unless there is another god here that we don't know about. If that's the case, we are screwed." Zander took a bite of a chicken leg and I watched as he thought some more. Something Zander said tugged at my mind but I couldn't quite grasp what it was.

Brutus wiped his mouth with a linen napkin and then said, "I have watched him for years and he never goes anywhere that leaves a pattern. There is nowhere that he goes that would make me think he is going somewhere to ensure a spell is being strengthened."

"Do we know where he was heading when he left here?" I asked frowning. There was something that was right there but I just couldn't grasp it. I was so close to putting this puzzle together but something was slipping through my fingers.

Alba spoke up, "Well I've been doing my fair share of getting turned around in this large castle." I couldn't help the snort that burst out of me. She wasn't getting turned around that was for sure. She was spying on anyone and everyone, which had been incredibly helpful. I had spent my evenings with

Brutus while she spent hers spying. I missed dressing in all black and creeping around listening to people's secrets. Unfortunately for me, now that I was engaged to Brutus, it seemed that I could no longer fly under the radar. It would be noticeable if I disappeared into the night. "I heard a few servants talking about them heading to your father's country estate for the winter. One of them mentioned how much they hated it because the energy there gave them headaches so badly it made them ill."

"That's it," I gasped. "Whatever he is doing to the magic, he is doing there."

"I'm not sure I would jump to that conclusion from a conversation a few servants were having," Quinlan shrugged.

"I am positive. Growing up there were times my father would have to drop everything to go there. Sometimes he would be outright furious about it. Talking about how it should never be that empty. I never understood what he meant. We would go there and be there for days at a time. It was always a horrible experience. I hated going there. I had to spend most of the time locked in my rooms. I watched from my window strange people coming but I was never allowed to meet them." The room around me had grown quiet. Everyone was staring at me as they started piecing things together. It was as if the wheel turning in their heads were moving at the exact same pace.

"Alright. If it is there, what are we going to do about it?" Vilulf asked. "His country estate isn't anywhere near Havaror lands. King Havaror isn't going to be able to assist us with his army."

"We will have to send a small group to make it look as unsuspicious as possible. Cordelia and I will go to spend the weekend there. I will use the excuse of needing to speak to him regarding terms of our wedding and alliance agreement." Brutus was thinking out loud and it honestly didn't sound too terrible.

"No," Quinlan said at the same time Zander stood. I caught Draug's eye and he was unusually pale.

"No?" Brutus asked, confused.

"If Cordelia goes somewhere, we go as well. We are her guards. We will protect her," Zander said with Quin nodding his agreement. My heart swelled for a moment. Maybe things weren't changing as much as what I had thought. Maybe they were doing it out of duty or possibly out of loyalty. Either way, I was grateful that they wanted to come.

"Okay. So Brutus, Quinlan, Zander, and myself go. Draug, Alba, and Vilulf stay here. We need to keep eyes and ears here because Ragnor is still around. I don't know why my father left him but he has to be watched. Alba, continue to do what you've been doing just make Ragnor your target. If my father is planning on moving troops or attacking somewhere, I'm sure Ragnor is in the loop. He will mention something or slip up one way or another. Draug, you and Vilulf need to coordinate. You are aware of Brutus army and capabilities and Vilulf is aware of Zeke's. Let's see if we can come up with some type of plan to push my father back some. Maybe we can regain some land and return displaced people to their homes."

"Oh, I forgot to mention it but Ragnor informed me that he is here to watch over you and ensure your fair treatment while your father is away," Brutus scoffed. "If he catches wind of us leaving, he might leave as well."

With a devious smile Quinlan said, "Then let's make sure

he doesn't know anything."

I think we can agree that man is absolutely terrible at watching over you. I mean you have vanished from this castle multiple times and he hasn't even been around at all. He should definitely be fired. Quinlan's words trickling through my mind made me chuckle.

"If we are in agreement about this then let's prepare tonight and head out first thing tomorrow." Brutus said, raising his glass in the air. Everyone picked up their glasses and raised them in the air with his. The sunlight through the window seemed to hit them just right making an array of colors on the wall momentarily distracting me. "It's settled then. Vilulf, inform King Havaror about our discoveries and plans. We leave at first light tomorrow."

Chapter Nineteen

I barely made it to my room before collapsing on my bed. I didn't bother changing instead, I just pulled the large duvet over me and snuggled in. It was long before sleep crept in whisking me away to the only place I desperately wanted to be.

"I've been waiting to see you again, my zonlicht."

I stood frozen in my spot not wanting to turn around and see the state that he was in this time. I knew what he would look like and I knew how badly my heart would hurt for him. His voice wrapped around me and soothed my soul in a way that was probably unhealthy. This obsession I have had over him and the guilt that has only grown over the weeks since he was taken from me faded away. I let his words caress me. Even though his voice sounded weak and tired, there was a small thread of hope in it.

I slowly turned around and met his gaze. Those emerald eyes that haunted every waking moment of mine bore into me. His dislocated shoulder had remained in place after I had fixed it. He had new cuts and bruises but the old one seemed to be healing.

Chapter Nineteen

"You've been waiting for me?"

"Of course. What else would I do while chained to this wall." He wheezed a laugh that was rough and sounded like there was something wrong with his lungs. Immediately he started coughing and then turned his head spitting out blood. The cold was already sinking into me. It was so cold that I felt it in my bones. How did he survive being chained down here? My emotions started to overwhelm me as the guilt I had over losing him only seemed to increase.

"I think I'm going crazy," I said, walking up to him and wiping the blood dripping from his chin. "I think I'm torturing myself over you. You were my first genuine friend and I didn't protect you. It was me they were coming for and you were trying to save me and then..."

I didn't have it in me to say the rest. We both knew or at least I knew since he was just a figment in my dream. The sound of his flesh rang in my head just as it always did when I allowed my emotions to take control. I felt tears falling from my eyes and I stared at the ground because I didn't deserve to look at him. Even if this wasn't real, I didn't deserve to gaze upon his beautiful face.

He leaned forward and nuzzled my head with his trying to touch me in any way that he could. "Hey now. What's this? You can't be crying. You fought. Gods. You fought so hard and you were beautiful and magnificent. Every glance I took to look at you almost took my breath away. One day we will be fighting side by side again. I thought that there was only one thing in this realm that I wanted." His voice started to shake and I felt myself instinctively lean closer to him. "I thought I wanted to go home. Now though, I want you, Cordelia. I think a part of me knew that a long time ago and I just couldn't quite admit it to myself. You are my home, my zonlicht"

I stepped up even closer to him making our chests touch and carefully wrapped my arms around his waist. I wish I would have held him like this before. I wish we would have stolen so many more moments together. He was so thin now and I wondered if he would ever be able to regain his muscular form that he once had. I let myself feel his body against mine and at that moment his stomach made a terrible gurgling sound.

"Sorry. I haven't eaten since the last time you were here," he laughed.

My heart twisted again and I stepped away from him. "That was so long ago. You haven't had anything since then?" Without a second thought, I had food, water, healing balms, and anything else I thought might be helpful. I fed him and helped him drink until he said he couldn't consume anything else. I looked at what I had brought and realized he hadn't eaten as much as I had hoped.

"You really did a number on your shoulder. The bruising is going to take a while to go away." His clothes were in tatters at this point. Exposing more of his blood crusted flesh than what it covered.

"It was worth it. It might end up dislocating again by the time I get that chain out of the wall. I started working on the other side. It's a lot looser but still hurts everytime I yank on it. Eventually I will break free of these chains and all those that attacked you will pay. I think they know it and that's why they are trying to keep me as weak as possible. Little do they realize that my zonlicht is my saving grace, coming to me, feeding me, healing me, and warming me." His laughed was rough but sounded better than the first time I had heard it.

I looked at the wall and the chains wishing that there was something I could do even though part of me knew it was pointless. The next time I dreamt, he would be here all the same. So instead

I focused on the things I couldn't change, I focused on making him as comfortable as possible, feeding him, and taking care of him the best that I could while we talked. I told him everything that had happened recently and our plans. I told him how my father had stopped advancing and it had me on edge. I didn't know what had caused my father to stop moving his troops but I knew he wasn't done. He wouldn't be satisfied until everwhere was his. Even Zeke's and Brutus's lands were in danger. I finally told him that Brutus believed I was a goddess and for a moment I thought I saw something like recognition flash in his eyes. When I ran out of things to tell him, I let the comfortable silence fill the air around us.

He watched me the whole time making small comments here and there but mostly he just seemed to be taking it all in like he was just savoring each and every moment we shared.

When he said, "You are so brilliant. I can't believe that some how fate brought me to this realm and I met you. I know you will save everyone. I have faith in you even when you feel like all is lost, I am here and I believe in you." I let out a sigh and stepped up close to him again. My hand shook as I reached up and traced his jaw line. He had lost so much weight but he still looked so handsome. His eyes closed at my touch and before I could stop myself, because this was just fucked up, I stretched up on my toes and kissed him. It was soft at first and I swear his breathing stopped. I pulled back so our lips were just a whisper to each other. Trailing my fingers from his jaw into his hair, I carefully placed my other hand on his chest and felt his heart racing. I thought about how he pushed me up against the wall and kissed me that day. My heart had beat just as hard. Then all I could think about was kissing him again. I brought my lips up against his and began kissing him with more passion than before. A deep moan escaped him and then he finally began kissing me back. Somehow even though his arms were in chains, he managed to take over. He devoured me and I allowed it, loving every second. It was as if all the built up emotions had risen to the surface and were consuming both of us.

I knew I was fucked up to be dreaming about making out with him. Not only was he gone and this was a dream but he had been tortured and beaten. He was chained up to a wall and here I was wanting to do so much more than just kiss him.

I don't know how much time had passed when he pulled away. It could have been hours or seconds. He stared into me with those emerald eyes that I loved so much but this time flecks of peridot shone through. It had been so long since I saw them that I almost started crying. I forgot how beautiful his eyes were when they were changing.

"You don't know how long I've wanted to do that," I whispered.

"Kiss me again," he demanded. His voice was rough and I couldn't help but comply.

"Helvig," I whispered against his lips. He was straining against the chains. I watched the muscles on his arms ripple and I couldn't help but wonder what that would feel like if he were healthy and on top of me. "Can I touch you?"

He made a slight choking sound and then rumbled out. "You can do whatever you want to me. I am yours."

I felt hot. So fucking hot. My body was an inferno ready to explode. I kissed his lips softly and then slowly made my way down his neck speaking between kisses. "Tell me what you need. If I could get you free, I would. If I could bring you back to me, I would. Tell me what to do right now because I'm lost without you."

I pulled my body up against his and pressed myself into him. His skin was cool underneath my touch. He felt shaky and weak and part of me felt guilty for even touching him. I started to pull back from him but his words stopped me.

"Don't. Please don't go. Just sit with me for a while. You don't have to touch me or do anything you don't want to. You don't have to do anything at all. You are perfect the way you are. Please just stay."

Hot tears pricked my eyes. Of course I would sit with him. Oh my gods. Fuck me. He's been standing and straining this whole time. I was such an idiot.

Helvig made a grunting noise as the chair appeared beneath him forcing him to sit and pull on his chains.

"I'm so sorry. I should have gotten you a chair sooner."

He let out a small chuckle and laid his head against the cushioned back. "Now this is luxury. I can't thank you enough for everything you have done for me but I need you to come here and sit. I might not be able to hold you just yet but I will. I promise one day, I will hold you and shelter you from everyone else in all the realms. Those that have hurt you will regret breathing."

"I don't want to hurt you though." Gods did I want to sit with him though. He looked so weak and exhausted but I just wanted to hold him.

"You aren't going to hurt me. Please don't make me beg because I will most definitely beg you. If I could get on my hands and knees, I would."

I gingerly-ed crawled onto his lap making sure I didn't put too much weight on any part of him. There was enough room in the chair for me to straddle him comfortably. Sliding my arms behind his back, I pulled myself up against him. It felt good to hold him and apparently he liked to be held. The sigh he released made me feel things I had never felt before and part of me that felt like something slid in place.

I placed my head against his chest and listened to his heart beat.

I felt him kiss the top of my head and then nuzzle me softly. We sat like this for a long time and I might have even dozed off once or twice which was strange since it was all a dream anyways.

"I wish you were real. I wish this was real." I whispered when I thought he was finally asleep.

"My Zonlicht," he whispered back. "I..."

The pale morning light shining through my bedroom window was blinding me.

"Did you hear me? You gotta get ready. It's going to be time to leave soon." Zander was standing next to my bed shaking my shoulder.

"I heard you. Just give me a couple minutes," I groaned. I felt like I hadn't slept at all. That was how it always felt when I dreamt of him though. I knew I should probably tell someone about the dreams tormenting me but I couldn't bring myself to do it. It felt like a violation of mine and Helvig's privacy. I knew that reasoning was so fucked up because he was dead and it was just a dream. What was even more fucked up was making out with him while he was chained up. My subconscious was seriously so fucked.

The things he said to me soothed part of me and I couldn't tell if I was having these dreams to make myself feel better or if I was only tormenting myself further. Either way, my guilt only grew. I just had to remind myself that he wasn't real and I was probably going crazy.

Chapter Twenty

⸎

One more day. It would take one more day until we reached my fathers country estate. We had already been on the road for five days and I was exhausted. I hadn't slept at all and it was starting to take a toll on me. Brutus brought a carriage along for us to ride in but I didn't like the idea of being in such a closed off space where I couldn't see our surroundings. We were heading into my fathers kingdom and I wanted to be completely aware of our surroundings. I tried to use my magic to just move us there but I wasn't able to do it with all of us. Plus, we then wouldn't have horses if we needed to make a quick escape and I was drained. So riding was our only option.

Brutus tried reassuring me that with our power combined no one would be able to attack us. I had asked him what kind of power exactly he was able to wield. I knew he took Zeke's thunderbird but he had acted like that was a surprise to him. However, he just avoided answering my questions. I saw him manipulate the fire and make things appear out of thin air, which was similar to what I could do. So I asked him about that. He laughed and said it wasn't the same but still wouldn't answer anything. My frustration with him was growing more and more each day. How was I supposed to get better if he wouldn't answer anything or willingly give me information?

Of course, Brutus had a plethora of guards surrounding us but that still didn't make me feel safe. Zander was to stay by my side and Quinlan would stay with Brutus at all times, since Quinlan and I could communicate over long distances. Quinlan and Brutus rode in the carriage while Zander and I rode on horseback behind the carriage. It was more than fine with me since the longer I looked at Brutus the more I wanted to shave off the rest of his stupid hair.

My father had orchestrated my kidnapping and it was because of him that Helvig was killed. I hadn't been powerful enough to save him and because of my weakness he was most likely tortured and then murdered. I could still hear the sound of his flesh in my mind and gods did it break me each and every time. Lately, though, the pain seemed to ebb and rage was slowly replacing it. I would get revenge for what had happened. It might seem petty to some but it mattered to me even after all this time.

Zander stiffened behind me, "There's a rider approaching from up ahead."

"HAULT!" the lead guard shouted. After a few moments, Brutus exited the carriage with Quinlan behind him. The lead guard approached and spoke softly to Brutus giving Quinlan nervous glances.

Apparently the rider is the same messenger that Brutus sent ahead of us to inform King Rovini of our arrival.

Okay. Why does everyone seem upset?

The rider delivered Brutus's message and left immediately. He was quickly tracked down and given a message for Brutus. King Rovini stated that we are not welcome at his country estate and he will return to Brutus's castle in two weeks to discuss everything.

It had to be because he is recharging the spell or whatever it is that he is using to block the magic. He doesn't want us to discover what he is doing.

What I don't understand is how some are able to access their powers like you and Brutus but then other fae are unable to access any of the magic that should be in their bloodline. If he was blocking it wouldn't it be blocked for everyone?

That's a good question. Maybe it's because Brutus and I are direct descendants of Gods and Goddesses? Also, I was never able to move people or myself from one place to another and now more recently I am. So I think that must be because whatever he has done is weakening. If we could stop him completely, everyone would be able to access their magic.

I watched as Brutus spoke with his guard and then walked over to the rider. He pulled something out of the pocket of his cloak and blew it into the rider's face. Purple smoke surrounded the rider for a few moments before Brutus waved his hand causing it to disperse. He then whispered into the rider's ear and then gave him a new horse. I watched dumbfounded as Brutus continued speaking to the rider as he walked him to the back of our caravan and helped him onto his new horse. The rider nodded once and then Brutus slapped the rear of the horse and they took off.

I moved our horse towards Brutus but before I could speak he started laughing. "You should really see your face right now. I used a powder that will make the rider forget the last hour. He will not remember approaching us, talking with us, or leaving us. He will continue riding thinking that he should cross paths with us on this route. Eventually he will end up back at the castle. We will continue on to your father's estate and tell him that we didn't see the rider."

A powder that could make him forget the last hour of his life... gods. That was kind of scary. "How do you know about that powder and what were the words you whispered to him?" Brutus sighed and tried to hold back a slight grin. "Does it bother you that you truly don't know what I am capable of?" I thought for a moment before I replied. "Honestly, no. It doesn't. I'm just curious. If we are cousins like your father thought, then maybe I have some of the same capabilities that you do."

Brutus shook his head, "No. Our fathers were brothers–yes. However, they had very different magic."

My heart beat sped up. "Can you tell me about my father?"

Brutus gave me a sad smile. "Unfortunately, I don't know much about him. I never had the pleasure of meeting him and at the time I never thought I needed to know anymore about him. All I know is the few things my father told me; he admitted that at times he had been jealous of your fathers capabilities. Apparently your father could create land anywhere, even in the farthest blank void of space your father could create planets. Other gods would request his help when building the realms that they desired. He could create whatever kind of worlds and landscapes they wished. He could pull continents out of oceans and create worlds where emptiness lay before. Yet, it never went to your fathers head that other gods needed him. He was humble and kind. The kind of guy that someone could go to for help and he wouldn't say I told you so or belittle them. From my understanding he

240

wasn't just a good God but also a good man."

My heart swelled hearing these kind words about my father. I wondered what he would think of me now. "What happened to my parents?"

"They went into a deep sleep after creating this realm and apparently creating you. They were probably planning on waking from their sleep and bringing you into this world. Afterall, they did create this realm for you. Well according to my father they created this realm because they wanted some place new and special for their children. Since you are their child that means they create this realm for you. I don't know if they had children prior to creating this realm and I don't know how long they had been together. Technically, this should be your realm and not King Rovini's."

I stayed quiet for a short while as we continued on to my fathers– err King Rovini's estate. My birth parents must have really wanted me. I smiled at the thought of them waking up and meeting me but then my smile fell when I realized that they missed out on me as a baby and a child. They would be meeting a full grown woman and they had missed out on everything that made me who I am today. "What's wrong?" Brutus had been watching the emotions change and dance across my face.

"It's nothing. Do you know where they would have gone to sleep?" Maybe, after all of this was over, I could go and see them. I could sit and tell them about my life and everything and when they wake, it would be as if they knew me. I didn't know if they could hear in their sleep but I could hope.

"I don't. That would be a great question for King Rovini though. I would assume that your parents slept in the same place that you were found." Brutus stared off into the distance and my gaze followed him. There was nothing but trees ahead of us.

Zander shifted and leaned close to me. "I will help you find your parents. Once we figure all of this out, I will be able to shift for longer periods of time and you can ride on my back. We won't have to worry about being shot at or killed for me using my dragon form. We could cover great distances quickly." He looked as if he was picturing flying in his shifted form. I briefly wondered what it would feel like to ride a dragon high in the sky.

"I think I would like that. Quin can be in his Phoenix form and we could spend the time searching and exploring the world that my parents created." One day I would be able to hug my mother and I wanted that almost more than anything.

"The estate isn't too far from here. We should be able to see it after we crest over the next ridge," I said as we started climbing the small mountain. After traveling for days a small rush of anticipation ran through me as I felt a pull towards where I knew my father was. Zander glanced over at me but didn't ask any questions. I needed to figure out how to mind speak with him like I could with Quinlan but it was as if I kept running into a brick wall. I either needed to figure out a way through or around that wall or Zander needed to figure out how to let me in. I was confident that once we made the connection we would be able to keep it open like Quinlan and I did.

Brutus says he feels something up ahead. He thinks your father is working on suppressing the magic again. Quinlans words whispered through my mind making me wonder if it was because of whatever my father was doing.

I can't say that I disagree with him. I've felt a pull towards my father for a little while now. It's like he is calling to me.

I don't like that. Have you felt that before?

I thought for a moment and realized that I had indeed felt this way before. I felt this way whenever we came here. It had been a much more faint feeling back then or maybe my memories of it had just faded.

Yes. Each time we visited here...

What could that mean? Why would I feel this way? Was it just from him suppressing the magic or was it something more?

Zander's hand rested on my knee for a moment. "My Queen, why are your emotions screaming at me?"

I huffed a small breath and gave home a reassuring smile.

"I feel a pull towards my father or a pull towards whatever it is that he's doing here. Stop calling me your queen. I am not your queen and you are not duty bound to me. I am just Cordelia to you and you are just Zander to me."

Zander frowned and then turned to look up ahead of us. "I don't like that."

I didn't bother with a response because I didn't think anyone liked that. The closer we got it became like a hum inside my chest telling me to hurry.

We crested the top and the sight before us took my breath away only not in a good way.

There were fae chained and hanging upside down. Their throats were slit and buckets sat under them catching blood. My father walked through the bodies and dipped his fingers into some of the buckets. The blood shimmered in the gleaming sunlight.

Get out of the carriage. Get out and come see this now.

Come see what? Quinlan was asking me as he stepped out

of the carriage. I heard Brutus and his footsteps approaching from behind.

What the fuck. Quinlan thought and asked out loud at the same time.

"Huh. I've always wondered how he did it." Brutus said, breaking my focus on the hanging bodies before us.

"I'm sorry but what?" I turned to look at Brutus.

"You know what is going on here?" Zander's voice sounded surprised. Nothing should surprise us anymore but yet here we are being surprised.

"All of those fae have strong and powerful magic in their bloodlines. I can feel it and I believe your father is using the very essence of their being, their life blood, to perform whatever ritual he does to suppress the magic in the realm. He might even be pulling the power from their blood and just discarding their blood. I doubt it though. It seems like he would be the kind of person into blood magic too." Brutus shrugged like it was just so obvious.

I turned and stared back at the hanging bodies gently swaying in the breeze. A shiver ran down my spine and I couldn't shake the really bad feeling I had.

Chapter Twenty-One

✦

I couldn't look at the fae dangling around me. How many had my father murdered like this over the years? It had to be thousands of fae dead so he could continue to repress the magic here. I felt my stomach twist and my lunch felt like it was going to make a reappearance. Gods. He... he was a monster. He was truly a terrible monster that had to be stopped. I should have worked harder to stop him. I should have figured out a way to kill him. All of these innocent people would have been spared if I would have ended him a long time ago. My brother could be king. He would have been a way better king than my father.

Brutus sent guards ahead of us to announce our arrival. We had waited a short while before heading towards the front door. We had to weave through the hanging bodies to reach the front gate. The closer we got the harder the pull inside me became.

I have a bad feeling about this. Something is wrong. I don't know what but something is seriously wrong. I glanced over my shoulder at Quin and he just nodded his head at me. Did that mean he also felt like there was something seriously wrong? I mean obviously something was wrong. This place was filled with dead bodies but besides that there was something else happening.

Out of nowhere I felt the tingle of my magic. "Uh guys. Something is happening. I feel like…" just then Zander reached out and grabbed my arm. The moment his hand touched my skin I felt my magic surge through me. I couldn't breathe suddenly. It was like the inside of me was being ripped apart. Someone was screaming. It was a blood curdling scream that would have sent shivers down my spine if I hadn't been in so much pain.

The front gate flew open and my father stood before us. "WHAT ARE YOU DOING HERE?!"

My head was starting to hurt from the screaming.

Quinlans voice flooded my thoughts. *You have to stop screaming. I can't help you if I don't know what is happening. Stop screaming and talk to me.*

I was the one screaming?

There's so much pain. Quinlan. I feel like I'm being torn apart.

"She needs help! We came here to discuss our agreement and the wedding but someone needs to help her! WHAT THE FUCK ARE YOU DOING THAT COULD DO SOMETHING LIKE THIS TO HER." Brutus was yelling at my father and suddenly I couldn't stay on my feet. Zander wrapped his arms around me just before I fell.

"Take her inside to the top floor. She will be able to recover there. There is a meeting room at the end of that hall. We can meet there in a few hours." My fathers words sounded distant. Everything around me went blurry and I couldn't keep my eyes open any longer.

The first thing I noticed when I opened my eyes was the pain had stopped. The second thing I noticed was the shouting coming from outside my childhood bedroom. I didn't remember anything after the excruciating pain hitting me as we walked through the dead fae.

I felt the steady pulse of Zander's emotions. He was concerned and angry. I could hear shouting outside the door of my room. Was that my father shouting?

I stood and felt weak instantly. How long had I been out of it? When was the last time I ate?

Can you come help me to the door?

I hated having to ask for help but I knew that Quinlan wouldn't judge me for it. He might tease me when everything is said and done but he would never judge me.

Suddenly the door opened and Quinlan was walking in with Zander, Brutus, and my father behind them.

Relief flashed across my fathers face just as Quinlan reached my side.

"Cordelia and Brutus, you need to meet me in the council room just down the hall. I will be waiting. Don't keep me too long. My patience is very thin today after your escapades." With that said, my father turned and walked out of the room. For a moment, I thought he had been relieved that I was okay but he was already back to his assholiness self.

"Both of you can join us, I don't care what he says." I nodded at Zander as Quinlan led us out of the room and down the hall.

Before we could enter, Brutus grabbed my arm, halting me. "Has that ever happened to you before while being here?"

I frowned and thought for a moment. "No. That had never

happened to me before but there were times that I felt tired or weak. I can remember a couple times that I was too weak to leave my bed."

Brutus gave a quick nod mouthing "blood magic" and walked into the room my father was apparently waiting in while the rest of us filed in behind him.

"Now that we are here plus a few extras," he gave me a pointed look. "I gave explicit instructions to your scout erm– messenger– that you sent a head. There is no way that he didn't run into you on your way here. So why did you come? I am busy and do not have time for this."

I started to speak when Brutus spoke over me. "I think we should just cut to the chase here. We have things to discuss regarding the wedding and our arrangements. You leaving unexpectedly was not part of the plan."

King Rovini tensed before speaking. "If you think that is a good enough reason to interrupt me and disregard what I had commanded you to do, then I suggest you start looking for a better reason. If I didn't still need what you are capable of, you would be dead already. You are lucky that SHE isn't dead because of what you pulled. You're lucky that you came when you did and we were able to get her up here before it got worse."

"Dad," I said, the word heavy on my tongue and I couldn't help the shiver that went down my spine because he wasn't my dad. "We know what you are doing here. We know you are trying to suppress all the magic in the realm. I figured out that you did that here and now all my memories of coming here are making more and more sense. Only this time, we will not allow you to suppress our magic. I won't allow it."

My fathers boisterous laugh made me jump. "Is that what

you think I do? That I am so obsessed with everyone's magic so I figured out a way to suppress it? Oh Cordelia, I needed that laugh. You are such a bright girl but you truly have no idea about anything." His shoulders shook and he held his chest as his words tumbled out between laughs.

"I… Is that not what you are doing?" I didn't understand and now I felt stupid. What else could he have been doing here?

"Is that also the same conclusion the rest of you came to?" His eyes danced around the room looking at each and everyone of us. "It is. All of you came up with the same solution? There weren't any other solutions in the running? No one else had a different idea?"

No one spoke as my father looked around the room. His burst of maniacal laughter made me jump and I hated it. I also hated how my father was belittling all of us.

"Well then since we got this all wrong. Tell us what you are actually doing then." Brutus's voice was laced with venom. Apparently he also didn't like how my father was acting.

"To be so young and so naive," he shook his head and relaxed his shoulders, almost slouching into his seat. "It's pretty simple. I'm honestly surprised you haven't figured it out yet. Your father was pretty close to figuring out my plans but then your mother ran off on him." The words were barely choked out. He was laughing so hard and holding his stomach.

Has your father always been looney or is this a new development? Quinlan was thinking the same shit I was. My father had absolutely lost his marbles. Maybe he had a split personality that I didn't know about. Before I could speak up Brutus had stood and slammed his fist on the table.

"DO NOT SPEAK ABOUT MY PARENTS. YOU KNOW

NOTHING ABOUT THEM."

My father's laughter died off and he straightened in his seat. He glanced down and adjusted his shirt and then his crown. "Oh, dear Brutus. I'm afraid you are the one that knows nothing. I could tell you so many things about your mother that even your father didn't know. Did Hypnos ever tell you about my father? No. I didn't think so. He probably didn't think I was important enough to tell you about. You see, your father knew exactly what my father had done to me. He HELPED my father deceive me. It's why I had to finally take my revenge when your father was getting too close to discovering what I was doing." I had no idea what my father was talking about and by the looks on everyone else's faces they didn't either. The air in the room felt suffocating and everyone was in fight or flight mode.

"What did you do?" Brutus bit out with barely restrained violence.

"Oh calm down. You are just as hot headed as he was. It made it so much easier to get to your mother. I just had to wait until she needed a bit of space from him. She snuck out alone and enjoyed spending time laying on the hill near your lake. That is where I happened to run across your mother. She was kind and sweet. I had no idea what she saw in your father and I actually felt bad for what I was about to do to her." My father stood and glanced around the room. "Do they know what you did to Ezekiel Havaror?" We seemed to all nod at the same time assuming he was talking about Zeke's thunderbird.

"Good. Less explaining then. Your father could do the same thing. He could also repair souls that he had torn apart. Have you figured out how to do that?"

"No," Brutus gritted out. "What are you getting at? What did you do to my mother?"

Brutus is going to kill him before we get any real answers. King Rovini is going to tell Brutus something terrible about his mother and then Brutus is going to kill him. Then we will never know what your father has been doing here. He's distracting us and purposefully deflecting.

I reached over and placed a hand on Brutus's knee. I gave him a firm squeeze and left my hand there. We were united in this even though part of me still loved my father even though he had taken me from my parents, I felt the familial bond with Brutus. Our fathers were brothers. We were cousins and maybe if things had been different we could have grown up together.

"In due time, Cordelia, I'm sorry if this changes things between us but it's time you knew the role that you are playing in all of this." Our eyes locked on each other and for the first time in a long while, I saw that same hate in my father's eyes that he had when I was just a child. Brutus reached down and placed his hand over mine. We were in this together. Whatever this was, I had Brutus and he had me.

"I would have left your parents alone if Hypnos hadn't still been working with my father. He was keeping tabs on me and had discovered just how close I was to locating something that my father took from me. It never truly belonged to him in the first and yet he still took away my chance of having it. I knew I had to take Hypnos' eyes off of me. I needed to switch his focus from me to something else. Your mother just happened to be the perfect target. Your father had been so in love with her he didn't see her as the weakness she was to him. I had been working for years to figure out how your father could rip souls apart. Once I thought I had it perfected, I did it to myself. Of course, I didn't have quite enough power in me to do it correctly so I had been gravely injured. I almost killed myself actually." His eyes looked distant as he remembered that day and his light chuckle sent shivers down my spine.

"What did you do, Rovini? What you were trying to duplicate could go wrong in so many ways. What did you do?" I whipped my head toward Brutus. I could sense the hint of fear coming from him. I hadn't ever been able to feel Brutus's emotions but now they were almost palpable. It was like he was forcing them down my throat.

"Come." My father raised his hand and motioned to the door.

Ragnor came swaggering in with a grin across his face. I froze. Ragnor was supposed to be at Daemonger's castle. He walked over and stood next to my fathers chair.

"You see, I tore my soul apart. I had duplicated myself and almost killed myself in the process. Luckily for me, my duplicate was strong and was able to heal me and keep me alive. Then I glamoured him. He is me and I am him but we are also separate. Everything about us is genetically the same but we are two different people. Let's remove the glamor, shall we?" King Rovini's grin was wide as he stood and motioned hand over Ragnor.

Before my eyes, Ragnor began to change. He looked exactly like my father.

"You created your own clone? A twin of sorts?" Zander breathed out. I didn't know if I should be afraid or if I should be amazed.

"What did you do to my mother?" Brutus didn't even flinch at the two identical men now standing before us. He probably knew what my father did before he showed us. After all this was his specialty.

"After I had created Ragnor, I discovered that although we are the same he is his own person. With his own conscience and personality. He didn't share my memories either. So what better way to get revenge on Hypnos than to rip apart his beloved's soul and that is exactly what I did the day I found your mother laying on the hill. I tore apart her soul and created a woman that looked exactly like your mother but was not your mother. I took her with me out of your kingdom and left her in a village. It just so happened that King Havaror happened upon her and fell in love. As for your mother, well I sent her to be in the realm of the gods."

Everyone stared at Brutus waiting for him to react to do something but he just sat there.

"So what is it that you're doing here?" Brutus growled. Okay. So I might have thought he was going to do something crazy and his response was a little anticlimactic.

"My father took something from me and I simply want it back."

"Yes, we all know he took your magic and all of your power." I snapped, unable to hold in my frustration any longer. I felt overwhelmingly frustrated by everything suddenly. It was like someone else's emotions were fueling my own. I was frustrated that my father killed all those fae not to mention that we still didn't know why. I was frustrated at this game he was playing and that I truly never really knew my father. He had all these secrets that I was never aware of. I knew myself well enough to know that I was frustrated because I felt helpless and useless. Slicing pain soared through my chest. The last time I felt this helpless was when Helvig was taken from me, but I couldn't think about that now. I had to focus. There was no room for self pity. Not here. Not now. Not ever. I had to move past this.

"So close my dearest. He did not take all of my power as you put it nor did he take all of my magic. I decided that this realm would be mine shortly after I realized I was stuck here. My father might have taken most of my power from me but he wouldn't be able to take this realm. That was created with MY magic. I sent him back to the realm of the gods. Buying myself time before he came back after me which I'm sure he is going to after what I did to him. He would be furious with what I did to him and his favorite child. Unfortunately for him, he created a barrier so that I wouldn't be able to go back and no one could come here. No Gods or Goddesses can cross the barrier. My father thought he was teaching me a lesson by stealing my power from me but really he just taught me how to be resourceful. Turns out the little bit of power he left for me has come in handy. I can drain the blood from fae with powerful bloodlines and siphon the power from their blood to fill my reserves. Of course, it doesn't come close to the power that I deserve but I'll get that soon enough with Brutus's help of course." A chill swept through the room.

"You drain them and take the magic that is in their blood for yourself? Just for you to simply have?" The wide grin on my father's face was an answer enough to Brutus' question.

"Do you know where your magic is?" I asked quietly. My voice was hardly above a whisper but the room was so quiet it sounded like I had shouted.

This is bad. This is bad. This is bad. Quinlan wasn't meaning to project his thoughts but he was starting to panic. I could feel Zander's unease through our bond and all I was getting from Brutus was anger.

"Of course. I do. Most of it in this room right here or at least it will be soon." King Rovini's smile was wicked. How could it be in this room? Did he get to that temple without us knowing?

Brutus stood up and stretched his arms. He walked towards the edge of the room where the floor to ceiling windows stood. "Why do you need me and what do you want me to do?"

"I thought I made it pretty obvious. I am unable to fuse things back together. I will need you to give me back my magic. In return I give you Cordelia." My fathers eyes never left mine as he spoke to Brutus.

"Even if you found your magic and it's supposedly here in this room, I can't fuse your magic back into you. First off, trying to merge your power back into your body is like ripping apart and putting back together souls. Magic is tangible like souls as far as I know. I don't know how your father was able to pull it out of you but I would have no idea how to put it back in. Secondly, why would I want to give you more power? You're already taking over this realm without it and annoying the shit out of everyone else. Why do you need more than you currently have?"

My father slammed his fists down on the table causing everyone to jump. "BECAUSE IT'S MINE!"

Chapter Twenay-Two

The room was silent after my fathers outburst. No one dared move or speak. I could see the facade my father had been wearing was cracking. He was close to the edge and unpredictable.

Thump. Thump.

I glanced towards where the sound had come from.

Thump.

What is that sound? I asked Quinlan without looking at him.

I'm not sure.

Ragnor began laughing and turned to my father. It was still odd seeing them together. Looking at Ragnor and seeing him as my father's twin and not the image of the man I had come to know him as. Though there was subtail difference, Ragnor had pure malice in his eyes. Most people might not be able to notice the difference but it was there in their eyes. Ragnor's looked almost empty whereas my father's held life.

"The new fae must have arrived," Rangor chuckled as he walked towards the windows that faced the back of the property.

"The new fae?" I choked out. Oh gods. They were bringing more here to be slaughtered. I stood rushing towards the window.

Guards were carrying unconscious fae and dropping them in a row by the back garden. Other guards were constructing the equipment they used to string the fae upside.

"What did you do to them? Are they still alive?" I could feel the panic floating up into my chest. I looked at Brutus wondering where our guards went. They could help us stop them.

"Of course they're alive," Ragnor's words came out condescendingly. "We need their blood to be fresh. That is when the magic it wields is the strongest."

"Stop this. Stop it right now. You can't do this. I won't let you." I turned towards my father and fisted my hands at my sides. At my words Zander and Quinlan came to stand behind me.

"You won't let me?" My fathers laugh was dark. "You can't stop me, Cordelia. You are weak and untrained. You have little to no control over your own magic. Sit down and shut up."

Suddenly, my body was jerked against my will and I slammed back into my seat. I couldn't move. There was nothing physically restraining me yet I couldn't even turn my head to look at my men. My breath started coming too quickly. I had to stop him. He couldn't continue to kill innocent fae. The more I struggled against the hold on me the more frustrated and desperate I became.

"What are you doing to her?" Zanders' words sounded distant. I could faintly hear Quinlan but I couldn't make out what he was trying to say to me. The panic was starting to overcome me again and I felt like I couldn't breathe.

Cordelia. I can't move either. I don't know what is happening but I believe your father has more power than we realized. Cordelia. Breathe. Breathe. You have to breathe and calm down. We will figure something out. Just calm down before you pass out again. You are so strong. You have this. Quinlans words reminded me other everything Helvig had been saying to me in my dreams and suddenly everything seemed not so bad. I could breathe a little easier.

Brutus' voice was too loud inside my head. I couldn't hear what was happening around me.

Focus on me. Look at me. Open your eyes and look at me.

I opened my eyes and they immediately locked on with Brutus.

Just focus on me. I won't let anything bad happen to you. I promise. Try to take a breath and hold it.

I focused on his words and shoved the bone deep panic away. I had to be strong. For some gods damned reason these men looked towards me and Helvig would expect me to be strong claiming that he knew I could do it or some shit.

I let the warm feeling of my magic deep inside me calm me. The power was humming just waiting for me to tap into it. It took one quick thought and then we were all standing outside next to the unconscious fae. My father and Ragnor stumbled into each other but my men didn't falter.

"I am not weak," I smiled at them as I waved my hands towards the unconscious fae. They vanished before our eyes. Vilulf and Draug were going to have quite the surprise. Sorry not sorry.

"You will not kill any more fae. You, father dearest, are no longer in charge." My smile widened.

"THAT MAGIC AND POWER BELONG TO ME! I TOLD YOU NOT TO USE MAGIC. DO YOU KNOW WHAT YOU HAVE DONE STUPID GIRL." My fathers screaming words pulled the guards out of the shocked stupor they were in. I glanced towards Brutus who looked just as confused as I did.

Ragnor was whispering to my father. "What do you mean my magic belongs to you?" I asked tentatively.

Ragnor turned and walked towards me. "It seems we have much to discuss. I thought the punishment you received for disobeying orders had taken care of this little problem. Apparently you are more stubborn than I had realized." At the mention of the punishment I had received over the years, the scars on my back began to ache. I knew it wasn't real pain and it was in my head but it still caused panic to rise inside me once again make me freeze in place.

"Do your men know about how truly pathetic you are?" Ragnor raised his hand and gestured towards me. Suddenly, my clothes disappeared and I stood before everyone naked. I moved to cover my breasts just as a force whipped me around exposing my back and scars for everyone to see.

Do not cower. You are beautiful inside and out. Your scars are beautiful. Wear them proudly. I will kill them for what they have done to you but you do not cower. You do not bow to anyone, not even me.

That voice inside my head couldn't be real. Tears pricked my eyes. Not because I was on full display for everyone to see but because of his voice. I closed my eyes and opened them slowly. I dropped my arms from hiding my breasts and moved my hair over my shoulders as I straightened. I revealed my scars and in all their glory for all the men and guards around me to see.

Finding strength that I didn't think I had, I said, "Here they are Ragnor. I know how much you enjoyed looking at them. I also know how much you enjoyed it when I received them." I glanced over my shoulder to look at him. It was all a game. Who could get into who's head. Who could break the other person without faltering.

"You did that to her?" Zander's words were just above a growl. He was vibrating and I could feel the anger rolling off him in waves. Quinlan was stuck in a half stepping position. His foot frozen in the air. I knew now that Ragnor was the one that had restrained us earlier. I slowly turned and stepped towards Ragnor. Risking a glance at my father I saw his eyes filled with hatred. Not shame or embarrassment for his daughter being naked in front of all these men but hatred for who I was. I looked at Brutus and something akin to shock and pride flickered through his eyes. I turned, seeing all the guards gawking at me. Our guards had been coming around the house, from where I had no idea, but at the sight of my naked body they stopped.

"Yes. Princess Cordelia Rovini is covered in scars. Take in your fill boys." At my words, the rage Zander was emitted sky rocketed.

"DO NOT LOOK AT HER. CAST YOUR EYES TO THE GROUND BEFORE I REMOVE THEM FROM YOUR HEAD," Brutus shouted. Shadows began to swirl and gather around him. One guard chuckled and said, "Like he's in any position to do such a thing."

A shadowing black tentacle whipped out from Brutus and snaked its way through the guards. The man let out a scream as the tentacle changed shape and plucked his eyes out of his head. The guards around him not only dropped their eyes to the ground but also fell to their knees and bowed their heads. Not one of them was risking that happening to himself. Interesting that Brutus could still manipulate his shadows even though his physical body was held in place.

"Now I believe it's time that we sit down and have a proper discussion. Not one full of half truths and riddles." I approached Zander and slid my hand across his arm. "First, you will release my men and then we can head inside to the kitchen and get something to eat. There you will tell me exactly what the fuck is going on and answer all the questions that I have. Otherwise, I might just do something you won't like." I winked at my father as I slid Zander's cloak off of his shoulders. I knew his anger was not only coming from his own emotions but from Zantos as well. I could feel the fury rolling off him and I knew if I was still exposed when he was freed, he would immediately shift and begin burning everything to the ground. I pulled his cloak around me and whispered to him, "I'm okay. I promise."

I turned and walked towards the house with my head held high. I do not bow for anyone.

I cast a glance over my shoulder as I stepped through the door. The smirk across Ragnor's face sent chills down my spine. Before I could look away from him, I was falling.

Everything around me was pitch black as I fell. My hair whipped around my face and my arms pinwheeled. It felt like I had walked off the top of a castle and was free falling through the air.

I landed with such force the air whooshed from my lungs. My arm was throbbing from being the sole object that kept my head from bashing into the ground. I slowly peeled myself up and stood on shaky legs.

What. the. Fuck.

I was standing in the forest near my fathers castle. More specifically I was standing in my clearing near the river. I spun in a slow circle not understanding what had happened. Did I bring myself here? No. I couldn't have. Could I? I hadn't thought about it and I had never fallen like that before.

Before I could finish my complete 360 a throat cleared.

"I don't have very long. Time is slowed down to practically a standstill for everyone else while you and I have a little chat." The tone of Ragnor's voice made my stomach turn.

"How?" My voice cracked, betraying me and all my emotions. I was afraid in this moment alone with him and now he knew.

"Your father may not have very much magic but that is his own fault. I, on the other hand, have plenty of powerful magic. I decided to bring you to your favorite spot. After all, you did spend many nights sneaking out to come here." He winked at me as he raised his arms and walked around the clearing. I hadn't known he was aware of my nightly escapades, but now it made me wonder just how much he knew from over the years. "You see, Cordelia, you and I have a goal in common. You and I both want to stop your father from blocking the gods out. Our reasons may differ but we want the same thing nonetheless. You will help me achieve that."

"If you're so powerful then why can't you stop him on your own?" I wasn't stupid. Out of my father and Ragnor, I trusted Ragnor the least. He was far more vindictive and manipulative or at least I thought. He was violent and always scheming and at least I knew there was some part of my father that had a soft spot for me. "Ahh. I would have many many years ago. Before we had even found you and discovered that you hold part of his magic inside of you. Alas, when I was created, your father ensured I could never go against him. I am physically unable to use any magic against him without hurting myself."

I looked around the clearing taking it all in. Some of my most precious memories were here. Such as when Helvig and I swam in the river together. I turned and stared into the river. A sharp pang of longing sliced through me. I listened to Ragnor as I stared into the water.

"Mmhmm." I hummed pretending to not care about what he was saying. I turned around looking at my clearing. Something was pulling at me telling me that this wasn't real. The red flags were waving and I was trying them. The woods were farther away than I remembered and the river didn't sound quite right.

"You have always had such potential, darling. I'm sure by now you've figured out that Brutus is your part of the family and your father isn't quite the family you thought he was." He raised an eyebrow at me expecting a reaction. I didn't give him one. "Your lack of reaction confirms it. If you and I come together, we could take down your father once and for all. We both deserve to be in the realm of the gods. You know there's a part of you that longs to go see it. We will never be able to do that as long as your father continues. We must stop him and I believe the best way for us to do that is together." Ragnor had moved closer to me. I wasn't sure when he had done that but suddenly we were just an arms length away. This was a world he had created in my mind after all so he had complete control.

"Say I agree with you. Then what? How exactly do you

plan for us to stop him?" I took a step to the side and walked towards the river. I could feel Ragnor at my back. His breath was on the top of my head as his arms wrapped around me. I felt my whole body stiffen. I couldn't move. Was he going to hurt me again? Would I be able to stop him? I didn't like him touching me and holding me like this. I reached for my magic but couldn't feel it. Oh Gods. This was wrong. This was all wrong. The water wasn't the right color. The sounds were wrong. The woods were wrong for this time of year. The leaves on the trees weren't the right shade and my magic felt buried so deep within me that I couldn't touch it.

"Don't panic now my beautiful girl. I can feel you reaching for your magic. Don't worry. I won't hurt you ever again. I had to do those things in the past because of your father. He demanded it of me but I never wanted to do it. I have always loved you and I never wanted to hurt you. I truly am so sorry, Cordelia. I hope one day I can make it up to you." I felt the lightest brush of his lips next to my ear and I instantly recoiled. I was not his to touch like this.

"Don't touch me," I broke free of the hold he had on me but something was telling me that he let me break free. "I don't believe you and I don't trust you. If you have had all of this magic this whole time then you wouldn't have ever needed to do as my father said. I saw it in your eyes everytime you hurt me or punished me. Even now outside in front of all those men, that was all you and you enjoyed it." I dug deep down for my magic again. This time it was as if I had just barely brushed it.

"This is all far more complicated than you know. I didn't always have magic. It didn't start out this way. Cordelia, please just listen. Gods be damned. I forgot just how obstinate you could be. If you and I don't work together then your father will come after you. You have his magic within you. That is why he forbade you to ever use your power. You have had both yours and his that he is owed dwelling inside of you and every time you tap into it, you are combining and mixing them according to him. Eventually, they will be melded into one unit, if they haven't already, and when he takes his magic, he will strip you of yours as well. It will make him even more powerful than before his father took it from him in the first place. I don't even want to think what will happen to you if he does that. He barely survived what his father did to him. I don't know if you would survive him doing something similar to you." Ragnor had the audacity to look upset by all of this. I took a step back from him shaking my head.

"I will never allow him to take anything from me, not even his magic if it is actually inside of me." I'm not sure when I realized it but I came to the conclusion that we were not in my clearing. This was all an illusion that Ragnor had created. His magic was much more powerful than mine and that made me very weary. I dug deep down and lunged for my magic.

"If he finds the correct temple and gets a hold of..." I finally reached my magic and used as much power as I could to break the hold he had on me. I felt like my body was flying backwards into the sky as everything turned pitch black. Suddenly, it was as if I was slamming into my own body. I fell into the doorway of the house and instantly started puking. By the time I finished, Zander had reached me.

"We are done here," I said with a quick thought. I gave one look to my father knowing what I had to do. In an instant, I had transported our whole party back to Daemonger castle. At the same time, I sent my father to the furthest part of his kingdom. It was at least a two week journey on horseback from there to his country estate. However, he didn't have any supplies. It would take him a few days to make it to the nearest village first. Then he would have to make his way back taking at least two weeks considering he was a king and inexperienced at practically everything normal including riding a horse. Hopefully that would buy us some time to figure some shit out.

I reached out to Vilulf and told him to find Alba and Draug and meet us in the throne room. Quinlan and Zander were asking me a million questions but I couldn't focus on anything they were saying. My mind was reeling. What had Ragnor been trying to do? Why was he trying to touch me like that and did he actually kiss my head? A cold shiver crawled up my spine. That was disgusting and now when I thought about his words and saying he wanted us to work together... what did he really mean by that? He brought up that Brutus and I were related and then talked about him and I working together. Did he want to be with me? Oh Gods, he was repulsive. Aside from the fact that he was the twin of the man that raised me and that he did terrible things to me. He had abused me more than once. I felt my stomach turn over and I thought I was going to start puking again.

Once we reached the throne room, I flung myself into the beautiful and comfy throne that Brutus had made for me. Well I had requested it be made but Brutus had allowed it. I needed to sit for a while or else I was going to pass out and that was not what we needed. Vilulf came bursting into the throne room. A moment later Alba came in with Draug behind them.

"So I'm hoping this meeting is to discuss the sleeping

fae that randomly appeared in the courtyard?" Vilulf said questioningly. One eye brow was raised and his arms were crossed. Draug came to stand next to him and for a moment I thought they seemed to be standing abnormally close. Draug normally kept his distance with everyone except me on occasions but with Vilulf they were a hair's breadth away..

His words caught my attention and I realized that I was a terrible person. I was so caught up in everything else that happened, I had completely forgotten about all those innocent fae we had rescued or rather that I had sent here while they were unconscious.

"I am going to defer to Brutus in regards to the fae," I said with a sheepish smile totally pawning off the problem that I caused onto him and he knew it. Brutus shook his head but I caught the small grin on his face before he turned away to speak to a servant. "I have much to tell you about our visit."

We all took turns filling Vilulf, Draug, and Alba on everything that took place while we were away.

I had filled everyone in on the conversation that took place in the illusion. To Zander, Quinlan, and Brutus it had looked like I simply stumbled and then decided to leave. They had no idea that Ragnor had frozen time and captured my mind which scared me more than I would like to admit. At anytime, he could do that to me and no one would know.

"Well that is not good. He is using extremely old and powerful magic. It is not common that someone can even enter minds let alone force illusions. We need to all start practicing closing our minds and keeping him out. We obviously don't know the full extent of his capabilities and we cannot risk being vulnerable to him." Brutus had begun pacing but stopped to look at each of us before continuing.

"I think we need to bring King Havaror here. I know he had a melt down before but he needs to be aware of these developments and we need to figure out what we are going to do about your father."

While I didn't disagree with Brutus about bringing Zeke here, I just wasn't quite ready to deal with him yet. We would also be able to reunite him with his thunderbird. Even if Brutus didn't know how to put the two back together, at least Zeke could see his thunderbird.

"There is something else that you all should know. I received word that your father's men have been sweeping through villages and leaving no one behind. They are either immediately killing them or they are taking them captive and having them work in their camps. It's the first time in years that they have started doing this. Back when your father first decided to take over the very first neighboring kingdom he left utter destruction. It seems he is reverting back to that." Brutus's words left a chill on my flesh. We hadn't been gone for that long, yet this short amount of time seemed to have changed so much.

"I do agree that Zeke needs to be involved in this but I don't think we should bring him here just yet. If you aren't able to fuse his thunderbird back into him, I don't know what kind of impact it will have on him to know that his thunderbird is this close to him yet so far away. We do have some more time before my father makes it back to his country estate. I think I have a plan though, we will confront my father's troops, camp by camp starting with the smallest. I will speak and give them the option to either join us in stopping my fathers reign of terror or die. If they choose to join us they will be forgiven of any trespasses against the realm seeing as they were forced by my father. If they choose to fight, then they will die. Hopefully, by starting with the smallest camp, we will have the least amount of casualties. We will send one of his men to the next camp to prepare them for our arrival. Hopefully, they will not fight us and they will make this easy. Once my father doesn't have an army behind him, we will see just how powerful he thinks he is. I will take Vilulf with me to talk to Zeke and we will get this settled once and for all." I glanced at Vilulf who didn't look hopeful. "Until then let's take care of the fae we rescued and get some rest. I don't know about all of you but I am looking forward to a hot shower, actual clothes, and my bed," I said standing up and heading towards the door.

"I'll walk with you," Alba said softly. She slipped her arm through mine and we walked down the hall together. After a short while she pulled me to stop. "How are you holding up? Don't tell me you are fine because that was a lot. Seeing all of those dead fae, facing your father, dealing with being stripped down in front of all those men, and that shit with Ragnor. That is," she blew out a breath. "A lot." I hadn't told her about the voice I heard when I was stripped down in front of everyone. I also had told anyone about the way Ragnor treated me. How he touched me and wrapped his arms around me. Nor did I mention the way he had kissed my head. I felt the shame from it all creeping up as I thought about it again.

"It has been a long few months. You're right though. I am not okay. I am barely hanging on but we have to figure this out. We have to make things right again for all the innocent people," I said with a sigh.

"I have faith in you. I know you will figure this out and

make things right. Just know that it isn't all on you. You do have us in your corner and as your honorary best friend, I will back you no matter what." My heart squeezed at the sentiment. I gave her a tight smile and headed towards my room. I was desperate for some space and a hot shower was calling my name.

Chapter Twenty-Three

I tossed and turned for what felt like hours. I had felt relaxed after my shower but once I laid down I became restless, my thoughts were consumed by Ragnor and my father. I had a bad feeling I couldn't shake that I was still missing some piece to the puzzle and it would cost us gravely. I stood and began to pace trying to piece everything together. Although my father had given us answers to questions we weren't asking, I felt as though he let on to a lot more than I realized.

What could I be missing? What exactly was my father searching for in that temple? What was Ragnor's angle in all of this? I know what he had said but he was a snake. There was no way he told us everything he was planning. He was still hiding things and between him and my father, he was the more dangerous one.

I knew I needed sleep. I had been up for days, aside from the random passing out in the front lawn after seeing all the dead fae, and it was starting to take its toll on me but I couldn't help thinking that we needed to go to Zeke immediately. My gut was telling me it was more important than ever to get started on our plans. That time was of the essence here. We had been stuck for weeks not making any moves against my father. Granted, he had only been moving his army a little bit here and there. He didn't order any more attacks. Yet, still there was this feeling that I couldn't shake. I was restless and we needed to do something about it.

I dressed quickly in tight leggings and a long sleeved black shirt. The shirt had lace up the sides leaving my skin exposed and I loved it. I grabbed my cloak and slipped my boots on. Vilulf would probably be asleep but I don't think he would feel the urgency I felt and I couldn't fault him or anyone else for sleeping. I had blocked my emotions from Zander and I knew he wasn't happy about it. I wanted him to sleep though. Sneaking past him and out my door I headed for Vilulf.

The hall was empty as I crept down it. For a brief moment I wondered if I should knock to be polite but then that would risk one of my men hearing the knocking. Zander was part dragon after all and had incredible hearing. I'm sure the others did as well.

I decided to forgo knocking and entered his room. It was dark but it was set up similarly to mine. I easily made my way through to his bedroom. I saw him lying facing away from me. His arm was thrown over someone else in the bed that was covered up by the blanket. It didn't surprise me. The room smelled of sex. At least someone was able to get some around here.

I touched his shoulder but he didn't stir. Gods. He had to be exhausted.

"Vilulf," I whispered.

The figure next to Vilulf moved in their sleep. A small purring sound entered the room and then the blanket moved to reveal them.

"Draug?" I said in surprise out loud without really meaning to be so loud.

Both men shot straight up in bed revealing their very naked bodies.

"My Queen," Draug breathed. "Is everything alright? Are you okay?" He was completely naked by my side assessing me in a flash. Vilulf was also naked and completely exposed because in Draugs haste he had pulled the blanket off of Vilulf and onto the floor.

"Yes, I'm fine. Shit. I'm sorry!" I felt so embarrassed. I had witnessed their looks for each other and I didn't take the time to stop and think twice about it. I hadn't even stopped to ask them about it. They stood close together and gave longing looks that I caught more than once yet I had been so focused on my problems I never thought to ask if they were together.

Vilulf cleared his throat. "We should have told you then you might not have just snuck in here."

"As it turns out, Vilulf is my fated mate." Draug shrugged and gave a loving smile towards Vilulf. "And I would bet money you would have still snuck in here even if you had known."

"Or as Draug likes to refer to it, we're soulmates. I don't like that term as much as fated mate though." Vilulf chimed in.

Remembering the first time Vilulf saw Draug I couldn't help but ask, "Is that why you froze when we walked in the room after I brought you back here?"

"Yes, I knew as soon as I saw him. It was quite a surprise. I have been waiting a long time to find him."

Draug leaned over and kissed Vilulf on the top of his head. "And I have been waiting even longer to find you."

My heart swelled with joy for them but it also ached for myself. I didn't know why I felt that ache but it was the same ache as when I thought of Helvig.

"I am so happy for you two. I shouldn't have interrupted though. I couldn't rest because I had a bad feeling and I thought that we could go to Zeke immediately. I will take Zander with me if you prefer? After all, you two haven't really had much time together and you both deserve a break."

They both shot me a look that said "shut up" and before I could say anything else they were already getting dressed.

"That's okay, my queen," Draug smiled. "We have spent time together over the last few days and this is more important than anything else."

"I am ready to go whenever you are. I suppose since you snuck in here, we aren't telling everyone we are going?" Vilulf asked with a knowing look.

"I was planning on telling Quinlan after we left but now that Draug is here..." I trailed off hoping they would get my intentions.

"I will tell everyone of the change of plans in the morning. Please keep in touch." The last part of Draugs words were directed at me but his eyes bore into Vilulf. The love they already had for each other was apparent. Vilulf stepped to Draug embracing him so lovingly it made tears swell in my eyes. I want to be loved like that and the only time I had felt cherished like that was my dreams with Helvig when he just wanted me to sit with him. Before Vilulf let go, he tilted his head and gave him a passionate kiss. I realized I was being a complete creep and intruding on their private moment, so I quickly turned around to give them some privacy to say their goodbyes. Still, I loved that they found each other. No matter what happens in our future, at least they have each other.

"Shall we go?" Vilulf's tone sounded strong but I could detect a hint of sadness.

"If you're sure?" I asked again, wanting to give him one last out before we left.

He held his hand out to me. I took it and felt the world shift around us. When I opened my eyes, I saw blackness with bright specks everywhere. I looked at Vilfulf and he was frozen in time except for the wind in his hair and clothes. I didn't feel any wind but I could see it when I looked at him. The world shifted again and we were suddenly upside down. It took me a moment to realize that we were not actually upside down but we must have been redirecting for our landing here at Zekes tent.

"I'm not sure I'll ever get used to that feeling. It feels like you threw me on a dragon, had them fly as fast as possible while spinning."

"I'm sorry?" I laughed aloud. Again, I didn't bother knocking and just entered Zeke's tent. I should probably start caring about people's privacy but call it a character flaw I can worry about later... maybe.

Zeke was asleep but tossing back and forth.

"My King," Vilulf strode forward to wake him.

"I'm not in the mood for your bullshit, Vilulf," he mumbled before rolling to face the tent wall.

"How about my bullshit?" I said, shoving his shoulder.

Zeke jumped and stumbled out of his bed getting his feet caught in his sheet and falling face first on the ground.

"Cordelia, I'm sorry. I am so sorry for how I acted. I don't know what came over me. I won't do that again. I promise. We talked and I am perfectly fine with not being together. I mean unless you want to get back together. If you do I would be open to that completely but if not that's okay too," he was rambling and I hadn't ever seen him ramble before. Normally he was calm and composed. This was a refreshing side to him that made me smile.

"Come on. We have business to discuss, a battle to start, men to hopefully not kill but kill if we must, and a war to end." I said over my shoulder as I exited his tent. He was naked and for some reason I really didn't feel comfortable being around him while he was naked. Even though we had been together before and I had just seen Vilulf and Draug naked without a second thought. I stood waiting outside his tent and within minutes he came bursting through the flaps.

"Let's walk?"

I explained to him what had happened and the terrible gut feeling.

"I agree with giving them the option of either joining us or fighting. It will give them an honorable death at least. Where do you want to start?"

"Well I think we start with my fathers smallest group of soldiers. They might not take what we are saying seriously and no one will join us. If that is the case then a small number of men will die compared to starting with a large encampment. We will leave one or two alive to spread the word about what we are doing. Hopefully by the time we reach the next ones, they will make the right choice."

I didn't like the idea of killing them because I knew my father forced men that fit certain criteria to join his army.

Chapter Twenty-Three

They might not have chosen this life, so I was giving them a choice.

"The smallest one will take us two days horseback—"

"We can go now. I'll move us there. Gather your twenty best men and then I will move us." Something I hadn't mentioned to anyone was how much more powerful I felt after seeing my father. I didn't really know why I had kept it a secret from everyone, but I felt like the only person I could tell was Helvig and he was dead so there's that.

Vilulf nodded. "I will start gathering them and we will meet there." He pointed to a clearing in the tents.

I watched Vilulf in his full armor head off through the tents. He was a handsome man; Draug and him made a very handsome couple. I wondered if what I had heard about sphinx matings were true. I had once heard that sphinx had multiple matings and would mate in what they called packs with multiple mates. Would Vilulf and Draug take on another make eventually or would it just be the two of them?

"You think only twenty men will do it?" Zeke's question pulled me from my thoughts.

"It's their smallest camp. We'll be fine. Plus you have me and I can do a lot more now than I could before. Don't you remember when I saved your ass last time?"

"Their smallest camp is well over two hundred men." Zeke looked unsure. I hated the fact that he didn't trust me to be able to do this. I hated that he was questioning my calls. Part of me just hated that this was something I had to do and I knew my feelings were misplaced. Any smart person would question this. I knew that but it still stung.

I thought about the fact that two hundred men could die by my hands tonight. Shit. I don't know how many I was expecting but two hundred was a bit shocking.

"By the look on your face, I'm guessing you thought they had like thirty men?"

"I don't know what I thought. I guess I didn't give it too much thought before but now the idea of killing two hundred men makes me want to throw up."

"I would be worried if it didn't."

We continued walking in silence for a while. "Is that what you are wearing?"

I glanced down at my outfit and smiled. "Yah. I was wondering something though… I want to wear Helvig's sickles knife swords things."

"You know saying you want to wear something as dangerous as those but calling them sickle knife sword things is not reassuring."

"I know. I still want them."

Zeke let out a long sigh and laughed.

"I think he would want you to have them. Honestly, I think he was probably closer to you than anyone. Myself included."

I closed my eyes and tried to close off the hole in my chest. "I still don't know what he was and you do."

"Yah but he didn't tell me because he wanted to. I think he would have told you, if he had the chance."

We entered his tent again and Zeke went straight to the back. The last time I saw them they had been displayed. This time they were laying haphazardly on the floor partially under a box.

He grabbed them and then stopped picking up a couple other small items.

"His harness is probably a bit big but we might be able to adjust it. He never wore this but he cherished it. I think he said it was a family heirloom and I'm not sure what stone that is. That's saying a lot considering the vast amount of stones and gems my kingdom has."

Zeke helped me into the harness and attached the sickle blades. I held the necklace in my hand and rolled it around. It wasn't perfectly smooth. It almost felt like there was something carved into it but it was so dark I couldn't make out any markings. I pulled it over my head and tucked it into my shirt.

"Let's go see if Vilulf has gathered everyone." I patted my chest feeling the necklace. We headed towards the clearing when Vilulf came towards us.

"We are ready. Oh nice. I like the new additions," Vilulf motioned towards the blades.

Once in front of the twenty men, they looked at me confused. "Did you tell them anything?"

"Nope. I figured I would leave that up to you." I sighed slightly annoyed with Vilulf's answer. If I didn't like Draug so much I would have punched that smirk off Vilulf's face.

I sighed and turned towards the men. "Most of you might know who I am. I am Cordelia Rovini. King Havaror's previously betrothed—"

"Goddess. She is also a goddess but she probably wasn't going to tell you that."

I shot a glare at Vilulf and elbowed Zeke as he laughed.

"Yah. So apparently I'm a goddess too. Anyways, we are going to give King Rovini"s men the option to join us or fight us. If they choose to fight us, they die. If they choose to join us they will be forgiven. They were not given a choice when they were forced to join King Rovini's army. They will be given a choice now."

The men visibly paled but did not say anything. I knew they were thinking the odds were against us and they were being led to their slaughter. They didn't know me though and they didn't know what I was capable of. They might have heard but they were about to see it all first hand.

"Everyone needs to be touching each other."

I didn't know if that was the truth or not but it seemed to have worked before so we would try it again. I hadn't moved this many people at once so I was a little nervous. If I had to make multiple trips, I didn't know how that would play out if we had to battle two hundred men. Still I pushed through my doubts and waited until Vilulf gave me the all clear.

Taking a deep breath, I felt the now familiar feeling of the world shifting under me. King Havaror's hand was on my back while Vilulf was holding my hand. The men were standing behind us with their hands touching each other's backs. One man touched Vilulf's back to complete the circuit. It was interesting that none of them touched me or King Havoror.

Once again the world around me disappeared as blackness took over. The bright speckles looked more like spheres this time and they were full of color. Part of me wanted to reach out and touch one but I didn't dare.

We turned upside down and suddenly we were standing on a hill facing hundreds of tents below us.

Chapter Twenty-Four

I gazed down at the men who were unaware that their path in life was about to change. It would either come to an end or take on a new meaning. It was still night out and most of them were sleeping. The few that were on look out duty apparently weren't very good at their job.

"Should we wait for morning or just go in now?" Vilulf looked from me to Zeke.

"Do you have to touch someone to use your magic?"

"Mine? No. I don't have to touch them." Vilulf looked confused as my change of subject and I couldn't help but grin.

"Perfect. Pick any of those men and tell them that King Havaror and Cordelia Rovini are on this hill here to talk. All their men need to be gathered and ready. It is mandatory that everyone is part of the conversation."

"You think that will go over well?" Zeke chuckled like he was the master at negotiations.

"Probably not but I'm not sending anyone down there. They will probably be killed and I don't plan on losing anyone."

"As you wish my Queen."

At his words the men behind him stiffened and looked at me warily.

I watched as Vilulf concentrated on a man in the center of the tents. He froze and then began looking around. He took off and ran to the nearest look out who blew a horn. Suddenly the whole camp looked like a bunch of ants running around. In moments men were lined up with their arrows drawn and aimed towards us. A man with a ridiculous helmet covered in large feathers walked up and grabbed a blow horn from the man next to him.

"He isn't going to make this easy is he? Come on, everyone hold hands."

When Vilulf gave me another nod, I moved us down directly in front of the archers. Their surprise gasps filled the air. This time Vilulf stepped directly in front of me to shield me from the archers.

"Captain Bammiette, I see you are still not good at following orders. I believe you were directed to gather all of your men for a conversation not a battle," Vilulf announced.

"I do not have conversations with the enemy."

I laughed and stepped forward but before I could speak he began shouting, "King Havaror has Princess Cordelia held captive!"

Gods. I didn't know this guy and I already didn't like him.

"Hi. Yahhh… no. I am not being held captive."

He was still shouting about me being a captive and my patience with him was waning. I moved myself to stand next to him on the bench he was standing on. I slapped him hard on his back and didn't remove my hand.

"HI. SHUT THE FUCK UP FOR LIKE TWO GODS DAMN

SECONDS. I AM NOT BEING HELD CAPTIVE. I CAME HERE TO MAKE YOU AND ALL OF YOUR MEN A DEAL."

I turned and saw Vilulf's wide eyes. Zeke had pulled his sword from his sheath ready to attack at the first sign that I needed help.

I moved myself to stand directly in front of my men.

Slowly, more and more men began to surround us but the soldiers with me remained stoic and strong.

"It's going to be annoying as fuck to have to yell all of this for them to hear me. They're all talking now and I don't know if they would even shut up enough to listen."

Zeke stepped forward and gods was the grin on his face sexy. Maybe I shouldn't think that anymore but I couldn't help it. His skin was rippling with energy. For a brief moment I wondered what exactly he could do but then he opened his mouth and scared the shit out of me.

"QUUUUIIIIIEEEEEEETTTTTTTTT!"

Silence fell among the men and everyone stared at us. Zeke turned, bent down, and picked me up. I sat on his strong shoulder with one of his arms across my shins to help balance me.

"I AM CORDELIA ROVINI. YOU WERE NOT GIVEN A CHOICE WHEN YOU WERE FORCED INTO KING ROVINI'S ARMY. I AM GIVING YOU A CHOICE TODAY. YOU CAN EITHER THROW DOWN YOUR SWORD AND JOIN KING HAVAROR. YOU WILL BE FORGIVEN FOR EVERYTHING YOU HAVE DONE UP TO THIS POINT. YOU WILL BE PROVIDED ACCOMMODATIONS AND ABLE TO START A NEW LIFE. THAT IS OPTION ONE."

I watched as no one moved. No one set down a sword. No one said a word. Okay. So maybe I had hoped they would all be willing to throw down their sword and just join us.

"IF YOU DO NOT CHOOSE THE FIRST OPTION THEN YOUR SECOND OPTION IS TO FIGHT US NOW AND DIE. I WILL NOT SPARE YOU IF YOU CHOOSE TO FIGHT. ONCE YOUR CHOICE IS MADE, THERE IS NO GOING BACK. SO CHOOSE NOW WHETHER TO THROW DOWN YOUR SWORD OR TO DIE. ANYONE CHOOSING TO JOIN US MOVE FORWARD NOW AND YOU WILL BE PROTECTED."

Silence fell and still no one moved. I glanced over my shoulder and saw my men preparing for battle. "You guys won't be fighting."

"PRINCESS CORDELIA," Captain Bammiette. "YOU HAVE BETRAYED YOUR FATHER, YOUR KINGDOM, AND THESE MEN. WE WILL NOT SPARE THOSE WITH YOU BUT WE WILL HOLD YOU CAPTIVE FOR YOUR FATHER TO TAKE JUDGEMENT ON. I HOPE YOU HAVE SERIOUSLY CONSIDERED THE CONSEQUENCES FOR YOUR ACTIONS BECAUSE—"

I had heard enough. I raised my hand just for show and then used his own sword to go straight through his mouth.

His body slowly fell to the ground and the echoing silence seemed to stretch on forever.

"SO. NOW THAT JACKASS IS DEAD, FEEL FREE TO MAKE YOUR OWN CHOICE. I WASN'T GOING TO LET HIM CHOOSE FOR YOU."

The men all looked around at each other. No one laid down their swords. Instead someone rang out a scream and they charged us.

"Gods dammit." I sighed and closed my eyes. I moved us to the hill. The men all stopped and looked around.

"THIS IS YOUR FINAL CHANCE." I had told them once their choice was made that was it but I couldn't help giving them another chance. I so badly wanted them to choose laying down their swords. I so badly wanted them to choose right. These men had been part of those sweeping through villages and towns. Yet, I had hoped that maybe not all of them were bad.

Still no one laid their swords down. Instead they began swarming the hill. My heart dropped to my stomach and I felt the disappointment start to sink in. This did not go how I thought it would.

Zeke set me down, "I'm sorry. I know you had hoped for more than this."

I closed my eyes and felt the tears well from what I was about to do. I listened to the men screaming their battle rage out as they swarmed the hill and moved quickly towards us.

I heard one of our men gasp and I could hear them tighten their grip on their swords. Their leather gloves creaked like a plea for mercy in my ears.

"I'm so sorry," I whispered. The sound of screaming changed from a battle cry to horror and pain. I wasn't able to kill all of them at once so I had to do it in waves. Wave after wave I used their own swords to kill, forcing the next wave of men to not only witness this but have to crawl over the bodies.

I felt the hot tears rolling down my cheeks and my vision blurred as I killed them

I left five men standing a few feet away from us looking scared shitless. They still hadn't dropped their swords and they weren't begging for their lives to be spared.

"Consider yourselves lucky. You will be spared today. Go

and spread the word of what happened here today to the nearest camps. We will be making our way through each camp giving them the same choice we gave you today. Make them aware of this choice and the consequences." Zeke spoke to these men as if the hundreds of men laying around us weren't there. He didn't show an ounce of remorse or emotion. In this moment, I saw him for the strong king he truly was. He was a leader.

I looked over my shoulder at Vilulf through my tear filled eyes. He was speaking with his men. Some of them looked proud while others were puking. I didn't know if it was because they thought they were going to die or because I killed all of those men in just a few minutes. Would they be scared of me now? Would they look at me differently?

Zeke wrapped his arms around me and brought my head to his chest. "Shhh, I know. I know you hated that. I know you had hoped for so much more. I'm sorry. Next time will be better. Shhh. Please don't cry."

I stood there sobbing into him. I hadn't wanted to kill all of those men but I knew it had to be done. They were going to keep killing innocent people unless I did something about it. All I wanted in this moment was to be back sitting on Helvigs lap. I wanted to smell him and feel him under me. I wanted his comfort but I knew I would never get it. Maybe in my dreams but not in real life. The sun was beginning to rise and I knew we needed to go back. I pulled away from Zeke and gave him a thankful smile. I didn't think I could talk at the moment.

"Do you need to rest before we head back?" Vilulf asked, putting a hand on my shoulder.

I shook my head and moved so we could all touch. I didn't

want to be here any longer. I didn't want to look at all of the bodies. Vilulf grabbed my hand and Zeke placed his on my lower back. The men formed a circle around us and just like that we were back at Zeke's camp.

"Let me carry you to some place to rest," Vilulf said.

"I can walk."

"I know you can walk but you just used so much energy. You have to be exhausted. I know I would be and I haven't had to use half of the amount of power that you just had to use. Please let me do this for you."

"I do not deserve to be carried. Not now. Not ever again."

"You aren't being serious right? Fine. Hop on my back."

"Seriously?"

He stepped in front of me kneeling to the ground. Before I could move, he grabbed my legs and stood. I wrapped my arms around his shoulders and let out a small laugh. Vilulf galloped through the tents laughing and sounding slightly psychotic. I knew he was making a show out of this as he weaved around the tents in no specific direction. Before I knew it, I was laughing hysterically. For a brief moment I forgot about what I had just done. I forgot about who I was and what I was destined to do for this realm. I was just me and Vilulf was just my friend.

We got a few stares but suddenly men started kneeling with one hand over their heart. They kissed their fingers tips and then touched their forehead.

"What are they doing?" I whispered as Vilulf came to a stop.

I slid down his back and turned in a circle looking at all the men surrounding us. More and more came and knelt.

"Word spreads quickly around a camp like this. I'm sure they heard about you and what you did back there."

I stood there watching as what looked like the whole camp came to us. Silence fell upon us and then everything was in slow motion. The whole world grew darker before becoming brighter again.

"Wow. Look at you my dearest." His voice made my skin scrawl.

"Where are you?" I knew Ragnor had somehow taken over my mind again but I couldn't see him.

"Turn around," he said. I felt his lips touch my ear and I froze.

"What do you want?"

"I just wanted to let you know that I don't care what you do with all of your fathers' camps. You could kill every single man of his and it doesn't make a difference to me. If it is important to you then I want you to go through with this but don't forget about my offer. I want it to be me and you. I have big plans for us and thanks to you moving your father; I am one step closer to reaching my goal."

"Fuck you. I will not align myself with you and whatever you have planned."

"You say that now but time will tell. You are a Goddess, my dearest. You will out live everyone around you. Have you thought about your future? Not the next one hundred years but the next one thousand? I'm a patient man despite what you may think. We have time."

With that the world came spinning back to normal. All the men were moving back at normal speed as if I hadn't even blinked.

"Are you okay?" Vilulf asked next to me.

I jumped, forgetting that he was there.

"Yeah, I'm fine. Tell them they don't need to kneel. I'm just

Chapter Twenty-Four

Cordelia."

The look on Vilulf's face said he didn't believe me. I didn't blame him though because I wasn't okay. I had just killed hundreds of men and had another face off with Ragnor. Ragnor was right with one thing though, I would outlive everyone here.

"Let's gather the men and head back to let Brutus and everyone know how it went. From there we can move to the next camp."

I saw the flag on the top of Zeke's tent and took off towards it. I needed a moment to try and catch my breath. I busted into his tent and was relieved to see he wasn't around. My knees felt weak and I slowly lowered myself down to the floor. It felt like the world was closing around me and I couldn't breathe.

I closed my eyes and let myself fade away from reality.

Chapter Twenty-Five

"**O**h, Zonlicht."
    I felt his arms wrap around me as he pulled me into his lap. I knew I must have passed out. I was here dreaming about Helvig again and it felt like a relief. For these brief moments I could pretend. I could pretend that I wasn't on the verge of falling apart. I could pretend that everything was okay.

"What happened, My Zonlicht," Helvig asked while he nuzzled my head.

I slowly turned and saw that he wasn't chained to the wall by his arms any more.

"You're free? How did you get free? Why are you still down here? Let's go."

"No. I'm not free. I ripped the chains out of the walls and it took almost everything out of me. Unfortunately, I didn't have enough time to regain any strength before the guards came in. They chained my feet to the floor now."

I glanced down and saw his ankles had shackles on them. I reached down and touched one. A guttural scream escaped me.

Helvig ripped my hand away and brought it to his mouth.

"How are you wearing those? That was the worst pain I think I have ever felt. It was like the chain was sucking my soul out of my body. Everything burned."

"It isn't easy but we all carry our burdens." *His smile didn't reach his eyes. "Now tell me what makes your eyes puffy and your face streaked from tears? Who do I need to kill? I will fix whatever it is, I promise."*

I wished that he was real. That all of this was real. It was easy to be with him and tell him all my problems. He knew me better than anymore and as crazy as it sounded I almost wished I would never wake up. That I could stay dreaming of Helvig for the rest of my life. If I couldn't be with him while awake then I didn't want to be awake and alive. I would rather be comatose and sleeping... dreaming of him.

"I killed hundreds of men tonight." *I watched his face waiting to see the judgment but it never came. Of course it didn't. Helvig was perfect because he was just a figment my mind had created.*

"I'm sure you had a good reason to do that," he said hesitantly.

Before I could compose myself, the words came tumbling out, "I'm probably going to end up killing thousands of men within the next couple weeks. I gave them the option to put down their swords and join King Havaror or fight. They chose to fight. I tried to help them. I can still hear their screams because I wasn't strong enough to kill them all at once. I had to kill them in sections. The ones that witnessed it still attacked. Not that I want them to join our side out of fear but they knew they were going to die. They were willing to die. They were wanting to die. They had to know that there was no way they would survive." *A sob burst out of me and I began crying again. "I cry so much now. I don't ever remember crying this much in my life. I have these moments where I feel so out of control that I can't even breathe."*

We sat in silence while Helvig ran his fingers through my hair. Eventually my crying ebbed and I relaxed in his arms again.

"You are so strong. It's one of the things that I love about you. Don't you remember what I told you? You are benevolent, thoughtful, intelligent, gracious, and compassionate." I remembered those words. It's what he told me in the alcove the day we kissed. Those words made my heart feel like it was going to seize up.

"You are perfect. You have always been perfect and you will always be perfect. Even if you fall or make mistakes. You are still perfect because of all those things I love about you. You gave them a choice and they chose wrong. What else could you have done? Let them kill you or your men? Let them go on ravaging villages? No. Never. You're upset because you care. You didn't want them to die. You wanted them to live good long lives. You care about this realm and the people here. If you didn't care or if you weren't upset about taking their lives then you would be just as terrible as King Rovini. You are good. I promise that soon I will be by your side and you will no longer have to face these things alone. I know you have your men and Zeke but it isn't the same as what we have. They don't understand what you're going through nor do they understand the weight of the power you wield. Just being able to do something like that weighs heavily on your soul. Just don't pull away from them. Try to talk to them when I'm not there. They will do what they can to help you through this. Lean on those around you and once I am with you, I will never leave you again."

Suddenly, I was ripped away from Helvig and everything was black. I was falling and deja vu tore through me. Fucking Ragnor.

I landed in my spot in the forest or at least what he tried to make look like my spot. I was fucking furious.

"Cordelia, my darling," he said in a sickeningly sweet voice. "I have been trying to bring you to me for a while now. What were you doing that made you so disconnected?"

"It's none of your fucking business!" I spat. "Let go of my mind now."

I was vibrating with anger. The fucking audacity of this guy to come at me again. This time he took me from Helvig and the rage within me was at a boiling point.

"You know I don't really care how many men you kill. It makes no difference to me. I have bigger plans than this realm. Your father might have an issue with it but once you and I are together he won't be able to do anything about it. Tell me, have you made your choice yet?" I watched as Rangor walked towards me casually like this was an everyday occurance.

"I'm not sure why you think I would care about what you do or don't care about. Whatever your plans are, I will stop you and if you think that I will have anything to do with you. Gods. You are fucking delusional. After everything you have done to me you fucking psychopath, I will never be with you. I will always fight you." Just as he was in reach of me, I hauled back and punched him. The world around us started to fall away but not before I heard his last words.

"I love a woman who fights me. It's all the more pleasurable when I force her to submit."

Zeke and Vilulf were just walking into the tent when my eyes flew open. "I'm sorry," Zeke said softly. "I didn't realize you were sleeping. We didn't mean to wake you."

I ignored Zeke and looked Vilulf directly in the eyes. "I need you to teach me how to stop someone from accessing my mind."

"I can't. I don't know how and I have very little access to

my abilities. I don't even know where to begin in that regard."

Without missing a beat I looked at Zeke. "Do you have the same ability that Voronion does? That whole mind trick thingy?"

"I do not. What is going on?"

"I need to learn how to block Ragnor from accessing my mind. He just fucking accosted me from a dream I would have much rather been in." I didn't bother looking at them as I braided my hair and stormed out of the tent. Glancing over my shoulder at them I said, "Gather anyone who is coming back with us. We need to get back to the Daemonger Kingdom and I need to speak with Voronion."

"Of course," Vilulf bent quickly and then took off to find those that would be coming with us. I still didn't think I would get used to people bowing to me. I wasn't a queen or anything special. I was just Cordelia, yet none of them saw that. They saw me as a goddess and it was only going to get worse after what happened with those men. I had easily killed them and everyone here knew that.

Chapter Twenty-Six

I stormed through the halls on a mission. No one had seen Voronion in days apparently. That irritated the shit out of me because I finally needed that slimy piece of crap for something. Brutus hadn't even noticed that Voronion was missing which was also frustrating. He had been spending all his time with my men and Alba prepping and preparing for a war. I still wasn't sure why he thought a war was coming. Like hello, I fucking murdered a shit ton of men. Who is going to attack us? Yeah… No one in their right mind and if some crazy person decided to attack it would be over quickly. Brutus wasn't thrilled with my words. His frown had only grown deeper as I spoke until he finally said, "And you're just okay carrying the weight of that many deaths?" Of course I wasn't fucking okay but sure. I would do it if I had to. If killing all of them finally brought peace and justice to the victims of this realm then that is exactly what I would fucking do.

"I need to find someone who can teach me how to block Ragnor from my mind. I did it without meaning to with

Voronion once before. I need to amplify that so Ragnor can fuck off." I stated as I walked into Brutus's bedroom. It was huge and dark. Deep red curtains hung against black walls.

"Ahh yes. I have been thinking about that," Brutus said, rolling over in bed.

"And?"

"I don't have a solution. I have just been thinking about it."

"He can get into my head at any time, Brutus. Any fucking time. I have to figure out a way to stop it."

"It could simply be that we can't stop him. He is incredibly powerful. Much more powerful than any of us had realized. What I don't understand is why he hasn't used his power to take over the realm instead of King Rovini. It would be easy for him. Why this whole time was he hiding?"

"He doesn't care about this realm. He said that himself. Apparently, he has bigger plans than this place. I don't know what he is planning but it clearly isn't good."

"Do you think you have reached your max potential of your power yet?" Brutus raised an eyebrow and folded his arms over his chest.

"Maybe. I don't know. I can move more people every day. This morning Vilulf needed to speak with Zeke so I sent him to Zeke's camp without going. I told him I would retrieve him this evening. I don't know if he made it there or not yet. I could have left him stranded somewhere far away but I have a feeling that he was placed directly in Zekes tent. My accuracy has increased and my stamina as well."

Hmph was all he said.

We sat in silence for a long time, both lost in thought.

The sound of tinkling bells reached my ears. Her laugh was always so infectious.

Cordelia, you must focus my darling... This realm will fall. There will be many deaths, a great orange light will fill the horizon, and all will seem lost. You have to find him. It must be soon or else it will be too late. Stop them from destroying the barrier.

Your mind is yours and yours alone. Only you can allow someone to penetrate it. Simply deny them access. It is truly that simple.

Her voice began to fade away and the sound of bells reached my ears again. Remember the barrier. You are the only one that can complete the barrier.

The doors to my bedroom crashed open. I didn't remember going back to my room or getting into bed. "Quinlan has been trying to get in contact with you. King Rovinis forces are about to take Lanasia and are still on the move," Alba said breathlessly.

I sat up in shock. I thought Ragnor had said he didn't care about this realm. Could my father have gotten word out that quickly? Surely he couldn't have traveled that far already?

"Which camp took the city?" I slid my feet into my boots and began lacing them.

"Well, all seven of them that had previously surrounded the border are all moving in at the same time."

I paused, lacing my boot. "Fuck. You're joking me right?"

Alba narrowed her eyes. "I'm being dead fucking serious and honestly that's not even the worst part."

"What could be worse than thousands of men taking a fucking city right under our noses?"

"It seems that their directed paths lead straight into major cities. Not to mention the smaller ones they will decimate on the way. All seven are moving in fast. They are on a mission but I haven't been able to pinpoint exactly where they are going. We have just a general direction."

I knew where they were going. My father had wanted that temple. It felt like my blood was running cold. "We are going to have to move fast. Get everyone to the throne room. I'll talk to Quinlan."

Quin?

Oh I see. You finally decided to stop ignoring me and let me in. You know it gives me a headache when you do that. It's like I'm beating my head up against a brick wall.

Now isn't the time for that. Alba told me what's happening. Everyone is gathering in the throne room. We will need to move quickly.

Once everyone was gathered it was pure chaos. Everyone had an opinion about what we should do and no one seemed to agree.

Eventually, I couldn't take the arguing any more. Standing up I said, "I have already created a plan. It would take days to move Brutus's army by foot to one of the camps. If I move an army, I will have to rest which means they will battle and good men will die unnecessarily. So I will go. I will move from camp to camp giving them the ultimatum I gave the first camp. Either they lay down their swords or I kill them all." I started walking out of the throne room as everyone started talking again. It seemed they weren't a fan of my plan but it was the best one we had.

I could feel Zander's worry and his anxiety. I stopped and turned looking him straight in the eyes. "You will come with me. Maybe Zantos would even let me sit on him." My small attempt at lightening the mood failed miserably. Zander just nodded his head but Draug and Quinlan lost their absolute shit. They were furious that I wasn't taking them too. The thing was though, I couldn't risk losing them. Draug had just found Vilulf. I wanted them to live a long beautiful life together. I had watched Quinlan die once already and I was not willing to watch that again.

"We leave in 10 minutes to inform Vilulf and King Havaror."

Alba had approached me and wrapped her arms around me. "You know you don't have to do this without us. We support you. We are all here for you."

I kept my voice even. "I know."

I didn't want them to witness the horrific things that I could do. I didn't want it to change our friendship and I didn't want to see the judgment in their eyes when they saw what I was truly capable of.

I walked to the conservatory and stood outside the doors.

"I thought I would find you here," Brutus said as he leaned up against the wall.

"Yah. I keep thinking that we need to get Zeke here and try to connect him with his thunderbird. Other things keep on coming up and I keep putting it off. After this though, we have to try."

"Are you going to tell me what's really on your mind?"

I glanced up at him and his smile was small but I caught it. "This is what's on my mind."

"No it's not. You're worried that we will think you are a monster or that if we see what you are capable of we will think you are a monster. What you fail to see though is that we already know who you are and what you are capable of. We do not think you are a monster." He patted my shoulder and walked away. Words seemed to fail me as I stared at his back. How could he have known that?

I waited a few moments before heading to find Zander. I knew they were all here for me but they would never be able to understand what I was going through. Having the fate of the realm resting on my shoulders was unbearable at times. Knowing that my actions would directly impact everyone made me sick to my stomach.

I spotted Zander standing in the courtyard waiting for me.

"You ok?" He asked as he reached out for my hand.

"I'll be fine. I just hope that this time goes better than last time. I hope men actually listen and lay down their swords."

Chapter Twenty-Seven

I slept for almost two days after going from camp to camp with Zander. We didn't get to all seven before they had taken multiple villages. I had been utterly exhausted physically and mentally but I still didn't feel rested. I had dreamt about the time I had spent with Helvig in my father's castle and when I awoke, I found myself incredibly disappointed in reality. I closed my eyes again and laid back down. Already my dream was slipping from my memory but I didn't want to forget. It felt so real. The way we had laughed together as we walked the streets of my city. The way his emerald eyes twinkled with mirth when he dismissed Lance as I slid into our alcove. The alcove where he made me feel more alive than I had wanted to admit. I hadn't even admitted it to myself at the time. Now laying here in my bed alone, it was the only thing I could think about. It hadn't been real this time though. It had only been a dream. It felt different than my previous dreams about him but it was a dream nonetheless.

My mind wandered to all the men I had killed in the name of peace. I was just as bad as my father. If Helvig had still been alive, he would hate me. He would be disgusted by me. For a brief moment I wondered if this realm would be better off without me and if I was just adding to the carnage. It wasn't that I wanted to kill myself. It was more that I just didn't want to exist anymore. Not after everything I had done. Not after being so weak for so long. I thought about Helvig again. Was he waiting for me in the afterlife? Maybe the next battle I wouldn't defend myself. I could get distracted and not notice someone coming to kill me. It could be over so quickly if I let it.

You awake now? Quinlans voice was so loud in my head that I jumped.

Yes. You scared the shit out of me. I flipped the blankets off of me and stood. I had been practicing keeping Quinlan out of my head so that I could keep Ragnor out of my head too. It really upset Quinlan when I shut myself off from him. I hadn't figured out how to keep my mind open to him but closed off to Ragnor yet. The more I practiced the more I felt like I would figure that out soon. I needed a quick shower to freshen up and then I would start my day. It would distract me from myself and that's exactly what I needed right now. Well by where the sun was in the sky, this day was almost over but I would still check in with everyone. Although what I really wanted to do was just lay back down and let my dreams consume me.

Good. Ragnor arrived yesterday demanding to speak with you. We didn't allow him to bother you though. Apparently, he still doesn't know where you sent King Rovini and he is furious. He was spewing off in his rant and gave us some useful information.

Oh really? Like what?

He apparently has to stay close to King Rovini or else he starts to get ill. They haven't been able to figure out why it happens but the longest they have gone apart was 3 weeks before.

That's very interesting. I wonder if anything happens to my father?

He didn't say and no one asked. We did not tell him where you sent King Rovini though. We all acted as if it was news to us that they had been separated.

I'm sure he saw right through that.

He did but we've all stuck to it. So there isn't anything he can do.

If he gets seriously ill then that would leave my father very vulnerable, right? It seems to me that he has relied on Ragnor a lot more than any of us had realized. How are the fae we brought here? It's been awhile since I last checked in on them.

The fae that you rescued are doing okay. They don't remember much. They remember the guards coming and getting them. They were taken to a camp where they were drugged. Those that tried to fight were beaten and then drugged. They are very relieved to be out of that situation but most are not happy to be in the Daemonger kingdom. Some have started working in the village though. It could be a new life for those that want it.

Hmm. It definitely could be... I'll meet up with everyone for dinner.

I contemplated Rangor's situation as I got ready for the day. I would check with everyone and then go and get Zeke. It was time to loop him in on everything and I felt prepared to get him. I felt like something was wrong though. I didn't know what but it was a feeling I just couldn't shake. I gasped as a sharp pain slid through my chest. I had to move my shirt and

303

look at my skin to ensure there wasn't something stabbing me. At one point it felt as if someone was trying to rip my heart out of my chest.

After my shower, I ignored the pain that had turned into a dull ache and headed to meet with everyone for dinner. When I entered the dining hall and took a seat, Brutus looked towards the door after me.

"Is Alba coming?" he asked as he started putting food on his plate.

"Uh I don't know. I haven't seen her since the other night." A sense of dread washed over me as I spoke.

"She went to meet you to see if you needed anything while getting ready? She left right after you spoke with Quinlan," Draug chimed in.

"I haven't seen her. Maybe she took a different route to my bedroom?" Even as I said the words, I didn't believe them. "I'll go see if I can track her down." I stood and started quickly walking from the dining hall.

"I'll come with you," Zander said, worry dripping from his words. "I can feel your reeling emotions right now."

"No. I would much rather you head a different way. Maybe she got distracted by something." I tried to give a reassuring smile but I think it came off as more of a grimace.

"Shall we all go looking for her?" Vilulf had stood now too and was giving Draug a look that I couldn't quite decipher.

"I'm sure everything is fine. We'll be right back. Zander and I will know if one of us finds her. We will sense the relief in each other when it happens and then we can meet back here. Stay and eat. If she comes back, Quinlan can inform me," I said, turning back towards the door and picking up the pace. I couldn't shake the feeling that something was indeed happening but I didn't want everything to end up okay and it was just me having another overwhelming moment of emotions. I had too many of those recently and I didn't want everyone to start looking at me differently because of them. I didn't want them to think that my emotions made me a liability.

Zander and I turned opposite ways in the hall. We would make quick work of finding her and then head to dinner. I just had to keep positive. As I passed a stairwell that was hardly used I felt like something was calling me to it. I paused for a moment before I turned and headed up the stairs. I was no longer heading towards my room but there was something telling me I needed to go this way.

I followed that feeling, twisting and turning down hallways I hadn't traveled before. I thought I had recognized another hallway that I passed but I couldn't be too sure as I heard what sounded like a scream and practically ran past the hallway.

I ran as fast as I could when I came to a large wooden door. I could hear Ragnor yelling at someone. Then I heard her muffled cries. I tried to open the door but it was locked. With one quick thought, I was on the other side.

The taste of bile rose to my mouth. Three guards were holding Alba down on a table as Ragnor was bent over her. She had blood across her face and I was sure she would be bruised. Her clothes were ripped and I could hear the fabric tearing more as she continued to try to fight them off her.

"I told you we would all take turns until you tell me what you know bitch. I wasn't sure if I would be ready for a second round but luckily for me my men took longer than I expected. Now either tell me where King Rovini is or this time I won't be taking you in your pretty little pussy." Ragnor's words caused another round of bile to rise, burning my throat.

"Get off her!" I tried to shout but my words came out more horrified than angry. What had they done to her? Oh Gods. What had they done? I reached for my magic but it was gone. How was it gone? I tried to leave the room with Alba but I couldn't. I couldn't bring anything to me and I couldn't go anywhere.

Ragnors head whipped around and a smile split his face. He stepped back from Alba and turned towards me. He didn't even bother tucking himself away as he took a step towards me.

"No. GO! GO Cordelia. Run." Alba had looked angry before but now she looked terrified.

I don't know where we are but I need help. Quinlan?! QUIN? CAN YOU HEAR ME?

"Tsk. Tsk. Tsk. The look on your face says that you just realized you have no access to your magic. Such a shame. Don't worry, when you leave this room you will be able to access it again. Unfortunately, you won't be leaving this room any time soon. No one can get in or out of it unless I allow it."

"Let her go!" I said more firmly this time. What kind of magic did he possess? Every time I thought I knew the extent of it, he did something new that surprised me. How did he take away all of my power?

"I wasn't done with her yet but," Rangor snapped his fingers and two guards stepped away from Alba. The last one yanked her to him and put a knife to her throat. He smiled at me, "So you comply with me. You didn't think I would just let her come to you? Oh no, You see I figured you out. Your weakness is people. Not just any person though. Oh no. People you deem as innocent like poor sweet Alba here."

My hands were trembling and I didn't know if it was from anger or fear.

"First, you are going to come to me and let me touch you. Then I'm going to fuck you. I have waited years to be able to fuck you and I am done denying myself. I was hoping you would have accepted my proposition already and we would have been able to just naturally come together. Waiting doesn't work for me any longer. From now on, I'm just going to take what I want," Ragnor's voice almost sounded crazy like he giddy from the idea of raping women.

"No. No fucking way am I letting you touch me!" I shouted at him. I had to think. I had to be able to get us out of here without my magic. I could fight. I knew how to fight. I looked around the room for anything I could use as a weapon. The odds weren't very good but if I could get Alba out of the position she was in or at least get the knife away from her throat... As if he had been reading my thoughts Ragnor began to laugh.

"Don't even think about fighting. If you don't do as I say, I will have her throat slit before you can even say her name." Rangor held a hand up to the guard holding a knife to Alba's throat. "I spent years trying to kill you and you would never die. So I attempted to train you. I thought I could turn you into a warrior. Someone that would be feared. Yet, You always showed exactly what you were going to do on your face. You gave it all away. After a few years of training you, you started to grow up and I realized what a deliciously beautiful woman you were becoming. I have fantasized about all the things I want to do to you for so long."

My eyes met with Alba's and she shook her head moving

the word "go". Just then the guard pressed the knife into her throat slightly causing a trickle of blood to run down her neck. Her eyes widened for a moment before resolve sank in. She had accepted her fate that quickly.

"Stop! Don't hurt her!" I screamed at the sight of her blood.

"You know what you need to do then, Cordelia." Ragnor held out a hand to me. What else could I do? They would kill her.

"Give me your word that you will not kill her or hurt her anymore." I tried to sound strong but I didn't feel strong. Alba was shaking her head no at me and trying to talk but the guard holding her had stuffed her mouth with rags so her words were muffled.

"You are lucky that I am in a rather good mood. I'll make you a deal. You do as I asked already AND agree to marry me while also performing a mating ritual that will force the mate bond between us and I will give my word that no harm will come to Alba. If you betray me, she will be the first of many to die." My whole body had started to shake. My hands were trembling and I wasn't sure if I could move.

I had to do it though. I couldn't let them continue to hurt her. My men would come. Zander would have sensed something was wrong when I ran down the hall after hearing her scream. Quinlan wasn't able to reach me anymore. I wouldn't return to the dining hall. There were too many red flags for my men to ignore.

"Deal." I said without hesitation. Alba's muffled cries grew louder as I stepped towards Ragnor. My skin crawled as he touched me and my muscles screamed at the horror waiting for me. He looked almost exactly like the man that I grew up thinking was my father and it only added to how fucked up all of this was.

"Now that's my good girl. I knew one day you would welcome me. I have always loved the look of your legs in pants. I think that your father did too and that was why he only wanted you to wear dresses." My mouth was filled with chalk and I could no longer talk. Ragnor slid his hands around my back and under my pants. He squeezed my ass and then slowly knelt in front of me pulling my pants and panties down. He lifted one leg and then the other, removing them from me. As he returned to his full height, he walked his fingertips up the outsides of my legs. Each touch from him sent another wave of nausea over me. When he reached my hips, he grabbed the hem of my shirt and pulled it up over my head. I didn't bother to fight. I couldn't give them a reason to hurt her. I looked around the room hoping I would see something that could help us. There wasn't anything in here. There wasn't anything I could use to help us or to buy us time for my men to get here. If I fought him, they would kill her. I looked at Alba as tears slid down her face. She was screaming something but I couldn't hear her any more.

Alba's muffled screams had faded away and the room seemed to grow darker. It was like my body was shutting down and going numb. An icy chill ran over my skin causing goosebumps to cover my arms. Ragnors hands slid over my stomach and my breasts. He bent down and kissed my neck and then my collarbone. Suddenly, Ragnor picked me up and laid me in the same spot and position that he had Alba in just moments ago. He lifted my legs up and brought my knees up to my armpits for his two guards to hold. They slid cuffs around my wrists that burned.

"Mmm. Your pretty little pussy looks so delicious. I have

waited so long to taste you and to feel you. I can't wait to fill you with my cum." He groaned as he inserted one finger into me. I knew Alba was screaming and trying to encourage me to fight. I wouldn't though. I couldn't let them hurt her. I glanced over at her and our eyes connected. There was so much pain written across her face as she tried fighting the guard even though the knife was at her throat. She could fight and do as she pleased. They wouldn't hurt her now. Not after the deal I made.

Ragnor slapped my face so hard that it caused me to bite my tongue. The metallic taste in my mouth was a welcome distraction from the pain the guards were causing on my legs. I would have bruises there later but they would heal. "Look at me when I'm touching you. You don't fucking look at anyone else but me. I'm the one doing this to you. Your pleasure is because of me and no one else!"

He inserted two more fingers and groaned again. "You're so tight for me. I just need you a little more wet and then the real fun can begin." He began ramming his fingers into me so hard that my whole body was jerking on the table. I could feel the uneven wood digging into my back and the sharp sting of it scratching into me. I felt the wetness of my blood slide down my back as Ragnor continued his brutal assault.

The pain was blinding. I closed my eyes as the tears started to fall from them and pictured Helvig's emerald eyes. In this moment, I just wanted to be in Helvig's arms.

Chapter Twenty-Eight

The sounds of the room had faded away from me. My eyes were open now but they remained unseeing. If I closed them, Ragnor would slap me and demand I look at him. All I could focus on now was the pain. There was so much physical and emotional pain. I tried thinking of anything else but I couldn't. There was just so much pain.

Suddenly, Ragnor was removed from my body. It took a moment for my brain to process what was happening. I didn't know how or why but when he was removed from me it was as if all my senses came flooding back into me in slow motion. The room was too bright. There was shouting and screaming but all I could focus on was the pain and smell of blood, sweat, and sex in the air.

I rolled when the guards let go of my legs and fell to the floor. Slowly, I crawled under the table and pulled my legs up into my chest. It was so bright but I could make out legs moving and that's when I realized there was fighting going on.

I saw Alba rush out of the door that had been busted down. Now was my chance to run too but my legs felt weak and numb. They were tingly from being held in that position. I was slow but I managed to pull myself out from under the table and into a standing position. My eyes never left the opened doorway as I held onto the wall and forced my legs to move. They had gone numb from being held like that for so long but I wouldn't stop to give my muscles a chance to wake up.

Once I was out of the doorway, I didn't bother looking back. I wasn't even sure where I was or where I needed to go but I just needed to get away. As the feeling came back into my legs, I began moving faster and faster. I lost all rational thought as I started to run. I had to get away. I had to go.

The only thought I had was to run as far away as I could get. I turned down a hallway that I recognized and found myself outside of the conservatory. I burst through the doors and kept running until I stumbled and fell to my knees in the dirt.

I can't do this anymore. I can't. I just wanted peace for this realm. I wanted to watch my children play in peace one day. Why? Why was wanting that too much? Why did all of this responsibility fall onto my shoulders? I am no one. I have never been anyone. I just wanted to be loved and even that possibility had been taken away from me. No one would ever love me now. Zeke wouldn't even want me now. It didn't matter though. I hadn't wanted Zeke anymore anyways. I had let him go and I was fine with that decision. I had cared for him but I didn't ever truly love him. No. It was Helvig I had fallen in love with. It had been Helvig the whole time. I just hadn't realized it until now. Until it was his eyes I pictured to get me through that. The hole in my chest seemed to have opened so wide I thought it would consume me. The pain and the grief from everything was so much... too much. I sobbed and sobbed into the ground. My wrists burned from the cuffs. I needed to get clean. Wasn't there water in here? My thoughts were scattered and disjointed. I couldn't move to find a place to clean myself even if I had wanted to. I felt like I was dying.

I pulled my legs up to my chest and held myself. I could still feel Ragnors hands on me. I began to vomit. It was like a faucet had opened up. I puked until I was dry heaving which only made me sob harder.

My mind was going so fast that my thoughts were spinning out of control. No one had ever loved me. Not my father. Not Lance. Not even Zeke had loved me, it had just been some fucking pheromones. A flash of Ragnor's breath on me went through my mind and the thought of his hand between my legs flickered. I started vomiting again until I was dry heaving once more.

"I don't want to be here anymore. I don't want to do this anymore. I don't want the pain anymore. It's too much." My voice was weak and strained. I had so much constant pain my whole life and I was tired of it. The pain of never knowing my mother, all the abuse I had endured over the years, the loneliness, and losing Helvig. Flashes of what Ragnor had done to me kept appearing and the pain felt like it was surging all over again.

I had a chasm of black inky darkness filled with pain and anger inside of me. The pain would end if I made it stop. If only I had my dagger with me, I could stop all of the pain right now with one quick slice. I could join Helvig in the void.

I couldn't stop sobbing. My heart hurt, my soul hurt and my flesh hurt. I was shaking violently as I laid there in a puddle of my own puke.

"I'm sorry. I'm so sorry," I said to no one and everyone in this realm at the same time. When I could muster up enough strength, I would find a dagger and end this all. Tears flowed from my eyes and I sucked in a sharp breath as I came to terms with how my life would end. It would be my choice and by my own hand. Brutus and my men would make sure my father was stopped. They would take care of this realm and they would take care of Alba.

I should have told Helvig that I loved him that day. The day he was taken from me before we even had a chance to begin. I should have told him what he meant to me and how much I had grown to love him. "If there are any gods listening to me, please tell him that I love him. Wherever he is, if he has passed on or is somewhere out of reach in this realm. Just tell him I love him." The words were barely coherent as I sobbed.

I closed my eyes and let a shaky breath go. I had to get up. If I was going to die it would be my own decision and I was going to do it. It was time.

I felt a wind on my body and the faint scent of oak and ocean filled me. I let out a choked cry because I finally knew who the scent belonged to. Helvig's scent caressed me and touched that dark chasm in my chest making some of the pain I was feeling recede. I sucked in his scent once more hoping that if it was all in my mind, maybe I would forever smell him.

The scent of oak and ocean grew stronger and I let out a strangled sound. I sounded like a wounded animal but honestly at the end of the day that was exactly what I was.

Just a wounded animal. I closed my eyes and laid there taking in the comforting smell. My mind stopped flashing images of what had happened and slowly all thoughts seemed to have stopped completely.

Everything around me had gone quiet. I heard the thud of footsteps approaching but I couldn't move. Somewhere, far off, I could hear my men screaming for me. They were searching for me. They were too far away to be responsible for the footsteps approaching me. I still didn't move. Maybe this person would kill me. I didn't care anymore. I didn't care what happened to me. I just wanted to lay here smelling the wind.

I heard the sharp intake of breath and then warm arms wrapped around me. I was gently pulled into a lap. The arms were strong and steady as they held me to a man's chest. He was warm and comforting. I let out another choked sobbed because this couldn't be real. It wasn't the wind that touched my cheek bringing the scent I loved. It was the warm fingers brushing the tears from my cheeks. I couldn't breathe. I didn't want to open my eyes and be disappointed.

He held me so close to him like he was afraid if he let go I would disappear. His lips brushed my cheek and his voice cracked as he spoke, "you're safe now. I'm here. You're safe. I'm sorry. I'm so sorry it took me so long but I'm here now."

The sound of his voice wrecked me. I jerked and moved my hands from my chest to clutch his shirt. I pulled myself into him even more and continued sobbing. I still hadn't opened my eyes. I couldn't. I was so afraid he would disappear and that I had truly gone crazy. More footsteps were thudding closer but he didn't move. He just sat there holding me, whispering against my cheek, running his hand in my hair, and rocking us gently. Not even at their collective gasps did he flinch or move.

Eventually, my sobbing ebbed and my breathing started to even out. Only when I had the occasional quickened breaths from crying so hard did I attempt to open my eyes. It was brighter than I had expected and it took me a moment to realize what I was looking at. His shirt had been ripped open and there was blood splattered across his chest. But his sepia reddish brown skin was glowing. A small sobbed broke from me because I knew this skin. I had known his scent and his touch. I knew his voice and soaked in every word he whispered to me. Every word calmed part of my soul telling me on a deeper level that I would be okay. There was still pain and I would ache for days, but somehow I knew if I was with him I would be okay. But seeing his skin up against mine did something to me. I couldn't look away from his chest. I was afraid to look away.

Gentle fingers touched my chin and lifted my face up. I stared straight into a beautiful pair of emerald eyes sprinkled with peridot.

This couldn't be real. I wasn't losing my mind anymore. I HAD lost it, someone would have to lock me up in the crazy bin because I was hallucinating.

"Helvig?" My voice cracked. "How are you here?"

"You brought me to you. Your soul called out to mine and pulled me to you. Just like you've been doing for months now only instead of you coming to me, I came to you." He brushed the hair away from my face and kissed the top of my head. I sat there soaking in the moment with him before reality came creeping. My brain was slow and my body was even slower. I felt like I was in a fog and the only light I could find was his beautiful eyes.

"What did you say?" Horror slid through me as his words registered. Just like I've been doing for months now? For months I've been going to him? No. No. No. No. He has to be wrong. I've left him there. He's been so sick. Oh gods. No. "YOU'VE BEEN CHAINED IN THAT PLACE FOR MONTHS?"

A grim look came over his face. "I'm still chained there but I'm not what's important. I think—"

I cut him off. Panic began to override my mind and body. "What do you mean you're still there?" I was shrieking at this point as I touched his shoulders and his chest. I could feel him. He was here holding me so how was he still there? Maybe part of me was trying to focus on him so I didn't have to focus on what had happened to me.

He let out a long sigh and then pulled me closer to him. He sure as shit felt like he was right here. "The same way you came to me but your body was really somewhere else. I know it's confusing. I should have explained it to you the first time you came but seeing you like that. I couldn't do that to you. Then each time you came I just couldn't bring myself to add more weight to the burdens you were already carrying."

"WHERE ARE YOU!" I screamed at him, jerking my body away from him for a moment. "WHERE THE FUCK ARE YOU?"

"CORDELIA? We're here. We can't come closer. Can you come out? Are you okay? Where's Alba? I can't feel you anymore." Zanders' voice sounded so distant.

Helvig pulled me back to him as I continued to scream at him. "DO YOU KNOW WHERE YOU ARE OR NOT?"

"My zonlicht, I'll be okay. You need to calm down and

breathe for a moment. Your bleeding and probably in shock from everything–"

"NO! YOU DON'T GET TO TELL ME HOW I FEEL. DO YOU KNOW WHERE YOU ARE OR NOT? You know what, it doesn't matter. I'll find you wherever they have you. I will find you and I will burn it all down." Tears were streaming down my face. I grabbed Helvigs face and pulled my forehead to his. I wasn't worried about my back or any other part of me. I would heal physically and the rest of the pain I knew I was disassociating and deflecting it. "Is it all real? Everything you've said? I wasn't making it up? I wasn't dreaming?"

"Everything has always been real between us. Please take care of yourself until we are together again. There's something you need to know."

"I'm fine. I'll be fine. I'm so sorry. If I knew that you were really there and I wasn't dreaming, I would have found you already. I would have done that first. It would have been my first priority. I thought you were dead," I choked on that last word. The tears were threatening to spill over again.

"Shh. Don't cry. I need you to please listen… They have divine galena. It's what coats the chains and they had it in a powder form the day we were attacked. It could kill you if they use it correctly. I don't think they know how to use it or else I would be dead but that hasn't stopped them from trying." The light surrounding us was beginning to fade and my eyes widened.

"NO! You can't leave me. I'm not ready. No." I wrapped my limbs around him. I could feel the panic rising within me and suddenly I didn't feel so strong. "Please." I begged.

"Remember, you bow for no one. You are so strong. Stronger than you know. You are mine and I am yours. We

318

will be together soon," Helvigs lips brushed mine. The light around us had faded so much I could see the trees behind him.

Helvigs eyes were wide and I could see the fear in them. My heart broke all over again watching him slowly fade away. His mouth was moving so fast but I couldn't hear him anymore. Before I could take my next breath he was gone and I fell to the ground.

The sound that left my chest was inhumane. I screamed everything from inside me out and into the ground. I felt so angry that I couldn't contain it. I let out another wail when I heard Zander again.

"My Queen," he said gently. I felt the cloak drape over me and then his hands were wrapping around me. I kept screaming and thrashing like a wild animal but Zander didn't falter.

Vilulf stepped forward and placed his hand on my head. "I'm so sorry." Then everything went black. I felt like I was weightless and floating through nothing. The feeling was calming like when I would lie on my back in my river and stare at the stars.

I didn't feel the anger that had been simmering inside me since I was a small child. I felt relieved for a moment. I felt nothing and I was okay with that. Maybe I could stay here forever. I closed my eyes and let myself drift off into the nothingness. I liked being in this void.

I hadn't opened my eyes but I knew I wasn't in that void anymore. I knew because the pain radiating from my back was the first sign. The second sign was how much my vagina hurt. The third sign was the anger that had been simmering inside me my whole life had turned into a rage ready to boil over. Slowly, Alba's words reached my ears.

"I'm almost done removing the wood from her back. Once it's removed, she should be able to heal on her own like she normally does. Physically, she will be fine. Mentally. I don't know. Being hurt like that isn't something someone can just move on from and everyone reacts differently. We all handle it and deal with it in our own ways."

"I should have fucking been there. I should have fucking gone with her and I shouldn't have split up from her." Zander's voice told me that he was angry and blaming himself but I couldn't feel his emotions. I reached out trying to find the thread that connected us but it wasn't there. It felt like a brick wall was built around my mind and there was no one getting in or coming out.

"This wasn't your fault. It isn't anyone's fault but Ragnor and Voronion's. They are the ones that did this. They are abusers, rapists, murderers, and the only people to blame." Alba had stopped messing with my back and I felt a sheet being pulled over me.

"I'm supposed to protect her. It is my duty and I failed her!"

"Zander! Calm the fuck down before you shift in here! We can't afford for you to shift inside again! You've already destroyed two rooms and you could hurt her if you do."

"I'm trying but my dragon is riding me hard to shift and burn the world down. I've never felt him like this before. Not even when our mate was killed." Zander's words were filled with growls and snarls as he struggled to keep himself in control.

"So let's go burn the world down then," I said. My voice came out a small whisper which sounded rather pathetic and not how I felt at all. My throat felt raw and I knew it was from all the screaming I had done.

"You're awake! What hurts? What can I do? Do you need water? Are you hungry? I can go get–"

I cut Zander off. "I want to talk to Alba alone please. You can get me some water and let everyone know that I'm awake."

"Are you sure? I shouldn't leave your side. I can have–"

"Just go get her water. She will be fine if you are gone for a few minutes." Alba sounded just as annoyed as I felt.

I waited until I heard Zander's footsteps fade and the door shut.

"How are you feeling? I managed to get all the wood out of your back but I would imagine it still hurts like a bitch. It took awhile and some of it was embedded pretty deep. I had to wait for your body to push it closer to the surface before I could remove it all."

I let out a small chuckle. "It definitely hurts but not as bad as having broken ribs. My back will be fine."

Silence filled the room for a moment and I couldn't bear to turn and look at her.

"Everything is fuzzy and there are blank spots in my memory. Can you tell me what exactly happened?" I asked. It actually wasn't fuzzy at all. I remembered everything clearly but I needed to know if what I remembered had actually happened.

I heard Alba's sharp intake of breath and then she gently asked, "Do you remember what Ragnor did to you?"

I pinched my eyes closed for a moment and let out a breath. "Yes. I remember…" I let my voice trail off. I don't know why I couldn't say the words. It was on the tip of my tongue but my mouth couldn't form the right word. "What I don't remember is how it stopped or what happened after. I remember running down the hall and I remember a bright light." I also remembered smelling Helvig and I remembered him talking to me but his words couldn't have been real. He couldn't have been real. My memory made it seem so real but it was like a dream that was just out of reach.

"Oh. Okay. Uhm. I don't really know how to explain any of that. I was being held and then suddenly there was this bright light. It was shaped like a man but it was like staring into the burning sun. It was so bright and the heat that radiated off of it was unlike anything I had ever seen before. It ripped Ragnor away from you and then burned even brighter. You could smell Ragnors flesh burning from where the thing touched you. The men started freaking out and trying to fight it. Then I heard Zander on the other side of the door. The force of Ragnor being tossed towards the door broke it down. I ran. I'm so sorry. I didn't even look back. I just ran and ran. I didn't even know where I was going. I just ran until I couldn't run any longer. I ended up in the pantry in the kitchen. I hid behind a shelf. I know that sounds pathetic and I can't even explain why I did that. It was there and I just hid behind it. I stayed there until I heard Brutus calling out for us. He shouted our names and said that Ragnor and his men were gone. I waited until I saw that it was really Brutus and came out. They hadn't found you yet. Brutus wrapped a cloak around me and tried to talk to me about it. I insisted that I was fine and told him I didn't want to talk about it. He respected that and didn't ask any further questions. We searched everywhere for you. When we finally made it to the conservatory, we knew you had to be in there. That same bright light was coming out from the cracks around the door. When the men opened the doors it was like stepping onto the sun itself. Even Quinlan thought it was excruciatingly hot but they didn't hesitate to come in. Zander insisted that you were at the center of it. I don't know how he knew maybe it had to do with his dragon eyes but I couldn't see anything from how blinding the light was. It was like a barrier was there keeping everyone away from you. No matter what they did or how hard they tried to get through they couldn't. Not until the light started fading. Then we could finally see and hear you. Zander covered you with his cloak. You were making these sounds that I'm pretty sure would haunt demons' dreams. Vilulf used his power to shut your mind down. Now you're here with me."

I knew the light was Helvig. He had come for me because I had somehow called out to him and brought him to me. I felt the rage and panic starting to bubble up again. My hands were shaking as I turned over to sit up. "How are you handling all of this? You seem so calm and put together." I looked at Alba for the first time and a small sad smile crossed her lips.

"The first time I was raped, I wasn't calm and put together. I screamed and screamed until they began beating me and then I learned to stop screaming. After that, I began plotting my revenge. I vowed that one day I would make sure they paid for what they had done to me. I was raped everyday from the day that your father killed my parents and took our kingdom until the day that King Daemongers men joined up with the camp I was in. Brutus's men are not allowed to rape and apparently have morals, ironically. Growing up I had always heard about how horrible the Daemonger Kingdom was, in reality they saved me. A group of men were caught gang raping young girls when the Daemonger army came. They killed them and then searched each tent. I had been tied to the bed when they came in. I will never forget their kindness." Her eyes looked far away as she recounted those times. "Anyways, it never got any easier. Each time was just as bad as the first time but I learned that it hurt me more if I dwelled on it. Instead I focused on the things I would do to those men if I had the chance. The day before you arrived in the camp, I had my first chance at one of them. I had been tasked with the job to refill the water jugs in the captain's tent. I walked in and he was sleeping. I picked up his dagger and stabbed him. I kept stabbing him over and over. A soldier came in and saw what I had done. He gently pried the dagger out of my hand and asked me if the captain should have died the day they came to our camp. I couldn't even answer him. I just nodded my head and looked at him in horror at what I had just done. I was in shock that I had killed him. He told me to stay there and left the tent. I thought for sure I was going to die that day. Instead a handful of soldiers came in with a tub and other women. The soldiers put a blanket over the dead body and the women helped bathe and dress me. When we left the tent, two of the soldiers were posted at the entrance. That night the captain's tent caught fire and he was burnt to a crisp. I can't tell you what to do or how to feel. All I can tell you is that you aren't alone."

She gave my hand a squeeze and stood. "Let's get you cleaned up and dressed."

I couldn't find any words as she helped bathe me. Anger and sorrow had filled me and tore me a part on the inside. I didn't know how to express how I was feeling or to even convey any words to her. It wasn't until she pulled out one of my favorite jumpsuits that I finally found the words that were caught in my throat.

"No. Not that today. We have shit to get done and a world

to burn." Alba didn't even question me. She just nodded her head and went back into my closet. I followed her and grabbed my black leather training pants. They were tight enough to let me move swiftly but not too tight to restrict me. I pulled them on and then grabbed a loose fitting black long sleeve shirt. I pulled Helvig's necklace out and laid it over top of my shirt. I walked back into my room and put on Helvig's blades. There was something so comforting about having them on my person. I wasn't sure if it was because they were Helvigs or because I could use them to protect myself. I would never be unarmed again. I had grown too comfortable here and was careless. In my father's castle, I was always on edge waiting for the next time Ragnor or Emon would attack me. Here people bowed to me as I passed them in the hallways. Everyone respected me and no one dared speak to me unless I addressed them let alone try to attack me. I would never be weaponless again. Quickly, I pulled my hair up into two buns on top of my head ignoring the ache that raising my arms caused in my back and abdomen.

"Well you look like you're ready to kick some ass today." She smiled but it didn't reach her eyes. To someone who didn't know her, she looked happy. To me though, she looked haunted and I realized for the first time that this was how she always looked. Before, I had easily taken her cold demeanor towards people for the fact that she was royalty. Now, I knew it was from everything she had been through. I wondered if that's how I would look too.

"Thank you," I said, turning towards her. "Thank you for sharing your story with me. Do you remember the regiment that held you before the Daemonger army came?"

"They called themselves the black knights."

We stared at each other for a moment not needing any words to communicate between us. She knew what I would do to them.

A knock sounded on the door.

Chapter Twenty-Nine

I opened my bedroom door and came face to face with Quinlan.

His eyes widened for a moment just before he launched himself at me. He engulfed me in a hug and started shaking. "I can't hear you anymore. I thought you had died or some shit. I should have gone with you. I shouldn't have let you leave alone. This is my fault. I failed you and will spend the rest of my life making it up to you."

"Hey!" I said, slapping the back of his head. "I don't want to ever hear you blame yourself again. Actually, I don't want to hear anyone blaming themselves over this ever again. It isn't your fault nor Zanders. It isn't Vilulfs nor Draugs either. Now. If you could let me go that would be great. My back hurts and you are making it worse."

"Shit. Sorry." Quinlan said backing up. "You look…"

"Badass?" Alba filled in for him.

"I need to talk to Brutus and then I have plans for today." I smiled at him and he gave me his dazzling smile back. I was so thankful that he couldn't hear my thoughts because then he would know that I was barely keeping control over my rage. I didn't want anyone to feel or have any inkling as to how I was really handling everything. I knew they all blamed themselves and I didn't want them to feel worse. They weren't the ones I wanted to hurt.

"Oh. Okay. I think Zander was on his way there. We can stop by Vilulf's room and then head there too." Quinlan gave me a side eye but I pretended like I hadn't noticed.

"I can get Draug and Vilulf." Alba said, stepping into the hallway.

"You can't!" I said, panic filling my voice. Was she crazy? She couldn't go alone.

"It's safe, Cordelia," Alba gave me a reassuring smile. "Brutus has posted guards everywhere. These two are assigned to me."

I stepped into the hall and saw two men with shadows spilling out from behind them standing there. My whole body tensed and I felt like my throat was starting to constrict. I stared at them for a moment making sure they weren't the men from the room. Definitely Brutus's men which was good but still they were men. I gave them a weary look before I caught myself. I had to keep it together. I put on a brave face and turned back to Alba.

"Okay." It was all I could manage to say. Luckily, that was all I needed to say. Alba knew. She nodded her head and let us know she would meet up with us quickly.

"Brutus assigned men to you as well. Draug and Zander weren't very happy about it. I figure the more men we have around you the safer you will be." Quinlan was talking nonchalantly as we walked but my spine stiffened at his words.

I didn't need men around me. I didn't want men around me. I had my men and those were the only men I wanted nearby.

Quinlan continued talking, making me relax, "Draug and Brutus came to an agreement that they have to stay 10 yards away from you at all times. The only time they can approach you is if you request it or if you are hurt and need assistance." Atleast Draug seemed to have some sense about the situation.

I stayed silent as he kept rambling. I wasn't sure if he was nervous and felt the need to fill the silence with words or if it was because the connection between us was silent. I need it to stay that way. I didn't trust myself to open it. If I did and he heard or felt the rage simmering just beneath the surface, well I didn't know what he would do. I did know that I didn't want to find out. I didn't think I had ever heard Quinlan talk this much. My mind began to drift back to Helvig as we walked. All the pieces had finally clicked and I remembered everything. "How long was I asleep for?"

"Two excruciatingly long days."

"TWO DAYS?" I shrieked. Helvig had been chained and starved and tormented while I slept in my warm bed for two more days.

"Yes?" Quinlan scrunched his eyebrows as he opened the large brown door to Brutus's war room.

Brutus and Draug were arguing over something as we stepped in. Zander was standing between them with his arms crossed. The room fell silent as I walked in.

"Glad to see you are up and moving," Brutus said walking towards me. He stayed a little more than an arm's length away and looked me over. "Do we have special plans for today?"

Draug had walked up to me and hesitated before smoothing down his beard. I gave them both a nod and headed toward the seat closest to the windows.

"We have much to discuss but I think it's best for us to wait until everyone else is here. I don't want to have to repeat it and I would rather hear all of the opposing arguments at one time."

"Ok, then we can discuss something else until then. How are you feeling?" Brutus asked while walking towards his seat.

"I'm fine." My words came out harsh but I didn't want to get into what happened any more than necessary.

"Fine?" Draug asked, crossing his arms.

Before I could answer the door flew open. Vilulf came storming in with Alba hot on his heels.

Relief flashed through Vilulf's eyes as he looked at me.

"I hope you aren't too upset with me. I didn't know–"

"I'm not upset with you at all. Actually, I am incredibly thankful for all of you. Please come sit. I have some things I need to inform you all of and I don't want to waste anymore time." I could sense the weariness and unease in the room. Sitting in my chair a sharp pang shot between my legs and I couldn't help the wince that crossed my face. If anyone noticed, they didn't say anything.

Draug pulled a chair out for Vilulf and gestured for him to sit. Once he sat, Draug took the seat next to him. I watched as Vilulf leaned towards Draug out of instinct. Alba took the seat on my right and Quinlan took the seat on my left. Zander on the other hand remained standing directly across from me. He was tense and I could tell that Zantos was still giving him a hard time. I had a feeling Zander wouldn't be able to sit through this meeting and that was okay. Zantos would get his fury out soon. I would make sure of that. Soon I would be making a lot of people pay for their past deeds and I planned on Zantos joining me.

Brutus cleared his throat and I realized they had all been waiting for me to begin.

"First, does anyone know how Ragnor was able to completely take away all of my magic and power?"

"I had a feeling that piece of shit did something like that!" Quinlan burst out. He must not have known I wasn't able to use my power until now. I didn't know what Alba had told them or even how much of their words she remembered. In a situation like we were in, the trauma in it all can make you block things out.

"I found ancient words carved into the back side of the door along with a crystal that I have not seen before." Draug shifted in his seat and pulled out a small metallic shimmering crystal setting it on the table.

"Divine Galena!" Zander and Brutus said at the same time.

"Well that takes care of my second question," I chuckled.

"What was your second question?" Alba asked with her eyebrows pinched together as she stared at the divine galena.

"I was going to ask if anyone knew what divine galena is."

Brutus stood and walked to a cabinet. He pulled out black leather gloves and slide them on. He carefully picked up the Divine Galena and examined it.

"How do you know about it?" Zander asked me.

"I'll explain that in a moment. First, I would like to know how you both know about it and what exactly you know."

"I don't know about it per say. A memory flashed in my mind telling me what it was. It was one of Zantos' memories." Hm. I wondered how old exactly Zantos could be. Was he alive when my parents were creating this realm?

"My father warned me of it. I normally wouldn't speak about this in front of other people but I believe we can trust everyone in this room." Brutus's eyes bore into me making me feel like a petulant child.

"Tell us about it then," I said, crossing my arms and leaning back in my chair.

"This stone is Divine Galena. It is found deep in the realm of the gods and it has the power to render even the strongest god helpless. It drains all power and can even kill you. My father told me a story of chains that were coated in Divine Galena. They were used to hold gods that were being questioned about something they had done. Depending on how it is used, it could even kill a god. This should not be here in our realm."

Silence filled the room and all I could think about was touching the chains when I visited Helvig. He was experiencing that same pain right now. That's how they were holding him captive and the fact he was in constant pain made me almost lose my mind. The rage had almost reached its boiling point. I would burn everything down until I found him and those responsible for torching him. Slamming my fists against the table I stood suddenly.

"You all wanted to know how I knew about it," I turned and looked at Vilulf. "Helvig told me it is coating the chains that are holding him captive at the moment. He has been held in a dark, dirty, and cold dungeon for months being tortured and on the verge of death. He was the source of the bright light you saw. He was what came to save me. I thought I was having dreams about him but it fucking turns out I was going to him. I didn't realize it at the time but I know now. He doesn't know where he is located but he is out there somewhere being tortured as we sit here. As I slept for two fucking days, he was being held and tortured. So here's the fucking plan, I am going to my father's camps, the first being the regiment that call themselves the black knights, and I am going to kill them all. I am not offering them a choice. They do not get a choice at life after the things they have done." Alba turned to me. Her eyes were wide and her mouth was hanging open "Alba, if you would like to come and watch the show, I will be more than happy to bring you. If there is someone in particular that you would like to take revenge upon, you will have that option. If not, I will take them all out. Secondly, I will go to each of my father's camps and ask for information on where they are holding a captive. They will be given a choice. They can either tell me the information I am seeking or they will die. None of the men in those camps deserve redemption. The so-called good men sit by and allow the bad men to do terrible things. I do not care how many men must die. I will kill thousands of men to get Helvig back. Once I have him, they will all be begging for mercy. Brutus, I want you moving your men into the territories that my father has taken as we move across the land taking back the kingdoms. Your

men can help the villages and cities get back on their feet. Vilulf, I want you and Zeke doing the same thing. They can question the villagers and anyone else they see on where a captive might be held. It is an underground, cold, and damp dungeon. Zander, you will let Zantos take his revenge on the black knights and you will not feel one ounce of guilt or remorse for it. Quinlan and Draug, there might be times that I am distracted and not paying attention. As much as I want to trust the people around us, you never know when a seemingly innocent villager could decide to attack. Especially since I am Cordelia Rovini and my father's men have pillaged, raped, and murdered their loved ones. I want you two by my side ready for anything at all times. I plan on leaving tonight. So everyone needs to rest up and prepare themselves for what comes next."

"Do you think killing thousands of men will solve anything? Truly? Do you really think it will help heal you?" Zander's words cut through me. How dare he. How FUCKING dare he question me about this. After everything I have been through, he wants to talk about me healing.

The room was silent as everyone stared at me waiting for a response. This is what was going to happen whether they liked it or not. I started to stand from the table when Brutus cleared his throat and then stood, "This Helvig that you speak of, who is he to you?"

Brutus crossed his arms and leaned next to the windows.

I stared at his black eyes trying to find the right words. Who is Helvig to me? He is my best friend. My confidant. The one person who knows me better than anyone.

Looking around the room, I let out a breath. "He is everything to me and I will stop at nothing to get him back."

With that I turned and left the room. Brutus' men stayed a good distance behind me but I couldn't help trying to put more distance between us. I stepped into my room and closed the door, locking it in one fell swoop.

Closing my eyes, I tried picturing where Helvig was. It had been two days since he came to save me and who knows what he had endured during that time. I knew I hadn't gone to him, yet I opened my eyes slowly, hopefully.

Moving to my bed I laid down and thought about the night

he had been taken from me. The memories were fading but the one thing that would never fade was the sound of his flesh. I couldn't help but wonder what had happened to him. What did they do with the Divine Galena exactly that made him so vulnerable?

The last time I saw him in the dungeon he was chained to the floor and those chains hurt so much when I touched them. How was he able to deal with that amount of pain?

I pictured his perfect face, sepia skin, and emerald eyes speckled with peridot. He was so beautiful and so strong. He could have been arrogant and it would have fit him well yet he wasn't. He was reserved and calm. He was patient and kind. Did he know that we were soulmates? Of course he knew. If I had to bet, he has known for a long time. When did he find out and why hadn't he said anything to me? Would I have believed him if he did?

The world around me faded away as I found myself standing in that dungeon. As soon as I felt the stone beneath my feet, I took off running to him. He was chained to the ceiling by his hands this time and a puddle of blood was underneath him as he dangled a few inches off the ground. My heart seized in my chest at the sight of him.

"I'm here," my voice croaked. I reached my hands up and touched his chest. I didn't know where all the blood had come from and I didn't want to risk hurting him more. I tried to move him to my bedroom but nothing happened. I didn't know if it was a me issue or the chains blocking my magic from moving him. I was stronger now than the first time I tried to move him and it infuriated me that I couldn't move him now.

335

His head pulled to the side a bit as he tried to see me through his hair. Reaching up I slide his hair behind his ears. My eyes met his and I watched as his whole body went rigid.

"You," he wheezed. "Have to leave. He knows about us now. It's a trap." My blood ran cold.

"I will not leave you as long as I am in control."

I glanced at the ground and before I knew what I was doing exactly the ground began to move towards Helvig's feet. I watched in amazement as a small mound formed under our feet. It grew tall enough that his arms were no longer raised above him but hanging at his sides instead. Helvig stumbled at having to stand holding his own weight again. I wrapped my arms around his torso and steadied him.

"I won't allow you to suffer any more than you already have. How do I get these chains off of you? I can't touch them."

Helvig didn't respond. Instead he buried his head into the crook of my neck and inhaled deeply. He nuzzled the side of my head before pulling back and kissing the top of my head.

"I don't deserve you," his words were barely a whisper above the rattle in his chest.

"How do I get these chains off of you? They're coated in divine galena aren't they?"

"You can't. The only way for them to come off is by the person that put them on, commanding them to come off. You have to get out of here before he comes back. He was waiting on you to come. I'm sure he knows that you're here already."

"I will kill Ragnor for what he has done to not only me but to you as well. I will kill him and then beg the gods to bring him back just so I can kill him again." I felt that rage beginning to boil over again. Helvig looked like he was about to say something when the ground around us began to shake.

"Shhh. Be calm, my zonlicht" He pulled me close to him carefully making sure the chains never touched me. I took a deep breath trying to calm my anger. The ground around us calmed as I took in his scent. Everything about him calmed and soothed me. For the first time since the incident, I didn't feel any pain anywhere. Not even emotional pain and maybe it was because I was so wholly focused on him but it was a relief to not feel like I was drowning with emotions that I didn't fully understand. He had been calling me zonlicht for months now. I had never asked him what it meant because I had always assumed it was something my subconscious had made up. Now knowing it wasn't something I made up but an endearment from him, I was too nervous to ask him what it meant.

"It's my fault you are here. If I would have been stronger, this wouldn't have happened to you."

"Listen to me. None of this is your fault. It isn't fair that it all fell onto you but this has been a millenia in the making. You didn't deserve any of the things that have happened to you or anyone else." He pulled me closer and kissed my head again.

"I'll get you out. I promise. I won't stop until I get you out. Where are your wounds?" I slid my arms around his body searching gently.

"I'm fine. I'm already healed. You do not need to worry about me. I know that you have so much on your shoulders and I don't want to burden you with any more worry. I know you are doing the best that you can and you need to know that I want you to take care of all the innocent people before me. I don't need to be your top priority, they do and understand." For a moment we didn't say anything. We just stood there holding each other in a comfortable silence. His stomach growling made me realize just how selfish I was seeking comfort from him when he was being starved and tortured. Who knew the last time he ate, probably the last time I fed him, and here I was being comforted by him.

"I should have done this as soon as I got here." I closed my eyes out of habit and brought a table and chairs into the room. Then I filled the table with food and drinks. Hopefully Brutus's kitchen staff wouldn't be too upset over the missing food. Then I turned to the only doorway into this room and filled it with rocks and dirt from my river. Next I studied the spot where his chains were attached to the ceiling. There wasn't anything I could do about the chains themselves, I had tried so many times in the past to move the chains, but now I realized I could move the dirt that surrounded them. In one quick moment I had the chains removed from the ceiling and loose on the floor. "At least this should make you more comfortable and take them longer to get in here."

Helvigs smile melted my resolve. A part of me couldn't believe that it was really him sitting in front of me. All this time longing to see him and be with him and he was right here the whole time. Zander's questioning words from earlier floated through my mind as I watched Helvig carefully eat.

"I want to go to all of my fathers camps and kill all the men. Do you know what they do with their captives? They rape them. They beat them. They do terrible things to them. Even the men who don't do those things stand by and let it happen. I want his whole army to pay. I want to walk through and slaughter each and everyone of them. Then I want to hunt Ragnor down. I want to make his death slow and I want to watch the life drain from his eyes." My words had been a soft whisper of confession in the beginning. By the end, anger enveloped each word as I spoke.

Helvig sat back in his chair and stared at me for a moment.

"Would you like to know the moment I started falling in love with you? Although I think I loved you before I even knew you, there is this one moment that just plays on repeat in my head."

His words felt like a bucket of ice had been thrown on me.

"When," I said breathlessly.

"It was the night I caught you sneaking into the village for the first time. I knew you were fierce and more than capable of handling yourself. Yet part of me feared something happening to you. I saw you give that poor beggar money and when you made me wait while you had your meeting, I couldn't help but stare at you in awe. You were betraying your father and your kingdom. You were going against everything you were raised to believe in and follow. You weren't doing it out of spite either. You were genuinely just trying to do the right thing. You wanted to save innocent lives. You knew that this realm had seen too much death and chaos and you became a hidden beacon of hope. Word had been spreading throughout your fathers camps that the enemy had learned of their plans. Many camps had to turn around and many orders were canceled. The men in those camps weren't upset. They were relieved and some were even hoping their regiments would be sent home for the winter. Not all of them are bad men and many of them didn't get the choice. If they speak up against their superiors, they will face consequences that could involve their families being harmed. Later when we went to the river together, I couldn't help but feel so lucky to be there with you. I think about us in that river almost as much as I think about when I kissed you in the alcove."

I had sat frozen to my spot as he spoke. I hadn't known that camps had to turn around due to orders being canceled because of me. I mean I knew that orders had been canceled because of how angry my father had been. There were many times I gave important information that changed everything with the war. I hadn't known that the men in my fathers camps had been relieved either.

When I didn't say anything, Helvig began eating again. My mind was everywhere and nowhere all at once. My body had already healed everything from Ragnors brutal assault and I couldn't help but wonder if being so close to Helvig had something to with that. There was a phantom pain that I couldn't shake, I adjusted my position in my seat so that my back wouldn't touch anything. I watched as a small drop of water trailed down Helvigs neck from the goblet he was drinking. My mind wandered off to us in my river.

"Will you tell me about your home?" I asked.

"Our home," he corrected. "I want you to come home with me when we get the chance."

A smile filled my face as I sat forward in my seat. "You really want me to come with you? I thought I couldn't go wherever you're from?"

Helvig chuckled and I felt its warmth deep inside me. "I have so much I want to share with you, my zonlicht. I am the God of Light, my love. Well not THE God of Light. My father was still very much alive and the head of our court the last time I visited."

Helvig was a god? There it was, the last puzzle piece of Helvig had finally fallen into place. I thought I heard someone calling my name and before I knew it, I was being pulled back to my bedroom.

Chapter Thirty

Fuck. I opened my eyes and heard Zander outside of my bedroom door. Gods damn it. I was getting somewhere with Helvig and Zander had to fucking ruin it.

I stood and stretched looking around my room. It felt empty and lonely without Helvig. I would be correcting that soon though. Very very soon. First, we were going to purge all the evil men from the camps. Then, I would find Helvig. I walked to my door and opened it coming face to face with not only Zander but Quinlin as well.

"Is everyone ready to go?" I asked, pretending to be more confident than I actually felt. I had finally figured out how to keep the guys out of my head and my emotions. I realized I just had to build a wall in my mind and they stayed out. If I wanted to let them in, I unlocked a door and opened it for them. I'm not sure when exactly I had figured it out but somehow I had been doing it easily.

"That's what I wanted to talk to you about," Zander started.

Quinlan leaned back and folded his arms across his chest. Was he mad at me?

"What is there to talk about?"

"I understand your anger. I do. I really really do. However, I don't think killing all those men will make you feel better. I think that you will regret it and be really hurt by it in the end." His gaze held mine for a full minute before I finally looked away.

"Let's get ready to go and I'll think about what you said." I gave him a small smile and walked past him. Quinlan still hadn't said anything so I did what any mature woman would do. I grabbed his nipple and twisted. "Now, what the fuck is your problem?"

"Shit!" Quinlan shouted, grabbing his nipples and looking shocked that I did that to him. "I agree with Zander. I don't think killing everyone will help cool your fucking inferno of a heart."

Ouch. That one stung a little.

I leveled him with a glare before turning and striding down the hall. I noticed Brutus's men were following us and for the first time I didn't mind. Maybe seeing Helvig and knowing it was really him did something to me. It made me feel lighter and dare I say happier. I was still completely pissed that they took him and the rage that was burning through me was still sitting there just waiting. Like a ticking time bomb but I had it under control. There would be a time and a place for me to release it and it wasn't here.

Everyone was standing inside of the throne room. Brutus looked menacing like normal and for the first time I noticed a deep dull purple aura around him. I wasn't sure what it was but it caught me off guard. I stood staring at him for a moment before turning to see that Draug and Vilulf had a dark green aura around them. When they touched their aura's seemed to burn brighter and mix with each other. Was that their bond?

Before I could dwell on what I was seeing, Alba spoke and broke my train of thoughts. My gaze flickered over to her to see that she didn't have an aura. Interesting. Did that mean she didn't have a mate bond waiting for her? Did whoever was meant to be her mate die and that's why it wasn't there? Maybe I was getting ahead of myself. I didn't even know for sure if that's what the auras meant.

"Alright, there has been a slight change of plans. I've been thinking about a lot of things that Helvig and Zander said to me. I will not just be plowing through camp after camp, I guess. We will go to the black knights first and they will all die. Zantos will be able to take his anger out on them. Going forward, I will give them a choice to either join us or die. It will be their choice to either live or pay the consequences for their actions. I understand that most of them didn't have a choice to join my fathers army but that doesn't excuse their actions going forward. They didn't have to rape and murder innocent people. Those that didn't could have spoken up. They could have stopped the ones that did. They chose to turn a blind eye to the brutality happening around them. So they should consider themselves lucky that I am even willing to spare them at all."

"What about finding Helvig?" Alba's voice spoke again. She had asked it once before but I hadn't answered it.

"I can take us to him and once we take care of a few of the camps, we will go to him and get him out. I don't know what is waiting for us outside of the dungeon he is being kept in but whatever it is, we will get through it. I can't move him with my power because he is being chained with divine galena. So we will have to fight our way out."

"I have a list of camps that are on the move towards large villages. I don't know what their motives are but I don't think they have good intentions. I think those are the ones we should focus on," Brutus said, pulling out a list of camps and their coordinates.

I nodded my head and moved all of us without warning to the black knights camp. It took almost nothing from me to move us all to the camp. My power had felt stronger over the last few weeks and I had thought it was from just getting better at using it. Now though, I felt like I had more power in me than ever before.

They had black flags flying underneath my fathers flags. The stench was enough to make me want to vomit. "What is that smell?" Vilulf said scrunching his face up.

"The decaying bodies of dead and dying captives. They are held in large cages and aren't removed when they die. When it's time to move the camp, they leave the bodies where they are. They don't even bother giving them a proper burial or anything." Alba's words sent a chill down my spine. If it was true, then by the smell that would mean lots of dead bodies.

No one had noticed us or if they did they hadn't cared enough to do anything about us.

"Where do you think is the commander's…" my words trailed off as a teenage girl came running half naked through the tents crying. She was attempting to cover her breasts as she ran and kept looking over her shoulder.

I moved myself directly in front of her path and startled her accidentally.

"You have to help me," she begged. "He was trying to… he was attempting to… he will kill me because I ran." She broke into tears again.

Alba walked up and gingerly wrapped her cloak around the girl. "Don't worry. We will take care of him. Can you tell me where Commander Shnoh's tent is?"

The girl's eyes widened even further. "That's where I just came from. I don't want to go back. Please don't make me go back."

"Do you see the men standing over there?" I pointed to Brutus, Zander, Draug, Vilulf, and Quin.

"Yeah," she said hesitantly.

"Most of them are shifters and one of them is THE King Daemonger. They are here with us and I promise that they will not let anything happen to you." I tried to give her a reassuring smile but it felt very forced.

"Okay," she breathed. "His tent is this way."

We followed her through the mud and past buckets of urine and feces. The longer we walked the worse the camp seemed to get. Then I saw it between the tents. A large cage filled with people. My steps faltered and I almost fell. Quin grabbed a hold of me.

"What is it?" he asked. Trying to follow where my gaze had been.

"Is that really a fucking cage full of people?" I shouted turning towards the girl.

"That's where they hold us when they don't need us for something."

"Are you fucking kidding me? Where the fuck is that piece of shit commander? I swear, I will make each and every one of these fucking disgusting pieces of shit pay." I had taken off walking angrily. Finally, The commander's tent came into view. I knew it was his because of the sheer size of it and men standing guard.

The men turned towards me as I approached but I didn't bother letting them say anything. I was too angry to focus my power on them so I did what I knew best. I beat the shit out of them with my bare hands. Once they were both knocked out thanks to the pummel of one of their swords, I stepped through the tent flaps and into the vipers den.

The commander was naked sitting in a chair while a girl who couldn't have been much older than 18 was on her knees in front of him. My stomach rolled but I held down the vomit that threatened to make an appearance.

"I think the commander has had enough for today," I said, making my presence known. "Get your clothes on and step outside where my friends will keep you safe while I have a word with Shnohs here."

The girl hesitated for a moment before scrambling to her feet.

Shnohs didn't even show one ounce of concern as she left the tent.

"Cordelia, darling, I have been waiting for you to make your appearance here," he said, smiling at me.

"Get your ass up and let's go to the cages," I stated.

"I suppose you're going to make a show of this aren't you?" he stood and went to gather his clothes.

I snapped my fingers to get his attention, "No. You don't get the privilege to dress. You will go like this. Zander!"

Zander and Quinlan stepped into the tent.

"Fuck. You could have warned us. I wasn't expecting to see an old shriveled prick today." I glared at Quinlan while

347

suppressing a laugh.

"Let's take him out to the cages." I smiled and turned walking out of the tent.

Vilulf had let a few soldiers know to gather everyone near the cages. I wasn't sure how he knew that was where I would want to go but Vilulf just had a way of knowing things.

The men standing around looked at us as we approached with Commander Shonhs hands bound. I watched as they put their hands on the pummels of their swords waiting for a sign from the commander to do something.

"Open the cages!" I shouted but none of the guards near the cages moved.

"Did you really think you could come in here and make demands. None of them know who you are. They're all just waiting for a sign from me before attacking." Shnohs' laugh made me grind my teeth.

"I am Cordelia Rovini. I am here to make you pay for the sins of your past. It's time those in the cages get the revenge they are rightly due." I raised my hand for show and snapped my fingers. In an instant the cages had disappeared.

"Anyone that was harmed by the men in this camp now has the chance to take your revenge. I will not allow any harm to come to you. Here stands King Daemonger willing to accept you into his kingdom and provide you with a safe haven until we can get you home."

Those that had been in the cages looked scared and confused. I waited a few moments before turning to Alba. Maybe she could provide them with the reassurance that they needed. To my surprise, a woman stepped forward. Her clothes were ripped and her long brown hair was matted. You could tell that she had once been beautiful but now her face was swollen and covered in bruises.

She bent, picking up a rock and then threw it at Commander Shnohs. I watched as it connected with his chest. She picked up another and then another as tears streamed down her face. Slowly, more and more women stepped forward doing the same. They all looked like they had been abused at some point recently and my heart broke for them. They screamed and cried as they threw rocks at the commander. He was screaming and begging for them to stop. He was pleading with us. Asking for mercy and saying he would join our cause.

I felt Brutus rest a hand on my shoulder. I turned to look at him as he bent to whisper to me. "I know this seems brutal and savage but I think this will help these women heal. What you are doing for them means more to them than you may ever know." I watched the tattoos on his exposed skin twist and turn moving across him. It took me a moment to realize that it was his shadows. He had wrapped his shadows around himself. "Now before you have your fun with the 457 men in this camp and before you release Zantos, I would like to have my own fun. It's been a very long time since I have let my shadows out to play."

I nodded my head at him and turned back to the women. "If there are any men that you know the names of or can point out to us that deserve this same fate, please do so and I will make sure they are brought forward."

I felt the tension in the air increase around us and for a moment, I didn't think anyone was going to say anything. Then women began stepping forward, pointing, and stating names. I didn't even have to try and guess who they were pointing at because the men that were accused began running.

Draug grinned before running after them. He truly enjoyed the chase and brought each man to the center faster than I could track. They began begging for their lives but I didn't want to hear it. I turned and walked to the back of the crowd. The women began stoning the men. Maybe I did have a frozen heart because I wasn't phased by any of it. They deserved so much worse than what they were getting.

Eventually, the screams and sounds of rocks hitting faded away. It was silent as the rest of the soldiers stood looking terrified.

I didn't feel like giving a speech anymore. I didn't feel like taking their lives. The anger in me had seemed to slip away some. It wasn't my revenge. I wanted revenge on Rangor not these men and Ragnor had made it perfectly clear that he didn't care what I did with the camps.

"Vilulf, let the men know their choice. Those that choose to switch sides need to show they are truly willing to do so by walking into the cages that I relocated on the other side of the tents. You can let them now that the cage isn't for holding them, but for protecting them," I said while walking over to Zander.

Brutus grinned from ear to ear as he snuck away as Vilulf spoke. I was curious where he was going considering he wanted to let his shadows out to play.

"It's time," I said.

Zander and Quinlan both walked quickly over to a clearing not too far away. I watched in amazement as they both changed. Zander became a large fierce dragon, Zantos, and Quinlan turned into his phoenix.

Alba had approached the woman and was explaining to them about what would happen next. I waited for her signal before moving the women and Alba to Zeke's camp. Once they were cleared from what would soon become a waste land I walked to Zantos. He had seemed on edge from the moment Zander released him. As soon as I was close to him he bumped his face against my chest and snorted. His hot breath seeped through my shirt and tickled my skin.

"You ready to let out some of your frustration, big guy?" I heard Quinlan let out a squawk as he took off into the air.

Suddenly the sounds of screaming filled the air and I turned in their direction. Zantos nudged me again and lowered himself down to the ground.

"Climb upon my back and I will show you what is happening," Zantos' voice echoed through my head.

"How did you do that? I have my mind closed off to everyone."

"You have your mind closed off to those that do not belong in it currently. I am Zantos and will always be able to communicate with you and your bonded mate even if you attempt to shut me out."

I narrowed my eyes at him as I climbed upon his back.

As soon as I was seated and holding on, he took off into the air.

Chapter Thirty-One

T he wind blew my hair and there was an exhilaration humming through my blood that I had never felt before. I felt connected to Zantos in a way I hadn't known was possible. I felt like I had always been meant to ride on his back like this. I let go of the spike I had been holding and flung my arms out wide feeling the wind wrap around me.

"That is where the puny men's screams are coming from."

Zantos words pulled me out of my momentary distraction. I looked down to see some men walking into the cages as others tried to sneak past them and make a run for it. Brutus was waiting in the shadows for them. I watched in awe as the shadows slinked off his skin and formed creatures like the ones I had seen in the village. They consumed the men leaving husks of skin behind. Brutus looked like a demon king. A chill and fear started to slide through me before he looked up directly at us. He gave a small smile and then the feeling had disappeared. Was he capable of making someone feel fear in his presence like that? There was so much about Brutus that I didn't know but we were family and I was safe with him.

"Are you ready to release that pent up anger yet?" I asked while rubbing the scales at the base of his neck.

"I have been waiting for you to allow it."

"Well the wait is over. You may begin." I leaned down and rested my forehead on him. His scales were hard and smooth. I opened my mind and heart to him and he began his descent.

A rush of excitement and anger filtered through me. Zantos had been waiting for this moment for a while. He let out a deafening roar just before his fire ignited the commander's tent. The men that chose not to go to the cages began running now. They reminded me of ants scattering around after you accidentally step on their hill.

Quinlan shrieked in the distance. He dove almost straight down before swooping and swallowing a man whole. I wondered what the armor and sword would do to his insides but Quinlan didn't seem to be bothered. He flew around gracefully picking and choosing who would be his next meal with care. Zantos on the other hand had turned the whole camp into a blazing inferno. I hadn't been paying attention to what exactly he was doing but now I could see. He had flown higher admiring his own work. Satisfaction hit me as I studied what he had done. He encircled the camp with a wall of fire. The men that were running had nowhere to go. They were trapped. The only decision they had was whether they wanted to be burnt to a crisp by the fire wall or if they wanted to die by a dragon, shadows, or phoenix. Draug and Vilulf were standing next to the men in the cages watching the show.

Zantos let out another deafening roar before he landed hard on the ground. He let out another stream of fire before he began tearing men apart with his teeth. For a moment I had to remind myself that these men deserved it. It was brutal and disgusting. They had never stood a chance against us. Helvig's words rang in my head as Zantos raised his head and blew another stream of fire. I was the beacon of hope. I was the beacon of hope for the innocent that had suffered at the hands of these men.

The men were trying to fight off Zantos but they weren't prepared to face a dragon. Their swords did nothing to his scales. His tail swept them away just before he would turn his head and blow his fire at them. The air smelled oldly like barbeque and it took me a moment to realize that it was all the burnt flesh I was smelling. I hated to admit it but it smelled a hell of a lot better than when we first entered the camp.

Once all the men were done, Zantos allowed me to get off of him. I felt the air change and then suddenly Zander was standing there in all his glory breathing heavily.

"I feel much better and Zantos is incredibly content now." A grin crept across his face and I couldn't help but admire just how beautiful he was.

I smiled as he wrapped his arm around me and we began walking towards the cages. Everyone else was already waiting for us.

"I'll transfer the men to your castle and then we can head out to meet up with Zeke. I think he still needs updated on my plans and then I want to go get Helvig."

"I think that sounds like a great idea, but I would like to grab some clothes. It's going to be cold once we are away from the fire." Quinlan said, feigning a shiver.

I rolled my eyes and immediately moved the men that chose to switch sides as well as Zander and Quinlan back to Brutus castle.

I figured I would give them a few moments to get some clothes before I brought them with us to Zeke's camp.

"So how do you feel?" Draug asked as we stood assessing the damage.

"I feel pretty good, I think." I hadn't spent too much time dwelling on what happened today. The men that were stoned deserved it. The men that chose to switch sides were probably genuinely good men and the men that chose to stand against us deserved to die.

"For what it is worth, I am proud of you." Draugs words hit me like a ton of bricks. I whipped around and looked at him. My mouth fell open and words seemed to fail me. "You are good, Cordelia. You have alway been good and you continuously choose good even when choosing bad would be easier. You could have just walked in here and killed everyone. It would have been quicker and easier. I bet Zantos wouldn't have hesitated if you let him have free range of this camp the moment we arrived. Yet, you chose to give them an option. A lot of the men that chose the cages seemed young and hopeless."

Vilulf reached over and wrapped his arms around Draugs waist. "I think there will always be good in you. I can't imagine how you are feeling and everything you have been through. I'm proud of how you handled today though."

I didn't know how to respond to them. I wasn't used to people being open with their emotions like this. I also wasn't sure how to deal with them telling me that they are proud of me. Do I say thank you? Is that something you say thank you for? So instead of saying anything, I just gave them a small smile and walked towards the cages. I looked over the men and they looked completely defeated. It wasn't just from today. It looked like they had given up a long time ago.

"How many of you willingly chose to join my fathers army?"

They kept their eyes cast down and no one spoke up.

"None of you?"

Finally a boy who looked no older than 16 spoke up. "The army came through my village and forced us to come with them."

"I'm sorry that happened to you all. I hope that going forward you will be presented with more choices and are able to have more control over your lives. We will be going to King Havaror's closest camp. From there you all will report in. Some of you will probably be asked to stay and others will be released and sent home. It is going to be King Havaror's decision though. He is a just and fair king so I know that he will listen to whatever your concerns are and take them into consideration."

I glanced over my shoulder at my men and then took us all to Zeke's camp.

Zeke's camp was bustling with men everywhere. Clearly, Alba had informed them that we would be coming because as soon as we appeared one of Zeke's high ranking officers came over to address us.

He had the men line up and head to a nearby tent to record their information such as name, age, and what city they originally came from. Vilulf and Draug headed off in one direction together. Quinlan stayed with the men from my father's camp just to ensure that they were being treated carefully.

Zander and I walked to find Alba and Zeke. As we walked past the warriors of the Havaror army, they bowed as I passed. "Why in the world are they all bowing to me?"

"It's a sign of respect, I think. King Havaror probably told them to bow or something like that." Zander said, shrugging his shoulders.

We turned a corner and I saw Alba storming towards us. She looked furious. Before I could ask her what happened, Zeke came barreling after her. What the fuck.

"Cordelia, you better tell him to stay away from me!" She shrieked.

I rushed to Alba's side and pulled her behind me. I didn't know what was going on with Zeke but I remembered when he had a melt down with me. Maybe he was doing something similar with her.

"This doesn't have anything to do with Cordelia. Alba, I just want to talk to you. Why is that too much to ask for?" He shouted at her.

"Whoa! I don't know what the fuck is going on between you two but you do not get to shout at her like that!" I said, shoving my finger into Zeke's chest. "You need to back the fuck off and if she wants to talk to you she will come talk to you. Otherwise, stay the fuck away from my friend."

Zeke was physically vibrating with anger. I heard a low growl come from Zander behind me and the hairs on my arms started to stand up. The air around us began to change and feel charged. Electricity began to ripple around Zeke and I actually felt scared that he was going to do something really bad.

"Zeke," I said, my voice barely a whisper. "You have to calm down. I know you don't want to hurt us but you will if you don't calm down."

"Ezekiel, this only makes me want to stay farther away from you. It makes me want to never see you again. If you want to change that, then you need to back up and give me space," Alba shouted at him.

Zeke looked from me to Alba and back. He let out a long sigh and rolled his shoulders. In a typical Zeke move he scrubbed his hand down his face. Slowly, I felt the air around us return to normal. Alba leaned close to me and whispered, "Please just drop it. I'll tell you about what happened later. I don't want to talk about it right now."

I nodded my head with my eyes never leaving Zeke. There was something about him that was keeping me on edge. He seemed to be a loose cannon and I didn't know what to do about that.

"You good?" I asked him.

"Yeah. I'm good," he grunted unconvincingly.

"Good. We have shit to take care of. Starting with getting Helvig back."

"Vilulf told me about Helvig still being alive. He said you've been going to him like what you did with me and that he's being held captive?" All the tension had melted away from Zeke revealing sorrow and regret.

"As soon as everyone is settled here, I want all of us to go and get him. I don't know what we will run into when trying to get him out so it's best for us all to be prepared for a worse case scenario." I looked between Zeke, Alba, and Zander.

"I'll stay here and continue helping the women get themselves together. Find me when you get Helvig back." Alba quickly took off and didn't bother looking back. I chanced a glance at Zeke and saw him staring after her.

Chapter Thirty-One

"Do I want to know what was happening between you two when we first got here?"

"No. She'll tell you when she's ready," Zeke growled out. It seems he was in a pretty shitty mood but whatever was going on between him and Alba would have to wait.

Chapter Thirty-Two

I took a deep breath, anxiety filling my chest. In just a few moments we would be finally getting Helvig back. Months of thinking he was dead and now we were really going to get him back.

Vilulf leaned down closer to me. "I have known Helvig for years and when I thought we had lost him, I cried. It was the first time I have cried since my first battle. He is an honorable man. One I would consider worthy of you and for what it's worth, I'm glad that it's Helvig and not Ezekiel. Something about you and Ezekiel just didn't sit quite right with me but now I know it's because you were always meant to be with Helvig."

I had grown to really care for Vilulf over the last few weeks and his words only made me appreciate him that much more.

"It's time," I smiled as Quinlan finally joined us. "I know that Helvig might hate the part of being a damsel in distress but he is. He is pretty helpless with the divine galena on him. I cannot use my power on him while those are still attached to him. I don't know where exactly he is or where the doorway will lead us too. So everyone needs to be fully prepared for an attack. Protecting Helvig and getting him out is our number one priority. If you have to change forms in order to protect him, do it without hesitation. Any questions?"

"I think you made it pretty clear that rescuing Helvig is our number one priority, but I want you to know that I won't let anything happen to you either. If I have to choose between you and him, I'm always choosing you," Quinlan said, folding his arms just waiting for me to argue with him. I wouldn't though. I knew where his loyalty was and Zander probably felt the same way. The difference between the two men though was Zander understood that I needed Helvig. I had no doubts that he would do everything he could to get Helvig back. I also knew he wasn't doing it for Helvig but for me.

"Let's go," I said and then quickly moved all of us to Helvig. I watched in amazement as the world around us fell away and we were turned upside down for a moment. Vilulfs face twisted with discomfort as we came to a stop in the dungeon Helvig was being held in. Like usual, Vilulf turned and began vomiting. Draug stood by his side patting his back.

The room was cold as usual but something wasn't right. I felt my heart start to beat faster as I rushed to the cell that Helvig was kept in. As soon as I entered the room, it felt like my body had been hit by a brick wall. He wasn't there. I turned to look at the doorway only to find that the dirt and rocks I had piled there were gone. It had only been a few hours since I had seen him. I looked back at his cell again hoping I was wrong. That I had just missed him. The table and chairs from earlier were still there. The table had been knocked over and broken. One of the chairs was broken as well. Did Helivg break it trying to defend himself? He was fucking gone. Again. They took him away from me again. I was just getting him back and he was gone.

"He's not here," my voice cracked. "THEY FUCKING TOOK HIM AGAIN." My heart was pounding and my breaths were coming in fast and short. Too fast and too short. It felt like the room was spinning.

Zander wrapped his arms around me and pulled me to his chest. I began beating his chest, the anger and panic hitting an all time high. Zander didn't even flinch though. He held me firmly in his arms. "We will find him. I promise. Brutus has already sent his shadows out in search of him. They can't have taken him far. The blood in the hallway is still warm. I bet he put up quite the fight. Let's head out, ok?"

I had stopped trying to fight Zander at some point and let myself just feel his heartbeat against my cheek. Helvig would have fought them the best he could. He was probably still trying to fight them. I had to fight for him too. I couldn't just stand here and have a melt down. I had to pull myself together and hunt down the bastards that thought they could take him from me again. He had said before that it was a trap and I hadn't paid him any attention. Now though, I was starting to wonder what exactly he was talking about.

"We might be walking right into a trap. Helvig told me before that I shouldn't be here because it was a trap but nothing happened. Maybe this is the trap they had set–" Zeke cut my words off. His eyes had changed colors and I knew he must have been talking with one of his commanders

"They took Lanasia," he whispered.

I felt my heart seize up in my chest. No. No. They couldn't

have.

"How?!" I screeched. "How the fuck did they take Lanasia? We took out the camps along that border. How could they have taken it so fast? What about the neighboring villages or the ones that were along the main road that they would have passed?"

My father had been planning on taking Lanasia and moving quickly to a temple. At the time he had believed that his magic was there. I didn't know what everything meant back then. Now I knew that I was harboring my fathers magic or at least part of it. So was it the rest of his magic that he believed to be in that temple or was it something else entirely?

"They destroyed everything on their way," Zeke turned to look at me. He knew I would take this hard but he didn't know just how hard.

I would eavesdrop on my father's conversations and then sneak out of the castle and head into the village to the docks. I would leak information to our enemies to try and save lives. My father never knew what I did but one night I had overheard his plans to take Lanasia and then head to a temple. I acted swiftly and was able to pass the information on. Troops had been moved and they were able to stop my fathers attack. It had been a stalemate ever since then. Well until I came through and destroyed my fathers camps. I thought that move had pushed them back further and gave us more of an advantage. It seems though we had only relaxed and let them slip right through. Helvig had been with me that night. Not on purpose. He had followed me and discovered what it was that I did. It was that same night I took him to my river. The memories began flooding me and my heart ached.

"I've made the command to move my troops to stop them

from going any further." Brutus said. His tone was even but it was laced with malice. A promise of vengeance.

"Zeke, what about the temple?" I had begun shaking. This was bad. This was so much worse than any of them knew.

"What temple?"

"There is a temple not too far away from Lanasia. Did my fathers men take the temple or is it still under our control?" I was frozen to my spot as I watched him. His eyes flashed colors again as he asked his commander about the temple.

His face dropped and I knew before he said anything.

"They took it. It seems they stopped advancing once they reached the temple."

I felt the world fall from around me. If they had found whatever it was they were looking for, my father would be more powerful than we could deal with. We weren't just dealing with a sick man now. I could hear Zander, Quinlan, Vilulf, and Draug arguing over what we should do next. I knew Brutus and Zeke were communicating with their men. None of it mattered now though.

"We have to go," I said. "There isn't anything we can do about it now. My father was searching for something in that temple. If it was there, then we are all screwed."

My body moved through the doorway on its own. My mind was racing as I was trying to piece together what my father wanted to do with Helvig. Why had he kept him this whole time? It wasn't just a coincidence. My father had to know that Helvig was a God. Why was that important to him though? What did he want from him?

I didn't have to look behind me to know that everyone had followed me. I had somehow become their leader and they all followed me. I still wasn't sure how it had happened but it did.

I moved through the dark hallway. I didn't bother looking in the doors as we passed. I knew Helvig wasn't there. I followed this invisible line that seemed to connect us. I opened the door at the end of the hall to find a stairwell that led up. It was dark but I could tell there was a light somewhere up higher.

I took the stairs two at a time. Running up the stairs for what felt like a lifetime and there hadn't been one door or window yet. I froze and turned to look behind me. Everyone was following but something was wrong. Something was happening. I could feel the shift in the air.

"Cordelia," Brutus sounded far away.

Suddenly a pain like I hadn't known before sliced through my chest. I looked down to find there was no wound. I grabbed at my chest as the pain continued to increase. A scream wrenched from my throat and I couldn't breath. My eyes were wide as I suddenly felt a pain in both my wrists.

Brutus grabbed me as I began to fall to my knees. The pain was unbearable but there was something much worse happening. I felt that invisible line to Helvig begin to waver and I knew deep down that something was happening to him. I opened myself up for the first time in a long time to my men. Draug let out a growl as he felt the pain I was consumed with. Quinlan could hear my racing thoughts and I knew Zander was already reading all of my emotions.

"It's Helvig. They're trying to kill him and it might just kill Cordelia in the process," Zanders' words were breathy. If anyone knew what it felt like to lose their soul mate, it would be him.

I didn't feel the pain in my chest or my wrists any more.

The pain that was coming from the bond between us was indescribable. Suddenly, the pain began to ease and it felt like the bond was fading. I let out a breath finally getting some relief only for my heart to begin aching. Helvig was dying. HELVIG WAS FUCKING DYING.

I pushed out of Brutus arms and began stumbling up the stairs. I was moving as fast as I could but it felt like my arms and legs weren't listening to my brain. I began pushing love and warmth into our bond. Pain was radiating from it but I tried my best to ignore it. I fought past the pain and pushed every memory of us through it. Every moment that made me fall more and more in love with him. I loved him. I loved him with all of my being and if he died, I didn't want to be here anymore. Not without him.

I could see a door and pushed myself faster. I don't know when Zander had wrapped his arm around me helping me run but he had. We burst through the door and I felt my lungs give out. We were in the library at my fathers castle. THE FUCKING LIBRARY. I paused for a moment trying to pinpoint where exactly in the library we were. This was my fathers private section. It had always been forbidden for me to come here. He even went as far as putting a gate up to keep me out. It stung me if I tried to touch it. Gods be damned. The gate had been coated in divine galena. I felt the pain from the flickering bond again reminding me to keep going.

Forcing myself to keep going, I pushed deeper into my fathers private library. Letting the pain of the bond pull me to him. I continued to push love and happiness, life itself, into the bond.

I could hear the commotion of everyone behind me but I couldn't be bothered looking at them. My eyes were locked on to a door at the back. He was there. I knew he was.

Zander let out a roar as he surged forward. He shoved the door open, breaking it just in time for me to come barreling through.

Chapter Thirty-Three

I stumbled into the room and immediately rushed to where Helvig had been suspended with blood running down his body. I didn't even bother looking around. My focus was solely on him.

"HELVIG!" My voice was shrill as I reached out to him. Zander let out a dangerous roar just before he shifted, releasing Zantos.

I untied the ropes that held Helvig, noticing the chains were gone and held him as he dropped. The weight of him was much more than I had anticipated and we fell to the ground together. He was splayed over my lap, still bleeding.

"Open your eyes, please. Please open your eyes," I cried out to him. I ran my hand over his face.

"Perfect timing my beautiful daughter," King Rovini said. "I knew I could count on you to arrive just as planned."

My stomach turned as I looked up at the man who had raised me. The man that had taken me from my actual parents. The man that had lied to me my whole life, who had killed innocent people, who had taken Helvig from me.

"What did you do to him," I croaked.

"He will probably be fine. Well maybe. That just depends on whether or not the bond between you two is strong enough to sustain him until he heals." Ragnor's cold words sent ice through my veins.

Zantos wrapped his tail around us as he faced off with Ragnor.

My father moved closer toward Ragnor and smiled but it seemed wrong. His face twisted aa he suddenly pulled a sword out of thin air and stabbed Ragnor straight through the heart.

My mouth fell open as the only sound that pierced the air was from Ragnors body hitting the floor. I looked around the room, for what I honestly couldn't tell you. Was all of this really happening?

My father dragged Ragnors body over to a small pit in the center of the room. Then he picked up his head and tossed it in. Brawntly appeared, dropped something into the pit and then lit it on fire. My father tossed Ragnors body into it and stood with his arms held out chanting words in a language I didn't understand. I looked down at Helvig as tears fell from my eyes. I could still feel the faint pulse of our bond. He was still here with me. I bent over him and kissed his cheeks.

"I'm so sorry. I'm so sorry I left you earlier. I should have stayed. I should have brought everyone here sooner. I should have gotten you out. I'm sorry." I kissed him again and placed my forehead on his.

Brutus's voice filled my head. "You have to get out of there." I hadn't even noticed that Zander and I were the only ones in here. I looked at the door to find that it was fixed and closed.

I could hear them pounding on it on the other side.

I looked back to my father and saw streams of all different colors coming out of the fire from Rangor's body and into my father.

"What are you doing? Please. Just let us go." I begged.

Brawntly came sauntering over and laughed at me. He stayed just out of reach of Zantos who let out a roar.

"Don't worry. MY father isn't going to harm you. He discovered a way to ensure you don't receive his magic at all, dear cousin." Brawntly began laughing like a madman. Cousin? How was I his cousin?

I looked back to the man that held all the answers. This was his game we were playing. I realized that now. I had thought Ragnor held all the power but I had underestimated my father. Ragnor might have held my fathers power but my father had planned out everything. Suddenly, my father threw his head back as the last of the glittering colors seeped into him.

A loud deafening crack sounded through the air. Wind began whipping around the room blowing my hair every which way. I held tighter onto Helvig as Zantos let out a whine. I felt his wings come out and cover us. The room began turning brighter and brighter. I watched as Brawntly had to cover his eyes but myself and my father didn't flinch. It was Helvig's blood making the room glow like that. I wasn't sure how I knew it but deep down inside I knew what my father was doing. His father had taken away his power and sealed this realm off leaving him stranded here. My father had gotten his power back and now he was going to break down the barrier between the realms.

It was so loud and the wind had turned brutal even with

Zantos doing everything he could to protect us.

"I love you," I yelled but my voice was barely a whisper in the air. "If we die, I hope you know just how much I love you."

Helvig's emerald eyes opened and all at once everything stopped. The wind had stopped and the light had returned to normal. He reached up and gently caressed my face.

Zantos moved his wings and we were once again exposed. I looked around to see that Brawntly and my father had moved toward the balcony.

Helvig gasped as he sat up but quickly moved and shifted into his true form. He was at least 8 feet tall and glowing as bright as the sun. Part of me thought I should look away but this other part of me couldn't bear to take my eyes away from him. The light seemed to seep out of his radiant sepia skin coming from deep inside of him.

I scrambled to my feet and watched as Helvig moved towards my father and brother. He was almost too fast for me to track. Just as he reached the balcony doors the air around them shimmered. Helvig was thrown backwards as fire erupted out of nowhere. I felt Zantos at my back and heard Helvig yell, "BAYLOR! DON'T DO THIS!"

The walls weren't burning but the air itself was burning. It was as if the air itself now held an orange glow.

"I'll make sure to stop by to say hello to your parents. It's been long time since I've visited The Court of Light." My father smiled before grabbing Brawntly's hand and walking into the fire.

"Fuck," Helvig's knees knocked together and he hit the ground hard.

I rushed to his side, "Helvig what the fuck is happening."

Flames erupted from the wall and shot out in all directions.

Zantos covered us with his body.

Helvig reached a shaking hand up and caressed my cheek as I leaned into his touch. "He broke the barrier. He fucking broke the barrier and he's going to take his revenge out on The Realm of Gods. If you thought things were bad now, it's only going to get worse." Helvig spoke softly to me while still bleeding from his chest and stood. "We have to go, *my zonlicht*. We have to go now before this portal closes. It will take us directly where it took them. Otherwise, we will have to find another portal and they don't all lead to the same place."

"You're fucking bleeding out from your chest. We can't just leave," I could feel my panic raise as I watched the blood pour from his chest. He wasn't clotting.

"He poured a liquid form of divine galena over me before he cut me. I won't heal until I get to the spring of cleansing and that, my love, is not in this realm." Helvig grabbed my arm and pulled me towards the fire. I glanced back towards the door just as Brutus and Zeke burst through it.

"This realm is in your hands now. Take care of it, we might not return," Helvig said to them. As he laced his fingers into mine, walking us into the fire.

About the Author

Aspen F. Sapphire has always enjoyed reading and writing stories but have only recently begun sharing her stories with the world. When she's not lost in a world she has created, she enjoys spending time with her daughters and husband. She loves to travel and explore new places that inspire her to write.

Also by Aspen F. Sapphire

Being Bright - The War Between Bright & Dark Book One

In the realm of Bright, Princess Ixia's world falls apart when her parents, the beloved King and Queen, are brutally murdered. Framed for their deaths, Ixia flees. Desperate and with nowhere else to go after exhausting all other options, she seeks the Dark Realm. As she finds her place in the dark domain, Ixia begins to find shocking truths that shatter her beliefs about the Dark fae. She discovers unsettling secrets concealed by her parents long ago, setting her on a journey to find the truth to set things right. The Dark Fae King challenges everything she thought she knew. As their bond begins to deepen, Ixia struggles with conflicting emotions, torn between loyalty to her kingdom and her feelings for the very person she was taught to fear. In this tale of deception, love, and redemption, Ixia must navigate the complexities of taking back the crown while clearing her name and her heart's desires.

Milton Keynes UK
Ingram Content Group UK Ltd.
UKHW010634040324
438885UK00001B/21

9 798869 144850